DEATH SINGER

ASCENSION QUEST
VOLUME 1

RANDY ELLEFSON

Evermore Press
GAITHERSBURG, MARYLAND

Evermore Press, LLC
Gaithersburg, Maryland
www.evermorepress.org

Death Singer / Randy Ellefson. -- 1st ed.
ISBN 978-1-946995-68-1 (paperback)
ISBN 978-1-946995-69-8 (hardcover)

CONTENTS

ACKNOWLEDGEMENTS

Maps by Randy Ellefson

Cover design by Christina Myrvold

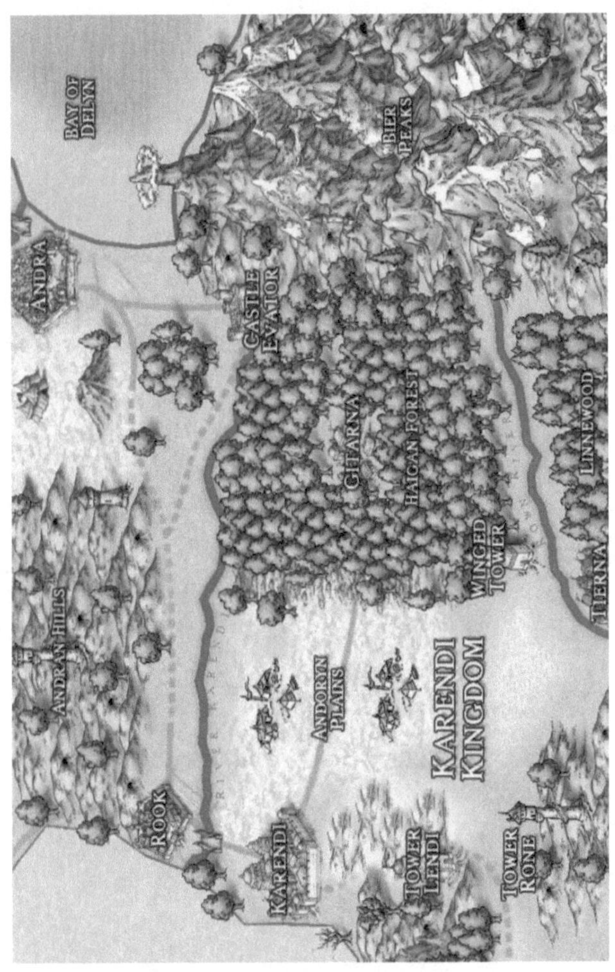

Partial Map of the Kingdom of Karendi, on Lurien

View a larger, full color map online at https://fiction.randyellefson.com/ascension-quest-litrpg- series/death-singer/

CHAPTER ONE

Max turned his back on the three people giving him the finger. He couldn't make out their faces anyway, with them being backlit in the noisy Baltimore club as Steel Panther blasted from the loudspeakers. They'd been flipping him off all night while he was on stage with his band, Burp the Worm, cranking out 80s metal tunes on his axe-shaped guitar. It wasn't the first time the flip-off fest had happened. He'd always thought being good would get him support, not jealous people eager to see him fail. Today, he wasn't in the mood for the haters. It was time to go home.

With his last glance at the stage to ensure he'd grabbed all his gear, he strode over to his guitar case and crouched down as much as his black leather pants would let him. Max took a last look down at "Kat," the prized electric guitar he'd built. She was all silver hardware and black paint except for a silver area on the bottom, where it looked like a blade. And he knew people hated him for this above all else.

He zipped the case closed and rose, casting a last look at the club where drunk people were wobbling into each other and slithering out into the darkness. Last call had come, and he felt a little inebriated from the shots two hot girls had brought him on stage. He slung Kat over his shoulder and stepped out of the club with a last wave at his bandmates, who were busy with their own gear or hanging out with people.

His black leather boots crunched on the parking lot's gravelly asphalt as he strode toward his banged up, red Dodge Charger. As he neared it, three figures stepped out from behind a van parked beyond it. They took up positions on either side of the Charger and blocked the way to it. The blond held a hockey stick, but the short one and the overweight one had nothing in their hands. With the streetlight above backlighting them, Max recognized their silhouettes from inside and stopped. They weren't really going to attack him, were they? This was getting out of hand.

"Hey dickhead," the blond one called out, his voice echoing off the stone walls of the surrounding buildings.

"Give it a rest, guys," Max said, suspecting that was the ringleader.

"We're gonna give *you* a rest," said the chubby one, the voice revealing she was female.

Max rolled his eyes. "Clever. Maybe you should be a poet."

"Fuck you, dude."

The short one finally spoke. "You think you're so much better than us."

Max sighed. "Maybe that's because I don't go around flipping people off or accosting them at their car. Come on, guys. They just did last call. Go get another beer and see if you can get laid before it's too late."

The blond guy glanced around before yelling, "Get him!"

They rushed at Max, who stepped back and saw from their body language that they weren't kidding. He turned a little too late and ran, but they had a head start. The soft guitar case bounced haphazardly on his shoulder. He lost a precious second getting it into one hand, where it was almost as awkward. Running from these bozos irritated him, but 3-on-1 and unarmed weren't good odds. With the footsteps closing in, he risked a glance back just as the blond with the hockey stick swung it at his legs and tripped him.

Max fell too quickly to break his fall, one knee slamming painfully into the asphalt as his hand slid on loose gravel. The guitar case fell to one side. As he reached for it, the short one kicked it away. The girl stomped on his other hand. Pain, anger, and fear of broken bones tore through him. As they laughed, he rolled onto his back to see them surrounding him. He held up his injured, bloody hand and saw it shaking, whether from adrenaline or pain, he didn't know.

"Get the guitar!" the blond one in front of him hollered.

"No!" Max yelled, struggling to his feet. He moved left toward the short one who'd picked it up, but the blond one swung the hockey stick to keep him back. "You'll never get away with stealing it. Everyone knows it's mine."

The blond one sneered and walked toward Kat, limping for some reason. "We're gonna smash it to pieces, not get caught with it. This is what happens to arrogant motherfuckers."

Shock tore through Max. After all these years of taking care of Kat, her being destroyed was the worst thing he could imagine. To think he'd gotten upset when he'd scratched the back of her on his belt buckle until he'd learned to pull the front of his shirt over his waist. And now three dumbasses were gonna break her? Over his dead body.

"Leave the guitar alone," Max demanded, as the short one pulled it out of the case.

"Leave the guitar alone!" the girl mocked. Only now could Max see she had long purple hair braided on one side, and a nose ring attached to an earring. He wanted to yank it out of her face.

The short one dragged Kat across the gravel, likely scratching the paint.

"I'll give you whatever money you want," Max pleaded, cradling his injured hand. "Come on. That guitar is priceless."

"It's about to be worthless," said the blond one.

The girl laughed. "Hey! We *are* poets!"

The short one raised Kat over his head by the neck like she was an actual axe. Dread filled Max at the impending motion of it slamming into the ground. He lunged forward. The blond one jabbed him in the chest with the hockey stick hard enough to make Max gasp at the pain. But Max yanked the stick out of the guy's grip with his good hand. Suddenly Max was the one with a weapon. He ran toward the guy holding the guitar over his head and cocked his arm back to swing.

Pain exploded across his right temple as a flashing light blinded him. He never saw the ground as he fell hard to his left and slammed headfirst into the asphalt, which stunned him. His ears rang. A punch. From the blond one. Max hadn't seen it coming and now couldn't see anything. He dimly heard the crack of Kat being smashed into the ground. Once. Twice. And the sound of wood clattering. Laughter. He tried to lift his head but couldn't. Or his arm. His legs wouldn't move and felt impossibly heavy.

Crunching footsteps neared him and stopped. Max feared what they were about to do to him.

The girl said, "Shit, dude. I think you hit him too hard."

"Yeah. Yeah, I think you're right. We better get the fuck out of here before somebody sees us."

"Let's go."

The footsteps rapidly faded away. Max blacked out with a groan of pain, despair, and helpless fury.

CHAPTER TWO

Max opened his eyes to see tall trees just feet in front of where he stood. A rocky dirt path led between them and through a forest with low bushes scattered throughout. A glance around revealed more of the same, the trail behind him, too. The turning motion caused him to notice coarse fabric rubbing against his skin. Looking down, he saw a plain, long-sleeved tan shirt belted at the waist with a rope. He also wore similar pants that reached to his ankles. And it felt like he had no underwear; a quick touch down there confirmed it. Brown fur boots completed the outfit. He otherwise had nothing else with him.

He'd never been much of a nature buff, but the air smelled pristine, with a pine scent. His sinuses hadn't seemed this clear in forever and he took a deep breath. He felt relaxed and rested, as if after a good night's sleep. A slight breeze felt wonderful against his skin. Everything seemed almost too vivid. His sight was even clearer than before, even though he'd never needed glasses and presumably had 20/20 vision.

But he had no idea what he was doing here.

Confused, he tried to take a step forward, and while he could lift his foot, it went back to the ground in the same spot instead of forward like he'd intended. He tried again with the same result. Was something invisible holding him in place? He couldn't back up or go sideways, either. He extended his arms successfully, reaching around and up, but he appeared stuck in place. Though he didn't see anyone, he was about to call for help when a semi-translucent display of light appeared, hanging in the air several feet before him. Instead of an edge, it had an outline of glowing yellow light with rounded corners. It looked like a TV or computer screen, but there was no stand, and it wasn't hanging from a tree or crane or something. The image just floated there. It had no cables or apparent battery supply. Words of blue then appeared in the middle of it, a pleasant female voice reading them aloud.

Welcome to Llurien Online, the world's premiere virtual reality game. You must choose a character before you begin your adventure. Proceed?

"What the hell?" Max muttered, not remembering logging in. Or buying Llurien Online. In fact, he didn't even own a VR headset or whatever else he needed for this. He'd played MMORPGs before, just not the virtual reality kind. Maybe he was at a friend's house? No, he didn't really have any, and not one that would do this with him. And no one else was nearby in the game as if they were doing it together. Maybe he just couldn't see them until he made a character.

He'd heard of Llurien Online, which was based on several series of books set on a world called Llurien. The game had launched a while back, but between work, the band, and his nearly complete degree in classical guitar, he seldom had time for computer games anymore. He wasn't that good at them anyway, not having the patience for them—or dealing with other players attacking him. It was aggravating building up a character and getting loot only to have someone kill you and take your shit, not that all of them had that. Hopefully, this one didn't.

He'd seen enough games to know that the screen before him was a Heads Up Display, or HUD. In theory, in could be dismissed, but he left it there.

He sighed and looked for a logout button. As if reading his mind, one appeared in the upper right corner of his vision. When he turned his head, it moved with the motion. It looked greyed out so he couldn't click it, and he wasn't sure how to anyway. But just thinking about it caused the button to depress and release with no apparent effect. It certainly didn't log him out. He tried several times. Had the game crashed?

Frowning, he imagined taking off the virtual reality headset he assumed he was wearing in the real world, but nothing changed. He moved to do it as if he was wearing it in the game, but still nothing happened.

He sighed. "I can't really be stuck in a VR game, can I? Maybe I can save and quit after creating the character."

At his impulse to reach up and click the "Proceed" button, it clicked by itself.

A character creation screen appeared. In a row at the top were eight species from which he could choose. A unique color bordered each circular picture of a head. He noticed the colors were the red, orange, yellow, green, blue, indigo, and violet rainbow spectrum from left to right, with the human one at the end encircled by white. That one was already selected, which didn't surprise him, as his hands and limbs appeared human.

Below that row stood a human warrior that looked nothing like him, but he figured he could change it later in the process. The gender had been set to male and could apparently be toggled, though this was also greyed out. He mentally clicked a few times to be sure, not that he really wanted to switch it, so he moved on. As he read a description box on the screen's right side, the same pleasant female voice spoke the words.

Species: Human.

Summary: The eighth species of Llurien, humans were created by all twenty-eight of Llurien's gods, who realized no species equally represented all of their traits. They are, therefore, the most unpredictable. Evil to some, good to others, humans are sometimes called Antarians after the first male and female, Antar and Taria; Antaria is also the name of the continent upon which you stand. Their language, Antarian, is spoken throughout Llurien.

Species Strengths: Superior Versatility, Mastery, and Resilience. All religions are possible.

Species Weaknesses: -5% Luck, -1 Wisdom, -1 Morale.

Species Bonuses: None.

Class Restrictions: None. Dual classes permitted.

Proficiency Points Bonus: None.

The human player didn't sound interesting, but being able to choose any class or be dual class was attractive. And yet, playing something else was part of the fun of RPGs. The description suggested that the other species had not inherited the traits of every god. How would that affect game play? He had also noticed that all the options were called a "species" and not "races," and when he began clicking on the other seven, he saw that most of them had more than one race under them. Humans did not.

But what he immediately noticed was that the "Continue" button was greyed out unless he was on human. That didn't make any sense. Why have these options here if none were available? For a moment, he wondered if the game was in a beta or test mode, and that explained these not being available. But the game had been around a year or more. Was his account screwed up or something? Starting with a glitch was just what everyone wanted. That would explain the logout button issue. He irritably clicked through the other species again anyway, mostly to get a sense of what other players might be using if they weren't also restricted. And NPCs were likely to be these species, with him needing to fight some.

Several were taller than him, including one that looked like a humanoid descended from dragons. Another had the muscular and agile body of a male gymnast, while the third had webbed toes and fingers for its life in the sea. The rest were shorter, one reminding him of halfings, another like a goblin or another nasty species, and one having feathered wings in addition to two arms and legs. From the depiction, a final one appeared able to control spirits. Max saw an icon showing two blended figures. Clicking on it revealed a dizzying array of hybrids. It wasn't just humans crossed with other species, but each other, though some combinations appeared to be missing. None were available to him. Only human.

Max sighed and reluctantly clicked the "Continue" button to select human. He got a message that his wisdom and morale had both dropped by 1. The race restriction had indeed deflated his mood. The wisdom drop amused him because he had to agree that people weren't wise. Neither was he, really. No other stats changed and nothing had affected his body, so he didn't feel any different. He still couldn't walk anywhere.

Now he saw options for changing his appearance, his character before him on the floating screen. It looked nothing like him, so he decided to make it closer but with a slight makeover. Max replicated his long, straight blond hair that grew to mid-back. He also kept his blond mustache and goatee, tall height, broad shoulders, slender waist, oval head, arched eyebrows, and straight, slightly large nose. But he improved his jawline, added muscles, tanned his skin a little more, and changed his brown eyes to blue. When he hit the save button, he noticed he was getting several inches taller as the ground moved slightly farther away from his vision. The rest of the changes he wouldn't see without a mirror or unless he viewed himself on the character screen like this.

Satisfied, he clicked through to the next screen and found a list of classes, most familiar: fighter, knight, paladin, hunter, rogue, bard, healer, druid, wizard, sorcerer, monk, Coiryn rider, winger rider, and warder. He didn't know what the last three were, but they were listed as heroic classes. Each of them and paladin were inaccessible until higher levels. He also didn't understand the difference between a wizard and sorcerer, so he checked out each.

Class: Wizard

Summary: The most common type of magic user, wizards are those who must study and practice spells that use some combination of words, gestures, or materials. Species, races, or individuals who lack the discipline and opportunity for education cannot usually become wizards, though it is technically possible. The same spell, if cast more than once by the same wizard, will yield predictable results within a pre-defined range of possibilities as decided by the spell's inventor (almost always one of the gods). This includes mana cost, duration, range, time to cast, and more.

Class: Sorcerer

Summary: Sorcerers are magic-users who can perform magic by will, without training, discipline, or any predefined words,

gestures, or materials. Rarer and more powerful, they are also more dangerous to others and themselves due to unpredictability. The same magic effect produced twice by the same sorcerer might vary wildly in mana cost, duration, range, time to cast, and more. With higher levels comes greater control.

Being a sorcerer might've been okay if Max was fine with just winging it, but tactics went out the window when you couldn't count on the results at all. What if he tried to do magic, expecting it to affect everyone before him, and hardly anything happened? Or it affected allies? At higher levels, such things could be mitigated, but it sounded too risky at first. He'd also have to watch out when facing a sorcerer. He wouldn't be able to predict what they were about to do.

Max had known from the start what he wanted to be—a bard. They had strong melee, ranged, *and* magical attacks. And they were musicians. He wondered how much his real-world skill at playing guitar would impact what he could do. He wasn't a talented singer, but he could hold a tune. And with bards being an all-around class, it might be just what he needed playing alone.

He frowned. These games often had people playing in teams, but Max never did. It put him at a disadvantage and was one reason he quit online RPGs. Maybe he could team up with someone in here, but he doubted he would.

He resumed looking over the bard class, which came with proficiencies in light armor, simple weapons, hand crossbows, longswords, rapiers, and short swords. And he could choose three more now. He would receive a bonus to Dexterity, Intelligence, and Charisma with each level, and to Agility at every other level. The first would help him with archery, playing instruments, and thieving skills like picking locks or disarming traps. Charisma and Intelligence would help him resist mental effects like a charm or illusion spell. The Agility would help him in combat, and while pure fighting classes gained Agility with every level, they didn't get some of his other bonuses. He could choose three instruments to be proficient in, but would hold off until finding some, so as not to waste it on an instrument he didn't have. He selected the bard class and received another prompt.

Choose your name.

He'd never been one for just using his first name, but he wasn't adding his surname. He also didn't want to be one of those dorks with something stupid that they thought was funny. Having numbers after his name sucked, too. It took a minute to think of something related to music and his class. He chose Maestro Max. The words just appeared by themselves in the text box, followed by a Save prompt, which he mentally pressed. The display glowed briefly.

Congratulations! And welcome again to Llurien Online. Let the adventure begin!

The screen faded away, leaving him standing alone in the wilderness. He took a step just to ensure he could, and it worked.

"Great. One problem solved. Now for another if I can log out."

But when that thought caused the button to reappear at the corner of his vision, it hadn't changed. He mentally pushed it several times with no result. He swung his fist at it, not expecting to connect, and while his hand missed, the button depressed again with no resulting logout. Or anything else. Was it broken? That was a heck of a bug. How many other players were stuck in the game? Someone had to figure it out, unless it happened to everyone and no one could communicate with the outside world. That would be interesting. Something akin to claustrophobia lurked at the edge of his mind, this feeling of being trapped.

What he'd seen so far had piqued his curiosity so that part of him wanted to just keep playing anyway, but he couldn't help wondering what was going to happen to his physical body if he was truly stuck in here. First, he'd likely pee himself, so he had that to look forward to. After three days, he'd die of dehydration. Surely his parents would find him by then? Maybe he shouldn't worry about it, but then he noticed something else to worry about. A new element had appeared under the logout button.

Life Counter: 6 Days, 23 Hours, 47 Minutes.

"Life Counter?" he asked aloud. "What does that mean?" But the game didn't answer. He tried asking several ways as if to get the prompt correct, kind of like when he had to say "Alexa" before his Amazon device would do anything. But the game never responded.

As he watched, the minutes dropped by one. What happened when it hit zero?

CHAPTER THREE

Max stood there in the wilderness staring at the Life Counter as it descended. Would his character die when it ended? Did he only get a week to play? Did the counter stop if he *did* log out? Maybe this was another thing not working correctly, but he couldn't do anything about it.

He might as well choose his proficiencies and spells in the meantime. After wondering how to pull up his *Character Screen*, a tabbed window appeared floating before him as if reading his mind. This was more cool than creepy, but were there limits on the mind reading this thing was doing? He hoped so. Now he got a first look at his stats.

Name: Maestro Max.
Species/Race: Human.
Class: Bard, Level 1.
Reputation: 0—Unsung.
XP: 0.
HP: 16/16.
MP: 6/6.
Strength: 6.
Dexterity: 6.
Agility: 6.

Constitution: 6.
Intelligence: 6.
Wisdom: 5.
Charisma: 6.
Morale: 5.

He wasn't sure if these were good or bad, so he clicked the info button. After scanning the text, he found what he was looking for. It looked like his starting stats were from one to ten, with most defaulting to six. His race had cost him one point in Wisdom and Morale. If he was reading this correctly, his initial Mana Points were based on his class, and his Hit Points were his Constitution, plus ten for his bard class.

He moved on to perusing his proficiencies on the *Character Screen's* next tab, starting with whittling down the big list by ignoring things like ventriloquism or mountaineering. He needed something practical and immediately helpful and focused on survival. He finally chose *Hunting*, *Setting Snares*, and *Cooking*. Since it looked like he might be playing this game for a while, he flipped to the *Magic Screen* and saw several tabs for spells he could choose, including valenders.

"Valenders? What is that?"

To his surprise, he received a notification floating in the air.

Info: Valenders.

Summary: Valenders are simple spells that even untrained magicians can use. They don't require preparation and do not cost mana to cast unless they do damage. Your class and level determine how many valenders you know. Once chosen, they cannot be replaced.

He saw that he could choose two from the twenty options. He wanted to get this right. Since he had no armor, he carefully decided on *Weapon Ward*, which would reduce the damage he took from blunt and piercing weapons by 10%. And having no weapon made him choose *Hand of the Grave*, which gave him a ghostly, frigid hand he could touch a target with from twenty feet, inflicting up to 8 HP of necrotic damage.

You have learned the Valender, *Weapon Ward*!
You have learned the Valender, *Hand of the Grave!*

Before making spell choices, he realized he needed to know about the magic system to make smart choices. He didn't want to pick spells and then never be able to change them, like the valenders. Or if that's how it worked, he at least wanted to know that first. Not sure if it would get him any info or not, he asked aloud, "How does the magic system work?" and a window appeared.

Info: Llurien Magic System.
Summary: Even if untrained or unskilled, anyone who can perform magic is a magician, but trained and skilled practitioners are called magic-users (and to call one a magician is an insult). The two main types are wizards and sorcerers.

Wizards perform spells according to directions. An error causes spell failure; nothing happens and gathered energy is safely released. Failure sometimes causes lost mana but does not produce unintended side-effects. On reaching a level, a wizard gains access to all spells at that level. A set number of spells can be swapped out on the hot list except during combat. To cast, the player must have any needed materials. Only mana points (MP), which the player's mana regeneration rate

influences, and the availability of required materials, determine how many spells can be cast.

Sorcerers manipulate magic by willpower, not spells, and are unaffected by deity associations (see "Deity Supplement Option" once you've reached level 8). They can achieve whatever they imagine if they have enough mana and skill. But this often requires knowledge they may not possess. Materials can aid them but may not be required. They may not safely release gathered magic energy when failing in their objective, and magic can still happen with unintended side-effects and results, rather than being aborted altogether. Intentionally or not, they are among the most dangerous people alive.

Mana Regeneration in combat is reduced by two-thirds.

Max joked, "Now I know how to insult wizards and sorcerers."

He switched to the *Spells* tab of the *Magic Screen* and clicked Level 1. The other eight levels were greyed out. Over thirty spells appeared, including staples like *Detect Magic* and *Heal*, both of which he added to his hot list, leaving him one more slot. *Sleep* was a classic, but he didn't have the feathers needed. He'd need to keep an eye out for materials and buy them in towns when able. Many of the spells needed something he didn't have. He noticed that one god or another had created each spell but wasn't sure if that mattered.

On seeing the name *Orb of Doom*, Max smiled. The rock guitarist in him loved it, and when he saw what it did, he immediately chose it, partly because it was the only real level 1 attack spell for him.

Spell: Orb of Doom.
Level 1 Evocation.

Description: In the caster's hand, creates a fist-sized ball of energy that can be hurled at a target up to 100 feet away, inflicting 5-25 HP of damage. The orb is not affected by gravity. Dexterity and Agility affect accuracy. The energy is one of the four elements: air, fire, earth, or ice. The element determines the nature of the damage.

Components: Verbal—"Gather [Element]." Gesture—Throwing motion toward target. Material—The element.

Cast time: Instant.

Duration: Orb must be thrown within five seconds and will last until striking a target.

Cooldown: 5 seconds.

Sphere, Deity and Boost: Green, Tarrera (Goddess of Truth), +10% Damage.

MP: 2.

At Higher Levels: 5-10 extra HP damage per level.

With these chosen, he dismissed the *Spell Screen* and found nothing had changed while he'd been occupied with his character sheet. Was that because this was a starter area, or did time stop while he was looking at a screen?

Only now did Max wonder which way he should go down the dirt path—behind or forward? After wondering if he had a map, one appeared before him. It showed a green pine forest to the north, south, and west, the words Haigan Forest overlaid on it. More trees among the foothills stood to the east, too, but they stopped at a mountain range running north to south, the words Bier Peaks over them. He hadn't noticed the white-capped mountains through the trees behind him, but now he peeked through the foliage to see them looming overhead. That explained the rolling hills, the rocks in the path, and a few boulders amid the underbrush.

The path led parallel to the mountains, and he couldn't zoom out further to see what might be there. He likely had to explore to see more on his map. He dropped a pin on his location now to orient himself as he went. Then he started north, in the direction he'd been facing on appearing in the game, since that seemed like a hint of which way to go.

Before going too far, he wanted to try the valenders and spells, especially the offensive ones. *Hand of the Grave* probably needed a living target. Looking around and listening to the forest, he tried to approach some birds he'd been hearing. Within fifty yards, a bend in the path revealed a bird with a pale abdomen and green and yellow streaks on its back. It sat on a tree branch close to the way. He pulled up the *Spell Screen* again to refresh his memory before dismissing it and focusing on the bird. To his surprise, a sign popped up above it.

Antarian Sparrow. A common bird on the continent of Antaria, the Antarian Sparrow is invasive enough that some people try to repel them from (rather than attract them to) settlements and homes.

HP: 1/1.

Max prepared to do more than repel it.

"Feel the touch of Krairon," he said, holding out his open hand toward the bird. He felt a cold sensation down his arm before a ghostly copy of his hand floated out from his own. It moved across the distance separating them. Climbing steadily, since the target was above him by several feet, it headed straight for the bird, which flew away at the last moment, leaving the hand with nothing to grasp. The spell wouldn't last much longer, but Max saw nothing else alive to grasp except vegetation. He closed his hand to make the spectral one do so around the tree branch, but he missed and tried again before it worked. Dropping his arm, he walked up to look at the branch just as the spell ended. The tree's bark had white frost around it with a noticeable handprint, but it didn't seem damaged. His mana had dropped by one but regenerated to full in just seconds.

Looking around, Max went searching for another bird. After a minute of stepping over fallen branches and rocks, he received a notification.

You gained a skill!
Stealth.
Proficiency Type: Active.
Level: 1.
You gained 25 XP!

That surprised him. He had chosen a few proficiencies during character creation and figured he'd gain them on leveling up, but now he gained one from attempting to do something. Now he wanted to practice such things.

Having found another bird like the first, he focused on the task. This time, the bird didn't move as the hand closed around its body, which stiffened and trembled, the bird letting out a small squawk before falling to the ground and taking the spectral hand with it. Aline from a Dream Theater song popped into Max's head, about watching a sparrow falling giving new meaning to it all, and that if death didn't happen today, it would come soon enough. That applied to him just as well as the bird.

You have killed (1) Antarian Sparrow!
You gained 10 XP!
Loot corpse?

He gained more XP from the skill acquisition than killing the bird. Maybe this game wasn't all about murder. That was encouraging. The bit about looting a bird surprised him, but he said yes and received another notification.

Sparrow feathers (2)
Sparrow feathers with necrotic damage (8)
Bird breast with necrotic damage (1)

"Shit," Max muttered. "If I hadn't used that spell, I might've been able to eat the breast later." He remembered that the *Sleep* spell needed a feather, but he didn't swap out his hot list of spells yet. What would happen if he used the feathers with necrotic damage in a spell? The results could be interesting. And unexpected. He took all the loot in case it might be useful. He could always ditch it from his inventory later. There was nothing else in there now.

He next tried casting Detect Magic and *Weapon Ward*, both working without issue, but what he really wanted was another target so he could try *Orb of Doom*. Continuing down the path, he brought up the mini map to keep an eye on his direction, seeing that the places he'd been remained visible among the otherwise greyed out areas. The mountains were falling behind him as he turned west, deeper into the Haigan Forest.

He soon found another harmless bird, this one on the ground, and reviewed *Orb of Doom*. Since it had four versions, one for each element, he tried the air version first.

"Gather air," he said, raising one hand, palm up. A softball-sized sphere of swirling air quickly formed an inch above his grip. Eyeing the target, he made a throwing motion, and the orb rocketed across the space between with a whoosh. It struck soundlessly as loose dead leaves exploded into the air from the blast, several small branches flying up and backward. The force of it all startled him, but he frowned in disappointment when the bird hurtled upward, wings furiously flapping to escape as it vanished. He'd missed.

Max tested it on a tree branch, missing twice more but by less each time. He used a small rock for the earth version, snapping the branch off with a loud crack. His shout of excitement made him realize he needed to be quiet in case a threat lurked nearby. Without a source of fire or ice, he'd have to wait on the ice and fire versions, so he moved on.

Minutes later, the dirt trail opened into an oblong clearing fifty feet wide. A small hill stood toward the other end beside a large boulder, which something could hide behind. Max paused on the trail, then moved behind a tree. Maybe going through there wasn't wise, but he had seen nothing dangerous so far. The underbrush was just thick enough in the forest that he'd make noise if he tried to go around this. His mana was at full, but he had no other weapons. Stooping to get dirt in the middle of a fight wasn't good, so he grabbed some now and decided the earth version of *Orb of Doom* would go first if needed, then the air version second.

He stepped back onto the path and tried to quietly jog his way across, hoping his *Stealth* skill would help, but he hadn't gone far when the sound of large flapping caught his attention. The source was above the trees and toward the mountains. It sounded larger than any bird he knew of. And then he realized more than one pair of wings were flapping.

Kais, he guessed, realizing he should've studied the species descriptions at the character creation screen more. There were two races of the species, one benevolent, the other not so much. Only the sinister one concerned him now, so he pulled up its description.

Species: Kais.

Race: Daekais.

Summary: One of the seven original species, daekais exhibit the traits of the four Orange Sphere nefarious gods who created them: deception, greed, envy, and fear. They steal everything they can, and follow and ambush unsuspecting travelers. Daekais usually attack in numbers, the talons and bite poisonous. They excel at ranged attacks. From a distance, they can be mistaken for their more benevolent brothers, the morkais. Feather colors suggest their habitat: green for forest, gold for plains, blue for seas, and so on.

In the Divine Covenant, the gods turned two daekais into morkais, creating a new race. Now, the daekais are considered a race of the kais species.

Species Strengths: +1 Agility in the Air, +1 Dexterity, +1 Constitution.

Species Weaknesses: -1 Strength, -1 Intelligence, -2 Wisdom, -2 Charisma, -2 Morale, -5% Regeneration, -5% Attack Speed, -1 Reputation, Poor Concentration.

Species Bonuses: +50% Most Thieving Skills, +10% Poison Resistance, Assess Gems.

Class Restrictions: Any Heroic Classes (Knight, Paladin, Coiryn Rider, Winged Rider, Warder), Bard, Monk. Can be Sorcerers but not Wizards.

Feeling exposed and unable to hide, Max cringed when four of them crested the tree line. Each daekais was a three-and-a-half-foot tall humanoid with feathery wings of brown and green. Arched eyebrows added menace to the large, slanted, glaring eyes already on him. Unkempt orange hair was haphazardly shorn to an inch or two. The teeth were sharply pointed like their chins and ears. Garish baubles adorned most fingers, wrists, ankles, and their long, thin necks. The daekais had retractable talons on dirty, bare feet, and long nails on grimy hands. Above stained, tight leggings, they wore soiled, ill-fitting tunics that had holes in the back for the wings.

Max had no time to cast *Weapon Ward* before all of them raised a sling and fired stones that whistled through the air. Two soared by, but one struck his right shoulder and another his left thigh. Max cursed at the pain, which he wasn't expecting. Since when did games have that as an element? It really raised the stakes of playing. He didn't sign up for this shit. He *really* hadn't.

His health bar appeared for the first time, down a quarter already. He noticed that one of the kais wore a glove with two nasty looking hooks sticking out of it. All of them began circling him twenty feet off the ground. A message appeared as he focused on one.

Daekais. Level 1 Looter. 8 HP. Greedy, deceitful, and wanting easy prey, Looters are the most common class and want whatever you've got. Beware the poisonous talons and bite.

Two of the others were the same class, but one was level 1 and the other level 2, with 13 HP. They all seemed male, but he couldn't be sure. The fourth daekais had a different class.

Daekais. Level 1 Scout. 7 HP. Easily frightened, Scouts are tasked with finding easy prey but not engaging with it. Instead, they tell their tribe of your whereabouts, threat level, and potential loot.

Max wondered if the noise he'd made blowing up birds had attracted the Scout's attention. He had no loot, but they didn't know that and likely thought he wasn't a threat because he was unarmed. He eyed the path, but they saw his gaze and a Looter moved to hover over one escape into the woods, wings flapping gracefully to keep himself afloat. The Scout guarded the other exit. Max had to get out of here through the underbrush if needed. He was no match for the four of them, especially when they were moving targets. And yet two weren't moving any-more. He whirled toward one guarding a path, his hand pulling back.

"Gather earth!" he shouted. So fast that he almost didn't see it happen, dirt rose from the ground by his feet into his hand, forming a sphere of hard-packed earth. He hurled it at the Scout, who shrieked as it soared past, narrowly missing. Max almost turned and ran into the woods, but the Scout furiously rose and flew away, casting several frightened looks back at Max. The other daekais guarding a path resumed flying circles around Max. Had he realized the folly of holding still?

Three daekais remained and Max had only 4 of his 6 Mana Points left, though it was slowly regenerating. With *Orb of Doom* costing 2 MP, he couldn't get all of them, especially if he missed. *Hand of the Grave* only cost 1 MP, but it did 1-8 HP of damage compared to 3-24 HP for *Orb of Doom*. And what if *Hand of the Grave* didn't kill one? Only at maximum power would it get three of them. It was also slower moving, and they'd likely dodge the damn hand.

But then he had an idea. Before he could do it, two of the daekais fired at him. One missed, but the other hit his stomach. While he winced and doubled over, the level 2 Looter landed on the boulder and fired a shot that struck Max in the temple and knocked him sideways, a sharp pain making it hard to think. His health bar dropped below 50%.

"Gather air!" he said between clenched teeth. With the other daekais circling, he waited for one to fly past the boulder, giving him a chance to hit the second one if he missed the first. He finally threw the *Orb of Doom* at the sitting daekais, who leaned forward and flattened himself so that Max again missed. But the orb came close enough to the one flying behind it at that moment that the air blast still knocked him out of the sky. The daekais haphazardly flew into a tree, a red -3 HP rising from him after the collision. Then he fell to the ground, an additional red -3 HP fading up. The daekais struggled to rise, the health bar flashing red. Seeing this, the other one still flying around them fled.

Max's heart leapt. He might actually win this fight. The Level 2 Looter seemed to realize it, too, fumbling for a stone to fire. From the ground, Max snatched one rock that had struck him, wondering if stone would cause a more potent missile than dirt.

"Gather earth," he said, and a smooth stone *Orb of Doom* floated in his hand. "Let's see whose rock is better, motherfucker."

Chapter Four

The daekais' eyes widened, and he launched itself up off the boulder, flapping wings sending leaves and dirt scattering as he tried to escape. Max didn't wait for him to get too airborne in case the guy started zigzagging or something. He hurled the stone orb, which struck the daekais in the chest with a sickening crunch of shattered ribs. A red -15 HP floated up. The daekais flew backwards, legs and arms limp as he landed in a heap on his back. This time, another red damage indicator didn't rise, and Max suspected that this meant the guy was dead before he hit the ground. The daekais didn't move again.

Critical Hit!
You have killed (1) Daekais Looter, Level 2!
You gained 100 XP!
Loot corpse?

You gained a skill!
Critical Hit.
Proficiency Type: Combat.
Level: 1.
You gained 25 XP!

Max brushed aside the messages. By now, the other daekais who'd crashed had risen to his feet to stare in horror at his dead companion. Max noticed his own MP had regenerated to 1, just enough for *Hand of the Grave*.

"Feel the touch of Krairon," he said, extending his arm. As the spectral hand soared across the ground and grabbed the distracted daekais by the throat, his victim never moved. The daekais let out an awful shriek, peeing himself. Then he fell face first to the ground.

You have killed (1) Daekais Looter, Level 1!
You gained 50 XP!
Loot corpse?

Max let out a breath and looked around. The other daekais didn't appear to be returning. Not yet, anyway. Maybe they'd come with reinforcements. He hurried over to the bodies and looted them just by accepting the prompt to do so; he didn't have to rifle through their soiled, torn tunics or touch their grimy bodies, which he could now smell. Being this close afforded a better look, but there wasn't much that differed from the character creation screen image, except that each appeared distinct from the others like real people did. Only now did he notice that there was no sign of the stone *Orb of Doom* he'd thrown. Had it rolled away, disintegrated, or just ceased to exist when the spell ended?

He received two slings of poor quality, two knives of terrible quality that were obviously useless and he threw away, two pouches with twenty-two stones total, a bunch of daekais feathers, a poor quality pack of valend cards, three talons, and two teeth. He wasn't sure what the talons and teeth were good for, but suspected crafting. Maybe he could extract the poison. The cards just looked like tarots.

There were also two good quality talon gloves, which one of the daekais had been wearing. Each was a fingerless leather glove with two sharp hooks protruding beside the pinky and index fingers. These hooks seemed well fashioned, including the sturdy attachment to the glove. He couldn't tell what they were for, as they didn't look entirely like weapons, even if they could be used as one. They were too small for his hands, but he put them in inventory to potentially sell, or trade to another daekais for leaving him alone.

The daekais also had 10 circular, metal coins between them: 9 copper pieces and 1 silver. They felt cold, like real-world currency. One side read "Neistrum is Divine" and had the image of a money pouch with light shining from the top stamped on it. The other side read "Antaria, Llurien" along the top and had what looked like a date on the bottom. On that side, the copper coins showed a bird of prey with wings outstretched, but the silver piece showed a knight on horseback. The edges of both were milled, and Max picked at the ridges with his fingernail.

The other coins were rectangular gems with smooth edges—8 amethysts and 2 emeralds. They were unmarked and slick on the backside but had designs on the front. As he looked them over, a message told him they were niquerran coins, made by the mountain-dwelling niquerra, who used poor-quality gems as currency. He dimly recalled that niquerra were a race of the querra species. The gems had exquisite craftsmanship, the amethysts showing a fish, and the emeralds carved with what looked like a mountain goat. Wondering at the value, he looked at the message and tried to click the words "niquerran coins." It worked, and another notification appeared.

Niquerran Coins:
1 amethyst = 10 cents
10 amethysts = 1 emerald = $1
10 emeralds = 1 ruby = $10
10 rubies = 1 sapphire = $100
10 sapphires = 1 diamond = $1,000
10 diamonds = 1 obsidian = $10,000

Then he pulled up info on the other money.

Metal Coins:
10 iron pieces = 1 copper = $1
10 coppers = 1 silver = $10
10 silvers = 1 gold = $100
10 gold = 1 platinum = $1000

Math was never his strong suit and trying to remember what everything was worth wasn't helping, but he figured he had over twenty-one dollars. He did not know what anything cost. At least the game designers told him how much everything related to Earth money as a frame of reference.

He finally looked over all the baubles the daekais wore, but most had no value. He put them into his inventory anyway, figuring he might bribe the next daekais. His health bar had risen faster with the end of combat, as had his mana regeneration. This was now high enough to cast another spell.

"Mother Llurien," he began, "mend your child." He felt the soreness in his forehead vanish as his HP rose by 3. He'd need to wait a minute for more mana to get himself to full. With a glance at the sky, he jogged down the path and into the tree cover before slowing. From now on, he'd try not to make a sound. His *Stealth* skill would help. The stone *Orb of Doom* certainly made a noise on impact, so as much as he wanted to practice his aim, maybe it wasn't smart.

He walked north for half an hour, not seeing much else to trouble him. Along the way, he found a stream and quenched his growing thirst. He also practiced a bit with the sling, aiming at the water to minimize the sound of impact. He tried to save the smoother stones the daekais had. They looked to have come from a riverbed, based on their surface features, and he found a few similar ones in the water. Only now did he wonder what had made the trail he walked. Clearly, the daekais had no need. What else was out here? As he did this, he gained the *Foraging* and *Slingshot* skills at level one, each giving him 25 XP.

With the mountains further behind him, he hoped for some sign of civilization soon, like wagon tracks, an actual sign with directions, mileage, and a town name written on it, or even an abandoned building. But the next thing he encountered was a bunch of humanoid figures lying on the trail and to either side of it. He slipped behind a pine tree and visually scoured all around him. Nothing else seemed to be here. Most of the figures seemed awake and none gave a sign of detecting him as the quiet minutes passed.

They were the same size as daekais but had no wings. Their faces and chins were round but mishappen. They seemed thin, as if malnourished, with small feet and hands and a hunched back. Multiple sores oozed on their skin, maybe because they all wore soiled and torn tunics and trousers that fit poorly and didn't match. Dirty nails and unkempt hair added to their overall impression of filth, and Max could smell their sweaty bodies from here. As he peered at them, he got a notification.

Riven swarm. Named for their dual nature, riven hate themselves as much as everyone else. They are perpetually

dying from disease when not murdering others, and are torn between slumber and a frenzied state. Disturb at your peril.

"Great," Max muttered, wondering how to get by them. He pulled up a longer description.

Species: Riven.

Summary: One of the seven original species, riven exhibit the traits of the four Violet Sphere nefarious gods who created them: haste, hate, cynicism, and sloth. They are a perpetual plague on the land and live near settlements to prey on everyone. All shun them. They don't respect anyone's life, including their own. If disturbed from their seemingly perpetual sleep, they can become reckless, frenzied attackers who swarm and slice through everyone before them. When that doesn't kill, the multitude of diseases they carry will. A riven swarm is so formidable in melee that even armored knights just run, townspeople clearing out. They otherwise lack the will, focus, or energy to achieve much; a more determined one can easily amass followers among them.

Species Strengths: +1 Agility, +1 Morale.

Species Weaknesses: -2 Strength, -2 Constitution, -2 Intelligence, -2 Wisdom, -2 Charisma, -10% Luck, -10% Regeneration.

Species Bonuses: Charge Bonus, Identify Poison, Resist Cold, Resist Heat, +25% Attack Speed, +15% Physical Attack, +50% Followers, +25% Fearful Reaction.

Class Restrictions: Any Heroic Classes (Knight, Paladin, Coiryn Rider, Winged Rider, Warder), Hunter, Bard.

Proficiency Points Bonus: 1 point at creation and an additional 1 point every 4 levels.

Max leaned back and looked harder at the terrain. The decaying leaves of autumn were still everywhere. It wasn't like in his neighborhood, where the landscaping service came by and used leaf blowers to clean everything out. He'd be heard if he went anywhere but on the trail, and he wasn't backtracking. The only way forward was through them. They looked like they were settling down for a nap or just waking up. But since he couldn't tell which, waiting them out wasn't a plan.

He pulled up his *Magic Screen*, remembering the *Sleep* spell being there. He had plenty of feathers, the lone material needed, though some had necrotic damage. The spell worked from fifty feet away. With a radius of twenty feet, he might get them all. Their description suggested they were prone to sleep, anyway. The necrotic feathers were tempting, but he wasn't sure what that would do. What if they turned into zombies or something? He could make things worse.

He pulled out one of the daekais feathers and reviewed the spell. Before casting it, he wondered what would happen if they didn't all fall asleep. Would they realize magic had been used on the others? If so, and they looked for the cause, he'd have to stay hidden. He could always cast the spell again, except that it had a two-hour cooldown. If they stayed asleep for the full eight hours, that would work if not being ideal. Hoping for the best, he peered around the tree and retrieved a feather from his inventory. Holding it in one hand, he summoned magic power to infuse him.

"Feel slumber's call to rest," he intoned. Then he dropped the feather. As it fell, so too did the riven in the distance. They dropped, one by one, some tumbling into a comrade to lie in a heap.

You have made (14) riven fall asleep!

You gained 225 XP!

The XP gain surprised Max. Was it worth something to spare a life instead of ending it? Maybe the game designers were conscientious. He didn't much care but appreciated the idea.

Silently watching for several minutes, he saw no movement but heard snoring, even from here. He finally decided little risk remained. He cast *Weapon Ward* and ventured over to them. As he neared, the smell of sweat and feces nearly made him gag. He couldn't help a muted cough or two while burying his nose in his sleeve. Up close, he saw open sores on their skin and lice in their hair. He scrutinized the first few he came across and saw a weapon tied to the waist of several. As he focused on it, information popped up.

Riven Dagger: Double-bladed Dagger.
Quality: Very poor.
Rarity: Common.
Speed: Very Fast.
Physical Attack: +10%.
Magical Attack: NA.
Bonuses: -1 Intelligence, -1 Wisdom, +2 Morale.

The weapon looked like a regular dagger, except it had a blade protruding from both ends. Someone could stab up and down, or left to right, in alternation without having to change the grip. No surprise they rated it very fast. Most of these riven had one and if they swarmed like their description said, it was no wonder they were feared.

Since he still didn't have a weapon besides the sling, he eyed each riven who had one to see who it would be easiest to take the dagger from, based on their position. To his surprise, a quarter of them were female. He stopped and carefully untied the sloppily done knot of a ragged string that held a dagger to one's waist. What he'd read about the diseases they carried had him worried about contracting something. Maybe this wasn't a good idea. There was no telling how contagious they were and with what. If something was on the handle, he might get infected. But if he didn't have a melee weapon, that could be fatal in a hand-to-hand fight. This would do as a backup weapon to his fists.

After getting the knot undone, he looked around and grabbed a few leaves to lift the dagger itself with. A notification told him he'd just earned the Pickpockets skill at level 1 and another 25 XP, and then came the better message.

You achieved Level 2!
You gained 8 Hit Points!
You gained 2 Mana Points!
Class bonus: You gained Dexterity +1, Intelligence +1, Cha-
risma +1!
You gained (2) proficiency points!
You have (2) unassigned proficiency points!
You have (1) additional spell you can have in your hot list!

Max avoided celebrating aloud, given that he was straddling two sleeping riven. He had answered the question about gaining proficiency points with levels. It seemed that the game wanted to reward him for smart or skillful play and not just killing things all the time. He could get behind that, deciding how to advance and play the game. He wanted to choose new skills now, but this wasn't really the time.

Max began stepping over the small bodies, which were left, right, and centered on the dirt path. Most of the riven had skin problems like a rash. This close, he noticed what their clothes were soiled with—dirt, food, sometimes dried blood, and sweat stains at the arm pits. A few had darker ones along the crack of their asses and Max decided right then to stop scrutinizing them.

Riven dagger still in hand, he had made it most of the way by them when he froze. Slumped against a tree in an upright position sat a female riven, narrow, bloodshot, violet eyes regarding him with a mix of sullenness and muted fury. He was close enough to see that the pupils were horizontal slits. Was she asleep with her eyes open? Or was she awake? Max couldn't tell. The riven hadn't reacted. A rustle out in the forest caught his attention, and he decided not to stay in case something—like him—woke them. But he stared at her as he took another step over a body and felt his heart skip when the eyes moved with him. Max glanced at the others on the ground ahead of him and how many steps he had to take to be clear. Another five. If she moved, he was running.

He continued on, the riven turning her head to watch. The heavily-lidded eyes had opened more, her hand going for the riven dagger at her waist.

"Shit," Max muttered. He stopped looking at her and skipped over the remaining figures one by one until clear.

You have used the Stealth skill and gained 15 XP!

Max looked at her to see that she was rising. Apparently, she wasn't included in his successful use of the skill. That she had seen him hadn't impacted him being awarded for sneaking past the others. The *Sleep* spell hadn't gotten her because she was farther away.

Seeing her watching him, Max took off down the path at a quiet, careful run, avoiding any jutting rocks or loose branches and hoping to get some distance. Once he rounded a curve in the bend, the trees blocked his view behind. The sound of his own steps made it hard to tell if she was following. He just continued for five minutes before stopping, afraid to run too far in case he ran right into another threat. How quiet were riven? They were small and had little on them to jingle. Would he hear her coming? He listened for a bit and heard nothing, so he set off again, this time at a walk.

But he couldn't shake the feeling he was being watched. Maybe it was paranoia. Every time he reached a curve in the path, he looked ahead, seeing no one on it. But he also wanted to see how far it was before another turn because that's how long he'd be in sight if something was following him and came around behind. And that's when he decided on a ploy. A straight section over a hundred yards long lay ahead, so he went about halfway before ducking behind two trees that had trunks close together, providing him with better cover.

A minute later, she appeared, jogging down the path with more stealth, caution, and determination than he expected. Unless she ran past him without seeing him, he had made a mistake. Wasting no time on regret, he decided the sling might not do much damage even if he hit her, and he didn't want to get close enough to use that riven dagger. *Sleep* had too long of a cooldown to use again. That left him with *Hand of the Grave* and *Orb of Doom*. His MP was full, like his HP. He rearranged his hot list spells to remove *Sleep* from there and add the others.

She stopped halfway to him, listening and sniffing the air. She looked around as if suspicious. Did she know he couldn't have made it to the end without her seeing him? Was she smart enough to know he had to be hiding? Out of caution, he assumed so despite the dull look he'd seen in her eyes when closer. *Orb of Doom* might make enough noise to bring another threat here, one he didn't know about. How many HP did she have? Was *Hand of the Grave* enough to kill her? The spell was quieter. She continued toward him as he readied *Orb of Doom*, peering past the trunk at her.

Riven, Level 1 Brawler. 5 HP. The basic fighter class among riven, they are just as likely to stab themselves as you with their riven daggers because they only fight in one state—frenzied. Kill them from a distance if you can. And if you miss, run!

So he might kill her with *Hand of the Grave*. He switched the spell in his mind and waited for her to get within twenty feet, the spell's range. He also had to step back from the tree because he needed to stretch out his arm and was hoping to do it without sticking his arm out where she'd see the movement.

"Feel the touch of Krairon," he whispered, gesturing with the hand not holding the river dagger.

The spectral hand appeared and soared across the ground toward the riven, four feet above the path. Max wondered if only he could see it, but soon got his answer. She stopped, a look of alarm animating her ugly face. She backed away and Max feared she'd escape, so he stepped out, ready to pursue. Her eyes darted to him and back to the hand. Snarling, she retreated more quickly and Max broke into a run. She turned and ran, too, and with the spell only lasting ten seconds, he feared she'd escape. He'd have to wait to cast it again. She was faster than he expected and kept ahead of him until the hand vanished and he stopped. Hearing this, she did, too, turning back, eyes darting around for the shadowy hand. Then she seemed to accept that it was gone. A sinister leer split her face, revealing yellow teeth with half of them missing.

"Gather air!" Max said, holding up his hand. He felt the swirling orb hovering there before he hurled it.

Whether she saw it or just understood the throwing motion, the riven dove to the path and the orb sailed past her with a whoosh, hitting a tree branch behind her and cracking it. She got up and ran toward him, arms pumping up and down, the dagger in one hand reminding him of his peril.

Max cursed and ran.

CHAPTER FIVE

With the riven closing in behind him, Max knew he couldn't outrun it, to his surprise, given that he was two feet taller. The underbrush had grown thicker, so he plunged into and around the first few bushes. He nearly tripped until realizing he might be the one who went down, so he slowed. The riven followed, her pace had slowed so that she wasn't gaining. Maybe he could try Orb *of Doom* again and catch her by surprise.

He came across a wide swath of four-foot-tall bushes with violet flowers amid their large, shiny green leaves. They filled the gap between some close trees on one side and a boulder on the other, blocking the way. They were five feet deep, so he shoved his way through to the far side, the branches scratching his legs through his thin pants. Maybe they'd poke out the riven's eyes. The underbrush after was clearer, and he started onward only to hear a screech behind him.

The riven had stopped short of the bushes, eyes so wide that he saw the surrounding whites. Her violet eyes darted back and forth at the obstacle. He wondered what she was so afraid of. As he looked at it again, a message popped up.

Kyson bush, aka, "Death Bush." With violet flowers blooming from spring to fall, and red berries through spring, the ky-

son bush's leaves worsen any existing malady. The effect is worse on riven because of their perpetual illnesses. To keep them away, the bush is frequently planted as riven bane around settlements. Even frenzied riven will stop at the sight of it. Despite the nickname, it doesn't necessarily kill riven, though it can; the term is designed to inhibit them.

Max noticed she was so horrified that she didn't even appear to be considering a way around it. She had seemingly forgotten him. In her distraction, he whispered the *Hand of the Grave* spell again. She stood still while the hand grasped her throat. Only then did she seem to remember him, but it was too late as it choked her, a red -8 HP floating up from her as her health bar briefly appeared. She fell back with a strangled cry and thud on the hard earth.

You have killed (1) Riven Brawler, Level 1!
You gained 50 XP!
Loot corpse?

Only now did he realize he could've killed all those sleeping riven for far more XP, but it seemed too dishonorable. Murder. That's what it was. Killing someone who was actively trying to kill you was one thing, but it just wasn't sporting to kill defenseless people. Were they really people? They were just NPCs in a game. Computer code. And yet they seemed so lifelike. Maybe he was being foolish, but it didn't feel right. He knew some people played games with a very different personality than their real one, but he felt preoccupied with curiosity about why he was even in this game and couldn't logout. It distracted him from something like adopting a persona not his, not that he really wanted to. Not today.

He focused on the corpse from his position and looted her without getting close. All she had were 2 copper coins and another riven dagger, which he added to his inventory. He broke off some twigs from the bushes to take. Maybe he could just wave it in front of him and walk through the next group of riven, and they'd all back away, but he wasn't counting on it. He also took some berries and flowers in case he could use them for potions or crafting.

He wondered if he should do something with the body. Normally he wouldn't even consider it in a game, but the realism was making an impression. Burying her would take too long and he didn't have a shovel. Something seemed appropriate, but when he caught a whiff, he decided not to touch her. Maybe the game would make her just disappear like some games did.

Since he had a moment of quiet, he pulled up his stats and saw he'd amassed 560 XP. He still had two proficiency points to use, and looked over the skill list. Since he was already sneaking around, he added a point to *Stealth*. He wanted to use the other point for a weapon, but since he felt that the river dagger and sling were not items he'd be using long, he saved the other point.

With nothing left to do, he checked his map to see nothing had really changed. His MP were regenerating nicely, so he found his way back to the path and continued. As he walked, he practiced with the sling, saving the better stones he'd gotten from the daekais and just using rocks found on the trail. Hitting a thick trunk might make noise to bring more trouble, so he aimed at smaller targets and improved. The rocks skittering through loose leaves on the ground were more likely to be mistaken for small rodents or something else.

The trail led him northwest, angling away from the mountains, the foothills rolling underfoot. The trees were mostly evergreens with increasing numbers of deciduous plants. Why the game had started him here was not apparent, and he figured a settlement had to be around here somewhere. Maybe he was going in the wrong direction, but he'd been facing this way on arrival.

After twenty minutes, he heard the clang of metal ahead and shouting voices muffled by distance. He loped ahead, cresting a hill in a crouch until verifying nothing lay on the other side. The path continued over another rise and he saw the flash of a blade, the voices almost loud enough to make out the words. Questioning whether this was wise, he crept ahead and peered over the next hill, seeing information pop up as he took in the scene.

On the path, two human hunters—level 1 and 2—stood back from those fighting, hands on sword hilts. They had short bows strung over their shoulders. One had turned just enough toward Max for him to see a symbol of a hawk in silhouette on the worn leather armor. They seemed to be with the two level 1 human fighters, also clad in leather, who took turns assaulting another figure, their blades clanging. One attacker was a muscular woman. All were NPCs. Max focused on their intended victim, who wore leather armor under a tunic, which was emblazoned with a gate that had two trees flanking it.

Name: Norus Shadowmoon of Gitarna.
Type: NPC.
Class: Hunter.
Species: Human.
Level 5.

"Don't hurt him too much," said one hunter, laughing. "Need him alive."

The other hunter shook his head. "No. Just need him not to tell anyone we were here."

The first one laughed as Max frowned. He'd never liked an unfair fight, but him joining their victim wouldn't change that. Most of the attackers had about a dozen hit points except for the level 2 hunter at 24. While he watched, the woman fighter sliced into Norus' leg and Max had seen enough. As if reacting to his emotions, a notification popped up.

New Quest: Save Norus Shadowmoon.

Objective: Save the hunter Norus Shadowmoon of Gitarna from certain death by joining his fight against the forces of Evator.

Difficulty: Moderate.

Rewards: +1 Reputation in Karendi Kingdom (Gitarna). -2 Reputation in Andra Kingdom (Evator) if there are any survivors. 1,000 XP.

Accept?

Max was going to do it even before this, but now it was certain. He grabbed a small rock, knowing he was within range but concerned about his accuracy from here. They were close enough to each other that missing one might mean he hit another.

"Ward me," he whispered, casting *Weapon Ward* once again. It only lasted two minutes, but it could help. And he wasn't in combat yet, so his mana regenerated quickly.

"Gather earth," he whispered next, rising to stand atop the hill behind them. The ball of stone that formed in his hand felt like nothing, as if not real, but it would feel real enough when it struck. He made the throwing motion and ducked down behind the hill again as the orb soared at the male fighter, who had his arm back to swing at Norus. The stone slammed into his hip with a sickening crunch, a red -10 HP floating into the air as his health bar appeared, flashing red. With a shriek, the guy fell to one knee and dropped his sword, clutching the wound. Norus wasted no time slicing him across the neck, killing him. Despite Max ducking down, the woman fighter saw him and pointed before resuming her attack on Norus.

Both hunters turned toward Max, drawing swords, but only one—the level 2—ran for him. Fumbling for his sling, Max hoped to slow him so he could cast *Orb of Doom* again. He aimed and fired too quick, missing. He fumbled for another but realized he wouldn't get a second shot off. Backing away, he pulled out the riven dagger just as the hunter reached him and swung. Max tried to block with the blade, only to have it painfully knocked from his hand. His health bar appeared as a red -1 HP floated up before him. The hunter swung again and Max jumped back, losing his balance on the hill and falling to the ground, taking another -1 HP of damage.

"Gather air!" he yelled. Panic overcame him as the hunter raised the sword up to impale him to the earth. He sensed the orb in one hand and hastily hurled it up, catching the hunter full in the chest. A red -20 HP floated up as the hunter flew back and landed with a thud, unmoving. A notification popped up, but Max ignored it, though he noticed it said that the guy was dead.

Getting up, he rushed over to the body and grabbed the sword, and then crested the hill. Norus' red health bar suggested he didn't have long to live. The fighter attacking him had lost half his life, but the remaining hunter stood unscathed and now ran toward Max, who awkwardly held the sword. This wasn't like other games he'd played. He needed actual skills he didn't have, not to just use a controller.

The hunter swung at his torso. Max raised his sword, which his foe knocked sideways with a dull clang. He barely brought it back before him, only to have another blow do the same. The hunter smiled, lunging. Max hit the blade aside, but not enough. The tip sank into his left arm. He grunted at the awful pain. Fear, anger, and adrenaline surged.

Ignoring the damage indicator, he slashed at the hunter and caught him across the chest. The blade slid off the leather armor without hurting the guy. Before he could recover, his foe slashed across his belly. Only Max leaning back saved him from being disemboweled. The wound stung. His health bar flashed red. Max swung several times to force the hunter back, but it didn't work.

"Gather air," he said. The orb filled his left hand, where blood had dripped to from the arm wound. The hunter's eyes widened before he slashed again. Max barely raising his sword, which flew from his hand into the underbrush by the trail. Max hastily threw the orb, pain in his arm making him gasp. The range was too close to miss and the orb hurled the hunter away and onto his back, a red -8 HP floating up.

Max jumped on top and pinned the guy's arms to his sides with both knees. Then he punched him several times, doing -1 HP of damage with each, the hunter's red health bar flashing. That surprised Max, but he kept swinging until the man stopped moving. By that point, the guy's eyes and lips had swollen, his nose was broken, and Max could hardly recognize him. He ignored another notification, this one about the hunter's death, his breathing heavy. Norus killed the remaining fighter and fell to one knee, his health bar low.

An unreadable gaze met his.

CHAPTER SIX

Max sat atop the dead hunter, unsure how to feel as he ignored the notifications. The wounds in his stomach, left arm, and right fist had most of his attention, but he didn't have enough mana to heal himself. There was no risk of dying, but that pain had to stop. He felt relieved to have won the fight, and yet the sightless eyes of the hunter staring past him made him feel guilty. Max had never seen so much blood. That he'd beaten the guy to death freaked him out a little. He'd never been in a fight so violent. Most altercations he'd experienced had been over in a punch or two. None of this felt at all like a game. It was too visceral. And it would not get any better as long as he sat there on the dead man's chest.

He got up, legs shaking from adrenaline or because he felt a little faint. Only now did he notice the blood splattered on his clothes, his right fist covered in it. Something dripped down his face, and he assumed it was sweat until wiping it away and discovering it was blood, but he didn't have a cut there. It was the hunter's. To take his mind off it, he looked at Norus, who was watching him with concerned brown eyes while kneeling over a body and wiping his sword on the dead man's tunic.

"You okay?" Norus asked, voice deep and sounding masculine, an impression his brown stubble beard and square jaw aid-ed. His brow was thick and damp with sweat. On rising, he seemed over six feet tall, slender but muscled, his stance casual, as if he belonged in these woods.

Max nodded despite how he felt. "Yeah. You?"

"I'll be fine, thanks to you." A small vial appeared in his hand from nowhere—likely his inventory—before he drank it. Some of the wounds Max could see went away and Norus' health bar rose. He then pulled another vial out and nodded at the bodies. "Most of them should have healing potions if you don't. You earned them."

Max perked up and looked down at the hunter at his feet, seeing an option to loot the corpse, the word "corpse" making him frown. Couldn't the message say "body?" He sifted through the items, ignoring everything but a healing potion he pushed into his inventory, then moved to his hand.

Potion: Health.
Effect: Restores 1-5 HP instantly.

He quaffed it. The wound on his stomach mostly disappeared, but the others didn't change. Was the game smart enough to ensure the more serious wounds were affected first? He looted another body for two healing potions and consumed one, the rest of his wounds disappearing.

He asked, "Why were these guys attacking you?"

Putting away his sword, Norus replied, "I think we should get out of here first, before getting into that. There will be others not far behind. You can loot the bodies for gear. You need it."

Max nodded and first pulled up his notifications as Norus busied himself with his gear.

You have killed (1) Human Hunter, Level 1!

You gained 200 XP!
Loot corpse?

You have killed (1) Human Hunter, Level 2!
You gained 250 XP!
Loot corpse?

You achieved Level 2 in Orb of Doom!
Increased accuracy!

Quest Complete: Save Norus Shadowmoon.
You earned 1,000 XP!
You earned +1 Reputation in Karendi Kingdom (Gitarna)!

You achieved Level 3!
You gained 12 Hit Points.
You gained 6 Mana Points.
Class bonus: You gained +1 Agility, Dexterity +1, Intelligence +1, Charisma +1.
You gained (2) proficiency points.
You have (3) unassigned proficiency points.
You have (1) additional spell you can have in your hot list!
You gained access to level 2 spells!

Max struggled to feel any excitement about this and decided to worry about new spells and skills later. He once again felt relieved to take things without having to touch a body. Some elements of the game were so realistic, but this wasn't at all. He wasn't complaining. He had four bodies to choose from and focused on the level 2 hunter first, outfitting himself with a level 3 Asyander short bow, the best of the items. That guy's leather armor seemed in better condition, but one fighter had a better longsword and dagger. He donned the finest tunic, which had the hawk symbol on it. All the items were common and of good quality.

On realizing his inventory could hold all the items, he agreed with Norus to split it evenly. Maybe he could sell the extras. They halved the money, too, Max coming away with nine iron coins, six copper, and four silver.

Among the other items he took were a bunch of arrows, a coin pouch, a backpack with things like a coil of rope or a whetstone, and various foodstuffs—breads, fruits, dried meats—that he didn't recognize the names of. He'd have to take a bite to see what they were. Most restored a few HP, MP, or both. All of the dead had an acorn in their possession, too, so he took them in case they were useful. To his surprise, one hunter had a wooden flute that looked to be handmade, and poorly. But the bigger find was a piece of sheet music with a single melody of two similar phrases on it, chords written above the music staves. A message appeared as he looked at it.

Spell Song: The Song of Gathering
Key: A Major
Time: 4/4
Description: This old melody predates even the Empire of Antaria before it fell long ago. It will cause all who hear it to gather around the performer and become receptive to what he says. But it cannot make listeners do something that goes against their nature. The melody can be performed on an instrument or sung with the words, which have a stronger effect.
Duration: Continuous as long as it is played. Once stopped, the song will keep those who've gathered from leaving for five minutes, unless the performer tells them to go. Keeping them

present after that will depend on the caster's other crowd control abilities.

Level: 2.

Cooldown: 1 hour.

Lyrics: Come and hear the words of wisdom that will lift your heart anew. Hear the sound of hope and joy that gathers like the morning dew.

MP: 2.

Too bad Max had no idea how to play a flute. Maybe he'd spend one of his three music proficiency points on it. The sound could carry far, but he already wondered if a trumpet wouldn't be better because it could be used in battle or at ceremonies. And of course, he was hoping to find a guitar, or at least a lute or mandolin. He really wasn't sure what he'd be able to acquire, and he'd never actually played a lute before. It just seemed appropriate for the style period. He knew how to read music, at least, and started humming the melody for *The Song of Gathering* to himself.

Breaking his thoughts, Norus said, "We need to move on, and quickly. This is an advance scouting party. More aren't far behind."

"Should we hide the bodies?"

The hunter shook his head. "There's no way we're hiding that a fight happened here. We'll just leave them, but let's dress one of them in the clothes you were wearing. He'll seem like he was you, and you now look like someone from Evator. It will look like one person from Evator survived. If we are caught, maybe no harm will come to you."

Max nodded, unsure of the value of that ruse but willing to play along. "What about you? Shouldn't you put on something of theirs, too?"

Norus smirked. "My face is already known there. Such a ruse will not work."

The game made it easy to put the clothes he'd started with on one body without even touching it. He wanted to choose some spells and skills, but figured they could wait a minute. His HP and MP were nearly at full already, and he felt relieved to be properly armed and armored. Maybe this NPC could tell him what was going on. He suddenly realized how desperate he was for information.

"Let's go," said the hunter, continuing on the path. Max followed and they soon took a fork toward the west, deeper into the woods and farther from the mountains.

Max asked, "Where are we going? Can you tell me who they were? And you? Where is Evator?"

"In good time," came the reply, and they trotted for ten minutes before slowing to a walk. Max fell in beside him.

He had listened for sounds of pursuit or any movement from elsewhere, but he'd heard nothing aside from the usual sounds of a forest, mostly birds chirping and some insects. Half-buried and loose rocks continued to dot the dirt trail, but they became less frequent. They sometimes topped a rise, giving Max a view of green pines stretching in every direction, an occasional wide break in them suggesting a clearing or lake. They passed through streams of various sizes, crossing on wet stones rather than a bridge. He once saw an animal that looked like a deer.

Max finally asked, "Why did those men, and the woman, attack you?"

Norus replied, "I'm not sure how much you know, but this land belongs to the Kingdom of Karendi. To the north is a river that forms the northern border. Evator, in Kingdom Andra, stands on the other side. Those soldiers were from there."

"So they aren't supposed to be here?" Max pulled up his map and saw that these locations were now indicated, the word "approximate" on them. He imagined that if he reached one, it would be more definitive.

"Right. This is our territory. I'm one of several tasked with scouting for exactly this kind of trouble."

"I heard them say they wanted to kill you so you wouldn't tell others they're here."

Norus nodded. "If you hadn't come along, I'd be dead. I will see that you remain safe, but I must get to Gitarna. You should come. The town is my home and lies to the west in the middle of this forest. We have a mining operation in the mountains, one the produces great wealth for the kingdom. Andra has always coveted it."

"Do you think they're planning to do something?"

"Seems so. There's been more activity in this area than usual. Riven like to bother people, and there normally aren't enough here for them to also be here, and yet they are much more than usual. It has suggested we need to look for trespassers, and we've been finding them. A few other hunters have gone missing. I now know why. Either riven have gotten to them, or those of Evator, who the riven are here to prey upon. The daekais have also shown more activity. They're like carrion in that when you see daekais hovering over an area, you know people are there, sometimes dead."

"They don't actually eat people, do they?"

Norus laughed. "No, I just mean you can tell there's activity under them when they circle, like a moragul. The only difference is that moragul feed on the dead, so you can be certain there's been a battle if there are enough of them. With daekais, whatever's on the ground is probably still alive. If they were dead, the daekais would fire rocks and arrows into bodies to make sure of that before landing and looting whatever's left."

"Charming guys. I killed a few. That's how I got the sling I used."

"And the riven dagger?"

Max had retrieved everything he'd dropped in the fight and put the riven dagger into his inventory. He didn't intend to use it again except as a last resort, though if it had any diseases on it, he likely caught them already. Maybe the healing he'd done would eliminate anything minor. He wasn't sure how well that worked. He related his encounter with the riven.

Norus clapped him on the back. "That was smart, the *Sleep* spell. And grabbing riven bane. I keep some in my pack. Some of it grows around here, but there are versions that need to be planted. Querra are great with that. They'll grow that anywhere. They won't admit it because they're too nice, but querra hate riven."

"Doesn't everyone?"

The hunter said, "Yeah, but everything you see riven wearing came from querra, sometimes daekais if they find a body. They can't make clothes. They're too lazy."

"So they kill querra and take the clothes, not sell to them?"

"Yes, no one does business with riven."

"What about those riven daggers? If they can't make clothing—"

Norus nodded in understanding. "Jhaikan usually have those made for riven, just to let the little bastards cause more trouble."

"Have those made? Jhaikan don't create the daggers themselves?"

Laughing, Norus said, "No, they do nothing personally except hunt, torture, and kill people. They have slaves do that kind of thing. They aren't usually down here in the woods much, except for hunting someone."

"Who do they hunt?"

Norus smiled. "Me. Others out here."

Max blanched and glanced around. He might've done okay against the riven and daekais, but the jhaikan had seemed far more formidable. At least he was properly armed now. "So how much trouble are those of Evator likely to cause? Are they just probing, or do you think there's a real chance of an attack on the mining village?"

"Not sure. We sometimes let a lone hunter of Evator come out here unmolested, but this is much more. It's been a long time—years—since they attempted capturing the village. We must get to Gitarna and warn them to send reinforcements, including a large scouting party to secure the area. Make a show of force."

New Quest: Warn Gitarna of Evator's movements.

Objective: Warn the town of Gitarna that reinforcements are needed at the village Pendir.

Difficulty: Moderate.

Rewards: +2 Reputation in Karendi Kingdom (Gitarna). 2,000 XP.

Accept?

Max accepted the quest and saw Gitarna appear on his map. It looked like two days to reach there on foot. Trouble undoubtedly waited in between there and here. The village of Pendir didn't show on his map. If they were a mining operation, he might enrich himself there through battles. Maybe it was no surprise those of Evator were interested in it. Was he on the wrong side of this fight? What if there were good dungeons to explore, with tons of gems to be found? He shrugged off the idea. For now, it seemed wise to follow Norus. Once they alerted Gitarna, he might get another quest to be among those headed for the mountains.

As they walked, Max decided to go through the level two spells he'd acquired. He did so while not walking into a tree despite the translucent HUD hanging in the air in front of him. He already had access to all the new spells and just needed to figure out what to have in his hot list, and whether he had the materials needed to cast something.

One option, *Fauna Wall*, caused a hedge of riven bane to appear; he'd had access to the non-riven bane version at level one. That could be very useful for stopping the disgusting bastards. It had a duration of eight hours, long enough to surround himself, and maybe companions, while sleeping in the wild. And he could make it spring up in between him and pursuers. Or maybe he even surround them with it and then pick them off with other spells, his sling, or a bow. It was a solid choice if he saw signs of them around.

Sphere of Daggers would surround a five-foot space with swirling blades. *Hammer Blows* would give him a magical hammer to bludgeon someone from up to twenty feet away. *Archery Fiend* could make him or someone else an expert. *Camouflage* and *Invisibility* could keep him out of trouble. And a singing spell might be helpful with his bard class, since he'd never been particularly good at that, though it felt like cheating to him. Maybe he'd avoid that unless really needed it. He added *Hammer Blows* to his hot list.

Max still had three proficiencies to assign and picked over the list. He chose *Local History* because it suddenly seemed like he'd need to know things even if no one told him. The skill allowed him to pull up more information about a location on a map, like population, defenses, who settled it, and events going back a hundred years. He suspected it would grant him more info when he arrived somewhere.

World Lore got his attention now that he had met someone and encountered more species and animals. It would automatically give him information on anything that was mentioned, like a god or term he didn't know. That could save him precious seconds of trying to pull up info on a screen, assuming the details even existed. That left him with one more to assign. Some of the other skills beckoned, but he wanted to continue waiting until he needed one. *Horsemanship* seemed like a good idea eventually, but not now.

For an hour, he followed Norus and peppered him with questions, learning more about riven and daekais, two of the threats in the woods and mountains. The daekais called both home and used the peaks to hide their stolen treasures where others couldn't reach them without flying. They weren't industrious enough to build much, so they lived in caves, bigger trees, and places captured from morkais, or abandoned. They flew in more haphazard formations, unlike the more civilized morkais, and as a result, it was often possible to tell which was which from a distance.

The riven were less of a consistent problem, and easier to evade or inhibit with riven bane, which lined the main roads in the woods as often as possible. They cared only for causing death and destruction and had no use for the riches. No society would let in to use money anyway, making it useless to them. Daekais weren't allowed in either, but they coveted it all anyway. Daekais were known to follow large groups of riven, who might attack caravans, lay waste to everything, and wander off without bothering to take the loot.

A few times on their route, Norus made them pause as he listened carefully, whether for those of Evator in pursuit or other dangers. The bodies had almost certainly been found by now. Max saw he was sometimes leaving subtle tracks, though Norus wasn't, so he practiced not doing so. After a while, he got a notification for having gained the *Pass Without Trace* proficiency at level 1.

Max asked Norus to teach him tracking techniques. Before long, he'd unlocked that as a skill. He didn't find any daekais tracks, since they didn't land unless necessary, but he saw riven footprints in several places, usually a day or two old. He learned to recognize several animal tracks even though he'd never seen the animals themselves. This was when the *World Lore* proficiency proved useful the first time, as information on harts, tosk, and kerr popped up when Norus mentioned them. The female voice that read messages to him could be muted, too, so that he could still hear the hunter instead. He turned it off for now. His tracking skill rose to level 2 from doing it so much.

They came across a clearing fifty yards around, with knee-high grass. Fearing a repeat of the daekais attack, he and Norus waited a few minutes, watching and listening, but nothing seemed amiss. They finally prepared for trouble by loosening swords, the hunter cocking an arrow into his bow. Then they ventured across. They were halfway through when they heard heavy feet running through the woods behind them.

"By Kriseri's breath," Norus swore, and Max saw a notification that Kriseri was the Goddess of Peace, and patron of hunters.

"They found us."

CHAPTER SEVEN

Nodding at the woods opposite the approaching footsteps of a dozen people, Max suggested, "Let's run for it."

Putting his arrow away, Norus shook his head. "We'll never make it before they see us or easily find a hasty trail we'd leave. Might as well face them here and now. Listen, we only have a minute. You're wearing the Evator hunter's armor. Pretend you captured me and you're one of them."

"Won't they realize I'm not because they don't recognize me?"

Norus pulled out a rope and tied a loose knot before sticking his hands through and gesturing for Max to tighten it as if Max had tied it.

"Good point," said the hunter, as Max tightened the bond. "Say you're from Rook, a town far to the west in Andra Kingdom, like Evator. It's on the shore of Lake Napier, on the northern side of River Karendi, the border. The river is a little north of where we stand now. You were sent from Rook to join Evator, saw me across the river, and tried to capture me to make a good first impression when you got to the castle, having a prisoner. You did it, but lost your horse. We're headed back to find it and your gear, but now you can forget about it, having the reinforcements from them. This will explain our position, your ignorance of the area, and their ignorance of you. They may send someone after the horse for you, but they won't find what doesn't exist, of course."

"They also won't find hoofprints that don't exist." Max saw the warriors had almost reached the clearing.

"True. Discourage them from going after it. Most mounts in use by soldiers are trained to return home and you're confident it will."

Max nodded and added to the ruse. "I'll say I caught up to you at the people we killed, but that it was you who did it all. Only...." He hesitated, realizing a problem.

"What? It's a good idea."

"But won't they kill you for having killed their people?"

Norus pursed his lips. "I'm your prisoner and you want me taken to Evator."

Max held his gaze. That might work, and he was prepared to argue for it. "I'll get you out of this."

Norus met his eyes. "I'm sure you will."

New Quest: Free Norus Shadowmoon from the forces of Evator.

Objective: Captured by soldiers of Evator, Norus may never see the sun again unless brought out to be executed in the town square. Free him without getting caught, killed, or getting Norus hurt.

Difficulty: High.

Rewards: 1 Rare Item. 1,500 XP, +1 Reputation in Karendi Kingdom (Gitarna), -5 Reputation in Andra Kingdom (Evator) if caught.

Accept?

Max accepted the quest. While he had saved Norus, who owed him a debt, the hunter had also taught him so much that Max felt indebted to him. And now Norus was saving him from capture or death, if Max played this right. He felt determined to complete this quest.

The new *World Lore* skill allowed him to quickly absorb basics about Rook. As the footsteps neared, he pulled up the map and saw the town far to the west, the city of Karendi south of it over the river, and Evator to the northeast of where he stood. All were marked as estimated locations.

Norus also told him to change his class name through his *Character Screen*. That surprised him. His class would remain bard, but he could make it say "fighter" because that's what he was pretending to be now, and that's what other players and NPCs would see. He could also change his name, so he made it say "Maestro Max of Rook, Andra Kingdom." Any other stats, like his level, would remain unchanged if someone could peek at them. He'd have to remember this for two reasons.

First, if he stopped or started masquerading as something or someone else, he had to adjust these or bust himself. Second, he could not trust what the game said about others. Then he realized there was probably a spell to prevent that. That also meant another person could realize he was faking and catch him without Max knowing that they knew the truth. He'd have to look into this. But it intrigued him.

They turned to face the growing thump of running footsteps as a squad of nine warriors in leather armor appeared, the crest of Evator on their tunics. A few had swords or daggers drawn. A woman in the lead held a crossbow, while a man fingered the arrow in his short bow. All but one were human. The lone kryll among them was a head taller and loped along gracefully. The other female wore chainmail and was clearly in charge, so Max focused on her.

Name: Sergeant Kari Brightblade of Evator.
Type: NPC.
Class: Fighter.
Species: Human.
Level 9.

They slowed on seeing Norus and Max in the clearing, waiting for them. Max made a point of acting like he was relieved to see them, removing one hand from his sword hilt. Their weapons lowered, though the archers glanced around the clearing before fanning out, peering into the trees as if no longer concerned about Max but with other dangers. He glanced at the sky, something he needed to get in the habit of doing as long as daekais were around. The rest of the group walked toward him, expressions neutral. Kari seemed unimpressed.

"Greetings," she said without friendliness, stopping two paces short of him. She'd pulled her straight black hair into a tight braid, leaving her lightly complexioned face exposed. The sun had brought out freckles on her tanned cheeks, but her overall muscular appearance only stressed the girlishness of that. Nothing else about her was the least bit feminine. She had a square jaw, a slightly bent nose as if someone had broken once it and it had not properly reset, and flat cheekbones. Her dark eyes were a little too far apart and showed a distinct lack of warmth. This was no girly girl, but someone who would kick your ass and then spit on your body. Max had never seen a woman like this.

He nodded. "Well met. I had expected warriors from Gitarna. I'm relieved to see it's you. What are you doing on this side of the river?"

"I could ask the same of you."

Indicating Norus with his head, Max repeated the story they'd devised about tracking the hunter down, concluding, "I was trying to retrieve my horse and head for the castle, though I'm unsure of the way now."

Kari observed, "You wear the crest of Evator, not Rook, and I do not know you."

Shit. He shrugged casually, stalling for time. "You really know everyone in the castle and in town?"

Her eyes bored into his. "Every last soldier."

Max smiled and tried to bluff, a little surprised the NPC was this tough on him. "My armor needed replacing just before I left Rook. Nasty fight with some riven left it covered in disease spreading spores we couldn't get out. My commanders in Rook didn't want to give me new armor just to have me arrive in Evator and trade it in for something with the Evator crest on it. They gave me armor from Rook."

Her stony gaze swept over his attire. "That armor doesn't look new."

Thinking quickly, he added, "I think it's from someone of Evator that was reassigned to Rook a while back."

Her gaze didn't lighten, but she changed subjects as if having accepted that. "We had no word you were coming."

"That's not unusual, is it?" he asked, hoping that was true. When she ignored that, he once again felt she'd accepted it, but didn't acknowledge.

Kari said, "We found three soldiers of ours dead a fair distance back. There should've been a fourth, but there's no sign of him. Instead, we found a peasant with his face bashed in. He is unrecognizable." Her eyes narrowed. "He was about your height and build."

Max cocked an eyebrow as if wondering what she was getting at. Surely she couldn't possibly jump to the right conclusion?

"I haven't seen your missing soldier. I was chasing this one when he ran into the three and the peasant. He killed them all." Max stopped himself there, realizing that if they'd inspected the bodies, they'd have seen significant bludgeoning damage to some of them, and no one had a weapon that could do that. His spells had done it. He had to change the subject, but she was too fast.

"What did he use to smash one's hip and the other's chest?" she asked. Her clear eyes never left his.

Max tried to look surprised instead of disappointed and frustrated. "I don't know. I caught up at the end, just as he was bashing in the peasant's face. The others were already dead. Somehow, I doubt he's going to tell you what he did to them."

Kari walked over to Norus and yanked his tied hands toward her, scrutinizing them as Max nervously watched. "Not a scratch on his knuckles," she observed.

"Well, I forced a healing potion down his throat after our fight," Max lied, nodding at the damage to Norus' clothes, and cuts to his armor. "Didn't want my prisoner dying. What are you guys doing out here? Maybe your missing man is still doing whatever you expect him to. I assume you've been sidetracked by following us. Maybe he wasn't. If I'd known you were of Evator, I would've gone toward you instead of away."

She sighed, dropping Norus's hands to rejoin her men. "He was their corporal and shouldn't have gone off by himself, but it wouldn't be the first time he didn't follow protocol." She shook her head and frowned at her remaining soldiers, eyes moving between two of them. "Are you paying attention? I don't care how good of a scout or hunter you are, I don't want you scouting alone when you're an officer with a team in the field."

The two soldiers nodded, and Max asked, "Is that what they were doing? Scouting?"

She nodded, and Max sensed he was off the hook. For now. For an NPC, she was smart as shit. He was used to games being hard for the battles, not stuff like this. It was pretty cool, but maybe a problem, too. Bluffing NPCs would not be easy. He was usually an honest guy. Those lies hadn't come naturally, but he felt pleased with his performance. It had seemed like he was a wrong comment away from joining Norus as a prisoner, which would have the side effect of negating the quest to free him. Not for the first time, he forgot he was in a game, it was so realistic.

"We can send someone for your horse," Kari suggested.

Norus spoke up with a feigned smile. "Wouldn't bother. Those of Gitarna will capture it before long."

Kari turned back to the hunter. "What do your people know of our movements?"

"Why would I tell you that?"

"I'd rather know now than torture it out of you in Evator."

Max tried not to react to the idea. If Evator tortured people, they weren't the good guys here. "He's my prisoner, not yours, and—"

"Not anymore," she interrupted, "and we have operations underway that you're here to help with. I don't know whose command you'll be under, but since you're close to our territory, in our armor, and a soldier of Evator now, you'll do what I tell you to until we reach Evator and your commander is determined."

She turned away and told everyone to head out, taking a different path somewhat parallel to the one they'd used to get here, but more northeasterly and back the way they'd come. Someone took the rope tied around Norus' hands and led him away as if to send a message that Max had lost control of the prisoner. He sighed and followed, purposely not looking at the hunter so no one would see any silent looks between them, ones that revealed they were partners.

The plan had worked almost too well. He would need to devise a way to free Norus when they reached Evator, but it would not be quick or easy. A search for an escaped prisoner would likely result. Max would get both of them out of there and on the way to Gitarna, probably with people pursuing them the whole way.

Max needed information. He started by peppering his new companions with questions about the area, the village outside the castle, and the fortifications. He pretended he just wanted to know his new duties and what it was like, sometimes throwing in made up stories about things that supposedly happened back in Rook for comparison. And he learned a ton, bonding easily with several of the soldiers as he picked up on what mattered to these guys socially. He pretended to agree and tried to seem like he was just embracing his new home and the people there. He stifled his curiosity about the kryll out of an assumption that the species wasn't rare and gawking might attract attention. Kari at first looked at him suspiciously for the questions, but she seemed to relent as the soldiers accepted him.

As he did this, he received a few notifications of skills gained. He reached level 1 in *Impersonating* and *Charm*. His Reputation also rose a level to 2 and would help with his charm and crowd control. He felt eager to put them to the test.

The soldiers briefly talked about the unfolding plans to mount an attack on the mining village, so Norus had been right about their intentions. Max wanted to gather what info he could, but he sensed asking too many questions might be suspicious. He hoped for more time later and settled for learning that Evator was in the early stages of planning, doing reconnaissance. Depending on how long it took to free Norus and reach Gitarna, the town might send enough reinforcements. And Max realized he was in an ideal position to learn what the plans were. He needed to bluff his way into knowing the leaders and their plans.

They stopped to relieve themselves and only then did Max realize he needed to pee. The urge surprised him. The group took turns stepping into the underbrush to do the deed, the guys unabashed about it. Max normally wasn't very shy, but he only now really thought about having genitalia. With a smirk, he thought about how this wasn't part of the character creation process where he'd changed his body. How many guys would give themselves a huge tool? Chuckling to himself, he went over to a bush and fished around his pants for the prize, a little amused at the sizeable result.

Not bad, he thought, a little more fascinated by his junk than usual. *Amazing detail. Never been uncircumcised before. Wonder why they went with that. I won't admit to whether I got an upgrade or not. Huh. I wonder if there are magic items for that!*

He stifled laughter while noticing how realistic the stream of golden pee was in the sunlight as it sprinkled on a green leaf before splattering on the earth. He also felt the internal pressure to relieve himself dropping. If he didn't know better, he would've sworn this was real. It made him wonder if he could get aroused or have sex, and would it only be with other characters could it be NPCs? What if a player was underage? They were probably restricted. Could players get pregnant? Catch venereal diseases? It opened a Pandora's box of issues. He decided not to worry about it and shoved his manhood back in his trousers, annoyed and amazed to feel a familiar drip of pee going down the inside of his trousers because he hadn't given himself a good enough shake. Shaking his head in disbelief, he decided to pull up information on the kryll before talking to the guy as he intended.

Species: Kryll.

Summary: One of the seven original species, kryll exhibit the traits of the four Red Sphere neutral gods who created them: curiosity, aspiration, fairness, and peace. Lovers of nature, they are excellent singers with powerful, agile bodies. Some are pacifists while other strive to balance good and evil with action. They excel at melee and ranged combat, especially with their traditional enemies, jhaikan, but their endurance is poor. While skilled magic-users, they can be reluctant to draw energy from the environment to cast spells.

Species Strengths: +2 Strength, +2 Agility, +2 Dexterity, +1 Intelligence, +1 Morale.

Species Weaknesses: -1 Constitution, -10% Regeneration, -1 Reputation, -10% Mana

Species Bonuses: +10% Luck, +5% Magic Resistance, +15% Speed, +10% Physical Attack, +10% Reaction Bonus, +1 Spear Bonus. They receive bonuses for using kryllan weapons. Balance Bonus, Befriending Animals, Calming Presence, Direction Sense, Hide, Leave No Trace.

Class Restrictions: None. Dual classes permitted.

Proficiency Points Bonus: None.

As they continued, Max let himself look at the guy. The man's physique bore great resemblance to that of a male gymnast, ample muscles rippling under the tight shirt and leggings, over which sleeveless leather armor lay. Two silver bracers fit his forearms. He moved with practiced ease that made him seem ready to roll on the ground and to his feet in one smooth motion. He was dressed like everyone in the armor and tunic of Evator of Kingdom Andra, but he wore it all better, like a second skin. A symbol of two clasped hands lay below the one for Evator. He wore his straight black hair in a braid that reached his waist. Strapped to his back was a leather case with three pieces of wood, two of them shod with metal on the end. Max wondered if they were nun chucks. The kyrll's reddish eyes observed Max's curious gaze more than once, and soon he fell in beside Max.

"Is there something you want to ask me?" he asked, voice melodic. "I am Malonir of House Enomi."

Max had already seen his info, but pulled it up again.

Name: Malonir of House Enomi, Castle Evator.
Type: NPC.
Class: Fighter.
Species: Kryll.
Level 3.
The symbol of Solon he wears shows he is a solonon kryll.

Full of questions, Max settled on one he felt wouldn't reveal his ignorance of the species. "What do you think of Evator's plans for the mining village?"

"Do you mean, am I okay with the impending assault? The taking of others' hard work?"

"Something like that, yes. Don't kryll try to remain neutral?"

"That depends on one's attitude. I'm a solonon kryll, so I will defend the castle but not take part in attacking those who do not warrant it. I will not accompany them on their mission."

Max nodded as if he understood, but he was really reading the notification his *World Lore* skill gave him.

Solonon vs. Kriserian Kryll.

Among the four gods who created kryll are Solon, the God of Fairness, and Kriseri, the Goddess of Peace. Some kryll follow the way of Solon and dislike unprovoked actions against others. In such cases, they will aid the victims, even if that means betraying their comrades (who are committing the unprovoked action) by "changing sides." By contrast, kriserian kryll are such pacificists that in extreme cases, they won't even defend themselves. It is safe to assume that a kryll who is a member of the armed forces is a solonon kryll. Each may wear the deity's symbol to show their viewpoint.

Max quickly pulled up info on the god Solon, seeing the symbol of two clasped hands that lay on the kryll's armor. The symbol for Kriseri was a tree in silhouette, as she was also the goddess of nature. He'd have to keep an eye out for these symbols on any kryll he encountered so that he would know what to expect from them.

He asked, "But you are out here in lands that don't belong to Kingdom Andra."

Malonir said, "That is not, by itself, an act of aggression."

"Yes, but it can lead to one, especially when so many other soldiers are with you."

"This is true, but I took part in this to protect my peers should they encounter trouble, not to instigate aggression."

"And yet, the mission of this group is to scout the area before an attack. Doesn't that make you culpable?"

Malonir smiled. "I could choose to view it that way, yes, and one of my kryllan peers did so and remained behind. I accepted his viewpoint but attended, regardless. This group has been instructed to avoid detection, not purposely seek trouble. I therefore decided their mission was in keeping with my values."

Max nodded at the logic, some of which sounded like semantics, but he would not argue. What he wanted to know now was the attitude of such kryll in case he had to fight one.

He asked, "What would happen if they found a similar number of soldiers from Gitarna and attacked first?"

"I would abstain from combat unless personally attacked."

That suggested Max could avoid a fight with such a kryll simply by not attacking one. "Doesn't that bother your fellow soldiers?"

"No. They understand and expect nothing else from me."

"You would not intervene even if one of them was about to be killed?"

"It depends upon the circumstances. If one of them were defeated, and there was no need to kill them, and someone clearly intended to anyway, I would intervene to disarm the perpetrator. But if the combat is continuing and a killing blow is about to occur, so be it. I would be unlikely to intervene in time, anyway. People know better than to try to kill an unarmed person in the presence of kryll. We are known as impartial judges, so even if we do not stop them, we may testify against them for war crimes."

Max cocked an eyebrow and decided he liked kryll. They seemed honorable. And formidable. Something equally impressive then caught his eye.

Chapter Eight

In the distance, and briefly visible between the treetops, an enormous falcon with green and brown feathers, and what looked like a humanoid figure astride it, flew across the azure sky. Max cocked an eyebrow, wondering if he was imagining it. People could *ride* these things? It seemed awesome. And terrifying. What if it tried to eat you? He knew horses could be temperamental and kill people with a well-placed kick if you were behind it. What would one of these birds do? He kept looking for it, but didn't see it again. And he imagined no daekais were anywhere near with that monstrosity in the sky.

As they walked east toward the mountains, Max saw the tops of two towers through the foliage to his left. The farther tower's pennants had a silhouette of a brown bird with spread wings on a blue background. He recognized the Evator crest on his armor. A blue spire topped the tower.

The nearer one had a flat, wide top with no flags or pennants. The square sides were wider and taller. It rose to about two-hundred feet. The two sides he could see had openings large enough for a truck. Or one of those giant birds. The holes were staggered so that those no two were on the same level. Extending out from the bottom of each hole was a stone platform, on either side of which were two large perches of wood with netting in between. Max suspected this was to prevent a rider who was mounting or dismounting a bird from falling to their death if they slipped.

"The Florin Tower," said Malonir beside him, his eyes on it when Max turned to him, "sometimes called a Winged Tower, though those are a little different."

"How so?" Max asked, watching a giant bird with its rider land on a perch. He guessed, "Is the bird a florin?"

"A florin bird, yes. No perrin birds here. A Winged Tower has no ground floor entrance so that the only way in is by flying, magic, or climbing the walls. It keeps anything that can't do those from getting in. A Florin Tower is usually in a settlement where the ground entrance is protected by its location. A Winged Tower is out in the wilderness where it isn't, and winged riders want to know it's safer to land on the tower and go in. The towers help them on long flights, when they can't reach their destination without having to rest, which they'd rather do in a tower with their bird, not be on the ground."

Mac quickly pulled up info on winged riders to learn they rode the giant birds and either acted as messengers or warriors. "Can't say I blame them."

"Evator has many winged riders who patrol the plains to the north and west, and the Bier Peaks to the east. They check the forest as well, but the morkais are more suited to that. Both keep an eye out for daekais attacks, which aren't common, and any jhaikan movements."

"Not the riven?"

"No. There's enough riven bane planted south of the castle that they'll never get through it."

Unless they burn it down, Max thought. But he supposed the smoke would give away their presence. He asked, "Is Evator your hometown?"

The kryll shook his head. "It lies to the south, in the Kryllan Forest. Many kryll in this region hail from there. This forest is lovely, but nothing compares to the giant Evenorr trees back home. I've become used to terra settlements, but it has been too long since I saw nothing below me but branches."

"Terra settlements?" Max pulled up his map and saw the Kryllan Forest roughly shown. It sounded like kryll lived up in the trees, and Malonir's reply seemed to confirm it.

"Those built on the ground."

"What do you call those in the trees?"

"Only Evenorr trees are large enough to support them, so we call them Evenorr settlements."

Now Max wanted to see that, but he asked, "What are you doing here, serving Evator?"

"I am not truly serving them, or you could say I'm doing so temporarily. My chosen field of study is border relations between Kingdom Andra and Kingdom Karendi, especially in this area. Being here and among those on the ground aids my research."

"Field of study?"

"Yes. Every kryll has one. We are scholars, though not everything is learned from reading, of course. Someone has to write the books others read. I was fortunate to be able to choose my specialty."

"What's your goal? To write a book?"

"To understand, though a book, or at least a scroll, will certainly result, to preserve and share what I've learned. It may also come to pass that when tensions arise, I can help ease them due to the knowledge I've acquired. Humans are not known for their impartiality, but kryll are, and I may avert altercations with my counsel. That is a side-effect of my research, however, not the goal as you inquired."

"Should I assume that whatever a kryll is doing for a living is related to his field of study?"

"Generally, yes. Don't be afraid to ask. It is our passion, unless we were assigned a field, so we usually enjoy discussing it."

"Why would you be assigned one instead of choosing?"

"The kryllan community may have a pressing need to understand something and yet have no scholar for it. If someone does not volunteer, one may be assigned. To refuse is to risk banishment."

That was harsh. He wondered if players like him, who chose a kryll for a species, were required to know a field, or if they were given quests designed to make them understand something. Did they get to choose? That could be interesting, but he was glad to not have the requirement, at least for now. Maybe if he played the game again one day, he'd try that.

A few minutes later, the group stepped into an area that had been cleared of trees for a hundred yards in every direction. To the right, behind, and in front stood the forest. To the left rushed the waters of a river that hurtled toward them out of the Bier Peaks in the distance ahead. The whitewater spray was visible as a mist and could be heard crashing as it flowed away behind them on their left.

A wide, grey stone bridge straddled the river. Men in chainmail or plate mail guarded the open iron gates at both ends. Between there and Max's position, as he followed his group into the clearing, two wooden buildings that seemed like guard stations had been erected. A few soldiers stood idly by as if not expecting trouble, their demeanor remaining calm as his group strode into view. They no doubt recognized the matching symbol of Evator on everyone's armor, except for Norus, who seemed more relaxed than Max would've expected.

On the river's far side stood Castle Evator, a short way from the bank. Lichen covered the outer, grey walls, or bailey, that encircled the keep, which sat atop a fifty-foot-tall rocky mound. A multitude of narrow slots for archers to fire through filled the entire bailey wall facing him. There was no door. An army that attacked from this side would need to go around after making it past the river. Max wondered if tunneling under the water and castle walls might work, but there appeared to be enough solid stones jutting from the ground in this whole area, some up to ten feet tall, that they likely blocked the way underground.

At the keep's farther, southwestern corner stood the tower with pennants and blue spire. The nearer southwest corner had the giant Florin Tower soaring high above. The perches loomed overheard, with one of the giant birds of prey sitting on one and seeming to watch them. The florin bird looked like it could bite a limb clean off. Or his head. It gave Max the creeps.

Twin roads went around the bailey, on the far side of which lay the town. Max couldn't see much from here other than a lighter stone wall twenty-feet-high surrounding it among the rolling hills and grasslands. Buildings with blue or brown roofs, some of it painted and chipped or fading, peeked over the wall or stood upon a taller hill. His ruse would get him welcomed here, but it seemed like an escape would be difficult if he and Norus tried to cross the river.

Max followed the others across the low grass toward the water, nearing a ten-foot statue of a woman in the clearing's center. The statue stood on a round pedestal a foot high, and around her feet had been placed a dozen acorns and mostly green leaves with their stems. She stood facing the woods to the south, one leg slightly before the other. A hand was palm up as her bent arm extended before her. A small bird figure sat on her hand, wings out, beak down as if feeding from her. The woman's hair flowed down her back, a gown swirling around her. His *World Lore* skill popped up with a message.

Deity: Kriseri. Goddess of peace, freedom, and nature.
Titles: Lady of the Woods, Goddess of the Wilderness.
Patronage: Patron of Hunters.
Symbol: Evenorr Tree.
Sphere: Red. Co-creator of kryll species and myrradim afterlife.
Alignment: Neutral.
Season/Element: Winter/Water.
Power Day: Red Day, Water Week.
Court of Gods Month: 10-12.

To his surprise, his group headed straight for the statue as Sergeant Kari pulled a leaf from her waistband and laid it at the statue's feet. She whispered something Max didn't hear, though his impression was of giving thanks. He cocked an eyebrow at Malonir, who laid his own leaf and explained as the group continued toward the bridge.

"We leave an acorn before entering the forest," the kryll began, "as a sign of reverence and hope for the goddess' favor, that we will be safe and successful in our mission. On returning, we lay the leaf as a token of thanks."

Now Max knew why he'd gotten a few acorns as loot earlier. "I see dozens of acorns. How many groups are out there now?"

Malonir shook his head. "The acorns are collected by a priest of Kriseri once or twice a week. The count doesn't tell you how many are out now."

"Is it one acorn or leaf per group?" Max asked. He'd noticed several other soldiers also adding a leaf, but not all of them.

"At the least. Some prefer to give their own token."

Max opened his mouth to respond when the shadow of a daekais passed over him, its shape identifiable on the ground as it moved. Looking up in alarm, he reached for the sling on his waist, only to feel Malonir's strong grip restraining him.

"Morkais," the kryll said, nodding at the flying figure, who approached the castle and flapped his green wings before gracefully landing on the battlement. "The daekais seldom come this close. They know their more benevolent brethren are here, plus the florin birds that don't take a liking to them. And then there are all the archers."

Max nodded, relieved. "How close do they come?"

"Not within miles, usually, and only at night, even though they're afraid of the dark."

"Good." Max had always been comfortable in near total darkness. He used to walk around late at night in his parent's house with no lights on, thinking about one thing or another if he was upset about something. He could be as quiet as a cat. That could help his *Stealth* skill.

He followed the group past the soldiers, who nodded at them, a few jeering at Norus and making snide remarks about his town, Gitarna. They moved across the bridge and through the light mist from the rushing waters. On the far side, they took the dirt road around the western or left corner and turned north.

Both the castle, and the town in the distance, had him curious, as it all looked so real, just like the characters he had met. The river, too. People weren't poorly rendered, stiff figures often seen in games. They also weren't so perfect that they seemed fake, nor did they seem robotic in movements or how they interacted. He almost wondered if they were other players. He hadn't met one to compare, but he suspected he was about to meet some. In MMORPG simulations, others were always a danger after the opening levels, and he tensed slightly at the potential threats he might face now. Was he still in a starter area? He wasn't sure how he would tell.

As with the south side of the bailey, the west one had no entrance, which was on the north wall. The group had to walk around the northwest corner and idle guards to approach the fortified gates. The dirt road gave way to cobblestones and a large square lined with a half dozen wooden shops, the temporary kind offering refreshments for visitors or guards, who increased in number. When his stomach grumbled, Max realized he'd hardly eaten since entering the game, as he'd only snacked on some provisions he'd acquired. It was early afternoon, at least.

Remembering his *Local History* skill, he tried it out.

Settlement: Evator, town in Andra Kingdom, continent Antaria.

Location: Found midway and near the eastern coast of Antaria, Evator is the southernmost settlement in Kingdom Andra, the capital of which lies to the north. The town stands just north of the Karendi River and the Haigan Forest, to the east of which loom the Bier Peaks. These mountains separate Andra Kingdom from Kingdom of Rien to the east, just as the river separates Kingdom Andra from Karendi Kingdom to Evator's south. Evator has changed hands from each of these kingdoms and was originally built to protect against jhaikan, riven, and daekais incursions into the rolling lands north and west of it.

Population: The Duke of Evator rules the town of four thousand, where querra are the second-most population after humans. Karelia and morkais are here in lesser numbers, while few kryll and no mandeans are residents. Reformed races like

dariven and rhaikan are poorly tolerated, but can expect no real trouble unless overstaying their welcome or arousing suspicions.

Recent Events: An unusual number of soldiers from Andra Kingdom are currently in Evator, ostensibly for training in the woods and mountains. This may explain the increased patrols in the forest.

Important Features in Town: Built on a natural rock mound fifty feet high, Castle Evator occupies the southeast corner and includes a Florin Tower. The Querran Quarter is found northwest, near the Shrine of Scrylyn. The cemetery lies northeast. Though the land south of the river, in the forest, is Karendi Kingdom territory, the Karelian Guard of Evator is found there.

He wasn't sure if the information would be helpful, but he felt glad for it anyway. Max had noted the mostly open land to the west and north, stands of trees not big enough to be a forest breaking the plains. He saw another florin bird with its rider in the distance, and two more morkais briefly flying over the town's rooftops before they descended out of view. Another flew overhead from the castle toward the town, which lay a hundred yards away to the northwest. Beside it lay a road leading north and another west, presumably toward Rook, the distant town Norus had told him to pretend he was from.

Max felt a little nervous that his impersonation was about to be tested again. Would he acquit himself as well? Would anyone else be as suspicious as Kari? She seemed to have accepted him. Maybe others would take their cue from that.

As the group passed under the raised portcullis and in between the castle gates, Malonir said his farewells. He and others dispersed, some headed for barracks. Kari led Norus forward and nodded at Max to follow. He struggled to take in everything, trying not to gawk. He'd never been in a castle before, and he sometimes received too many notifications, like the one telling him two men were Coiryn Riders and what the symbol on their attire meant. But he found that if he didn't look at it, it went away in a second. Each could be retrieved later on a screen.

He and Norus followed Kari through the wide stone court-yard, where a few people went about their business or idly chat-ted. This included those dressed in finery and which he assumed might be nobles. Planters and statues of knights and other fig-ures dotted the manicured garden in which they stood, closer to the keep ahead. Various buildings lined the thick interior wall of the bailey, including barracks and shops. Off to one side were a half dozen smaller, wooden buildings that looked temporary, and where soldiers mingled, some of them practicing swords-manship or archery off to one side. Max needed to learn his way to understand how much pedestrian traffic might impede his rescue and escape.

They walked past two guards beside the keep's open doors and into the stone building. Nothing surprised him about the polished stones, parquet floors, tapestries, and wooden paneling because he'd seen many castle pictures online. They exited the foyer toward the Florin Tower on the right, then down a flight of dark stairs, lanterns lighting the way, the air increasingly dank and the décor more ordinary. Max suspected they were heading for the dungeon. He paid attention to everything he saw, from the number of guards to alternate ways out of this area. In theo-ry, he'd be rescuing Norus from here. To put the guards here at ease, he adopted a friendly demeanor, slapping one of them, who was ascending the steps, on the arm in passing.

"I brought you a prisoner!" he joked, and the man laughed.

"Maybe we'll let you torture him first."

"I'll stop by later. Don't start without me."

The guard chuckled.

They reached a room that seemed like the final stop before any cells, a male guard greeting Kari, who began relating info to him. A female guard took Norus and led him away. Max followed, making a show of inspecting with his eyes, and sometimes a hand, the solidity of the dungeon. He intended for them to think he wanted to make sure his prisoner would not escape when he was doing the opposite — figuring out what he was up against. Norus was finally shoved into a dim cell with fresh straw on the stones, a pee bucket hanging from a nail in one corner. The guard untied him, locked the door, and walked back to the others, leaving Max with the hunter.

CHAPTER NINE

Max whispered, "Any ideas?" through the black cell bars, which had rusted in places but looked sturdy. He discreetly tested several and only found a few that were a little loose, but not enough to provide an escape option. He had no idea how to get the hunter out of here.

Norus eyed the cage but keep his hands to himself. "If you knew how to ride a florin bird, yes."

Max nodded his understanding, intimidated by the thought of getting anywhere near the giant birds. "It's the best way, isn't it?"

"They're right above us and flying over all the trouble is the fastest and easiest."

That was true, but had other perils aside from controlling the mounts, which they might have to steal, an enormous problem in itself. "Would winged riders and morkais follow?"

"Depends on how stealthy we are to get out, but probably. It still beats a manhunt on the ground with morkais and winged riders helping from the sky, riven and potentially jhaikan on the ground. There are other threats in the woods, which are best avoided when in a hurry. If you're uncertain you can succeed, leave me. You need to reach Gitarna and warn them, whether or not you do it on florin bird."

Max nodded but didn't want to leave the hunter behind, even though he was just an NPC. And it wasn't only the quest XP and other rewards or a feeling of debt. He liked the guy, as odd as it seemed to like an artificial character. But something else was on his mind.

"Are they really going to torture you?"

Norus shrugged. "Maybe. They don't usually. I'm mostly going to rot here. They don't kill prisoners, either, especially given that they captured me in my own lands."

"You didn't actually commit a crime."

"Right. They may consider fighting and killing their people as one, but it would be bullshit. Wouldn't stop them from claiming it."

"What was that look you gave me in the courtyard?" Max asked. The hunter had stared at him silently for a moment as if to suggest he note something, but he hadn't known what it was about.

"Evator is amassing troops. Those extra barracks on one side aren't usually there. They're serious about an attack. You need to find out as much as you can and tell me. One of us can get to Gitarna, if not us both."

A message popped up.

New Quest: Learn Evator's Battle Plans.

Objective: Learn enough of Evator's plans to attack, seize, and hold village Pendir so that, if you complete the quest "Warn Gitarna of Evator's movements," you can provide enough detail for the town of Gitarna to have a tactical advantage defending Pendir.

Difficulty: Easy.

Rewards: 1 Rare Item. +2 Reputation in Karendi Kingdom (Gitarna). 1000 XP.

Accept?

He accepted the quest.

"Max!" Kari called from down the stone corridors. "Let's go!"

"I'll try to visit," he said, "but I don't intend to leave you here."

"Do what you feel is right."

Max nodded and left with Kari, who took him back to the courtyard and then into a building next to the barracks. He briefly met several commanders that included the lieutenant Kari reported to and their captain. They hadn't expected his arrival, of course, but before he even bullshitted them about it, one remarked that this wasn't uncommon unless the transferred soldier was important. And Max wasn't. The problem was that they gave him quarters in the castle barracks and wanted him on duty as a guard tomorrow, after he got familiar with the castle and town today.

Now he had to figure out how to get out of doing it. He doubted there was much to learn from working as a guard like an NPC instead of an adventurer. Surely the game wasn't about that. He needed to escape and find other opportunities, but with the day half over, he had limited time to explore. He would start with a castle tour to understand the defenses for exploitation.

As he and Kari exited toward the barracks, he asked, "You're to be my commanding officer?"

She looked sideways at him as if he'd said something stupid. "Didn't serve in Rook long, did you? You seem like some of this is news to you. You're assigned to a fireteam with three other soldiers. Corporal Iodin is your commanding officer, assuming he returns. He reports to me and the rest of my squad, which your fireteam and three others form. Our squad and two others are a platoon under the command of Lieutenant Makson, whom you just met."

"Got it," Max quickly said, trying not to seem too clueless. He knew nothing about military formations, but he realized a few things on hearing this. "Is Corporal Iodin the one who is missing in the forest?"

"Yes. The rest of his fireteam was killed. You're the only one in it right now, but we'll reassign at least one other today."

Max felt guilty on realizing he was standing there in Iodin's armor, and he wondered what would happen when the guy never showed up. "I'm sorry your fireteam, or one of them, was killed."

On seeing his expression, her grimace softened. "I'll ask someone to show you around. I must tell their families, since Iodin isn't here to do it."

Kari handed him off to someone else, who introduced him to a bunch of people. Max had always been bad with names, but being in the game solved that problem, since he could see names and more with a glance. They gave him a bed in the permanent barracks, in a room big enough for a platoon of three squads, nearly forty soldiers. Sneaking in and out would be difficult unless he improved his *Stealth* skill. He'd try it tonight, dreaming up an innocent reason in case he got caught. Maybe some soldiers, including him, were on duty at night. That prompted him to ask a ton of questions.

He learned that Castle Evator and the town of four thousand normally had over three hundred soldiers, enough for a battalion. This was high for such a small population, but the castle defended the border from two other realms. To the south lay the Haigan Forest in Karendi Kingdom, but no significant threats from the kingdom were likely to come through with the woods.

Rather, the jhaikan in the Bier Peaks and Haigan Forest were the main concern.

The daekais were more of a nuisance, seldom being able to mount an organized offense because they were all too driven by personal greed. They couldn't cooperate in large enough numbers for a true assault. That hadn't stopped everyone-for-himself hordes from attacking, but it had been a long time since that happened.

Riven were even less capable of being a genuine threat to a fortified location because they were too lazy and undisciplined. The daekais could just fly over everything, which accounted for the unusually high numbers of morkais and winged riders here to guard against that. Evator regularly received temporary troops from throughout Kingdom Andra. They would train against these nefarious species so that new soldiers came and went every season, making Max's arrival not a *huge* surprise.

On the other side of the Bier Peaks by the Namaeran Ocean lay the Kingdom of Rien, an occasional enemy of Kingdom Andra. Most warfare between them had been on the seas, but Rien had sent troops around the northern end of the mountains and then southwest toward Castle Evator before. Not doing so meant they would leave the castle at their backs as they marched north toward Andra, the capital. Some suspected such an attack might come in the next year or two, but that had been said for a decade now. It paid to be prepared.

The number of troops in Evator had quietly grown in the last two months because the duke was serious about attacking the mining town in the Bier Peaks of Karendi Kingdom—and keeping control of it this time. The makeshift barracks Max had seen stood out of sight except from above. The soldiers were mostly human and male, but both kryll and karelia were part of the defenses. The kryll were among the other warriors, but the Karelian Guard only kept watch at night across the river in the woods, since they could see well in the dark and needed little sleep. Max knew their presence was yet another reason flying out of here made the most sense. Sneaking out on foot meant trying to bypass the karelia. He arrived from the west and not seen them, but they were out there.

Having learned that Malonir had been reassigned to his fire-team pending the return of Iodin, Max hung out with the kryll for a bit and soon found himself in the castle courtyard again. As the sun fell, other soldiers joined them around a fire. Everyone was an NPC, making him wonder why no other players had made it here. Two servant boys handed out bowls of seasoned riva rice, Max's stomach growling at the aroma. He ignored the *World Lore* notifications about animals as he scarfed down a roasted tosk leg that tasted like ham or maybe boar, and a boiled terrin egg that was the size of his hand.

His eyes kept wandering to the looming Florin Tower, where two birds sat on perches. As he watched, another soared in from the north, a rider guiding it to a higher spot. He heard wings flapping and giant talons grasping the perch, a few voices shouting as it settled. A figure climbed off the bird's back as others helped remove a saddle.

"I can take you up there tomorrow to see them," Malonir offered, a wooden mug of frothy mead in one hand. They both still wore the leather armor they'd been in since meeting, but the kryll had left most of his weapons in the barracks, whereas Max just stuck them in his inventory.

Max turned to see the kryll's amused red eyes on him. "The birds are only for the winged riders, I assume?"

"Yes, except for the privately owned ones. They cost more than you'll make it a long time, too, so if you're thinking of buying one, may Adarra bless you." The kryll smiled.

Max's *World Lore* skill told him Adarra was the Goddess of Good Fortune, among other things. "You can't borrow one somewhere, like with a horse?"

"People assume you'll never return with it, or it will feast on you if your mastery of them is poor. And that the bird will not come home, even though they are trained to. So to rent, you'd need collateral—the entire sum needed to buy it. You get most of it back if you return."

Trying to sound like it did not intimidate him, Max asked, "Do they actually eat unskilled riders?"

"No. Perrin birds do. Even skilled winged riders have met that fate. Most places don't have perrins, including Evator."

Max thought that was just as well. He'd hate to try stealing a bird only to discover that only perrins were available. "What's the difference between perrins and florins?"

"Perrins are smaller, wilder, and not as easily controlled, even if supposedly tamed. Without a strong-willed rider, they just do what they want. People use them for war and they are more agile and vicious. The Florin Tower is named after the florins because that's typically what's in them. Perrins are rarer as a mount, but the name of the towers remains regardless of which is in them."

"There are no Perrin Towers," Max surmised. "Remind me not to get on one. How can you tell them apart? They look different?"

"Aside from the size, the florins are stockier and have much longer tails, but most people identify them by the end of their wings. Florin wings are serrated, like they have fingers. The perrin wings taper to a point. The perrins also have a sharp bend in the beak. They use it to snap the necks of their prey." Malonir chuckled when Max grimaced.

"I was hoping you would not say something like that."

Still grinning, the kryll said, "It's a quick death. Florins just use their talons. Another way to distinguish them is that florins hover in the air more often, gliding on the wind. Perrins are faster and more of a predator, so they are all fast turns, dives, and other aggressive moves. They hover little and are more likely to be flapping their wings often. These are some ways you can tell them apart from a distance."

Max hoped to remember that. "It's unheard of for someone to rent either kind?"

"In the big cities, you could rent a florin. No one rents a perrin."

Max looked up at the birds, wondering about travel issues, since there could come a day when he had one of these, despite what Malonir thought. "If someone has their own bird, and comes to Evator, I assume they can keep it here?"

"Yes, it's the only place you could, though some places won't keep a perrin. Are you thinking of asking an owner to borrow a florin?"

He hadn't been until the kryll suggested it. "No, but would that work?

Malonir shrugged. "You'd have to make a very good impression on someone, such as myself."

Max cocked an eyebrow, unsure whether the kryll meant Malonir had made such an impression on someone or… "Do you have a bird?"

"It is how I arrived from the Kryllan Forest."

"Is it really yours? I assume your, uh, salary is the same as mine."

"It belongs to my family. We have several."

Max stopped himself from asking for training. It was too soon to impose on the kryll, though the thought made him once again realize he was treating the NPC like a real person. But he wanted to plan for another bird on his own and see what his options were. He imagined a trainer would need to ride one while he rode the other. Maybe he could pay someone to train him and borrow Malonir's bird. Or maybe Malonir would train him and he'd find another.

But he had to be crazy to even think of it. He'd hardly ridden a horse before. He had a proficiency point left and would consider using it for this if the rescue via florn bird seemed workable. He gained another point with every level, so leveling up could make this more likely.

Before long, with a full belly and rapidly emptying mug of mead, Max got sleepy. It had been a long day. He was not only tired, but his feet hurt. He checked his stats and saw a fatigue debuff that had lowered his health a few points, which meant his regeneration wasn't keeping up with the debuff. He reluctantly headed for the barracks.

They stood next to the bailey wall. Nothing fancy about it existed, just large room after large room of narrow, low beds with thin, feather-filled mattresses. He pretended he knew how to stow his gear in a brown chest, which lay against the wall by his bunk. He really put the items into his inventory. To his surprise, a clean shirt and short pants were inside the chest, so he changed into them for the night and stored some of what he'd been wearing there. He wasn't sure if NPCs would wonder where his stuff had gone or if they were programmed to accept that he had an inventory that was normal for him. No one had acted like they were in a game of any sort, so he had played along.

Max checked the logout button and saw no change. Was he really supposed to sleep in the game? Would it even work? Once he fell asleep, would he essentially be logged out? Maybe that was the way out of here. Encouraged by the idea, he closed his eyes and tried to ignore the interesting day he'd had. The room was quiet except for two guys snoring. Anyone who entered did so quietly and respectfully. There was no machinery to emit hums or other sounds. He only heard two very low voices in the room outside this one.

But it took a while to fall asleep.

During the night, he rolled over in bed and was aware of his surroundings, casting a bleary eye around the room. The beds were still there. More soldiers occupied them. Dim, flickering torchlight still shone from the adjacent room that wasn't sleeping quarters.

In the morning, judging by the darkness of the room, he woke before dawn. The first thing he checked was his inability to logout. No change. No surprise. The Life Counter had dropped to six days, three hours, and 26 minutes, so he'd been in Llurien Online for almost twenty-four hours. He wanted to find another player, instead of an NPC, and ask what the Life Counter meant. He needed some answers.

As he stood up, he noticed his feet were still a little sore, as were his shoulders from the armor, which had chafed his skin in places. Only now did he check some of his notifications to see that his *Impersonation* skill had risen two levels to 3. And he had gained a level in *Charm*. He needed just over 700 more XP to reach level 4, but he was unlikely to get it soon without combat, which he wasn't expecting today.

Atop the chest, someone had placed a spare set of folded clothes without Evator's logo. They were likely meant to replace the supposedly lost ones that his non-existent horse had carried off. That lie had apparently been more useful than expected. He donned the mostly brown and tan tunic and trousers as quietly as he could. He probably wasn't leaving civilization today, so he just put the armor into his game inventory, adding a dagger to his belt. Then he slipped on a cloak that hung to his knees. Each item was of good quality.

Among them was a gold pin showing a sword crossing a heart-shaped shield. He'd seen every soldier wearing one yesterday and had noticed his stolen attire hadn't included one. Maybe it had fallen off in the fight with Iodin, a blessing in disguise—this was the symbol for the soldiers of Evator and it would have given him away as wearing the dead man's clothes. He should've been wearing a pin of Rook, but no one had commented on its absence. Had Kari noticed? She hadn't said anything, but that didn't mean she hadn't seen.

Shit. Maybe they aren't infallible NPCs, just smart, but able to make mistakes and fail to notice something that they could have.

As for the symbol, it was that of Coiryn, the God of Courage, and while universal, each soldier had the same pin. For a moment, he thought blending in with the townspeople today would be best, but he placed the pin on his chest. It might get him preferential treatment. He intended to enter the town for some solo exploring.

He practiced his *Stealth* skill a few times on his way out, since not waking everyone before dawn else was a great excuse for sneaking around. Then he entered the courtyard, grabbed some bread and fruit to take with him, his *World Lore* skill letting him know what to expect of each, like the nigs, a small nut in a shell that had to be pried open like pistachios, which they reminded him of. The round juna was a yellow orange with a skin that was poisonous if eaten. Being a soldier allowed him to take his fill in the courtyard, a perk he hadn't expected despite his small feast the night before, when it hadn't occurred to him that this came with the ruse.

He gave himself a tour of the castle grounds and interior as people woke up. The reconnaissance helped kill time until the town came alive. Along the way, he chatted up guards he saw, some of them initially looking like they were going to stop him until seeing his pin. He admitted to being a noob and found they would answer many questions about the use of one room or another. This included inside jokes and little known secrets like hidden passageways or shortcuts. He came away with a great understanding of the place, but some areas were still off limits.

On checking his *Map Screen*, he discovered a new one for both the town and castle, with the latter significantly filled out. Remembering a spell he had available, he asked a servant for a blank parchment and then discreetly cast *Map Structure*. A 3D rendering of much of the castle was revealed, though he already had most of it. What piqued his interest was that several areas were not rendered. Were they magically protected from discovery? Almost certainly. That made him very curious about what lay inside them.

He finally exited the keep as the sky turned less black, strolled through the courtyard, and then stepped through the open castle gates. The few merchants who had stalls here were still opening their businesses, waving him off when he stopped to look. The cobblestone road descended over the uneven ground toward the walled settlement, where the gates now stood open. Whether the pin on his chest helped, guards recognized him, or they'd seen him come from the castle, he entered town without incident. Nothing was open yet, so he strolled the streets partly to map them, dropping a marker on anywhere worth finding again. The settlement reminded him of the Maryland Renaissance Festival, with its mostly two-story buildings of stone and wood. While the ground was dry now, mud from the mostly dirt streets had been tracked over parts of any cobble-stones.

He saw both querra and karelia NPCs but didn't interact, mostly to keep a low profile. The fewer who knew him, the better, given his intended rescue of the hunter. As the town awoke, he finally saw other players, just not as many as expected. None seemed interested in interacting, and he felt the same. The low player count struck him as odd. He found the only store to buy a musical instrument and toyed around with a few, including a lute, but had nowhere near enough money to buy anything.

Max retraced his steps back through the town square, where a platform stood to one side by town hall, a fountain in the center. Four people ahead of him stood together on the left, watching everyone. What caught his attention was the human fighter's dark eyes meeting his and seeming to recognize him. The fighter held his gaze until Max looked at the others—a human woman in a healer's robe, a black human woman in a dark wizard's robe, and a kryllan girl dressed as a monk.

The healer saw him and perked up, green eyes intensifying so that Max almost stopped to turn away. He didn't like two people seeming to know him. He had the distinct impression they were looking for him, or maybe someone just like him. And in a game where players could hurt and kill each other, and there being four of them, he felt wary. He veered right toward another street, hoping they wouldn't realize he was doing it to evade them.

"Max Parker! Wait!" yelled one of the women.

He stopped, more from surprise than to obey. How did someone know his last name? His gamer tag was only Maestro Max. He turned to see them approaching. They didn't seem threatening, and he quickly checked their gamer tags to see how high their levels were.

Name: Thomp.
Class: Healer.
Species: Human.
Level 1.

Name: Lydia.
Class: Wizard.
Species: Human.
Level 1.

Name: Akio.
Class: Fighter.
Species: Human.
Level 1.

Name: Siren.
Class: Monk.
Species: Kryll.
Level 2.

The healer, Thomp, smiled reassuringly. Akio the fighter looked around as if bored and unimpressed, but he carried himself with great assurance, like he could kick everyone's ass despite being level 1. The wizard Lydia seemed more confused than anything and as if restraining herself from gawking. Only the kryllan monk, Siren, looked like she was enjoying being here from the spark of amusement and interest in her black eyes, her movements graceful and confident. None of this seemed in any way new to her.

Max was level 3, but his higher level might not help against four of them. Maybe he didn't need to worry, based on their demeanor. He tried to act like he wasn't positioning himself for a hasty exit, though the fighter seemed to notice, nodding as if in approval. That surprised Max, who decided against pulling a sword from his inventory. But he quickly checked his hot list of spells and swapped out a few, making sure *Sleep* was among those ready.

At a gesture from Akio, they stopped five feet from him, though the healer visibly chafed at that. Apparently, Akio was in charge. No one said anything for a moment, the healer's eyes intensely curious and scrutinizing him.

"You're not NPCs," Max observed. The healer looked confused. Max arched an eyebrow.

"Non-player characters," Siren remarked over one shoulder at the others. Then she smirked at Max. "They're noobs. Old, too."

"Sakura," admonished Akio.

Siren gave him a withering look. "Don't use my real name. Not cool."

"The rest of us did."

"That's because you're too boring to think of ones and don't intend to play the game anyway."

Akio sighed. "You're only here to help, and right now, the best way to do that is to be quiet."

Siren looked at Max and rolled her eyes.

Amused by her, Max got the impression they knew each other very well. Akio seemed like an authority figure to her. The names Akio and Sakura sounded Japanese. Were they family? What did she mean about the others not being here to play the game? Why else would they be here?

"Who are you?" he asked. "What do you want? How do you know my last name?"

Akio seemed ready to speak, but the healer, Thomp, gently laid a slender hand on his arm and stepped past him, kind green eyes on Max. She had shoulder-length blonde hair and gave the impression of having not customized her appearance much, as it lacked any decoration that females could do. The simple yellow robe had a brown belt at the waist, a symbol of half-peeled corn on it. Max's *World Lore* skill told him this was the symbol of Ko-jen, the Goddess of Rejuvenation, a benevolent deity. Despite that, her reply filled him with alarm.

"We're here to tell you why you're in this game," Thomp said, "because we're the ones… Well, I'm the one who put you in here."

CHAPTER TEN

Max looked intently at the healer, Thomp, questions swirling. How could another person put him in the game? What did that even mean? He didn't remember logging in, but he had assumed he had, not that someone else did it to him. Had he objected? Put up a fight? Why would she do such a thing? Thomp forcing him into a VRMMORPG would be wrong morally, legally, ethically, and probably in a few other ways.

And yet she didn't seem nefarious. If anything, she seemed kindly and pleasant, like someone's grandmother. He also already had the impression that the player behind the avatar was a lot older than her character looked. Was the healer's robe fooling him? That she'd controlled him entering the game brought something else to mind.

"Are you also the reason I can't logout?" he asked.

The healer exchanged a questioning look with the wizard and said, "I was hoping you'd be able to. I can't quite explain that if it's true, but maybe I can make some sense of it, if you'll give us a few minutes." She took a step closer, as if to add urgency to her next words. "It's very important we talk with you, Max."

When he hesitated, Siren said, "Your life may depend on it."

"Sakura," Akio chided her. The fighter's dark eyes matched his short black hair, his gruff demeanor somehow matching his compact, somewhat muscular body, on which he wore leather armor and trousers. He had taken the time to age his character to his 30s, perhaps in imitation of real life. Max couldn't tell the age, but he seemed older from the commanding way he spoke and carried himself. He was intimidating.

Despite that, Siren replied as if unphased by him, "What? It's true. And you guys have been through a lot to get to this point with him. More than he knows. So have I. He can at least listen to you."

"What is going on?" Max asked, eyeing them suspiciously. They were obviously in this together, not just the game, but having done whatever they'd done to him by putting him in here. "What do you want?"

"Is that a yes? You'll hear them out?" Siren asked. She had a distinct no-bullshit vibe that he liked and found appealing, like he could trust her to just get on with the truth. As a kryll, she was taller than him by several inches. A streak of red in braided, straight, black hair matched the red eyes the species typically had. Like many female characters in games, she was buxom, but not overly sexualized. She wore tight fitting leggings and brown leather armor much like what he had in his inventory. Her eyes were more slanted than he'd seen on Malonir, once again giving the impression that the player behind her was Asian.

As he hesitated, Siren, or Sakura, added, "When I said your life may depend on it, I didn't mean in the game. In real life. There's a good chance that if you don't listen… Let's just say you really need to."

Max eyed her, wondering if this was a put-on, but she seemed serious. His eyes went to the others, each wearing a grim expression that sobered him. "I suppose so."

The healer Thomp said, "We have a room inside—"

Max shook his head, wariness rising. "No. There are four of you. I'm not going into a room with you. Out here."

I might need witnesses, not that it would really matter.

The healer said, "We really need privacy, Max. The other players shouldn't hear what we're going to talk about. You would agree if you knew. You wouldn't want them to know what we say about your situation. We're not here to hurt you. Just the opposite."

"Easy to say," he said. He'd long been suspicious of reassurances that he should trust someone, even though she didn't say the dreaded, "trust me."

"Over there." Siren pointed behind the four of them to the marble steps of a two-story shrine, where no one stood or was passing near. "It's quiet enough. It should stay that way. Players don't go into churches much. I'll keep anyone who tries back."

Max sighed, which Thomp took as acceptance from the way she turned and led the way over, the others following, Max bringing up the rear. He went around them and mounted the steps so he could keep the shrine behind him, the rest in front, the sparsely populated town square over their shoulders. He felt caught between wanting his guard up and sensing they weren't troublemakers or, worse, griefers. He had to admit, only Siren acted like a player, her eyes discreetly assessing every passerby. The others ignored their surroundings altogether, as if only Max concerned them and they had no concern for their character's safety or status. Noobs indeed.

When everyone seemed settled in their stances, he asked, "So what's this all about?"

The healer pursed her lips and stepped closer to him, lowering her voice. "There's no easy way to tell you this, Max. In the real world, you are at Shady Grove Hospital in Gaithersburg,

Maryland. I am your physician, Dr. Thompson. You're in a coma due to head trauma to the back left of your head. You also have a contusion on your right temple, but this isn't the cause of your condition. We believe you should be able to wake up, but you have not yet. This is not unusual, as comatose patients sometimes do not wake immediately when they have otherwise recovered from an injury to the brain. We have faith that you will soon, but we're hoping to help you wake using this game's interface."

Max stared at her for several seconds before realizing his mouth was hanging open. He shut it. Her matter-of-fact delivery had been disturbingly believable, not like someone screwing with him. It also explained why he didn't remember buying the game or logging in, two facts no one could know. But she did. He resisted a compulsion to put one hand on the back of his head, where she said he'd been wounded enough to put him in a coma. He had never been seriously injured before. No one had to tell him that if what she was saying was true, he might never wake up. A chill went over him, not just mentally, but physically, his game body reacting to the news, which had the awful ring of truth to it. A host of questions came to mind, but one came out first.

"Is this why I can't logout?"

Thomp looked surprised, maybe more by which question he asked first than that he brought it up again. "I don't know. Is there no logout button?"

"There is. It's just greyed out. I can't touch it." He pulled it up, seeing it with fresh eyes, the significance making him go cold. *Holy shit. I'm in a fucking coma?*

She sighed and nodded as if to herself. "The coma may manifest that way. The game designers did not stop you from leaving the game. In fact, I believe that logging out will coincide with your awakening in real life and we'd want it as easy as possible for you to leave here."

Max thought about that for a second. "So if they aren't preventing me from logging out, then who is?"

She pursed her lips again. "You, I suspect." To his scowl of incomprehension, she added, "Sometimes patients' minds play tricks on them. You may have heard of phantom pain when a limb is amputated but the patient still feels it. Or people sometimes reject a transplant that should work, but it appears that their mind causes it to fail and require removal. The same thing may be happening with you, where you could click the button, but your mind is preventing it."

He absorbed that. "That all makes sense, but I don't see why I would do that. I've been trying to logout since I woke up in here."

"There could be many reasons you unconsciously reject it. Unfortunately, I'm not a psychologist, but maybe you're not ready to awaken, psychologically, or spiritually, maybe even emotionally, as if you cannot yet deal with the real-world repercussions of what has happened to you, and so you remain in the game."

"But I want to wake up, especially now that you told me this." Max mentally banged on the logout button to one side of his vision in frustration before stopping. The feeling of being trapped, which he'd forgotten about with everything that had happened since he'd started, suddenly returned. He felt his head spinning a little, so he sat down on the marble steps, but it didn't really help. His eyes sought Dr. Thompson's and the worry in them drove home his peril. He might be stuck in here forever. It occurred to him that he knew why she'd chosen a healer class.

Thomp added, "There is a possibility that you have to play the game in order to wake up. Maybe something about the journey in here will help you. I'm sorry we can't give you more guidance. This is unprecedented. We're really just glad you could be conscious in here. We aren't prepared for more than that to happen. It's all so new."

Max nodded to show he wasn't upset with them. "So this wasn't planned?"

"Not really. It had been discussed, but we were a long way from setting up anything when we gave it a try. We honestly didn't think it would work, so you sort of caught us by surprise."

That made Max wonder if there was some sort of glitch or bug that would disconnect him at any moment. Would he go brain dead? He tried to shrug off the worry but sensed it would dog him. He eyed the others, changing the subject for a minute.

"Who are the rest of you?" he asked, curiosity growing.

The black-skinned human wizard cleared her throat. Max took in her off-putting, resting bitch face expression and suspected she had worse things to say. She had brown eyes and straight black hair down her back. Her black robe accentuated her large breasts, but he had the impression she was a little overweight, the robe hiding that.

Her tone formal and lacking any warmth, the wizard said, "Hello, Max. I'm Lydia Anderson, an attorney your parents hired. I'm working to help with some legal concerns regarding your situation, which I came here to help explain. As Sakura mentioned, neither myself nor Dr. Thompson are really here to play the game. We have briefly joined so we may talk to you directly for a few minutes."

"So you'll be leaving?" he asked, wondering why he had an attorney. What had happened to him? He couldn't help adding, almost bitterly, "You'll be logging out?"

Lydia replied, "Yes, but not until we have answered everything we can."

Looking at the two players with seemingly Japanese names, he asked, "What about you two?"

The fighter looked him in the eye. "Detective Akio Nakamura of the Maryland State Police. I'm investigating the apparent crime that was committed against you, and which put you in the hospital. This is my daughter, Sakura. She is an avid gamer and—"

"And I can speak for myself," Siren interrupted, as her father frowned. "My dad can't be in here long because he's got a job, like the others, and he's too boring to do this, anyway. But I can spend a lot of time in here. I came to help you, to keep you company if you need it, and just to play the game with you."

She said it so matter-of-factly that a moment passed before sudden gratitude filled Max. It wasn't an emotion he was accustomed to, mostly because few people had done something nice for him. But the implied compassion of being here while he got devastating news, and then remaining after to support and help him, removed any remaining suspicion of them. While Sakura didn't act like she was being sweet—if anything, she seemed to take no shit—he felt her presence was the nicest thing anyone had done for him in a long time. And he suddenly had a much bigger problem than worrying about rescuing Norus.

More sincerely than ever before, he looked her in the eye and said, "*Thank* you."

Siren blushed slightly and looked away as if she hadn't.

Dr. Thompson said, "We have been concerned about how you might react to unexpectedly awakening in the game and felt it might help for you to have a companion. When Sakura learned of this, she graciously volunteered."

Akio smirked. "It wasn't that gracious. She just wanted a chance to play without paying for it."

Siren frowned at her father but didn't argue the point.

With an arched eyebrow, Max asked, "What are you talking about?"

Akio replied, "She couldn't afford a subscription. Your parents are paying for her to play with you."

Shit. My parents. How are they reacting to all of this?

Before he had a chance to ask, Siren said, "Come on, Dad, you're making me sound selfish. I honestly wanted to help, though he doesn't seem like he needs it. He's already level 3."

Max nodded. She was level 2, and what the others had said explained why they were all level 1. "How long have you been in?" he asked Siren.

"Shortly after you. I was grinding while waiting for these geezers to be ready."

"Enough Sakura," said Akio.

"Siren," she corrected.

"Okay," Max began, changing the subject again, "now that I know *why* I'm in the game, how did I get in here? I mean, don't I have to be awake to enter a virtual reality?"

Dr. Thompson replied, "We have connected you to Llurien Online using a neural interface, though the rest of us are doing it the old-fashioned way, with a headset that requires our eyes to be open. Newer simulations can have a neural interface as another option. This minor detail suggested to some of us that a comatose patient might join such a simulation and interact within it.

"We've connected you for several reasons. One of those is admittedly to see if it would even work, to connect your consciousness despite you being unconscious out there. It's something that we've been considering for some time before you came to our attention, but we didn't have a suitable patient. Until you. You are young and otherwise healthy. And you have played games like this before, from what we understand from your parents. We thought this might help reduce any shock at finding yourself inside the game.

"Another reason is that you are newly in a coma and have physically recovered enough to wake up shortly after entering the coma. We thought you had a good chance of this connection working. If someone has been in a coma for longer, such as several months, we feel it is less likely to work. You were an ideal candidate, if you'll pardon me for making you sound like a guinea pig."

"Isn't that what I am?" Max asked, trying not to sound resentful. Part of him thought this was cool, but the seriousness of it all overshadowed that. Dr. Thompson crouched beside him and laid one gentle hand on his arm. He grudgingly admitted she had a good bedside manner, or maybe digital-side manner.

"Please remember we're here to help you wake up. You have nothing to lose and everything to gain if it works."

He shook his head. "It hasn't worked."

"Give it time."

"Speaking of time," began the wizard, Lydia, "you need to be aware of the legal situation, Max."

Max turned to her and stood. "What situation?"

Lydia continued, "As far as your parents know, you don't have an Advance Directive. Is that true?"

"Advance Directive?" Max thought it sounded familiar but couldn't place it. Then a slow dread crept over him and worsened as the attorney answered.

"It's a legally binding document that specifies what happens to you when incapacitated, like you are now. You would have needed to create one and sign it while of sound mind, with two witnesses or one notary present."

He remembered now and shook his head, the feeling that he had no control over the situation surging. Why was an attorney here? He couldn't bring himself to ask, his mouth going dry. "I don't have one."

She frowned in resignation. "That's what we thought."

Knowing she was getting at something and frustrated that she wasn't just saying it, he asked, "Why does it matter? What happens now?"

"This is the part that's going to be hard for you to hear, and it's one reason we're talking to you, so you understand. According to the current laws of the State of Maryland, and in much of the country, you cannot be on life support for longer than twenty-one days. You had already been on it for about two weeks when we tried this, leaving you with seven days in here."

Another shock. A couple of them. He turned to Dr. Thompson. "I'm on life support? I thought you said I had recovered."

The healer replied, "We believe you're mostly out of danger. You are on IV fluids, since you cannot eat in your state. You also wear a catheter. The biggest remaining concern is that you are not breathing on your own, but we expect that to change with you awakening."

Max let out a big breath. The catheter meant someone had been looking at and touching his privates, which seemed a funny thing to be most concerned with, but he'd always been pretty private about that. He glanced at the doctor before realizing a nurse had probably done that. Not for the first time since hearing all of this, he felt a little vulnerable and didn't like it. Control had never been so important as it was now that it had been taken away.

His thoughts drifted to this life support restriction he'd heard of before. Many states had passed similar laws after a pandemic had caused mass hospitalizations that left people brain dead or worse, their families unwilling to let them die as machines kept them alive. The crowding had caused even healthier people to get denied care and sometimes die from preventable issues. With that pandemic lasting for years, the havoc led to a slew of U.S. laws restricting extended hospital care when there was little hope of recovery. But some states were more draconian than others. With an Advance Directive, you could stay on machines longer, but those without got less time to show signs they would recover. Years later, the laws were still on the books, and now a patient would get the plug pulled on them.

Dr. Thompson put a hand on his arm again. "The first good news is that your body has recovered enough to be mostly out of danger. The second is that we could get permission from Llurien Online to try this. And the third is that it worked, and you're here, and you seem fine. This is a mental projection of yourself, and while we can see you've altered your appearance, you otherwise appear mentally sound. We're almost there, Max. All you need to do now is awaken."

He got the point and tried to seem a little more positive for them. They had spent a lot of effort on his behalf, even if they had an ulterior motive of helping other patients, too. He could hardly be mad about that. But if he didn't wake up, he had to know how he was going to die, the thought sickening him.

"What happens if I don't wake up? When they pull the plug?"

The healer said, "Dehydration happens in a few days, as opposed to weeks for starvation."

Sensing she had stopped herself, he said, "Spit it out, doc. What happens?"

She sighed. "You would pass painlessly in your sleep."

So there it was. A slow wasting away, but not as slow as starvation. It's not every day you find out how you're going to die. A horrible sadness filled him. If it happens, this was how everyone would think he'd spent his remaining days, unresponsive and unmoving. A meat sack, not full of life. He felt as alive as ever inside this world, maybe even more so. The idea of dying because someone had unplugged him was so lame, so helpless, like he was some sort of appliance that no one wanted anymore. He was getting angry at being denied more time in life.

He said, "Technically, that means I have three additional days to wake up, not seven…" A sudden realization struck him, and he pulled up the HUD.

Life Counter: 5 days, 23 hours, 54 minutes.

"Is *that* what this Life Counter thing is?" he asked, certain he knew the answer. This was all making horrible sense. But he felt a little energy returning.

The healer nodded. "Yes. The game designers added that to give you a sense of urgency."

Max snorted at the understatement. "Well, tell them it worked. I'm motivated. Am I the only player who has that?"

"I think so, yes. We didn't get into many specifics on it, other than me insisting they not call it Death Counter, or several other awful suggestions they made."

Max laughed, not because it was funny so much as absurd, obnoxious, and… okay, it was a little funny. But he appreciated the healer's attempt to put a positive spin on the thing. It could've been worse. Now he wanted to know what the other options had been. "Time to Die?" "Countdown to Extinction?" "You're Dead in X Minutes?" As a Megadeth song started playing in his head, he turned to the attorney, another realization striking him.

"Can't we do an Advance Directive now? You're a lawyer. We have witnesses. You know I want life-saving measures taken, or whatever the lingo is."

She pursed her lips. "You have no legal standing in here. You can tell us what you want, but no judge will accept it as binding."

Max scowled. She wasted no time shooting him down. She could've been more civil. But griping about her personality wouldn't get him out of here.

"Yeah," he retorted, "but this is unprecedented." He began looking back and forth between her and the doctor, depending on who he was referring to. "You said so yourself. No coma patient has ever been in this position, being able to communicate with the outside world."

"That's true," Dr. Thompson admitted.

Max got the impression she didn't understand what he was getting at. "Isn't that the whole reason we need to be of sound mind when signing an Advance Directive *before* something happens, because we can't communicate *after*? Well, I'm of sound mind. You said so yourself. And I can communicate my wishes."

Lydia said, "But there's no law—"

"Exactly! This is so new that there's no law about this. The current law doesn't apply to me. It's about people who cannot communicate. But I can. We need a new law for this situation. In the meantime, I cannot be unplugged based on this law, whatever it is. We should challenge that, say it's illegal, that my unique situation must be considered. I have rights and they aren't being honored."

In the long silence that followed, the attorney cocked her head. Siren grinned at him.

"That's smart, dude." She whacked the attorney in the arm with the back of her hand as her father frowned at her. "You totally need to do this."

Lydia nodding slowly, eyes brightening. "You may be onto something. This could really change everything. For a lot of people."

Dr. Thompson smiled. "This proves beyond any doubt that he's of sound mind."

Max turned to the doctor, eyes intense with urgency. "Keep me alive."

She gave him a smile that had no trace of sadness in it for the first time. "I will."

"And I'll try to do the same in here," Siren said, eyes keen.

Noticing everyone looked excited except the dour Akio, Max aired an idea to see what they thought of it. "Maybe if I die in the game, I wake up."

Akio said, "Or you never do."

Chapter Eleven

Well, *that* sobered him. What if Akio was right that dying in the game could keep him from ever waking up? It might even cause him brain death or make his body think he was dying for real. It added an urgency to protecting himself. In real life, he seldom worried about dying, but in a game like this, the possibility of death was omnipresent. Maybe he needed to stay safe in the castle or town and not venture into the wilderness. And hide if daekais attacked the town. Some of these species he'd encountered were far more dangerous than others, but he'd gotten lucky in not meeting the more deadly ones. That reminded him of something.

"When I created my character, I couldn't choose my race. Do you know why?"

Dr. Thompson nodded. "I asked them to restrict it to human to minimize any shock at finding yourself in the game. Another species or race might've altered you in other ways and we needed to see you as yourself. *You* may have needed to see you as yourself."

Max grudgingly accepted that. This was a medical situation—a life or death one—not him just playing a game. If he ever got out of here, he could create a new character if desired.

He asked, "Do you think there's something I can do in this game that might help me wake up?"

"We don't know," replied the healer. "There's nothing specific to the game, and no modification designed for you, though now that we know you're fine in here, maybe we can work on something with the Llurien Online people."

"Better be quick."

She continued, "I'll schedule a consult with a psychologist to see if they have any ideas for helping you."

He almost laughed at the idea of a shrink coming in here to do therapy with him. Would that be a world first? What if someone attacked and killed the psychologist before she reached him? Or during a therapy session? Would *she* suddenly need therapy or be able to shrug off being killed? Maybe he'd be the one doing the consoling. He realized he was assuming she would be female. Maybe a guy would be better, or at least a woman who understood these games and felt unfazed by the violence in them. Someone more like Siren than Lydia, his somewhat wide-eyed attorney.

"Max," Akio began, interrupting his thoughts. The guy had seemed impatient and serious throughout. Max could tell he was tired of waiting to address something. "Do you remember anything about the attack?"

The question surprised him. He hadn't even known he'd been attacked until they told him, and he'd been distracted by the rest of this since then. Max searched his memory and drew a blank.

"No. When was it?"

"Two weeks ago. It took a while to get you set up in the game. Happened pretty quick, actually, from what the doc here tells me. Anyway, what was the last thing you remember?"

Max recalled getting ready for the concert, packing up, the planned set list, but nothing about arriving or the performance itself. "Driving to a gig."

Akio said, "You were found outside the club's rear exit with your empty guitar case. This was after the show. Your keys and wallet were still on you. Your car was still there, loaded with the rest of the gear, so we have doubts this was a robbery gone wrong, unless they only wanted your guitar. I understand it was a custom build? Well, we also found what looked like a few pieces of it, based on photos others showed us of what it looked like. If they destroyed it, it also doesn't suggest a robbery."

Max arched an eyebrow, dread overcoming him as he tried to focus on something other than the sudden image of himself lying vulnerable on the ground. "Pieces? My guitar was in pieces? Are you sure?"

Akio nodded, face as dour as ever. "It looks like your guitar was broken in whatever fight took place. We don't know what happened and were hoping you could tell us. If we catch them, the people responsible for this are likely to be arrested for assault, at the least, and if you don't survive..." He trailed off. A long pause followed.

"Murder?"

Hearing himself say the word made a chill pass over Max. Anger began to build. He felt helpless to do anything, upset that his memory was of no aid in catching the perpetrators. First, his mind wouldn't let him log out. Now it wouldn't help him identify his attackers and get them caught. And while he didn't remember, part of him knew exactly why someone had attacked him, if Akio was right and his guitar, Kat, had been broken—jealousy. Whether it was over Kat, his guitar playing ability, or both, envy had put him in a coma and the grave might be next.

It was unfair. He had worked hard to build his skills and the people who hated him did nothing but sit around watching TV, with their one hand in a bag of potato chips and the other stuffed down the front of their pants. He deserved to accomplish something, and maybe they deserved to get nowhere in life.

Akio corrected him. "Probably involuntary manslaughter."

Max paled. Something about the word "manslaughter" sounded gruesome. Grim determination to make whoever did it pay came over him, especially if he died.

Akio continued, "I'd like to get you some justice regardless of what happens with you here, but I might need your help. Your priority is obviously to wake up, but if you can start remembering what happened, that will help us solve your case."

"Sure. I will do everything I can." Max looked him in the eye and saw approval for his reaction.

Akio nodded. "Anything you say in here can't be used in court as testimony, which is another potential legal issue, but if you give me enough information to identify them, there may be enough to find, charge, and convict them. If you wake up, your testimony can be used, too."

"Got it."

To his surprise, Max felt energized. This conversation was a bit of a roller coaster of awful news destroying his morale and revelations that inspired him to be proactive. He decided to play this game for what it was worth. Maybe he could seek a healer in here and a spell would help his mind. He really didn't know what he could do to help himself remember or awaken, but he would not mope around. Screw that. If these were the last days of his life, he'd at least have fun and try to save his life and send those who did this to jail for the rest of theirs.

"One last thing," Akio began, breaking his thoughts. "Word has leaked that this has been successful, that you specifically are in a coma but in Llurien Online, a game anyone can access. We'll find the leaker and deal with them, but this was supposed to be kept quiet. The media knows and has run with the story, which is all over the news, worldwide. People can log into this game and try to find you."

Holy shit. So much for anonymity. That was just what he needed. What if someone decided to grief him—or even kill his character? The interference could stop him from waking up or remembering anything. Now he really wanted to just disappear. Maybe the wilderness was actually a better idea. Finding him would be harder. All of these years of hoping to gain fame as a musician, and now it had happened in the worst possible way, with a different consequence than paparazzi in the bushes. He almost wanted to laugh.

"It's another reason I'm here," said Siren, her eyes still going to every person who walked by, "to help you if anyone's bothering you."

All of this was making a lot of sense. He once again felt grateful for Siren's presence because he might need the help. He suddenly felt outnumbered and alone. Except for her. "Thank you. How long do you think you can be in here every day?"

She shrugged. "My dad likes to say I need to get a life, so a lot, probably."

Akio said, "She'll be your main point of contact with us. Anything you need to tell us you can pass on through her, and she'll bring our messages to you. We won't be able to come in very often and she tells me players aren't likely to stay in one place. I think that's wise anyway, given your notoriety. You should keep moving."

Siren added, "I can join your party and we'll be able to message each other even if separated."

"The rest of you could do that," Max suggested, wishing they could stay. He really didn't want to be so alone.

"Not worth it," Siren said, "since they won't be in often, if at all. We should reserve those spots because we only get six total in the party."

He cocked an eyebrow. "You think it would be okay to let other players join our party? Won't they see messages between us we don't want them to?"

"You and I can send private messages, too. And as for them seeing messages about your situation, we'd only let people join if they already knew and vowed to help, and we trusted them."

Max wasn't sure how they'd find such people, but he let it go and said, "Okay. I've been wondering—all of you looked like you were waiting for me. Where did you start the game? I was out in the forest and had to work my way here, going up levels in the meantime, but most of you are level 1."

Siren said, "They just opened this region of the game for you, so you would have fewer players to deal with, but once it's open, it's open for everyone. We'll start seeing more players in Evator. The rest of us were among the next to join in, but there are already over a hundred players that started here. Right now, we're sort of cut off from the rest of the gaming planet because otherwise, higher level players could come in here and just take over."

"So we can't travel too far?"

"Yeah. I think for now, we're stuck in this part of this kingdom and the one to the south, where you started. We can't cross over those mountains, and no one from there can get here. Not yet, but time is running out on that, too. We'll need to level up more before leaving, or this area opening and anyone being able to reach it. We don't know how long that will be."

Max wondered if it would open up before his Life Counter expired. "How familiar with the game are you? Is there a way to suppress player names?"

"Not very. I started after you, but I had a chance to read some things online before joining. I don't think there's a way to hide player names but will check. I don't think yours, Maestro Max, has been revealed."

"Let's hope not."

Now Max understood why they wanted to talk to him privately, but it didn't seem like anyone had been near enough to hear any of this. He wondered if those who glanced their way had any idea who he was. He felt a little paranoid and vulnerable, adding to the growing chip on his shoulder.

After a few last details, Max thanked all of them and everyone but Siren logged out, vanishing. It made him feel a little jealous. And trapped. He sighed.

Siren pursed her lips. "How are you feeling, hearing all that?"

"A little pissed. Worried. Determined."

"Good. Use that. I'd feel the same. I sort of do, even though it happened to you instead of me."

He eyed her, already impressed with her mindset. "How old are you?"

"Eighteen going on thirty."

That sounded about right.

Max wasn't sure what to do in the game after the revelations about his situation.

But he added Siren to his party via the *Party Screen*, which allowed him to send invites and remove people. Once she accepted, they confirmed that the messaging between them worked. He was listed as the party leader, though he could assign it to someone else if he wanted to. Both could see some details of the other's inventory and class, which is how Siren came to realize he was really a bard. He was listed as Maestro Max of Rook, Andra Kingdom, and his class said fighter, but he'd leave it that way for now. Both tried to change their names but couldn't. Now he regretted what he'd chosen. Unless someone else named Max joined this starter area, it would be much easier for others to identify him. It also seemed that he could no longer change his appearance, which had been true since character creation.

At Siren's suggestion, he changed the way party looting worked so that he had first choice of all loot. She was only in the game to help him, his parents paying for her account, and she intended to give him her money and useful items to him any-way. They decided that anyone joining the party had to agree to this and that their primary objective had to be aiding Max, even if this would be hard to find in someone. But there were people who felt bad about his situation, so if any such gamers could just be identified and vetted as reliable, it was doable. At the least, they had a plan of sorts.

As they walked toward an equipment shop, Max said, "I think the big questions are what I can do to wake up, or remem-ber the attack on me, and how much I should really play this game. Is it going to help me with those or get in the way?"

Siren replied, "I think you need to level up as much as you can, just in case you become a target for griefers. We can do that now. Maybe we'll have other ideas as we go along, but pro-tecting you is a priority, since we don't know what happens if you die in here."

"Yeah. I'm also wondering what to do about me being a city guard. Today I'm not on duty, but tomorrow that changes. How can I really play this game while I have this role?"

"I half-expect that the town is going to be attacked and you would be part of its defenses. The whole point of these games is to level people up, so why give you the option to impersonate the town guards unless it will benefit you? This attack could come at any time."

Max hadn't thought of that and appreciated her input. "That makes sense. My impression is that daekais are the most likely threat. But I can't tell if it would be more likely at night or not."

"Let's just get ready. Sell some stuff we don't need, see what we can buy. There should be a way to train around here."

They reached an equipment shop and scoped out items so he'd know how much money he'd need for them. Most that were worth anything were out of his financial reach. Combat was the best way to get items, but he wanted to avoid potentially dying now. Levelling up—and therefore protecting himself—was going to be difficult.

But Siren was right about training, which they found an unexpected way to do. A commotion outside the western gate led them to find people playing "Beat the Kryll." The game was popular among warriors because kryll were so adept with weapons. Several kryll were present for different activities, which included archery, sword fighting, the jhaikan staff, and a hand-to-hand fighting style called the Kryllan Hand. This was also the name of the bracers Max had seen Malonir and now these kryll wearing. A few humans were also here conducting weapons training.

"What do you think I should do first?" Max asked, eyeing the wide field and a stand of trees in the distance. Farther away, he spied what looked like a farm silo.

Siren answered, "The Kryllan Hand and swords. The others can wait unless you want basic proficiency. I already have it with the jhaikan staff. That's my main weapon, so I'm going to train that first."

"Let's do it."

Max had asked Malonir about the jhaikan staff because the kryll had been wearing one on his back. He'd worn it in three pieces that could be clicked together to form a staff longer than himself. Metal shod both ends, from where blades could protrude from the end like a spear, or the sides almost like a short scythe blade. Max hadn't seen them in the equipment shops. Where has Siren gotten hers?

All but eight people were NPCs. Max tried not to call attention to himself with interaction, but in watching, he learned he needed to challenge a kryll, who would then compete with him. Upon besting him, the kryll would offer tips and critiques, then a rematch. The game messages showed each kryll was at least level 10.

When playing this games before, he'd used a controller, but had to use his body now. This added challenges. He'd mostly been using magic with a throwing motion from little league baseball or football. Nothing prepared him for swinging a sword or parrying. He didn't even hold it right. For a minute, he considered spending a proficiency point, but the trainer corrected him without wasting one. He soon learned so much about techniques and when to use each that he struggled to retain it all until he earned a proficiency. Then the knowledge, technique, and skill became second nature. He reached level 3 with the long sword.

When his hands needed a break, he switched to the Kryllan Hand. The trainer loaned him a pair of leather forearm braces that were also called kryllan hands. They were usually made of magical steel, and with a spoken word, metal gauntlets formed over the hands. This allowed the wearer to continue fighting by hand when the opponent had a blade, avoiding the fingers being chopped off. For training, a wooden sword was used with the leather bracers and padded gloves. This fighting style took long-er to gain proficiency and then level it up once.

Tired and sore, Max made himself gain archery proficiency anyway. He already had a bow and arrows, but no idea how to use them until now. By early afternoon, he was exhausted and hungry, but he felt pleased, but he'd only gained 125 XP. The real benefit would be when he used the skills. Siren had also made progress with the Kryllan Hand and jhaikan staff.

"I need to logout soon," she said, as they walked toward the castle. "Now that I know I'll be in here a lot, I just need to take care of a few things. I can come back in a few hours to check on you."

Max said, "I appreciate that you're in here at all. Maybe you can read about the game. There are probably forums and other things with tips we could use. Anything helps."

"Good idea. Your idea about a healing being able to help you wake up might work."

"I hope so. You look as tired as I feel. We get debuffs for that and for being hungry."

"Noticed that."

"I might try to complete one of my quests."

"The one about learning Evator's attack plans?"

He knew they could see each other's quests because they were in the same party. "Yeah. It's non-violent and it will get me enough to reach level 4."

"I saw that. And there won't be many players in the castle. But I wouldn't rescue this Norus guy anytime soon. He's just an NPC, and while the quest is good, you'll bring a ton of pursuit and scrutiny."

Max agreed and they parted near the south gate, Siren dis-appearing seconds later as she logged out. None of the NPCs reacted to her vanishing, as if they hadn't noticed. Not until he headed for the castle did he realize he hadn't been alone since learning why he was really in here. He glanced around to see if anyone was following him, but fewer people were here, including NPCs, as he entered the castle grounds. It was time to make a plan, so he headed for the great birds in the southwest tower.

CHAPTER TWELVE

Max was about to ascend the Florin Tower when he decided to visit Norus first. He made it to the guard station without incident. One guy had been there the day before and recognized him. Another had been drinking with him and Malonir last night, so they just waved him in with a few jokes about how soon Norus would be drawn and quartered. Max pretended he would love to see that as he went past them. Security in here was light, but then maybe they figured only a fool would try something this far into the castle, which would be hard to escape. Or the prisoner wasn't that important.

As he stepped into the corridor leading to the cells, one guard called out, "Watch out for the niquerra!"

"He's a vicious little kerr shit!" the other yelled. The two cackled, their voices echoing down the shadowy hall.

Niquerra? As Max searched his memory, his thoughts seemingly prompting the *World Lore* skill to kick in with a reminder that appeared before him. He unmuted the voice narration so he could focus on his footing in the dim light.

Niquerra. A cursed race of the querran species, niquerra are master blacksmiths, stonecutters, and gem cutters. They are obsessed with wealth and trade.

That made Max pull up the info on querra.

Species: Querra.

Summary: One of the seven original species, querra exhibit the traits of the four Yellow Sphere benevolent gods who created them: inspiration, empathy, rejuvenation, and patience. Lovers of the wilderness, they are master chefs, gardeners, and engineers who don't believe in personal property, making them natural thieves, though they're offended at the idea that they stole something. This and their penchant for practical jokes taint their otherwise stellar reputation; they are very popular and excel at relationships with animals. They're skilled at ranged attacks and running for their lives because they know everything can out-fight them.

Species Strengths: +1 Agility, +1 Constitution, +2 Wisdom, +1 Charisma, +1 Morale.

Species Weaknesses: Restricted to Leather Armor or Light Chain, -20% Physical Attack

Species Bonuses: +10% Luck, +20% Regeneration, +5% Mana, +5% Magic Resistance, +10% Attack Speed, +50% Herbology, +50% Cooking, +50% Most Thieving Skills, Acute Smell, Acute Taste, Acute Feel, Assess Gems, Befriend Animal, Brewing, Detect Unstable Ground, 50% Evade Detection, Leave No Trace, Speak with Plants, Weather Sense.

Class Restrictions: Knights, Paladins, Coiryn Riders.

Proficiency Points Bonus: None.

Max had seen querra around town and they seemed cheerful and friendly, even harmless, but the niquerra description he perused made that race of them sound anti-social and hostile, holing up in their mountains and imprisoning anyone who wandered too close. What was a niquerra doing in the prison? From the way the guards had spoken of him, Max had the impression that this prisoner was the opposite of dangerous. If niquerra were the evil version, were they formidable fighters who stood their ground instead of running away like querra? Was that why one ended up in here? They seemed too small to pose too much trouble, but then the riven were the same size.

Max turned a corner and stopped before the next cell to see someone inside it. A short figure sat cross-legged against the rear wall in straw that looked older than what was in Norus' cell. Beside him lay a tipped-over pewter goblet and matching plate with the small bones of some animal he'd picked clean. Max had trouble making out the prisoner due to the darkness, which was worse here because the nearest torches hadn't been lit. As he stared, a notification appeared.

Niquerra. Level 10 Blacksmith. 190 HP. No blacksmith compares to a niquerra one. Everything they make is the finest available, but their true artistry lies in the forging of niquerran steel, whether weapons, armor, or butter knives.

Now Max remembered the bit about the steel. He wanted one of those weapons, but only adventuring was likely to turn one up. Only basic items had been in the equipment shops, suggesting he was still in a starter area. So did the convenient training area with mostly low-level trainers.

Max went to one torch up the hallway and brought it back, the golden light warming his face when he held it too close.

"Ah!" said the niquerra, his voice childlike in pitch. "Get that light away!"

Max held the torch aloft and took a better look, seeing the guy shielding his eyes with one arm that a long-sleeved, yellow shirt covered. The niquerra wore neat but stained green pants tucked into brown leather boots. Max couldn't see his face.

Name: Evanel Soulcutter of Lagoni.
Type: NPC.
Class: Blacksmith.
Species: Niquerra.
Level 10.

That last name was a little disturbing. Did they get surnames from an occupation? What could lead to that one? He had to be here for a reason, or the game designers wouldn't have made him exist.

Lowering the torch, Max asked, "Why does the light bother you?"

"Don't know much about niquerra, do you?"

"I guess not," Max replied.

"We see well without light. If you insist on having one, use a lantern and keep the flame low."

Hoping to not bother the guy into refusing to talk, Max returned the torch to the wall and came back without it. He didn't need to see much more, anyway. "Why are you locked in there? What did you do?"

"Nothing."

Not helpful. Struggling for an angle, Max asked, "They locked you up on principle? Because you're niquerran?"

"I suppose you could say that."

"Why don't you just tell me the reason?"

"Why? Are you going to let me out if you disagree with them?"

Max thought he was a little smarmy and answered, "I didn't say that. But there's zero chance if you don't tell me."

Evanel rose smoothly, as if rising from the floor was a frequent action. He approached with a rolling gait that made it seem like he'd roll upon the ground and back to his feet in one motion. He stopped short of the bars and looked up at Max, his round face serious and unsmiling. The cherub-like cheeks didn't grant him the cheerful impression of querra. Instead, he seemed matter-of-fact and like a young adult who might have little sense of humor. Max had thought Evanel's blonde hair was neatly slicked back, but now he saw it was really in a long braid.

"Haven't seen you before," the niquerra said.

"Same. But did you see many people before you were thrown in here?"

Evanel snorted, a smirk appearing. "You really know little about niquerra."

"What's that mean?"

"They had a bag over my head. Everyone always assumes we want to steal their gold, so—"

"Do you?"

Evanel winked and continued as if he hadn't been interrupted. "So they seldom let my kind see a settlement's layout if they can avoid it. They assume we're making note of potential locations for their wealth."

"I'll just assume it's true. So you've only seen guards that come down here and not me before."

Evanel shrugged. "I've seen a few other rooms when they take me out, blindfolded, of course."

Max figured they must want something from him to remove him from the prison more than once, unless it was for some sort of trial. He had no idea how the criminal justice system worked here and hadn't thought to look it up. Breaking laws wasn't part of most games. You not only got away with killing things, but were actively rewarded for it. But maybe it was different here and he could end up arrested himself. Some games started with you in prison. And if he really rescued Norus, a stronger chance of being thrown into one existed. What would happen then? Would he get a trial? Executed? A hand cut off?

He asked, "What do they take you out for?"

"They want me to make niquerran steel for them. I have refused."

Max figured he already knew from its description why those of Evator wanted it, given its superior quality. Did they desire it for an impending mining village attack? How long would it take a lone niquerra to forge enough weapons for it to help the assault? Or was the desire more generalized and not for this specific mission? He doubted any real-world effect would come from it, so why would Evanel sit in prison instead of doing what they wanted? Was it principle?

He asked, "Why refuse? Did they offer to let you go if you created enough from it?"

"They did not. They'll just use it on my kind, assuming they ever found our home in the mountains."

Max wondered if that was really the reason, given the hinted at difficulty of reaching Evanel's city. "It's hard to find Lagoni?"

"No human ever has and made it out again."

Technically, that wasn't what Max has asked. "So do niquerra kill people who find it? Is that true in Lagoni or everywhere?"

Evanel shrugged. "Sometimes. I can't speak for other settlements, but I think it is common. You need to be invited. But no one ever is."

Eventually, they had to invite someone, but he got the point not to show up unexpected. "If you lock people up in your settlements, then you can't very well blame them for locking you up in here."

Evanel chuckled grudgingly. "I suppose not. That doesn't mean I don't want my freedom."

"What if you traded one of Lagoni's prisoners for yourself?"

"I don't know that we have any prisoners that came from Evator. And I am not in a position to arrange that even if we did."

Max nodded. "Right. And not your job, I'm guessing."

Evanel shrugged. "Technically, no, but they would listen to such a proposal. Whether they would accept is not known. I don't think anyone has ever tried that before. It is a novel idea. Perhaps I will mention it. I assume you are a lowly guard and in no position to offer this."

Smirking, Max replied, "I have the ear of my superiors, but I have not proven my value here. Perhaps soon. Are you considered valuable in Lagoni?"

"I am still an apprentice."

"If I could arrange for a trade, they wouldn't take it?"

"I didn't say that."

Max considered. Making a niquerran friend might reap benefits. If he let Evanel escape while he was freeing Norus, and the niquerra made it home okay, Max could even get an invitation. Or at least boost his reputation with niquerra. Sometimes you had to look for these opportunities. He had played these games just enough to know that questioning an NPC like this sometimes benefited him. Maybe the guy could even repay him some time by forging something of niquerran steel for him. That piqued his interest.

He asked, "Could you make the steel here if you wanted to?"

"Not without the ore, which they claim to have. But I can tell they want to steal the formula for making the steel by watching, and no niquerra will reveal that. It is worth far more than my life."

Max could respect that. "If you got out of this cell, would you be able to escape the castle, even make it back to Lagoni?"

Evanel stared intently at him for several moments. "If I had a querra's clothes, no one would stop me from leaving. As it is, my neater attire might help give me away, though it is now more closely soiled, like querra, with their sloppiness." His disdain was apparent, especially as he added, "I could, perhaps, accentuate that on purpose in the coming days. Once in the woods, I would be fine, even with no other equipment. However, some supplies would be appreciated."

Max nodded. "Maybe I'll ask around about their intentions for you and if your story checks out, I'll consider helping you."

The niquerra held his gaze. "If you do this, and I do not think that you will, but if you succeed and you ever find my lands, I would ensure you are welcomed—and allowed to leave if you desire."

New Quest: Free Evanel Soulcutter from Castle Evator.

Objective: The forces of Evator have captured Evanel to force the blacksmith to forge niquerran steel or give up its secrets. Free him from his cell and ensure he escapes the dungeon.

Difficulty: Medium.

Rewards: 1 Uncommon Item. +1 Reputation among niquerra. 1,000 XP.

Accept?

Chapter Thirteen

Max accepted the quest to free the niquerra.

I knew I should talk to this guy, he thought, pleased.

This quest sounded easier than rescuing Norus. He could almost do it as soon as he bought some querran clothes, assuming he had the money. And he suspected he had nowhere near enough. He could distract the guards to get Evanel to walk out undetected, but he'd need to get the keys. Maybe he'd come down here with some ale or mead for them. It was something to worry about later, but quests that involved no violence were a relief.

He went farther down the hall to Norus. The hunter sat against the far wall, one hand on his ribs, the opposite forearm propped up on one knee. He looked worse than before, with a few bruises on his chin and one cheek. His health bar was down a quarter, which suggested he'd just gotten the beating. Max clenched his fist. Sure, he had his own problems, but this was not okay, and he had to remind himself this was just a game—or was it? No, not anymore. He was imprisoned here—and it was the only world he was ever going to know unless something changed. His survival depended on what happened.

If his attorney was successful in getting him a reprieve, that still wouldn't get him out. What if this was the end? Then everything he did was pointless and maybe he shouldn't bother. But he couldn't spend his remaining time getting drunk in a digital tavern—assuming that would even work—unless he gave up all hope. Maybe the best way to assert his will to live—and maybe unstick that damn logout button—was to go for it in here and "live" as much as possible. Would adrenaline wake him?

Regardless, freeing Norus was not exactly a priority anymore, because Siren was right about the danger it would put Max in. Still, he didn't want to see Norus getting roughed up. If Max was stuck in here forever, NPCs like this were his only constant companions. They were better than nothing. And dreaming up some rescue might take his mind off his own situation.

"What have you found out?" Norus asked, rising with a suppressed groan.

"Not much. Can you ride a florin bird?"

The hunter snorted in amusement. "Can you?"

Good point, Max thought, once again intrigued by the realistic interactions these NPCs provided. "Let me worry about that."

"Rode one once. Didn't care for it, but if it's a choice between that and here, I'll manage."

"Have you noticed anything about how often the guards change, like at what hour?"

Norus nodded and told him of the pattern as best he could, but with no sunlight, it was hard to tell when anything really took place. Max decided to discreetly ask around, as if interested in doing that sort of guard duty. He still had no idea where he would be assigned and how to get out of doing it tomorrow. What would they do if he didn't report for duty? Arrest him and throw him in another cell? That would be perfect.

He soon left Norus and chatted up the guards for a bit, gaining both useless and possibly useful info. The banter lightened his mood. Maybe he needed that for a distraction. He returned to the ground floor, passing servants and a page boy or two as he tried to act like he belonged wherever he was. Between his demeanor and being seen as a guard, no one challenged him, but then he didn't try to enter a place that gave him the impression he shouldn't. He sometimes asked what was in a room, explaining if it seemed necessary that he was new in town and starting duty tomorrow. And NPCs just coughed up information so that he started to think this was genius and Norus had done him a bigger favor than intended with this ruse.

This continued as he ascended the unguarded Florin Tower. The worn steps, some cracked, spiraled up in the round, central pillar of grey limestone. At each floor, they reached a landing about ten feet wide, where an arched wooden door led to a room that hugged the tower's exterior. Some doors were closed, but most stood open to reveal living quarters for a handful of winged riders. Max sensed there was more space inside out of view, but he didn't investigate.

A few other rooms held supplies for either the riders or the birds. This included saddles, straps, stirrups, reins, and related equipment. One stored food in open wicker bins on shelves, kegs of ale and bottles of wine neatly arranged nearby. Pewter dishes, goblets, and wine glasses were stacked or hanging from a rack near the wall. It became clear that people lived here and the tower would seldom be empty. Getting Norus and himself up here wouldn't be easy if people were pursuing them. Or at all suspicious. They'd have to come up in full view with everyone thinking they belonged there until the last moments when they somehow got onto a florin and flew away without archers killing them.

By the fifth floor, he saw into one room and through a window, realizing that he had reached the castle's top but not that of the tower. His legs were burning, and this seemed like another problem for an escape. Those who regularly climbed this tower were likely to not get winded or feel weak legs, but he and Norus would end up slowing down. That he needed a ruse was increasingly obvious.

While he leaned against a wall to catch his breath, a pair of winged riders strode past him, smirking at his wheezing. One smacked his arm good-naturedly. He felt they had accepted him as one of the castle's defenses. Their symbol of two outstretched wings graced the backs of their tunics. He noticed both men were short and slight of build, which raised another question. Did he or Norus weigh too much to ride one of these great birds? Certainly, they might need one for each of them. This was getting less likely by the minute.

As he neared the upper areas where the birds were, he expected to smell them. Maybe they'd be akin to horses, which could stink from a distance. This was not just feces and urine in a stall or field, but the horses themselves. But so far, the birds didn't seem to have any scent at all, not that he was complaining. He reached the first open door that led to one of their rooms and had a florin bird inside. The doorway was too small for the birds, who couldn't enter the tower's center where he stood as a result.

Max stopped in awe, mouth agape. The bird was about twenty feet tall, from razor-sharp talons to the top of its majestic head. He knew nothing about birds of prey, so he couldn't tell if it resembled a hawk more than a falcon or another variety. Its breast had a combination of white and light blue feathers. Based on what little he'd learned on TV shows about predators in the wild, this was probably meant to disguise it against the sky when seen from below. The feathers on its top were green. Was this like the forest kais and meant to hide it from above against the woods below it?

Its head was more than twice the size of his, the vicious-looking beak cream-colored. It hadn't been looking his way until his movement caught its attention, the head snapping in his direction with an alertness he found menacing. It eyed him for a few moments before the head turned mostly away, but he had the impression it was still keeping one eye on him, as if he could be a threat to it. Funny how he felt the same way about the bird.

Max would never approach one of these things without training in what not to do. In here, the beak had to be more dangerous, but the talons looked worse. Each had been shod in dusky black metal. In places, the solid floor had been designed like any other for people to walk on, but to make it easier for the birds, branches or logs as big as himself had been dragged in and placed in various positions. The bird was standing on two of them, its talons wrapped around. That a bunch of straw covered the floor didn't surprise Max because he'd seen some of it falling from the tower's open sides at various times since arriving, likely blown by breezes. An enormous opening in the exterior wall revealed one of the outside perches he'd seen from the ground.

Max was so caught up in the bird that he didn't notice the notification that had popped up until he was about to continue up.

Florin, Tamed. One of the great birds of prey, florins are found near many of Llurien's mountain ranges and wherever they have been bred in captivity or captured and tamed. They are the primary mounts of the winged riders. Approach with caution.

HP: 28/28

That was more HP than the few horses he'd seen in town or the bailey's courtyard, but not by much. It didn't surprise him when he thought about it. They might be hard to get close enough to, for someone to attack by hand, but maybe they otherwise weren't that hard to kill. Missile weapons seemed the saner approach, though the idea of hurting such a beautiful animal seemed wrong. The real worry was how much damage one could do to *him*.

Max continued up the stairs, passing similar rooms, some arranged the same way but others seemingly designed for that but missing the hay, logs, or both, as if they weren't currently expected to be in use. Two birds were in one room while most were empty or had just one. He was two stories from the top when he encountered a guard talking to a female winged rider. He was about to step past when the guard stopped him.

"What's your business up here?"

Max hadn't been accosted even once so that he felt genuine surprise. He tried to turn it into an innocent look.

"I'm new in town. Came in from Rook yesterday to join the, uh, defenses. I heard I might be assigned up here and was curious about the birds. Can you show me around? Tell me how to not get eaten by one of these things?"

Both the guard and rider laughed. With a jerk of her head, the rider indicated Max should follow, so he did, taking a moment to observe a notification he received now, just like he did a few minutes ago with the prison guards.

You have used the Charm skill and gained 15 XP!

The winged rider took up him up to the last floor before the top, showing him a glimpse of the rooms where birds were kept, explaining only a few details. Walking out onto the perch there intimidated him, even without a bird on it. The stones and grass were a long way down, only black netting to the left and right offering some protection if he fell. That seemed more likely as the breeze buffeted him. Max imagined the riders were used to far worse while flying and maybe didn't consider this intimidating at all. He tried to act casual, aware that he was trying to impress a female NPC. He suppressed a chuckle.

She took him to the tower's mostly flat top, which they sometimes used for landing and departing. Covered in hard wood, it nonetheless had hundreds of small dents that Max assumed the metal-shod talons caused as birds moved around on it. This area provided fewer opportunities to fall and was considered safer for cadets or more casual riders, like royalty. The more skilled winged riders poked fun at each other if using it, unless dire circumstances suggested it, like an injured bird, a half-dead rider, or some other emergency. They even assumed something was wrong if one of them landed there, others rushing to help unless the winged rider waved them off because everything was fine, at which point the mockery began.

Max wondered how he and Norus would get two birds up here for them to flee with. It wasn't happening. The birds would have to already be here. What were the odds he'd break the hunter free, and they'd get up here to find that? And he wouldn't get someone to just hold them here... unless he and Siren had a lesson or something planned, and she was up there and helped them escape. But then she'd get caught. He sighed. The rescue idea kept getting worse.

He spent an hour atop the Florin Tower, which gave the best view of the surrounding countryside. The white-topped Bier Peak loomed above the Haigan Forest and its mostly pine trees that stretched as far as he could see to the south. Rolling open land with random crops of deciduous trees lay in other directions. A couple buildings, usually of stone, stood taller than other one and two-story wooden buildings in the town to the north.

Directly below lay the keep, though there wasn't much to see of its stonework from here. In the keep's center, a ceiling of glass panels lay, but he couldn't see through them to whatever was beneath.

He learned much about the birds, the equipment needed to ride one, and what gear a winged rider typically had. He slowly grew accustomed to the enormous birds, partly because the woman told him how to behave, like talking slowly to it in a low voice, and feeding it a small piece of tosk meat when it let him pet it, which had to be done on its breast because it was so tall. With more normal-sized birds, which existed on Llurien, this petting would be done behind the head, but he'd need a ladder to do that with this giant avian.

As the sun fell and two visible moons rose into the twilight sky, activity atop the Florin Tower increased. He'd seen morkais from a distance since arriving in Evator. Now several landed atop the tower to give reports on how things looked to the east. He pulled up their description.

Species: Kais.

Race: Morkais.

Summary: A product of the Divine Covenant, the morkais race of kais exhibit the combined traits of the benevolent Green, Indigo, and Yellow Sphere gods who created them: truth, vitality, courage, and intuition; innocence, passion, expression, and unity; inspiration, empathy, rejuvenation, and patience. They are often mistaken for their nefarious brothers, the daekais, from whom the gods created them, a fact which causes some to not trust morkais. They are frequent messengers, scouts, and aerial protectors of travelers and settlements. Unlike daekais, they do not have poisonous teeth, claws, or talons, but the antidote to daekais poison. They excel at

ranged and magical attacks. Feather colors suggest their habitat: green for forest, gold for plains, blue for seas, and so on.

Species Strengths: +2 Agility in the Air, +1 Dexterity, +1 Constitution, +2 Charisma.

Species Weaknesses: -1 Strength, -1 Reputation.

Species Bonuses: Daekais Poison Immunity, +25% Most Thieving Skills, +5% Magic Resistance, +5% Physical Attack, +5% Magical Attack, +10% Sling/Dart Bonus.

Class Restrictions: Coiryn Rider, Winged Rider. Dual classes permitted.

Proficiency Points Bonus: None.

Up close, Max easily saw the difference between morkais and daekais. The morkais looked very similar to the daekais, except that everything sinister, suspicious, and sullen was absent. They were refined, well-mannered, bright-eyed, and clean, including their clothes. He suspected that some found them arrogant, just as they did with him, because they were enviable. But he liked them partly because he suspected they weren't into gossip and bullshit.

As he watched, Max overheard that all the morkais who'd flown south, near the mountains, were late to return, though no one seemed concerned. Several riders returned from their shifts as others prepared for their nighttime patrol, which he imagined was more dangerous. What if those daekais attacked a rider at night? How likely was that? That was yet another element that made him leery of a nighttime escape with Norus. And wouldn't the morkais give chase, too?

Max overheard several scouts say a small caravan from Rook was also arriving from the western road in just minutes. He turned and saw it in the distance, two rows of torches already lit beside the wagons. It looked like both banoth and horses were pulling them, but he couldn't be sure from so high up. He hadn't noticed the caravan before, but then he'd mostly been looking at the birds and the Haigan Forest to the south, sometimes the mountains to the east, and not west at the gently rolling lands on this side of the river. From this high, he'd already seen that there were multiple farms out the way. With this caravan arriving, he'd need to avoid interacting with people from Rook in front of anyone from Evator if they knew he supposedly came from there. A lie might trip him up.

He descended to the courtyard for another night of hanging out with guards, drinking, and eating with Malonir and the others. To his surprise, the ale was influencing him, and while he wasn't drunk, he enjoyed the much needed feeling of mirth a little buzz created. His exploits had distracted him from his situation, and now, when his mind drifted back to it, it seemed somehow less dire. Maybe the shock had worn off. Or maybe he was getting drunk? He should probably lay off the stuff.

As he chewed a mouthful of roasted tosk leg, the rest in one greasy hand, he eyed the darkening sky. He had never been one for knowing the constellations, so the sky didn't seem much different to him except for the pair of moons, one barren and bright like Earth's moon, the other dark, as if covered in vegetation or water. He couldn't tell which. Earth had dark constellations of interstellar gas that caused deep purples and blues in bands across part of the sky, but he'd never seen them, since most were in the southern hemisphere. But some soared overhead, beautiful, mesmerizing, and getting clearer as darkness consumed the sky.

Siren broke his reverie on sending him a message.

Siren: Hey. I'm back in. Where are you?

Max: Castle courtyard. Not sure if you can get in here, but you can try.

Siren: I'm close. On the way.

Max waited until he saw her at the castle gates before heading that way to see if she needed help entering, but she seemed to bluff her way past the guards. He was going to ask her what she said when three players twenty paces behind her distracted him, one carrying a torch that lit them up.

At nearly nine feet tall, one of them looked like the nefarious jhaikan species Max had seen during character creation, but this player was the supposedly reformed rhaikan race of them. He didn't look any less terrifying, dark scales visible on any part of his body that the black leather armor didn't cover. He seemed like a humanoid dragon. The guy's class was stalker, whatever that meant. He saw Max staring and bared wicked teeth in what might've been intended as a grin. Figuring it would tell him more, Max pulled up the species description instead of the rhaikan race one and let the game read it to him so he could keep his eyes on people.

Species: Jhaikan.

Summary: One of the seven original species, jhaikan exhibit the traits of the four Blue Sphere nefarious gods who created them: wrath, malice, cunning, and domination. Jhaikan are synonymous with evil, brutality, and pain. Masters of the long con, they can never be trusted except to look out for their interests at the expense of others, including their own kind. Unwelcome in all but the largest societies and fond of stalking the innocent and wicked alike in the wilderness, they get more dangerous the more pain they feel. They also eat people. Alive! For the horror it creates. They cannot be wizards, only sorcer-

ers, but excel at melee and ranged attacks. They make superb tanks.

Species Strengths: +2 Strength, +1 Dexterity, +1 Constitution, +1 Intelligence, +2 Morale.

Species Weaknesses: -2 Charisma, -3 Reputation, +50% Fearful Reaction,

Species Bonuses: +1 Spear Bonus, +1 Staff Bonus, +5% Luck, +10% Regeneration, +5% Magic Resistance, +10% Attack Speed, +10% Physical Attack, +10% Bludgeon Damage, +10% Additional Hit Points Per Level, Acute Smell, Stealth, Resist Cold, Resist Heat.

Class Restrictions: Any Heroic Classes (Knight, Paladin, Coiryn Rider, Winged Rider, Warder), Bard, Monk, Wizard.

Proficiency Points Bonus: 1 point at creation and an additional 1 point every 4 levels.

Max felt relieved that this players was a good guy. Supposedly. He doubted anyone really trusted a rhaikan from the look of them.

Flanking the guy was a karelian sorcerer and a kryllan rogue, both dressed in black leather, and it was clear they were together. The nickname "Dark Trio" popped into Max's head. They seemed headed in his direction but were struggling to talk their way past the guards. Since he'd already familiarized himself with the kryll species, he pulled up the karelian one.

Species: Karelia.

Summary: One of the seven original species, karelia exhibit the traits of the four Green Sphere benevolent gods who created them: truth, vitality, courage, and intuition. Long-living critical thinkers, and stronger than they look, karelia are brilliant and brave. They need to be after the Divine Covenant, which gave them the skills that have made them respected and feared, so much so that some places don't welcome them despite their altruistic, lawful nature. Karelia need less of many things: food, water, and rest. They learn spells faster and excel at ranged, melee, and magic attacks; the god of vitality who created them is also the god of magic.

Special: During the Divine Covenant, karelia accepted a role as caretakers of all supernatural and spiritual disturbances. They received innate, advanced sixth sense skills: Disrupt Spell, Spirit Sight, Identify Spirit, Identify Spell, Speak with Undead, 25% Resistance to Necrotic Damage, 10% Detect Illusion, 10% Resist Illusion, 15% Magic Resistance, and Detect the Supernatural, Cursed Items, and Unholy Perversions. Some can even separate their soul and return.

Species Strengths: +1 Dexterity, +2 Constitution, +1 Intelligence, +3 Morale.

Species Weaknesses: -2 Charisma, +10% Undead Aggro, -2 Reputation, +10% Fearful Reaction, Obligated to Accept All Quests to Resolve Supernatural, Spiritual, and Undead Disturbances.

Species Bonuses: +50% Mana, +5% Attack Speed, +5% Physical Attack, +15% Magical Attack, 3x Regeneration, +1 Accuracy, +1 Sword Damage, Detect Character, Detect Poison, Heat Vision, 50% Karelian Sleep Reduction, Night Vision, 20% Poison Resistance, Direction Sense, and Weather Sense.

Class Restrictions: None.

Proficiency Points Bonus: None.

The karelia was impressive and something Max might've liked to try. The metal head in him loved anything with undead. Or maybe it had nothing to do with his music preferences. Seeing these three players together, Max thought they had picked the three most formidable species.

Just as Siren reached Max, shouts rang out from the Florin Tower. He turned and saw three archers from there and atop the castle let loose with arrows he couldn't see, but they were aiming up. And then he saw the danger as he made out what the archers were shouting.

"Daekais!"

CHAPTER FOURTEEN

A bright-eyed Siren said, "Told ya!" as she pulled out an Asyander short bow and loaded an arrow onto it.

"You did predict an attack." Max didn't share her enthusiasm as he grabbed his matching bow from inventory. He also added his long sword to his waist. He could get killed, a fact she seemed to have forgotten from that gleam in her red eyes, which made her seem a little devilish right now.

"Sometimes you can see shit coming in these games." When she said it, a small rock from above struck one of the nearby guards, who fell to the ground unconscious as the stone bounced away on the ground. "Then again, sometimes you can't."

Seeing two kais with green wings fly overhead, one letting loose with another rock from a sling, Max said, "I think we need to take cover."

"Toward the barracks."

As they jogged that way across the courtyard, going east, Max took in the scene. Scores of kais flew from the east, from his left to the right. Only a few seemed brave or stupid enough to fly directly over the castle. Most that he could see were over the forest, farther south and bypassing his position altogether. Then they swooped down out of sight beyond the bailey wall on his right, in the caravan's direction. Was that their target? It seemed likely for them to go after the relatively undefended travelers.

Max could now tell between morkais and daekais from the way they flew, as morkais seemed elegant and in control of the finer points of style, while the daekais were haphazard and somehow crude. It was the difference between a gold medal gymnast performing acrobatic feats and one from a country who barely made the Olympics doing it. In the dark, he couldn't see their feather colors unless some of them came nearer the fires lighting up parts of the castle's defenses; they seemed mostly green and brown.

"The caravan," he said. "That's what they're after."

Siren replied with little interest, "Maybe we should go that way."

He glanced over his shoulder at the Dark Trio. The guards were ignoring them as everyone prepared for battle. The Dark Trio rushed past him toward the keep, no longer eyeing Max, if they ever were. Was he just paranoid after learning people knew he was in here?

He took cover near the barracks entrance. He and Siren took turns trying to hit a daekais as they flew by, but Max thought it was impossible until seeing an NPC archer strike one in a wing. The daekais shrieked and lost control, spiraling down into the courtyard. He landed on his feet in an area that had just been occupied by guards, who had all run to get bows. He stood alone, one wing held protectively close.

Siren fired, striking the daekais in the other wing. Max didn't notice how much damage she did. He fired but missed over the shoulder by two feet. The daekais turned with sling in hand and shot a rock that cracked against the wooden wall next to Max, who lifted his bow once more. Determination burning—he remembered how much one of those rocks hurt—he coldly aimed for the daekais' head and fired. The arrow struck him in the chest and knocked him backward so that he fell to the cobblestones. Only now did Max notice the notification of how many HP the daekais had left. It wasn't much, the health bar flashing red.

"Finish him," Siren, nodding at the daekais. "He's yours."

Max didn't really think so but cast the *Weapon Ward* valender, then ran out into the courtyard, drawing his sword. The flickering of firelights cast dancing shadows on the daekais. The thought of killing someone laid out on their back didn't seem very sporting. The victim seemed dazed and unlikely to pose a danger. Max hesitated and then retrieved string from his inventory, intending to bind the daekais, though he knew little about tying knots. Maybe he'd spend a proficiency point later. Would a daekais talk if questioned? Did they have anything to say? Was there a reward for capturing one? A boost to his reputation?

He knelt by the dirt-covered bare feet, which had equally disgusting—and sharp—talons protruding. Max grabbed one ankle, and the daekais yanked it out of his grip, kicking at him. Max dodged the foot and tried to grab it again, but the daekais sat up and swung a clawed hand that scratched him across his cheek.

"Ow!" Max gasped at the pain. He was never getting used to that. The game didn't have to be that realistic. A notification had appeared with a red outline, so he took the time to scan it.

Warning! A daekais has poisoned you!

Great, he thought, angry. What if that killed him?

"You little shit!" he growled. "I was trying to *save* you!"

"Die, human scum!" the daekais snarled, swinging again.

Max leaned back, evading the swipe. All mercy gone, he pulled out his dagger and stabbed the guy in the chest, blooding spurting from the daekais' mouth as horrified eyes went from the blade up to Max's face. With a last gurgle of breath, the daekais fell back to lie motionless.

"Goddamnit," Max muttered, feeling the bloody gashes in his cheek with his other hand. He yanked the dagger from the corpse and wiped it on the tattered daekais clothing, something he'd seen in movies. Did he need to do that here? Would weapons decay if not properly taken care of? It was another factor he didn't know. Dr. Thompson could have at least set him up with a bunch of info when she forced him in here.

A system message appeared.

You have killed (1) Daekais Looter, Level 3!
You gained 50 XP!
Loot corpse?

The XP surprised him. He got the same amount from a lower level daekais looter out in the woods. But then he realized an NPC had shot this one, then he and Siren did before he stabbed and killed it. The XP had likely been split. That could be both good and bad, depending on how fights went.

As he quickly looted the body, Siren knelt beside him.

"Come on. Get up. The morkais have the antidote."

"Forgot about that." Max realized they were likely sharing some notifications as party members. He rose and noticed his HP had gone down a couple points from the blow and now dropped another point, presumably from the poison. How long would that last? Long enough to kill him? The game had said nothing about duration. He was otherwise not feeling anything like dizziness or weak legs.

This time they ran for the keep as a swarm of daekais crested the outer wall beyond it to the south. One in the middle had golden feathers that made him stand out against the night sky. Max's first impression was that these had no interest in the caravan.

They began circling the courtyard, raining rocks down at everyone as Max and Siren reached the open doors, which guards were frantically pulling closed. Looking north beyond the daekais, Max saw scores of morkais approaching from the town, most appearing armed with bows rather than slings. To his surprise, the Dark Trio was right behind him and Siren. They made it inside as the doors crashed shut, a portcullis dropping and beams slamming over the door. Max thought there was little chance of daekais getting inside now.

Then he heard a loud crash of glass shattering high above them, women screaming. Siren met his gaze and together they charged up a flight of stone stairs that torches and lanterns dimly lit. The Dark Trio, another player, and some NPC guards followed. At the top stretched two hallways, one going down the keep's side and another across the keep's front.

And there stood a daekais, rising off the floor to stand with her back to them, a tinkling of broken glass sounding as it fell off her to the stone floor. She had crashed through the window and now lifted her sling at guards on her other side. Max and Siren knocked arrows, but the Dark Trio's rhaikan and kryll charged ahead, blocking their shot. Max frowned at the interference as their sorcerer followed.

He noticed the rhaikan swinging an axe that looked familiar as he suggested, "Maybe we should go somewhere else, away from them."

"Up," said Siren, and they climbed one floor from the commotion without waiting to see the outcome. Heading down a hallway above it, they found a stained-glass window twenty feet square, with a florin bird depicted, wings outstretched. The view faced the courtyard.

Max peered through a clear window panel. Just above his position, the daekais circled inside the bailey haphazardly, whether to evade arrows or from habit. In their center and a little below hovered the one with golden wings, kept aloft with methodical sweeps of his wings, his gaze at the keep. He slowly waved his arms as if gathering energy. Max focused on him.

Daekais. Level 10 Sorcerer. 138 HP. Among the rarest of daekais is the sorcerer, one of the few classes with enough influence over the unruly daekais to command respect, cooperation, and joint military action. Killing him/her won't stop an attack that's underway, but it will hasten a return to the every-daekais-for-themselves mentality.

"We need to kill that one," said Max, pointing.

"Others seem to have the same idea," replied Siren, as multiple arrows missed the sorcerer. "I think this is a boss fight."

"Shit," Max muttered. "I really don't need to be in one of those right now."

Siren glanced at him. "True. I'll protect you."

He glanced sideways at her, amused by a woman protecting a man. Her smirk suggested she was aware of it, too, and teasing. He turned back to the window.

Max saw the evil leer on the sorcerer's face as he thrust forward with both hands. With Siren, he dove to the floor as an orange shockwave of energy hurtled toward them. It shattered the window, the floor shaking. Max kept his head down, broken glass tinkling on the floor. He worried about shards stabbing him, but only small pieces remained. He felt minor cuts on his hands.

Looking up, he saw that every window along the hall had broken. He suspected others on different floors had, too. There were also several cracks in the limestone walls. What looked like a gargoyle fell past the window outside, crashing below with a heavy thud, a man's scream splitting the night air.

Max rose and peered outside. The circle of flying daekais had abandoned the maneuver and were heading for the keep. The sorcerer turned to face the coming morkais and repeated his gesture. As the orange arc of energy raced outward, it cast light on the bailey walls and pavement. The morkais saw it coming and scattered, but it struck two in the chest. From the way they fell, Max knew they were lifeless before they smashed into the ground with a sickening crack. The arc of light continued past them before dissipating.

Max said, "Whatever that spell is, it's enough force to kill."

"And probably split eardrums. I think you need to avoid that guy more than me."

Max nodded, noticing his HP had dropped another two points from the poison.

Three daekais dove toward their position. Max stepped out of the way as they flew through the big window one by one and right past him through a large opening in the wall. Max had already glanced in there past the stone railing to see a two-story throne room below. Two iron chandeliers with burning torches hung from the ceiling. Finally dressed people and their servants ran screaming as guards fired crossbow bolts at the intruders, one daekais immediately falling. As other attackers entered the building, a notification popped up.

New Quest: Clear Castle Evator of Daekais.

Objective: Daekais have attacked and infiltrated Castle Evator! Kill or subdue them all (40)!
Difficulty: Medium.
Rewards: 1 Unique Item. +1 Reputation in Andra Kingdom (Evator). 2,000 XP.
Accept?

Max accepted the quest, a nod from Siren revealing she had as well. It was obviously a group one, since 40 daekais was way too many for just two of them. Loading another arrow, Siren looked at the courtyard, where the sorcerer had turned toward them.

She said, "I want a piece of the XP from killing that."

Max wasn't so sure pissing off the sorcerer was a good idea, but Siren let fly with an arrow that missed. He quickly examined his available spells, unsure if he could change his hot list. Normally, once he was in combat, it was fixed, but he wasn't fighting anything at the moment. Would it let him? He tried and it worked.

"I'm gonna cast *Archery Fiend* on you," he said to Siren.

"What's it do?" She cocked another arrow.

"Makes you an expert archer for ten minutes."

"Perfect."

Max pulled out one of the daekais feathers in his inventory. While the spell didn't specify what feather type was needed to mimic an arrow's fletching, he wondered if it being from the intended target race would help. He touched Siren with the feather. "By the grace of Coiryn, may your arrows fly true."

The feather disintegrated and a soft, green glow briefly surrounded both of Siren's hands. She fired at the sorcerer but another daekais flew into the arrow's path. The missile caught her in the breast and seemed to kill her from the way she fell to the stone courtyard and didn't move again, but her health bar was only deep in the red. Someone would likely finish her soon enough.

Max swapped out his other hot list spells, keeping Heal, *Orb of Doom*, and *Sleep*. But he replaced the other two with *Blindness* and *Break into Song*, both of which he intended to cast at the sorcerer. Maybe the daekais would be less effective if he couldn't see or was busy singing. The latter amused the musician in Max. That reminded him of the *Song of Gathering*. Could he use that to make the daekais gather around him and listen to what he said? He could tell them to leave. Or fight each other for whatever loot they had.

Siren's next arrow struck the sorcerer in the abdomen and the victim's health bar appeared, not showing much damage. His eyes focused on them. Siren wasted no time pulling out another projectile as Max prepared to cast *Blindness*. He waited for the next arrow to fly, hoping it might distract his target, who turned sideways so that the arrow missed. Then he flew toward them with powerful thrusts. Max knew they were in trouble, especially when Siren fired another arrow and the sorcerer brushed it aside with a gesture, magic making it deflect.

"Dodge this," he muttered. Using two fingers to mimic pulling his eyelids down, he said the magic words, "See no more."

Chapter Fifteen

That the spell worked was apparent from the way the daekais pulled up, shock on his face. He was close enough for Max to see a milky white film cover the eyes. Just as satisfaction filled Max, the sorcerer curtly waved one hand, and the cloudiness vanished. Max's heart sank even as Siren lodged an arrow into the sorcerer's chest. Still hovering by flapping his wings, the daekais snarled in pain and ripped it out with a grimace, then healed himself. He made a furious swirling motion with one hand. Max watching in growing fear as all the glass shards around them rose into a tornado. He turned to run and saw a small tapestry on the wall.

"Siren!" he called, yanking it down. She dove for it, but the sorcerer was close enough to see what they were doing. He changed the tornado shape from a vertical vortex to a horizontal one. It swept under the tapestry's edge as Siren and Max dropped to the floor under it, pulling it tight.

In the sudden, musky darkness, the glass under the tapestry was still moving. It cut his face, neck, and hands before getting inside his clothes. Siren made a strangled cry of pain. They were going to get sliced to death. Her health bar appeared, then his, both halfway down.

"Mother Llurien, mend your child." The *Heal* spell raised Max from 14 HP to 17, but he was a long way from full at 36 HP. He received a notification.

You are still poisoned by daekais!

Max pulled a health potion from inventory and quaffed it, but by the time it gave him 4 more HP, he lost that much from poison and more cuts. Suddenly the swirling glass tinkled to the floor amidst a cry of pain that sounded like the sorcerer. Max threw off the tapestry, more glass falling with the motion. Outside the window, another arrow now protruded from the daekais.

Max raced to the broken window's edge. His next spell had a 15 feet range. He raised one hand, palm outstretched as he sang the words.

"Sing for me, earnestly!"

The sorcerer turned to him, eyes wide, then confused. The daekais perked up as if having an idea, but as if caught between rising joy and consternation. Then his mouth opened, and he began to sing in a high-pitched, nasal voice.

"Golden coin is all I see,
Shining bright and so fancy,
I will take it all for me,
Kill all those who don't agree.
Sparkling gems are so lovely,
Wear them oh so prettily,
I will take them all for me,
And kill all those who don't agree."

As the daekais sang what sounded like a children's rhyme, he looked both engrossed in the tune and perplexed that he couldn't stop repeating it. This continued despite various waves of his small arms as if to dispel it. A bloody Siren fired again. The daekais turned, but there was no evading at this range. The arrow struck him in the ear, but he just kept on singing as he thrust with his wings to ascend. Max tried to prepare another spell, but Siren was faster, enchanted, and the sorcerer was rapidly getting away as he turned and dove, then arced into the sky. Siren tracked him and let loose.

The arrow struck him between the shoulder blades and the daekais faltered but still rose and turned, seeming to head for somewhere above them, atop the keep. Max doubted the sorcerer was done with them. The *Break Into Song* spell would last 10 minutes and apparently prevented the guy from casting anything else.

"Shit," muttered Siren, looking at an ugly gash on her calf. "I want to kill that fucker."

"Let's see about finding him while he can't cast anything. Hold on a second." Max was down to 7 MP because he'd regenerated 2 MP during the fight, but he was technically not in combat now and his regeneration speed increased. He cast *Heal* on her to close the worst wounds.

Siren said, "Don't do that again. You need to live, not me. Cast it on yourself. And take this healing potion."

She gave him one and for a moment he hesitated, but then he accepted that her sole reason for playing was to help him, so he drank it. He also cast *Heal* on himself twice, since he could regenerate to full MP in about 16 seconds when out of combat. Now he was up to 30 HP.

Another daekais flew through the big hole from the stained-glass window, but this one landed, not seeming to realize they were standing just off to one side. Siren leapt at him with her dagger, catching him by surprise. He backed away frantically, but was no match for her onslaught. Max shouted a warning about the poisonous claws and couldn't tell if Siren had heard him, but moments later, he saw the notification for her.

Warning! A daekais has poisoned Siren!

Then the daekais was dead and Siren straightened, her HP already dropping.

Siren achieved Level 3!

Max noticed he didn't get the long message like when he leveled, but he could always ask her about stats. Interrupting his thoughts, another green-feathered daekais flew through the window and landed before them before Max realized it was a morkais.

"Hey," Max began, approaching him, "we're both poisoned. How can we—Ow! What the hell?" Max snatched away the hand the guy had just scratched with a short talon, drawing blood and costing him 1 HP.

You have been cured of daekais poison!

"Sorry," said the morkais, not really apologetic, "but it's faster and we're all in a rush." The morkais held up a talon and turned to Siren, who glanced at Max and frowned in resignation. The guy repeated it on her.

"How's it going out there?" Max asked, curious to interact with a morkais.

"Some are fleeing. But that sorcerer got inside. Need to kill that one, not capture. Think you can handle that? You silenced him, in a way." The morkais smiled as if amused by Max's spell.

"Why don't you guys kill him?" he asked, meaning the morkais.

"Fighting inside isn't that easy for us. The wings. He'll have to emerge." He nodded farewell, turned to the window, and leapt through it.

Max and Siren turned away to search the keep's interior. The throne room below them was in disarray, several daekais dead on the floor among crossbow-wielding guards. Max recognized Malonir and Kari among the fighters. Eight more daekais were flying about the ceiling, always moving, sometimes keeping the chandeliers between them and their targets. They fired rocks from slings but missed more often than not. Max had an idea and pulled out a feather, which he dropped over the railing into the room as he focused on the flying daekais.

"Feel slumber's call to rest."

One daekais saw what was happening to the others and flew out of another opening to escape into the black sky. The others stopped flapping their wings or moving any limbs at all. They crashed to the floor as if lifeless, except for the one that accidentally impaled itself on a spear that a statue held. It died moments later. Another landed atop a chandelier, which swayed violently and creaked in rhythm. The guards fired crossbows into that one, killing it and giving Max partial credit. He saw notifications that the fall had killed three more, with the usual offer to loot the bodies, including the one atop the chandelier. The keep's defenders below killed the rest, with Max receiving more partial credits.

You achieved Level 4!

You gained 20 Hit Points!

You gained 6 Mana Points!

Class bonus: You gained Dexterity +1, Intelligence +1, Charisma +1! You can raise two abilities of your choice by 1 point each!

You gained (2) proficiency points!

You have (3) unassigned proficiency points!

You gained (1) additional valender you can learn!

You gained (1) additional spell you can have in your hot list!

The part about raising two ability scores surprised him, but he'd worried about it later. Now he saw Kari staring up at him, eyes suspicious or angry. He couldn't tell which. Or what she could be…

Oh shit, he thought. *I just cast a spell in front of her and she thinks I'm a fighter, not a bard.*

"Come on," said Siren, heading for the stairs. She retrieved her jhaikan staff from her back and assembled it with a few clicks and turns of the pieces. "I want to find that sorcerer and finish him."

Following, Max said, "I'll hang back a little."

They ascended the stone steps, finding dead guards, daekais, and two dead players along the way. The shouts and clangs of steel persisted farther into the keep. From somewhere, Max heard a big whoosh of fire. A wizard? He'd seen no players but himself do offensive magic. By the time they reached the next floor where the fighting seemed to be, his MP and HP were at full and Siren's HP were nearly so.

"Shit," he muttered, realizing another problem. They started down a hall. "I bet that sorcerer has fully regenerated hit points. We'll have to start over."

"Unless someone is keeping him busy."

"Do we get anything if he heals all the way and then someone else kills him?"

"Probably not."

He eyed her for a sign of something but didn't see it. "How long until the *Archery Fiend* spell wears off? I can cast it again."

"Not long. It should say in your HUD. Get it ready."

Max nodded and kept his long sword handy. He'd look for an icon in the HUD later. Ahead, they could hear the higher pitched voices of daekais arguing amongst themselves, but no sound of fighting between them or anyone else. He touched Siren's shoulder to have her stay back, then peered around the corner. Five daekais were grabbing at various trinkets, some of which were ordinary pewter goblets or plates with little value, all scattered on the floor. They didn't seem too smart from what he'd seen, but he had an idea and stowed his sword, then pulled the flute from his inventory.

Siren put her jhaikan staff in inventory instead of on her back, so she could pull it out intact and not have to reassemble it. The bow appeared in her hands, and Max cast *Archery Fiend* on her.

Now was not the time to screw up. He only had one chance at this. There were only so many instrument types he really hoped to use—something guitar-like, and maybe a horn for battles or signaling. That would be two of his unused music proficiencies. A flute was as good as anything else for the remaining one. He could probably gain another proficiency later anyway. Having decided, he used one point for flute and instantly understood the basics of how to play it.

He began playing the *Song of Gathering*, his lips correctly forming the right shape to get a good sound as he blew into it. His fingers easily lifted and fell over the holes. He went through the melody once while listening to the commotion abruptly stop, feathers rustling. The sound of small feet coming toward him prompted Max to creep up to the corner while still playing. The daekais stood or padded toward him, the look of malfeasance gone from the faces, curious wonder replacing it. They now more closely resembled a morkais, just not enough to pass for one. Their attire, talons, and teeth were too unkempt and ragged.

As Max repeated the melody, two other daekais jogged into the room, their wings shuddering as if in pleasure. Another flew in from a nearby window and landed, then walked over. Wondering how far this flute could be heard, Max continued playing for another minute to see how many he could gather. Hopefully, the spell description was accurate or he and Siren were going to die. When no more arrived for thirty seconds, he stopped, seeing roughly two dozen daekais gathered, standing patiently, their faces optimistic and receptive, as if admiring him and hanging on his next words.

But two players had also arrived, as had a half-dozen NPCs, including three morkais. All of them looked equally expectant of what he had to say. Max flicked a glance at Siren, who seemed unaffected, maybe because she was in his party. He wasn't sure what to do about the others. Two more players arrived and Max noticed they didn't wear the same expression. It appeared they had resisted. Had they come to see what was going on?

Max ignored them and pointed at the enthralled players, telling them to leave. They obeyed without comment, the other players watching curiously but staying. Max then told the morkais to resume their work freeing Evator of daekais. He was careful to mention he meant the ones outside, so they didn't interfere with the ones present. The morkais quickly left. Max made anyone else enthralled besides daekais go before he addressed his target audience.

"You have come for treasure. Coins and gems. Rare items. Weapons. Armor. And Magic. But you are finding only baubles. Do you know who is hoarding all the wonderful loot you seek? The sorcerer! Does he deserve it more than you? No. You should find him and take what is rightfully yours. I know you are afraid, but there are so many of you and only one of him. If you attack him from different directions, in two and threes, he won't be able to survive. And the treasure. All that glorious treasure can be yours! Go now and find him!"

Max gestured at the windows and watched in growing satisfaction as the daekais practically ran from the room and hurled themselves into the dark sky. But one stayed behind, glaring at them. Max was about to think of another spell when a bowstring sounded beside him and an arrow split the guy's forehead and hurled him onto his back, dead. The other two players walked away, there being nothing else for them to do now.

"You got all but one," Siren observed, lowering the bow.

"It probably only worked because I used their nature against th—"

"Yeah, I get it. Oh shit! There he goes!"

Siren ran to a broken window and let loose at the golden-winged daekais as he flew past. Max came up behind her. The charmed daekais were distracting the sorcerer with their pursuit, but Max noticed their numbers were already halved. This wasn't going to work long. Their aerial speed and maneuvers were making Siren struggle to target the sorcerer.

"I'll leave you to this," he said, feeling confident he'd be fine on his own. It seemed like the battle might be winding down anyway.

"Don't get yourself killed," Siren said. "Reach out through the party chat if you get in trouble. Tell me where you are before your next fight."

"Right." Max turned away from her and went up another level. He passed more dead NPCs, another player, and daekais, some of whom hadn't been looted. All but the players could be and he took what he could, gaining mostly items like daekais talons and feathers, extra slings, and pouches of stones, plus trivial amounts of money. He hadn't seen a dead player before and suspected that if he died in the game, his body couldn't be looted, because this one couldn't be.

At the next floor, it seemed like no one was there, but tapestries hung torn, pictures were damaged, and furniture had been upended. Several cushions smoldered where he walked. He smelled burnt hair. He skirted the area and went in search of a lone daekais to engage. Until now, he'd been along the keep's front, but now he moved toward the rear and what he imagined were living quarters of the royal family.

And that's when he heard a muffled commotion ahead. He turned a corner to find another hall with bodies. The noises came from behind a closed door, where a woman's shriek split the air. Max pulled on the door's big, golden handle, but it wouldn't move. He slammed his shoulder into it and the door wobbled but didn't open.

"Help me!" a woman's voice screamed.

CHAPTER SIXTEEN

As the wall of flames rushed toward them, Ryan waited in horror. This would be far worse than that little burn he'd.

New Quest: Save Princess Jiera from Her Attackers.

Objective: Daekais have entered Princess Jiera's private suite in Castle Evator in their search for treasure. Save her life and stop them from absconding with her jewels!

Difficulty: Medium.

Rewards: 1 Rare Item. +2 Reputation in Andra Kingdom (Evator). 500 XP.

Accept?

Max accepted the quest, wondering when he would get to finish even one on his growing list. Then he looked over his spells for something to bash down the door, belatedly realizing that he had a spell to map a structure. That would've been more useful earlier. *Hammer Blows* was already in his hot list and might work for this. It was the only suitable choice. He spied a broken table and took a small piece. Holding it in one hand, he made a swinging motion as he summoned the energy and spoke the words that called on the god of inspiration.

"A blow for Daedras."

As the wood vanished from his grip, a white, glowing hammer appeared in the air two feet in front of him, adding light to the dark scene. He experimented with controlling the magical weapon, which moved in a way that reminded him of playing a sword fighting game on a Wii. If he raised his arm, the hammer rose. Winding back and swinging made the hammer do it. If he thought about it, the hammer moved forward. The spell description said it could extend up to 20 feet.

Max backed up and then swung hard at the doors, one of which came partially off the hinges and tilted precariously. At the loud bang, Princess Jiera screamed again. Max caught sight of at least one daekais inside. What sounded like a rock struck the door and bounced twice on hard stone. He swung the hammer again at the more heavily damaged door, which splintered so that it toppled. A rock sailed past Max's head from inside. He sent the hammer in and was about to swing it when he realized he wasn't sure where the princess was. Not wanting to accidentally strike her, he stepped up to the opening to see the interior.

He hardly took in the pink and purple fabrics on the pine canopy bed to one side, or the elegant, matching furniture along walls, before two rocks flew at him. One slammed into the hand he was using to control the magical hammer. He lost 2 HP, from full down to 34, and had a broken middle finger throbbing with pain. He realized he'd forgotten to renew *Weapon Ward* and didn't want to lose a turn on it now.

The two daekais inside were both level 3 Looters, a level or two above most he'd dealt with today. Both were ignoring Princess Jiera, on the opposite side of the room from them. They had upended several ornate jewelry boxes. Some contents bulged from small sacks at their waists. Both had crammed a hand into another pouch and now pulled out a rock, expertly fitting them into a sling.

Partially hiding behind the other door, Max moved the magic hammer toward one daekais and swung it. He grunted in pain. The broken finger hurt like hell doing that, but he smashed the daekais' hip. A red -8 HP floated up, a health bar appearing. The daekais dropped the sling and snarled, clutching the wound. Another rock just missed him, so swung at the other guy but missed, maybe because he was cautious to avoid hurting his hand. He paid the price with a rock to the shoulder. He healed himself and felt the finger mend even as he dodged another rock. Max crushed that one's shoulder and felt relief when that daekais dropped his sling. He stepped into the room, whacking each two more times in the head or chest and killing them just before *Hammer Blows* ended.

The princess ran to him, white nightgown hiding all but her bare feet and hands, her long red hair disheveled down her back. In her round, comely face, her green eyes still looked urgent. Was this really over? He hadn't gotten a notification of the quest to save her ending. He stayed on guard and told Siren where he was via the chat.

Past the princess in the tall room, another shattered window overlooked the outer bailey wall and the forest he'd started in, all in darkness. This was how the daekais had gotten in. He got his answer about the quest not ending when the someone soared past the opening. The golden-winged sorcerer saw him and Max cursed, knowing what was coming.

"Princess," he began, "you need to run out of this room."

"I'm not leaving you!" she said, as if still wanting his protection.

"Safer if you stay back." He ignored her next comment as he mentally dictated into the chat.

Max: Siren! Get the fuck up here! The sorcerer is back!
Siren: Don't kill him before me.
Max: Probably the other way around.
Siren: Then run.
Max: Too late!

The sorcerer plunged into the room, immediately snapping his golden wings wide to slow himself, air rustling the feathers. He landed amid the baubles, eyes darting to them and back to Max. He had a bloody gash on one cheek and less serious scrapes all over his arms and face. Still-wet blood seeped through various holes in his leather armor. A broken arrow protruded from his back at an angle that allowed Max to see it from in front. The sorcerer was down from 138 HP to 81.

Okay, Max thought, heart pounding, *so not impossible. Just almost*. He knew the most damaging spell he had was still *Orb of Doom*, even if *Hammer Blows* let him get more turns in from one spell. But every turn meant far more damage to himself. He had to aim for the head to disorient this guy, maybe give him a concussion so he couldn't think straight and might lose an attack from confusion. But his best bet was *Break Into Song*.

Even as Max started the words for it, the sorcerer's eyes rose to his and flashed in furious recognition. He thrust both arms toward Max, who flew up and back to crash into the wall above the doors. He landed hard on the stone floor, knees slamming into it. His back, shoulders, and head ached, his health plummeting from full at 56 HP to 30 HP. But he lost no mana from his interrupted spell. He struggled to his feet and cast heal, but when he only gained 3 HP, he felt stupid. He had to play smarter.

But he got a break. The daekais also healed himself, restoring 10 HP before Max's air-based *Orb of Doom* struck his left shoulder for 20 HP. The sorcerer spoke while pointing at him. Max instinctively dove to the floor, a glowing, orange bolt of energy hurtling toward where he'd just been. A loud crack made him turn to see an inch-deep hole, six inches wide, in the stone wall.

Max: Siren! Where the hell are you?
Siren: Down the hall! Coming!

"Gather air!" he said once more as he rose. Wind swirled in his hand before he hurled an *Orb of Doom*. The daekais turned but caught the ball of energy in one wing, a satisfying burst of gold feathers flying in all directions. A red -15 HP floated up. Max had only 12 MP left for spells.

As if he had learned from missing with a single missile, the sorcerer made a rising motion with both arms and all the rocks the other daekais has used rose. This included those in their pouches. Baubles lifted, too, as did anything smaller than his fist. Dread filled Max as over forty items hurtled toward him. He crouched into a ball, arms hugging his head. Pain surged from seemingly everywhere but his back. His health bar flashed red. With horrified eyes, he saw the pathetic 3 HP that remained after 30 HP of damage. In panic, he cast *Heal* again and rose to only 6 HP. He might not live long enough to use his remaining 10 MP.

"Hey asshole!" Siren's voice shouted. Max looked up in relief to see her fire an arrow that struck the daekais in the chest, knocking him back a step. A critical hit message floated up with a -10 HP. They had now knocked 35 HP off the 81 HP the sorcerer started with, leaving him with 46. Max still thought they were doomed. He quaffed a healing potion he'd taken from a downed guard on his way up here and rose to 11 HP.

The daekais made a rising gesture toward Siren, who lifted off the ground. Max wasn't sure what the plan was and wouldn't wait to find out. He cast another *Orb of Doom* that caught the sorcerer in the chest, snapping Siren's arrow, which was sticking out from it. Now the broken piece got embedded into him. The daekais fell onto his back, clutching at his neck as if struggling to breathe. A red -17 HP floated up.

Siren nimbly landed on the floor and ran up the daekais, firing an arrow into his neck at short range. Max didn't know if his *Archery Fiend* spell was still active on her, but he assumed so from the critical hit of 12 HP. The sorcerer's health bar went into the red. Max suspected his previous spell had crushed some ribs. The sorcerer looked confused, as if concussed, which might've explained why he hadn't done another spell yet. But now that changed as he feebly raised his arms. He lifted his head to look at them with hate-filled eyes that began to clear.

"Gather air!"

Max ran forward to ensure he didn't miss and hurled the swirling gas orb straight down at the daekais. The sorcerer's eyes widened in horror as the ball visibly crushed his chest with an awful crack, a spray of blood erupting from his mouth, a red -23 HP rising. He had seen other messages from daekais he'd killed in the castle and ignored them, but this one he read.

You have killed (1) Daekais Sorcerer, Level 10!
You gained 3900 XP!
Loot corpse?

Not waiting to see if the combat was really over, Max cast *Heal* on himself. He turned to Siren, ignoring other notifications. "Did you get 3900 XP for him?"

"Yeah. How much damage did he have before you started fighting him?"

"He was at 81 HP instead of 138."

She said, "That suggests we got half each and any damage before we started was from NPCs, not players, or they would've gotten some of the XP. Not saying they didn't, but we got a lot, so that might've been all of it. No way to know how much he was worth."

Max nodded, not really caring. That was the most he'd gotten at once. He was mostly relieved that he hadn't died. Only now did he realize how nervous he'd been. Was the sweat dripping down his back from nerves or exertion? All that thought about avoiding trouble and he stumbled into a freaking boss fight. Twice, since he'd already fought the guy.

He saw the princess cowering just outside the room, behind the lone door that was still standing. But she straightened as if realizing the threat was over. That prompted Max to check his notifications, some of which were more important.

**Quest Complete: Save Princess Jiera from Her Attackers.
You earned 500 XP!
You earned +2 Reputation in Andra Kingdom (Evator)!
You found the rare *Lose Your Head* scroll!**

Max wondered why that quest was so low in XP. Maybe the scroll made up for it. He suspected that the sorcerer hadn't been part of it and had just extended it, because the guy was so hard to kill that the quest XP would've been higher. Max held off on reading the scroll in favor of the messages. One answered the question whether or not more danger remained in the castle right now. He hadn't been watching the system messages about the count of remaining daekais and realized he should have before now.

Quest Complete: Clear Castle Evator of Daekais.
You earned 2,000 XP!
You earned +1 Reputation in Andra Kingdom (Evator)!
You received the Atorin Short Bow!

Max sighed in relief. He'd had enough danger for the moment. Like a subject in an email inbox, he could already see the headline of the next message in his queue before he opened it.

You achieved Level 5!
You gained 18 Hit Points!
You gained 7 Mana Points!
Class bonus: You gained Agility +1, Dexterity +1, Intelligence +1, Charisma +1
You gained (2) proficiency points
You have (5) unassigned proficiency points
You have gained access to Level 3 spells!
You gained (1) additional spell you can have in your hot list!

"Awesome," Max said, excited to gain two levels so quickly. He now had 74 HP and 27 MP. He was eager to look over his spells, but it could wait. Max asked Siren about her changes and learned she had risen two levels. She got a piece of the princess quest, though this didn't lower Max's XP reward. It seemed like she got some sort of partial credit when the sorcerer's arrival extended it and she helped finish him. They were both level 5, though he was already halfway to 6.

He finally unrolled the *Lose Your Head* scroll he'd received earlier and read it.

"Oh, *hell* yes!"

CHAPTER SEVENTEEN

Spell Song: Lose Your Head

    Key: E Minor

Time: 4/4

Description: This chugging rhythm is punctuated by dissonant chords that will sever the spine, jugular, and everything else at the neck of one target up to 50 feet away. It will also cause *Horrifying Visage* for the caster's enemies within the same radius. The riff can only be performed on a lute, mandolin, or similar stringed instrument.

Duration: Decapitation – instantaneous once the entire riff is played once. *Horrifying Visage* – for 2 minutes after decapitation.

Level: 7.

Cooldown: 1 hour.

Lyrics: None.

MP: 10.

Note: You are not advanced enough to perform this song.

"Love this!" said Max, laughing. He mentally dubbed it the *Decapitator Riff*. Too bad he couldn't use it anytime soon. He already knew that his player level and spell levels weren't the same. Right now, he was level 5 and could only cast up to level 3 spells. He might need to reach level 12 or 13 before he could do a level 7 spell.

He examined the Atorin Short Bow's properties and knew this magic item – his first – was the new range weapon of choice.

Item: Atorin Short Bow of Siaran Oak

Description: Atorin of Evator liked nothing more than hunting and killing daekais with this Siaran oak short bow. Only his legendary accuracy matched the stealth with which he tracked them to their lairs, or escaped once discovered.

Bonuses: +2 Stealth, +4 Damage, +4 Attack or +7 Attack against all in-flight targets.

Max would likely never get something better against daekais or the giant birds of prey. He almost wanted one of them to appear so he could test it. Raising his archery skill jumped up his priority list. It had been a long time since he'd gotten cool loot in a game and he'd forgotten the thrill.

He saw Siren's eyes far away and suspected she was going over her own stats and acquisitions, so he turned toward the sorcerer and looted the body. He nabbed 2 gold pieces, 4 silver, and 1 niquerran sapphire gemstone coin. That was worth $100, like each gold piece. He'd had almost a hundred in metal coins and a little more in niquerran ones before. Now he had over $500 and could actually buy something helpful, though the equipment shops didn't have magic items. He surmised that Siren would get similar loot from the sorcerer, and there was one item he'd gotten that stood out.

Item: Ring of Coiryn.

Description: Made by Priests of the God of Courage, a Ring of Coiryn is so potent that the wearer and any allies with 10 feet feel less intimidated by threats.

Bonuses: +5 Morale, 10' radius.

He wasn't sure how the morale would directly help him or even other players. Maybe the ring explained the sorcerer's behavior, which Max had wondered about. With the God of Fear being one of their creators, many of the daekais had shown more courage than Max had expected. Had they just been driven by greed? Or had the sorcerer's power emboldened them? He slipped the ring onto his right hand and grunted on feeling calmer and more self-assured. He hadn't expected to actually feel different.

He turned to Siren, "Did you feel anything when I put this ring on?"

"Yeah." Siren seemed to search herself for the words. "More like I can kick anyone's ass."

Max laughed. Of course that would be how she interpreted it. "It should work within 10 feet of me. Your turn to loot the sorcerer."

She nodded and soon handed him a dagger. It had a symbol of two wings in silhouette carved on the blade and inlaid in silver on the black pommel.

Max cocked an eyebrow, then nodded his thanks.

Item: Winged Rider Dagger +3.

Description: Every winged rider is given one of these daggers upon acceptance. This one has been magically enchanted to increase the wielder's strength.

Bonuses: +3 Strength.

Max equipped the dagger, this time not feeling surprised that his gear felt lighter and he generally felt more powerful. "I wonder what a daekais is doing with…never mind. Probably found it or killed a winged rider for it."

"Probably."

Max eyed the sorcerer corpse. "I bet this guy was causing all sorts of problems. It should be safer out there in the wilderness now."

"Or worse, if he kept all the daekais busy doing things for him. Now they might be everywhere."

He smirked. "We need to work on your optimism."

"I prefer realism."

"Funny thing to say in a virtual reality game."

Siren smiled and then offered to give him all the money she'd gotten from looting so far. He initially said no, that he could get it later if necessary, but when she remarked that she might not be in the game when he needed it, he relented. He now had $746 in various coins. Siren was proving to be his greatest asset. He felt grateful and wanted a way to show it. He would have to think of something. How do you repay someone when everything they do is for you?

When she went back into her screens to choose proficiencies, he did the same. He had five proficiency points but knew he could spend them at any time. At least one for riding a great bird was likely in his future, but it could wait. He used one point on his *Archery* skill, raising it to 2, before realizing he could just cast *Archery Fiend* on himself all the time. But then maybe there would be times when he couldn't, or he'd been in some sort of anti-magic zone. Everything else could wait.

In looking over the notifications about the daekais, he only now realized some of them had classes like Sharpshooter, Messenger, Sling Master, and even Perrin Killer. He got the impression it had been "all hands on deck" for the attack. And now he wondered how much damage they'd done inside the castle or around the town, or at the caravan. Had any players died? What became of that Dark Trio? The attack had likely been designed to help people level up and gain their first real gear and loot.

Max also had two ability scores he could raise. To decide, he pulled up his main stat sheet.

Name: Maestro Max
Species/Race: Human.
Class: Bard, Level 5
Reputation: 4 – Good Standing (Andra), 1 – Accepted (Karendi)
XP: 7645
HP: 74/74
MP: 27/27
Strength: 9
Dexterity: 10
Agility: 8
Constitution: 7
Intelligence: 10
Wisdom: 5
Charisma: 10
Morale: 10

He wasn't surprised that he'd reached full HP and MP with the few minutes they'd been standing there. Some stats were always rising with every level while others never did. How out of balance would he get? He might need to find ways to boost the others. He pulled up the bard description again to see that he'd get to boost two stats of his choosing by one point, every four levels. Even though he had the Strength bonus, he decided to raise it for increased damage. He also raised his Constitution, which would improve how many HP he gained with levels.

When he exited the screens and waited for Siren to finish, the princess approached with a trail of royalty and guards following. He realized they'd been waiting for him and Siren. Had the NPCs known they were looking at screens? If not, what did they think they were doing? He wasn't sure if the NPCs knew they were only NPCs. They didn't act like they did. He had noticed that when he went into a screen and wasn't paying attention to his surroundings, people didn't stop what they were doing and wait for him like some roleplaying games. This was the first time he'd seen NPCs wait in Llurien Online. He and Siren had been standing close enough together, and talking quietly, that maybe the NPCs thought he and she didn't want to be disturbed. He nudged Siren and turned to face them.

"Maestro Max," began the princess, laying one hand on his arm, "you have saved my life. You, too, Siren. I am in your debt for once and ever more."

He wasn't sure what to say and tried to play it off, using his status as a guard to do so. "Just doing my duty, Your Highness."

She smiled. "Don't be modest. My father will insist on meeting both of you. Tomorrow morning, we shall send someone to fetch you. Wear your finest."

"Of course." Max did his best head bow, curious to meet the ruler. But gaining notoriety might work against him if he later freed Norus.

The princess excused herself to see to the wounded.

Siren smirked at him. "I think she likes you."

He rolled his eyes. "Let's go loot the remaining bodies we can and see what happened to the castle, and the caravan, even the town. I want to know what these daekais can do when organized behind someone like that sorcerer."

Looting the bodies as they went, Max nabbed more coins, a hand crossbow, some bolts and arrows, a cheap bow he'd sell, and several slings and pouches of rocks. He'd have to start selling some of the useless stuff to clear up his inventory and make a few bucks doing so.

They learned that the caravan had been badly damaged, daekais making off with smaller items. A few people had died from being stabbed or shot with a crossbow, but the morkais had cured anyone poisoned. There weren't as many daekais bodies out here, maybe because flying away was easier. Witnesses said that's what happened when a good defense had been mounted, morkais pursing them into the night, with some already returning now, a winged rider amongst them.

With it getting late, Siren logged out, intending to return by morning. Max grabbed food and ale on the way to the barracks, fatigue setting in. That he'd only learned his situation this morning seemed long ago. He overheard talk of a bath under the bailey near the barracks, and since he was starting to actually stink, he made use of it, noticing how real it felt, from the pine-scented soap to the bubbles and ripples he made in the water.

He retired to his small bed, reviewing the level 3 spells, which cost 5 MP, on his *Spells Screen*. *Blade Master* would help him or a target, like *Archery Fiend* did. But he didn't see any attack spells except for *Light Beam*, which caused actual sunlight that hurt undead. *The Flock* summoned animals to defend him, while *Perrin Shriek* would make everyone think a perrin bird was approaching. That was useful against daekais. He wanted to shop for spell components tomorrow.

The logout button hadn't changed, but the Life Counter had dropped to just over five days. Now was the first truly quiet time he'd had since learning of his predicament, and sleep was a long time in coming. His mind drifted to him lying in a hospital bed, like where he was now in Llurien Online, but the similarity ended there.

Any anger about the situation had given way to him feeling tired, remorseful, and resigned. Almost like giving up. The repeated failure to log out was having a cumulative effect on his psyche, a feeling of being trapped growing. Maybe he should just play for a few days and forget about it. Immerse himself. Pretend this was all there was. But feeling so alive and able to make decisions and speak rationally about what he wanted, only to have it not matter in the real world, was infuriating.

That put a small spark back into him. There had to be some way out of here. Was Dr. Thompson right, that his subconscious was keeping him in here? Psychology had never been his thing, but now he needed to think about the reason he seemingly preferred being here to the real world. He drifted off to sleep, wondering if he knew himself as much as he thought.

The next morning, Max dressed in his cleaner clothes, adding the soldier pin. He wasn't expecting trouble and would change after his meeting with the nobles. He exited the barracks and ran into Kari, who marched up to him, her chainmail looking freshly polished, the blood he'd seen on it last night gone.

"Come with me, Maestro Max," she commanded, dark eyes hard, "if that's your real name."

He wanted to play dumb but knew what this was about as he followed her to one of the courtyard's unlit firepits, where no one else stood. Other guards were stationed in their usual places or milling about chatting over handheld breakfasts of fruits and breads. A glance at the sky showed a morkais flying overhead. He heard the call of a florin bird and looked at the tower where one sat on a perch. The bodies from the night before had been removed, some of the blood washed away. The keep's windows were still smashed, but he saw one of them reform before his startled eyes. A wizard had likely done it from inside. How much of the cleanup had magic users performed?

He asked, "Why wouldn't it be my real name?"

Kari turned to face him beside the stone firepit. "I'm questioning what else I supposedly know about you. How is it that a lowly guard can perform magic of that level?"

Realizing he should've been more prepared for this, he lied, "I've always had the talent, just never the desire to really learn it."

"Then how *did* you do it?"

He shrugged, not having enough info about the magic system to bluff well. "The spell isn't that hard."

Her eyes narrowed. "It's not the only one you cast. *Orb of Doom* and *Heal* were among the others my soldiers reported."

Max flushed and stifled a cocked eyebrow at her having investigated him. Maybe he shouldn't have been surprised. These NPCs were a pain in the ass. He noticed that she seemingly didn't include him in her statement about "my soldiers" because she didn't say "my other soldiers." Maybe it meant nothing, or maybe she was letting on that she didn't really see him as part of the castle's forces. An outsider. Someone not to trust. To prevent her from following him around or worse, he'd have to gain her trust, unsure what would work on her.

He decided to start with some honesty while saying as little as possible until he better understood how to bluff her. She was a little too tough, given that he was full of shit and she seemed to know. As an honest guy, lying wasn't a strong skill, but maybe he could use any honest vibe he gave off to lend himself credibility, as long as he didn't set himself up for being found out. He'd skirt the line between saying too much and getting caught, and saying so little that he looked like he was hiding something.

He admitted, "Those are beginner spells."

Her eyes narrowed. "So, you passed the tests to become a wizard, learned a few spells, and then decided to stop being one?"

"Something like that."

"To become a *guard*?"

He smirked at her. "You were just a guard not too long ago, I presume. I'm surprised to hear such contempt for your peers." Scowling, she opened her mouth, but he kept going to ward her off, trying to think of a backstory. "All right, I'll humor you. I had the talent and thought being a wizard would be right for me, but I changed my mind. All the wizards I knew just seemed like they thought they were better than everyone because they can do more than valenders. I also wanted to see the world instead of sticking my nose in a book all day, so I quit.

"And yes, I became a guard, not because this is what I want to do with my life, but to protect myself better with a weapon in my hand. I figured I'll do my time in service, get training and some experience, and then move on to making my own way. If you want to stay in Evator or even Andra for the rest of your life, that's your business. But me being able to cast a few spells is none of *yours* if you're going to be rude about it. Maybe you should see me as a great asset who can be more useful than whatever you have planned for me today, now that you know."

As he said it, he knew it was far longer than he'd intended, a side effect of thinking aloud.

"Well," she started, eyes hard, "maybe I would have if you had told me."

"We haven't really had a chance to talk before now."

Ignoring that, she asked with no lessening of suspicion, "Where did you receive your wizardry training?"

He didn't know enough about the setting to answer, so even though he didn't want to antagonize her, he retorted lightly, "Why? Hoping to get training yourself?"

"Can you even name the guilds in Andra?"

"Can *you*?" he asked, still dodging. Then he thought of a better angle. "Knowing where we can be trained doesn't mean someone's a wizard. Everyone knows where. Little kids dream of going to the capital or other places for it. You probably did yourself."

Her jaw clenched and he knew he'd won that exchange. "I don't trust you."

"You *should*. I saved the life of Princess Jiera. What more do you want?"

"The truth."

"You just got it."

She walked past him, brushing her shoulder into his hard enough to turn his body. "We'll see about that."

"What's that supposed to mean?" he asked at her back.

"You'll find out soon enough."

He sighed. Part of him didn't care. It was just a game — unless he got stuck in It forever. Maybe he had to take stuff like this seriously, just in case. Joining Norus in a cell wasn't on his agenda. It certainly wouldn't help him. But he'd just saved the princess and was due to get a reward in a little while. That should trump any trouble Kari caused. She was just a sergeant. She likely didn't have as much sway as she seemed to imply. Maybe she was just trying to intimidate him. He had to admit it sort of worked in that he was worried what trouble she was going to cause. Maybe he needed to free Norus and escape Evator while he still could.

What if she checked the wizard training places or guilds, or whatever they were called, and no one had ever heard of him?

He supposed he had some time to get out of town, unless magical communication meant an answer would be had soon. But did she have the authority to arrange that? Did she have to pay in coins for it? Did she have enough? Or would her commanders shoot down the idea because he'd saved the princess? Now he felt determined to make a good impression on the town rulers. He might not be a war hero, but he'd see if he could gain an "above suspicion" reputation to shut up Kari, if nothing else.

Game on, biotch.

Not long after Siren logged in, they stood in the damaged throne room, where two tapestries were missing. It looked like the place had been hastily cleaned, dark blood stains not completely removed, stray pieces of broken furniture that had escaped notice still there. The daekais body on the chandelier had also been removed, the idea of it remaining amusing Max. It might've been a nice decoration.

Several others stood in the room with them, including army officers above Kari, who was absent. He wasn't in the mood for her and focused on the two thrones, one each for the Duke of Evator and his wife. Less ornate chairs that weren't quite thrones sat to either side. He'd just heard that a prince was off in Andra right now, so the other chair must've been for the princess, but no royalty were present.

No other players were here, even though some had clearly been involved in the defenses. Had he and Siren had been signaled out? Or were others having this meeting in their own groups? Maybe he was only getting this because he was part of the town's defenses. It didn't seem like other players were guards. He had half-expected more people to be here but felt relieved they weren't. His identity being discovered worried him and he still didn't want to interact much. Footsteps approaching on the stone floor behind him caught his attention. He looked over his shoulder and saw a determined and grim-faced Kari striding toward everyone as if she had something important to say. Max cursed under his breath.

Chapter Eighteen

Once Kari stopped beside Max and Siren, an official-looking man in a dark robe banged the butt of a steel-shod staff on the stone floor, the dull thud booming off the walls. On the far wall, to one side, doors with giant birds carved on them opened.

First strode in the princess, a green gown swishing softly as she strode to the smaller throne. She wore light rouge and a gold pin pushed through her long, braided hair, having pulled herself together well. Next came the Duchess of Evator, whose refined bearing likely shone without the jewels and small crown on her greying, black hair. With one hand on his portly gut, the Duke of Evator shuffled in as if his black boots were too heavy, or he bore a weight greater than the gold crown on his balding head of wispy grey hair. The duke lowered himself onto the biggest throne with a groan. After some formal introductions, the duke praised Max and Siren for their role in the defenses, at which point Kari intervened.

"Your Highness," she began, "Maestro Max is under my command, and I have sent word to Rook of his bravery so that his hometown may know of it. I look forward to hearing the response from his previous commanders."

Wily bitch, Max thought, turning to meet her amused and triumphant gaze. He feigned a lack of concern, as if she wasn't going to catch him. How long would it take for a message that they'd never heard of him to return?

Kari added, "Of course, I would not have sent a messenger just for this. They needed to know of the daekais attack on the caravan to better protect the next one, though we don't anticipate another, now that the daekais sorcerer is dead."

"Yes," began the duke, "and we have Maestro Max and Siren to thank for this. Thank you for your service, Kari." She bowed, and the duke turned back to Max and Siren. "Is there anything we can do for you? Within reason?"

Max replied, "Your Highness, it was my pleasure to save Princess Jiera. While nothing is necessary, I think Siren and I would appreciate more training, such as in the Kryllan Hand and archery. I've also become interested in the florin birds and would love learning to fly. Only I know it costs too much for—"

"Say no more," the duke interrupted, holding up one hand. "It shall be done. Perhaps you will become a winged rider yourself."

Max tried not to grin as he bowed. One problem solved. Now, hopefully another...

"Thank you," he began. "I *would* like to pursue such an opportunity with the defenses of Evator. Would it be acceptable to resign my commission for winged rider training?"

The duke nodded approvingly. "You are ambitious! But you have proven yourself too valuable. Kari will ensure you're exposed to more adventures."

"I understand, Your Highness." Max bowed again, stifling his annoyance. But it didn't really matter, since he could just leave. Something occurred to him, and he floated the idea before thinking it through. "If I may be so bold, I've become better acquainted with the prisoner I brought to Evator. I know we're planning an attack on the mining village. What if I were to learn of our plans, and then stage a rescue of the prisoner, with he and I fleeing on florin back, as if I have betrayed Evator?"

Siren looked sideways at him, but the duke leaned forward. "What purpose would this serve?"

"He would believe I am friendly to him, an ally. We could travel to Gitarna or the village, where I'd give them false plans instead of the real ones. They would prepare for an attack that differs from our plan. Having gained their trust, I might also learn their plans and send a message back to Evator. Our victory would be assured."

Nearly everyone reacted out loud, whether in approval, surprise, or caution. Before anyone spoke, Siren messaged him in chat.

Siren: I'm not sure if that was fucking brilliant or stupid as shit.

Max: Thanks. I think.

Siren: If they don't agree, you can't rescue him.

Max: Maybe. I could do it and would just be disobeying if they tell me not to. I was going to do it anyway. Maybe this way, I can complete some of my quests without ruining my reputation here.

Siren: Clever, Max. I'll give you that.

Kari spoke up, "Your Highness, while this is a bold plan, it is not suited to one so low in our ranks. I propose I accompany him."

Max suppressed a groan at her interference before realizing her idea was stupid, for reasons he immediately stated. "With respect, sergeant, no one would believe you would break him out, and two of us doing it is even harder to believe. One rogue guard is one thing, but two? Even if people thought we were lovers." He smirked, and she rewarded him with a withering look. Then he twisted the knife. "And I'm new here, so few would expect me to be as loyal to Evator as yourself. Your reputation makes you a liability. If anything, start acting like you really don't trust me, and pretend to try stopping me when I do it."

Beside him, Siren chuckled quietly. He'd told her all about his encounter with Kari.

Siren: Still can't tell if you're brilliant or stupid as shit. She's gonna hate you even more.

Max: Yeah, and maybe make a stupid decision because of it.

Siren: Is that your plan? She just became more dangerous. That's the stupid part.

Max: Kind of winging it. But I just made any suspicion she airs about me sound like a ruse. No one's gonna believe her.

Siren: And that was the brilliant part.

Max: Are you flirting with me?

Siren: Don't make me take you outside and beat you.

Max: So you *are* flirting.

Siren: Quit. Pay attention to the bullshit you just unleashed. Things are about to get interesting.

As if to prove her right, the duke said, "Maestro Max speaks wisely. We'll consider this plan. For now, he has earned our trust to learn our battle plans. Ensure he is briefed. Siren, we shall not include you at this time and trust you will remain quiet about what you have heard."

She nodded. "Of course, Your Highness. I may wait in the woods to help Max once he has fled with the prisoner. I suspect doing this on florin back would be best."

"Indeed. Maestro Max, we will inform you soon about our decision. Thank you both again for saving my daughter."

With a wave of his hand, he dismissed, Max and Siren, who left through the double doors with Kari trailing, her boots thumping loudly. In the antechamber outside stood the Dark Trio, who were apparently next to receive accolades. Elsewhere stood a few other players.

"Well, Maestro Max," Kari snidely began as she followed them into the courtyard, "you've fooled the duke into learning our battle plans, but I'll eat a banoth tusk before I let you free that prisoner, whether you get permission to or not."

Max turned and smirked at her. "Thanks for letting me know you'll defy the duke's orders. Funny how you think I'm the one who's the problem here."

Her lips tightened into a straight line as her eyes flashed. "Be in the war room at midday. Someone other than me will fill you in." She stomped away, boots slamming even harder onto the pavement.

"Will do!" he said cheerfully, glad to be rid of her. Then he turned to Siren as they continued through the courtyard, where a banoth was pulling a wagon full of daekais corpses through the gate. It looked like a woolly mammoth to him. "Let's go get some weapons training."

"I didn't realize you were such a smart ass," she remarked, falling in beside him.

"That didn't sound like disapproval."

"It wasn't." After a moment, she added, "I can speak for myself, by the way."

Max arched an eyebrow before realizing she meant him asking the duke about training for them. He didn't remember exactly what he'd said, but hadn't felt like he'd spoken for her. Was she touchy? She didn't seem the type, but he said, "I know. He was just focused on me and I didn't want you to get left out. I was really asking for both of us."

"Yeah. Forget it."

Max stifled a sigh, unsure if she meant that or not. He didn't like head games with women, especially ones he wasn't even dating. He chatted her up with banter and then suggested they head to a magicry—a store that sells spell components and other items a wizard or sorcerer—or even karelia—might want. He'd seen one in town and wondered what the name meant until his *World Lore* skill told him. Having not stocked up in such a place before, he wanted to see what options he could give himself.

After an hour of bargaining with the querran shopkeeper, he came away with a healthy supply of herbs such as solanaen petals, liquids like drops of mynx blood, animal parts like enoni bones and moragul spit, fabrics such as vandin silk, and earth materials like daedrite flakes. He also bought pouches to hold these, one special item being a box that would freeze any liquid placed inside. An ice version of the *Orb of Doom* was in his future. He'd spent over half of his funds, leaving with him with 5 iron pieces, 2 gold, and one sapphire, or roughly $300. The shopkeeper exchanged some of those for smaller denominations that would attract less attention: 5 iron, 20 copper, 8 silver, 1 gold, 20 emeralds, and 8 rubies.

With his quest to free the niquerran prisoner, Max also tried to buy suitable pants, a shirt, and shoes for a querra but couldn't find them anywhere. He finally asked a querra, who volunteered to give him some at the training grounds in an hour but never showed up. Another querra did it, too. Siren learned they were notorious for getting distracted, so he approached the Querran Quarter at the town's northwest corner, where buildings were low like querra, and immaculately manicured. One guy finally gave him what he wanted while refusing payment. He tucked it into his inventory.

In between all of this, Max and Siren got more weapons training past lunch time. Courtesy of the duke, they received dedicated one-on-ones lessons in any weapon they chose. Each raised their archery and Kryllan Hand skills by one level. Max's skill with the long sword also went up one, as did Siren's jhaikan staff ability. Then she logged out and Max headed to the castle, spending an hour learning their attack plans and their scouting ahead of that. This made more areas appear on his map. He completed another quest, earning another 1000 XP and the Earring of Timonen.

Chapter Nineteen

Item: Earring of Timonen.

Description: Made by Priests of the God of Timonen, this rare item lets the wearer hear anything within a hundred yards as if standing just feet from the source.

Bonuses: +2 Wisdom.

Max used his *World Lore* skill to learn that Timonen was the god of patience, wisdom, and several other traits. He experimented with it while sitting on a bench in the castle courtyard, trying to look like he was tending to his bow. The challenge with the earring was tuning out sounds he didn't want to hear, but with practice, he could sort of turn down other sounds. The ring didn't limit him to line-of-sight, so eavesdropped inside the keep or barracks from outside. After focusing on a place or person once, it became easier, like they'd been added to a favorites list. He needed practice. Ethical usage meant using it on enemies or troublemakers. He'd tune out talk that didn't concern him.

After his meeting about the attack plans, a commander told Max to report to the Florin Tower for training. He felt increasingly excited and nervous as he ascended the stairs. How often did someone fall off? What if the daekais were near? Flying over the forest was probably not smart. Near the tower's top floors, a guard sent him to his trainer in one of the perch rooms, his booted feet shuttling through the loose straw. He eyed the opening to the perch. No birds were on it.

His trainer was the woman who'd explained things to him before the daekais attack. A brunette with brown eyes and straight, braided hair to her mid-back, she was just over five-feet-tall, slender but fit, even a little muscular. Her casual demeanor made him wonder how often she truly faced a threat in the skies. Maybe she was naturally confident.

> **Name: Flight Leader Loira Talonstrike of Evator.**
> **Type: NPC.**
> **Class: Winged Rider.**
> **Species: Human.**
> **Level 12.**

Seeing a dagger on her waist but no larger weapons, Max guessed she'd removed a bow and arrows he'd seen others wearing. She also had a bulging pouch, maybe full of stones for the sling tucked into her belt. In a bandoleer that fell between her small breasts were multiple knives, their design suggesting they were for throwing. Several were also along the outside of her thighs and calves. Two were missing. She didn't seem to have a sword or scabbard for one.

"Don't worry so much," Loira teased as she folded a green saddle blanket and dropped it on a pile of them. "From what I heard, you're braver than most."

Max tried to play it cool. "I'm just worried I'll get so good, so fast, that you won't feel you're really helping."

She snorted. "Good. You'll need that sense of humor. Let's go."

He followed her to the flat top of the tower, where the light, warm spring breeze tugged at his long hair, some of it going into his face. Even as he began to put it in a ponytail because it might blind him while flying, Loira told him to. The familiar act calmed him as he eyed the two giant birds that were already here and prepared. He supposed he needed to learn how to saddle one and put the reins on, but apparently not today.

Max suspected he'd gain a proficiency in riding great birds, but to take the edge off his fears. he burned one of his four remaining ones now. Along with sudden confidence, the point had a side-effect—the drop to the ground below didn't bother him as much. He also understood the birds' body language. One flapped its wings a few times and leaned forward, its head bobbing up and down as Loira approached. Max sensed it was her bird and it felt playful, anticipating a flight. The other one, which was a little smaller, was preening its tail feathers, sometimes stopping to gaze at Max before resuming. He now knew this behavior meant the bird was calm. This proficiency point had been a wise spend.

"It's a good day for a first flight," said Loira, coming to him.

Max looked at the sky with fresh eyes, realizing he'd be flying through it. More impressions struck him, like the importance of an updraft or how to identify the changing conditions of an approaching storm and its wind gusts. It was as if the air was alive with knowledge he'd never had before. It made him feel excited to take advantage of it.

"What do we do first?" he asked.

"Ditch the long sword. A shorter one is better if you really become a rider, but you won't need anything like that today. I don't want you encumbered more than necessary."

Max removed it into his inventory. She said she usually had a short sword and bow, both of which could be stored in the lightweight saddles the birds wore. Everything was intended to avoid weight and tiring them. Riders were skilled in wilderness survival in case they needed to land due to a bird's fatigue. They also hunted most food rather than bringing it.

When Loira gestured for him to join her, Max cautiously stepped closer to the bird's left side. As tall as a two-story building, the florin, named Ronon, loomed over him, but much of that height was the neck and head. The body reached over ten feet off the ground. The saddle's flaps hung down enough for him to reach one. The foldable rope ladder with its wooden rungs had three potential positions—lowered, furled while in flight, and a quarter unfurled. This last position had it even with the saddle's bottom edge and allowed Max to reach and lower it to use.

When he put one foot on the lowest rung, at his knee, the bird shift its weight to the right and its left leg moving toward him as if compensating for his weight. He climbed quickly, fingertips brushing the soft feathers. At the top, he put one hand on the pommel at the saddle's front. Then he swung his right leg over the cantle at the back to settle into position, sliding both feet into the stirrups with an effort. They turned a little when he tried. He remembered struggling with that from horseback riding.

His eyes darted between Ronon, Loira looking up at him, and the ground far below. He felt vulnerable because the bird could take off before he was ready. With poorly restrained haste, he began strapping himself in as Loira called up instructions. The pommel strap, made from banoth leather, went from one side of his waist in front, then across his crotch to the back on the other side. The cantle strap did the opposite. Once clicked in place, he tightened them and experimented with leaning in various directions to see how secure he felt. Loira was yelling at him to pull up the ladder.

"You'll need to get faster at that and strapping yourself in, which you always do first," she called up. "You won't always have time to be methodical."

"What now?"

"Take the reins, but don't pull. Ronon knows better than to take off right now."

"How does it know that?"

"I told him not to. They understand some verbal commands. And this is a school bird, used for training. He'll be more forgiving of your mistakes."

"Great," Max muttered, not sure what to think. He'd ridden school horses, which could be difficult. Sometimes one only cooperated because a trainer was there. The minute the trainer looked elsewhere, the horse could refuse to obey poorly executed commands despite knowing what you wanted. It knew you didn't know what you were doing, and it didn't care about your half-assed commands. Was this bird going to be like that? What if something happened to the trainer and Max was out there by himself? Maybe he'd spend another proficiency point.

Loira repeated some of what she'd previously told him about the two sets of leather reins. The top set connected to the upper side of a dusky metal ring around the bird's neck, at the right and left. The lower and longer set did so to the bottom. Whichever of the four points had the most tension controlled which way Ronon went. The trick would be using even pressure on two rings at once for something like a left turn that didn't change altitude. If he pulled harder on the top rein, they'd also ascend, the strength of his pull determining the degree. He supposed it didn't normally matter if they were entirely level when he did these. Ronon would adjust altitude by himself anyway based on the wind. *Mostly* level was more likely, regardless of Max's rein skills.

While his trainer stepped away to mount her bird, Max's mount shifted weight to one leg and then the other. It unnerved him a little, but he succeeded in not moving in the saddle. He checked out what else was with him. Two light saddlebags allowed for storage. A crossbow was stowed behind his right leg, a short bow behind the left. Arrows and bolts were stored in a special quiver designed to inhibit them from falling out and were attached to a saddle case.

When Ronon spread his wings and leaned forward, Max realized he was gripping Ronon hard with his legs. He tried to relax. Loira had told him that the birds responded to leg pressure but had been trained to pay more attention to the reins. The legs were mostly used to indicate speed, just like with a horse; a subtle or not-so-subtle heel would signal them to speed up.

Max was so caught up in trying to feel comfortable that he didn't notice Loira grinning at him until she called out. "You will follow! Use your reins to mimic what I do. You don't have to be perfect as he will follow me, but you will lead us back here."

He licked his lips, heart pounding, the azure sky and its light clouds beckoning.

Loira turned away, looking north as her bird turned that way, to Max's relief. "Fly!" she shouted, and the bird jumped forward and over the edge, wings flapping to raise itself aloft. Ronon spread his wings, leaned forward, and stepped that way, so Max pretended he was in charge of what was to happen next.

"Fly!" he called with one hand on the pommel for support, so he didn't accidentally pull back on the reins—something he'd learned from horseback riding. The bird leapt into the air. Despite expecting it, he lost balance and tilted back and down from the force before righting himself. This briefly distracted him from noticing the lack of anything below him except Ronon.

But once he secure with feet, posture, and hands on the reins, he looked down. And instantly regretted it. He looked forward and up, seeing Loira a hundred yards ahead and above by twenty feet. He pulled on the top straps, feeling Ronon comply. He also nudged the bird with his feet and Ronon flapped his wings a few times, catching the gliding bird before them.

As Max closed in, Loira looked back for several long seconds before turning away. They continued this way for ten minutes, during which Max grew accustomed to everything from the warm wind buffeting him to the way Ronon flapped his wings several times before gliding again. Wind currents caused them to rise and fall, sometimes more gently than others. Once, they dropped several feet, and it felt like being on a roller coaster at the big drop. Max had always loved that, so after initially being startled, he shrugged it off. Not being able to tell it was about to happen was one big difference.

By now, the rolling green grass lay five hundred feet below, farms off to their left, and stands of trees lining the cobblestone road that extended north from Evator for miles before giving way to dirt. A few horsemen trotted along, heading toward the castle. Max carefully turned around so as not to disturb Ronon's flight, seeing the retreating town, bailey walls, keep, and the forest behind it. The sight reminded him of the time he'd flown a camera-enabled drone that a friend owned. Off to the right loomed the northernmost extent of the snow-capped Bier Peaks, while eastward the ground lay flatter, another dirt road, this one to Rook, disappearing in the distance.

Max finally played with the reins, having the bird shift up or down, then left or right. He tried slowing him, then speeding up. Everything seemed fine, and he flashed a smile at Loira the next time she looked back. Something about her grin warned him and she suddenly banked sharply to the left, diving a hundred yards as Max tried to follow. Ronon compensated for his mistakes, but he fared well and enjoyed the drop this time.

They leveled out to continue mimicking Loira, who began climbing to more than double the previous altitude. Once stabilizing that, she banked right to the west. This time, Ronon waited for Max to give the same command, which he mostly got, just not as tight because the tilt and the awful feeling that he'd fall off. Loria smirked back, so he made himself do it, catching up as they straightened. They climbed again, with Max telling himself it didn't really matter how high they went if he fell off. He'd be dead when he hit the ground, anyway. Somehow, the thought didn't really calm him.

With the clouds getting close, they stayed below or went around at first, but then his trainer grinned again and dove into one to disappear. Max followed, worried about crashing into them, but he figured Loira wouldn't risk that and had gotten out of his way. Ronon probably had a sense of where they were, anyway. But Max heard the rustle of feathers in her bird's wings, two flaps, and the creak of the saddle, all courtesy of his new Earring of Timonen. He'd have to make use of that if fleeing winged riders, wild birds, or kais. It could help in the darkness, too.

Suddenly he heard a rush of air and the rustle above and to his right, rapidly nearing. But Loira was left of him. It couldn't be her, so...

"Dive!" he shouted, frantically trying to pull the lower reins. But Ronon's own self-preservation instincts kicked in and he banked and plummeted just before a huge shape hurtled into view through the mist. A pair of giant eyes locked onto him as the bird's head snapped toward his changed position. Two outstretched wings swirled the cloud into eddies, two wicked-looking talons slashing the air where he'd just been.

CHAPTER TWENTY

The large bird disappeared as suddenly as it had come, banking left behind Max and out of view in the cloud. His heart was still pounding from fear and adrenaline. If he hadn't been wearing that magic earring and heard the bird coming, he might be dead right now, though Ronon had moved to dodge, too. He had no doubt that the impact of those wicked talons would have broken his spine if not ripped him right in half. Would it come back? It hadn't born a rider. He'd noticed the beak having a sharp hook in it and knew it had been a perrin, the more vicious of the two great birds.

Now he was diving at a disturbing speed and plummeted out of the cloud. Max immediately spied Loira and her bird to his left, where they had leveled out. He pulled on the top reins to level Ronon. He saw no sign of the perrin, he heads whipping around. Had it gone back into a cloud? Did it know where they were? Ahead, he saw Loira turning toward him. And then he saw the perrin below as it circled back and rose, green wings hiding it well from above. Loira circled to fall in beside him.

"Ronon, follow!"

She rose into the cloud. Max hung on while his bird followed. They climbed deeper into the mist before gliding a while. He lost track of time, ears straining for an impending attack. The need for *Direction Sense* arose as he failed to understand where they were going. But he saw they were still going west after dropping out of the clouds. To the right, the Bier peaks loomed larger. For the first time, he saw an ocean, in the distance. The perrin didn't seem to be around, but Max felt nervous until descending far below the clouds, away from where it could hide.

Loira eased up and turned north toward a small lake, which they began descending toward. Max tugged on the reins to slow, resuming some control. Seeing the ground get closer didn't relieve him as much as he expected. Maybe he was getting used to being airborne.

Ahead, Loira's bird skimmed the water surface, the talons extending. Max saw it coming when the bird's legs dipped into the water with a splash, emerging with a four-foot long fish. Max sensed Ronon was going to do it, too. He braced for the impact, which wasn't as jarring as he expected. He followed Loira as her bird landed softly in an open area beyond the lake. Max figured Ronon knew how to land without him doing anything, but he gave a gentle tug on the bottom of the reins and then made the bird land when Max told him to, which mostly worked. The landing felt smooth. Both birds began ripping into their kill and eating, Ronon's body shifting. Only now did Max realize his hands were sweaty.

"Where do you think that perrin went?" he asked Loira, who was twenty feet away so that he had to yell. He glanced around on the ground and felt relieved that no trees were close enough to be hiding anything else, and the grass was also too short for that.

"Back to hunting. Remember that everything in the sky attacks from above and usually behind."

"It almost got me."

"They don't miss very often. It's good you heard it coming."

"I have a musician's ears," Max said, not willing to admit to the earring's properties. Only now did he realize that Ronon could've been struck in such a way that he lost control and crashed. Or the saddle might've come off and Max, still attached to it, fell to his death. It was just as well that none of this occurred to Max before now. How long of a walk back to Evator was it, anyway? Probably a day or two, with many other things on the ground to kill him, too, and while he was under-prepared. Presumably, he and Loira had to pass by that perrin to reach Evator again, and it might've been true on the grass, too.

"Hey," he called, "do they attack people on the ground?" He sensed the truth of it even as he asked.

"Of course. Animals, too."

"Great," he muttered.

While the birds feasted, Loira gave Max additional tips, including reminding him of the verbal commands, one of which he'd used to escape the perrin. He was to lead them back, but this time they'd go farther inland to keep away from other birds of prey this close to the mountains. And they would evade the clouds. With Max in front, Loira would occupy a common role for the final rider—greater responsibility of watching the skies for threats.

The return to Evator was largely without incident. They saw another perrin, or maybe the same one, from a distance, but steered clear. Loira had explained that the perrins were less likely to attack multiple mounted birds. They learned that this was more dangerous due to the ranged weapons the riders had. Maybe the other one had thought the surprise attack from the clouds mitigated the risk.

They saw another mounted bird, ridden by one of Evator's winged riders. The guy came close enough to have a brief, shouted talk with Loira about bird, daekais, and jhaikan sightings. Max felt braver as they neared their destination, so he pointed toward the forest. Loira nodded, so they spent an hour doing reconnaissance, during which he saw a few daekais and a patrol of morkais who waved at them. He saw nothing that might come in handy if he freed Norus. Either way, the rescue via florin back seemed more likely now.

He finally arced toward the Florin Tower and did what Loira had asked—he tried to land on one perch instead of the tower's top. The birds knew how to do it, so it wasn't like he had to take control so much as indicate his intention with the reins. Ronon handled it as gracefully as Max expected. Riding a giant avian wasn't so hard but firing arrows at something from a moving bird was undoubtedly hard, even with *Archery Fiend*. He rolled down the saddle, unhooked himself, and descended to the perch and its adjacent walkway, relieved to be standing. He said farewell to Ronon with a pat on his legs. The bird rustled his feathers.

Loira had landed on another perch and he joined her inside the building, asking questions about bird prep, or what to do after a ride. She taught him whatever he wanted for hours. His proficiency rose two levels and he regretfully left the tower for dinner. He wanted to master these birds and afford one. That meant questing, which meant leaving Evator.

Siren: Hey. I'm back just to check in.

Max: Not playing tonight? You missed your florin bird training.

Siren: Yeah, I'll do it first thing tomorrow. How was it?

Max: Awesome. If you're afraid of heights, use a proficiency point on it. I felt a lot better.

Siren: Wimp. Kidding.

Max: LOL. Any news?

Siren: No. It's the weekend. No legal update until at least Monday. Courts are slow, but they're hoping to use that for a temp injunction or whatever it's called.

Max: Has my body decayed? Turned putrid?

Siren: Not any more than it already was.

Max: Nice!

Siren: BTW, your parents said hello. They want to know how you're doing.

Max: Oh wow. Did you talk to them? That's awesome. I can't thank you enough for what you're doing. Tell them I'm doing great, all things considered.

Siren: Yeah, no sweat. Don't get all mushy.

Max: Mushy is kind of my thing.

Siren: As if. Anyway, they wanted to tell you the usual corny shit, like they love you, blah blah blah. But seriously, they're very worried and have sworn to do everything they can to help. In fact, they may even join the game so they can see you.

Max felt a rush of adrenaline. His parents had never understood gaming. Coming in here seemed oddly flattering, like he could share something he liked with them. But most of his enthusiasm stemmed from seeing them before his demise. After hours of sort of forgetting about it, his predicament seemed all too real again. His mother would probably spend the entire time crying while his dad tried to look stoic. Maybe it would just get embarrassing, but it gave him an idea. He asked Siren to tell his lawyer to add this to the story, that the chance to say goodbye was something that people like him needed and deserved. Maybe a public appeal would cause other lawsuits.

When the chat ended, he realized Siren's positive affect on his mood. A little kidding around really helped. He wanted to stay positive for a while and not brood. With the sky darkening outside and the two visible moons rising, Max strolled into town toward the bar that the castle guards frequented. The two-story Wily Tavern stood by town square, white walls below a wooden roof. Torches burned beside the stairs as he mounted them, leather boots clonking on the boards. A small veranda ran along the front, NPCs there ignoring him as he entered.

An orange glow from a fireplace lit one side near a foot-high stage no one occupied. Across from it stood the bar, elegant carvings of hunting scenes on it. Tables with joking people filled the space between. Beyond it all, a stairway ascended. He sat on a barstool, a buxom black-haired bartender asking his fancy. He took an ale and flipped her a coin, then surveyed the room. Many present were gambling with valend cards, which depicted the gods and species they'd created, plus the court cards. He had a partial pack of from the daekais encounter and had flipped through them. While some gamblers used coins, the querra here wagered with seeds. Several guards from the castle jail were drunk, a key ring foolishly hanging from a belt and giving Max an idea for later. Malonir was also here, making Max realize he should join the kryll, as they were part of the same fireteam. He was about to rise when the front door banged open.

The Dark Trio strode in and took an empty table, the big rhaikan flanked by the female karelian sorcerer and the kryllan rogue, who wore a symbol showing he was solonon and focused on fairness. Max wondered what reward they'd received by felt they weren't approachable. He didn't want extra attention any-way. The group didn't seem to notice him this time.

He once again rose to join Malonir, but the kryll stood with a lute in hand and soon mounted the stage to sit on a wooden stool. Max realized the spot was reserved for a performer, a painting of the god of expression on the wall behind. It also came with a free drink, for an ale maiden placed a frothy pewter goblet on a small table next to Malonir.

Max had poorly played a lute twice, the different tuning throwing him off. The pairs of strings hadn't helped, as he'd only played a 12-string guitar a few times, too. This one at least had frets, unlike some lutes. If this was the closest to a guitar he could find, he might need to burn a proficiency point. He looked up music proficiencies and saw a generic fretted instrument one rather than something specific. Would his real-world skills translate? He decided to test it tonight on hearing Malonir sing in a beautiful tenor. The room cheered after each of the three songs. Several karelia did so the loudest, asking for more and flipping coins to Malonir.

Approaching the kryll, Max asked, "What were you playing? You were great."

Malonir replied, "Folk tunes of my homeland. They appeal to the crowd more than the songs of my court."

Max wondered if he meant more classical-like music. "Gotta play to the audience. Mind if I borrow your lute for a song?"

The kryll beamed. "Of course!"

Max accepted the instrument and spent one of his music proficiencies. He immediately felt more comfortable with the lute's tuning, even though he hadn't used it yet. If only real life was this way. Despite this, he wasn't sure what to play due to the tuning. He spent a minute simplifying things to some strummed chords and then tried to do "Nothing Else Matters" by Metallica, but it didn't go over that well, partly because the Dark Trio jeered him. He conceded it didn't really work. He next tried "Back in Black" by AC/DC with better results.

"You suck!" yelled the rhaikan, banging one enormous fist on the table.

"Keep your day job!" the sorelia beside him said, cackling.

The kryllan rogue gave him the finger. Then the other two did, too.

"Some things never change," Max muttered. He needed to learn songs from this world. Then he realized something and chuckled. He began playing the *Song of Gathering* spell, the melody easier to play than chords in a different tuning. The crowd quieted as the magic enveloped them. Max casts a curious eye about the room, wondering if anyone realized he was using a spell. Malonir sat smirking and Max flushed a little, grinning back.

When he was done, he said to the mostly enraptured room, "Everyone should buy myself and the kryll Malonir a drink. And the women should give me a hearty kiss!"

"Fjora's kiss!" they shouted as one. Max's *World Lore* skill told him they'd invoked the name of the Goddess of Passion. He smirked as a buxom ale maiden planted a lush, firm, comforting, and arousing kiss that felt better than any real-world one he'd experienced. Okay, that settled it. He wanted to stay in the game for good. What was sex going to feel like? Was it even possible?

He returned Malonir's lute, enjoyed a few more kisses and drinks, and decided to leave before he got too drunk. But a line of enthralled fans stood between him and the door. Maybe that spell was too strong? He tried to make his way past, but several made him chug an ale. Malonir ran interference and pointed toward the kitchen, suggesting Max go out the back. Was he the first rock star of Llurien Online? He laughed and swayed, dodging wines and ales but accepting kisses from all but the bearded guy.

"I have to get out of here!" Max laughed and stepped into the kitchen, the aroma of fresh bread washing over him. A querran chef swatted a towel to make him leave. He meandering around a corner or two and out into a narrow alley behind the tavern.

The darkness swallowed him, but light from the main street to his right beckoned. He took two steps before seeing a huge, shadowy, humanoid shape ten feet ahead and blocking his way. The silhouette reminded him of that rhaikan inside. And when the figure lit a torch, the orange flames dancing over its scaly face left no doubt it was the same guy.

Behind Max, a foot scraped on the ground. He turned to see the rhaikan's karelian sorcerer friend emerge from the shadows, her black leather making her hard to see. The darkness hid her face, but her eyes glowed a subtle green, the same way some animals' eyes glowed red in the dark. The remaining member of the Dark Trio wasn't apparent.

"Look," said Max, slurring his words, "I've had enough dudes like you trying to kiss me for one night, and you're not my type anyway, so if you don't mind..."

With one clawed hand, the rhaikan unslung a black axe with a silver blade edge off one shoulder. Max stared in recognition at what looked suspiciously like the axe-shaped guitar he'd built himself. And yet, the strings were missing, though six tuning pegs at the axe handle suggested it could be strung. The handle looked nothing like a guitar neck, however. He wasn't sure what he was looking at and blinked in confusion.

"Well," started the rhaikan in a deep, booming voice, "if it isn't Max Parker. We've been looking for you."

CHAPTER TWENTY-ONE

M ax blinked. "How did you...?"

Oh shit. Siren's dad warned me about this. I knew these guys acted like they recognized me.

The nearly nine-foot-tall rhaikan spread his hands, each fingertip topped with a sharp talon. "You're famous, Max. Everyone knows who you are." Everything about him exuded menace, the serrated teeth reminding Max of a shark. But the black forked tongue that flicked out was more like a snake.

Name: Reaper of Evator.
Type: Player.
Class: Hunter.
Species: Rhaikan.
Level 5.
HP: 59/59.

Max glanced behind him again to get the girl's stats.

Name: Vixen of Evator.
Type: Player.

Class: Sorcerer.
Species: Karelia.
Level 5.
HP: 40/40.

Outnumbered and outmatched didn't bode well, but Max tried to diffuse the situation with humor. Though he knew Reaper meant everyone on Earth knowing he was in a coma, he joked about his tavern performance. "Did you want an autograph or something?"

Behind him, Vixen said, "You'd like that, wouldn't you? Conceited prick. We're gonna ram this axe up your ass. You'll probably get off on it."

Adrenaline tore through Max, the hostility over nothing familiar. Knowing most people could dish it out but not take it, he shot back, "Maybe I can sign your tits. Did you give yourself a boob job in the character creation? Tired of being flat-chested in real world? Or did you get a boob job there, too?"

Even in the dark, he saw Vixen scowl. "*Fuck* you."

"My place or yours?" he retorted.

She sputtered for a rebuttal. "You got a smart mouth."

"At least *one* of us does."

Reaper said, "That mouth of yours has always been a problem."

That brought Max up short. Had they interacted before? "What? Wait. How could you... who are you?"

The rhaikan seemed to grin, but the motion of baring more serrated teeth was hardly friendly. "Let's just say we've met before."

Vixen cackled. "Yeah, and it didn't end well for you last time."

"What's that supposed to..." An awful possibility occurred to him. *No, it couldn't be.*

Reaper added, "Don't recognize us? Can't say I blame you. We chose different bodies on purpose, so we could surprise you. More fun that way." He looked Max up and down. "You always acted like you were so damn creative, and yet here you are, looking just like you did in the real world."

"Yeah, not so fucking creative after all, are you, asshole?" Vixen's smugness could have curdled milk.

Max nodded to himself, recognizing the type if not the individuals.

"You're some of the jealous little bitches in the Baltimore music scene," he said, getting frustrated that even here, he was not free of these people. "I guess you can take the losers out of dive bars, but you can't take the dive bars out of the losers. You idiots came all this way, changed your species, your class—as if you had any class to begin with—but you still can't stop being bitter assholes. You think the world owes you something because you're content to sit around with one hand stuffed in a bag of potato chips and the other hand down your pants, while other people actually try to do something with their lives. You have no respect for people who work for something and think it's unfair when they succeed. And then you're gonna what? Show them how it really works? Talk shit about them behind their back? Try to get everyone to hate them just because they got somewhere? Why don't you do something with your miserable fucking lives instead of trying to destroy someone who already did with *theirs*?"

That felt good. *Really* good. He'd been meaning to say something like that for a long time now.

"I'm really gonna enjoy killing you," said Vixen, taking a step closer behind him.

Another jolt of adrenaline coursed through him, and he met her hostile gaze. "Same."

Reaper said, "You know, when we first found out you were in a coma, we weren't too worried you'd identify us after our last get together. But then we heard you were in this game and the cops were trying to talk to you in here, to find out who attacked you. So we came to pay you a visit."

Vixen added, "Yeah, we thought to convince you to keep your fucking mouth shut. And then we had a better idea."

Reaper laughed. "To quote an old Stephen King movie, sometimes dead is better. If we kill you and keep you dead, you can't say shit."

Max paled in shocked disbelief that his real-world attackers had entered the game to screw with him. It was so extreme. And so fucked up. What the hell had he ever done to these people? Anger began to build, and his drunkenness rushed away. "You're the ones who attacked me outside the club."

"Not as dumb as you look," said Vixen, gloating.

Max clenched his jaw. He didn't deserve this. They were the reason he was in a coma. In this game. And maybe dead soon. They knew he would die in real life if he didn't wake up. Siren's father said everyone on Earth knew. The attack in Baltimore could be called a crime of passion, but this? It would be first degree murder.

Would they even be punished? There were no real world laws about what happened in here. They hinted at some plan to keep him from respawning until he died in the real world. It was the perfect crime, killing where no law applied.

The cold anger grew. This all seemed vaguely familiar. And suddenly scattered images of that night in Baltimore came into his head for the first time. What they really looked like, but only vaguely. Hair colors. Their size. Body language. The tone of it all.

Reaper laughed, a deep guttural sound. "We were gonna kill you at the castle until that daekais attack interrupted."

Max doubted that, given Siren's presence and the guards. He tried to think of some angle to stop this. "You both chose noble species or races. Rhaikan are reformed. Karelia are benevolent. Killing another character for no reason will hurt you in the game."

Reaper snorted. "Nothing compares to you blabbing about our little incident at the club."

Max scowled. "Little incident? You putting me in a fucking *coma*."

Vixen said, "You whine like a little bitch."

"You're wrong anyway," Reaper drawled, ignoring the sorcerer. "I'm a jhaikan *pretending* to be rhaikan. She's a sorelia. Killing you won't affect us at all."

Max glowered, wondering how much cunning he'd have to take from these jerks. He didn't like not seeing things coming. Where was the kryllan rogue? Max glanced at the roofline above but saw no one.

Stalling for time, he asked, "What's everyone going to think of you coming in here after me?"

Reaper said, "They're never gonna know. You'll spend your time in here dead until they pull the plug and you die for real."

Anger grew at the cold intent now openly stated. "You're really going to make sure I die for real? Prison for murder is a lot longer than causing… an accident." Giving them the benefit of the doubt made him want to puke, but it was an angle. His eyes darted past the jhaikan. Getting by him wouldn't work.

Pointing the axe at Max, Reaper said, "And being free forever is even shorter."

That gave Max an idea. "I don't know who you are, anyway. I don't remember the attack."

Reaper snorted. "You expect me to believe that?"

"Why would I remember? I have a concussion and I'm in a coma."

"One you're never waking up from to identify us."

Max tried to remain calm, his eyes scanning again. "Where's your kryllan friend?" Then something occurred to him. "I have one, too. She's the daughter of the detective investigating the attack. Might want to think twice about screwing with her."

Reaper grunted. "Interesting. But she ain't here now, is she?"

Vixen said, "Aw, he's got a girlfriend. Have you tried sex in here? Maybe you'll get a chance when we skull fuck your corpse." She cackled.

A jolt of anger tore through Max. "I'm gonna shove my sword up your ass while you're still alive and then split you down the middle with it."

She laughed harder. "I think he's flirting with me!"

Knowing that escalating wouldn't end well, Max regretted letting her get a rise out of him, but he couldn't help it. It's not every day you learn people are intending to kill you… any second. Where was that damn kryllan rogue? What were they planning to do after killing his character? And would that kill him in real life?

Wiping a sweaty palm on his pants, he said, "If you kill me in here, the system will know your player names killed my character and there will be a record of it."

Silence greeted this before the sorcerer said, "They'll never know it was us because you're never going to regenerate to tell them."

Max eyed her suspiciously. A clue, at least. "You can't stop me from respawning."

Vixen snickered. "Can't we?"

Reaper lifted the axe and put the torch before it, so Max could see it better. "We used a 3D printer to bring your guitar into the game. Too bad for you we smashed it to pieces in the real world, but this one plays real nice."

Max's gaze hardened at the reminder of his beloved Kat being gone. He'd *known* the axe looked far too familiar. "It's an axe, stupid, not a guitar."

"Oh yeah?" Reaper turned the weapon to hold it like an instrument, dropping the torch, which bounced once on the ground. The axe handle changed shape to more closely resemble a guitar neck. Frets and violet-colored, glowing strings appeared. Playing "For Whom the Bell Tolls" by Metallica, with hands that were too big for the guitar, the jhaikan said, "This is your new theme song."

Max retorted, "Yeah, and 'My Own Prison' is gonna be yours."

Vixen asked, "Are you two done being clever?"

Hefting the axe like a weapon again, Reaper advanced. "I liked killing you for your guitar so much that, this time, I'm going to kill you *with* it."

Max fumbled for his sword, then realized a spell was better. He backed away to gain time until his boots got stuck like when he'd started the game. He glanced down, then behind in suspicion. The sorcerer had one hand outstretched toward him. On her cheeks and forehead, her lorenia lines and eyes glowed green in the darkness, revealing her use of magic.

He looked back and lifted a hand. "Gather air!"

The swirling vortex filled his palm while Reaper charged. Max flung the magic orb, which faintly glowed as it soared across the dark alley. Reaper turned one shoulder but the spell struck him there, doing 15 HP of damage and knocking him off balance. He stumbled into the alley wall.

A sharp pain between Max's shoulder blades made him gasp. He would've fallen forward if Vixen's spell wasn't holding his legs. His health bar appeared along with a -36 HP floating away—almost half his HP.

"Got 'im!" shouted a new voice behind him. "Critical hit *and* stealth bonus! Fuck yeah!"

Max looked to the side and saw the kryllan rogue, Iron Heart, holding a dagger that dripped with Max's blood. He'd come out of the shadows.

A roar in front of Max made him turn back. Reaper loomed before him, the axe raised with both hands. As the blade hurtled down, Max instinctively held up both arms to block, dread filling him at the obvious consequence. The axe sheared his left arm off at the elbow and continued down, slicing open his chest an inch deep. He screamed in pain and horror. Blood spurted from the severed limb with each heartbeat and flowed down his torso. His health bar flashed red. He hardly noticed the red -29 HP drift away.

"Yes!" Reaper crowed with delight. "Let's see you play a fucking guitar now, you cocky asshole!"

Warning: Your Health is under 5%!

Rage and desperation filled Max. He raised his other hand, a feather from his inventory appearing in it. He belatedly realized he should've cast this first.

"Feel slumber's call to rest!"

Two bodies fell when he dropped the feather. Only two, snoring before they hit the ground. The axe-wielding jhaikan stood before him, pulling the weapon back. Max's legs had been freed, but it was too late.

"You were mine anyway."

The axe hurtled toward Max's chest on the left side, slamming deep into his chest, a fountain of gore spraying out. Max flew sideways and crashed into the alley wall, everything going black as he crumpled to the ground. The horrendous pain in his torso was surprisingly fleeting. And he knew why as a silent scream of terror in his mind almost drowned out Reaper's next words.

"You're dead, motherfucker!"

CHAPTER TWENTY-TWO

Max whipped around in a panic.

"Shit! Shit! Shit!"

The alley was gone. So were the Dark Trio. And the tavern. So was the pain.

Gravestones, grey mausoleums of different sizes, and random trees dotted the grassy hill where he found himself. Bright moonlight pierced the dark sky and lit his surroundings far more than before. It seemed like he could see much farther than normal. Everything looked different, vegetation darker against the backdrop of other vegetation, so that it was harder to make out. A soft white glow emanated from the gravestones and the black metal fence surrounding the cemetery.

He appeared to still be in the game. Some elements like the hot list and compass were visible. And the Life Counter, which continued its descent.

Life Counter: 4 Days, 10 Hours, 34 Minutes.

That seemed only a few minutes after the alley. He'd started at 9am on day one and it had been after 10pm when he'd left the tavern. It didn't seem like his game time had been impacted. Normally in a game, if you died, you immediately appeared in the nearest graveyard, and that appeared to be exactly what had just happened. He began to calm.

The logout button was still greyed out. He hadn't considered that dying in here might free him, but the possibility was now eliminated, since he hadn't woken up. It was still possible that dying would kill him for real. Maybe there was a delay. He didn't feel that reassured. But there was nothing he could do about that if true.

He looked down. That his body was gone didn't surprise him. It should still be in the alley. He was standing. No, floating. A few inches from sparse grass and dirt. His feet were translucent, surrounded by a soft white glow. He held out both arms—there were two full limbs, not one whole and one severed. They had the same appearance, as did the rest of him that he could see. He touched his cheek, and it felt... weird. Like he was pressing on cellophane. It gave a little like actual skin, so he pushed where his cheekbone was, but it felt the same, not as though bone was under there. He quickly pressed his elbows, skull, and stomach. They all felt the same, as if his mass didn't change anywhere.

"I'm a ghost?" he wondered aloud, and his voice sounded familiar but like he was in an empty hall, slightly reverberating. As if to answer his question, a message appeared.

You are dead!

Your class has changed! If you regain your body, you will return to your previous class.

You are now a non-corporeal undead.

Class: Ghost, level 1.

You should examine the class description to understand your new capabilities and vulnerabilities.

Your current location is the nearest cemetery to your corpse. This could be a considerable distance, including underground or underwater. Your map now includes an arrow showing the general direction of your body. When within 50 ft, an X will show the exact position. One or more red arrows mark the direction of those who killed you; a red dagger icon will mark their exact position when you are within 50 ft of each. This will improve your ability to haunt them. Or enact revenge.

You may gain XP, level up, and perform some previous or new quests as allowed by your current condition. As your undead level increases, you may change to other classes of undead.

All proficiencies and bonuses associated with your life are unavailable and will remain so until you regain life. However, you have new proficiency points that can be assigned to your undead class. As with your life, your undead choices will still be there each time you die.

You cannot access your *Party Screen* or chat features with the living, but you can gain undead party members who will be permanently lost if you regain life; you may add them again the next time you die. You can also not communicate with the living until you reach undead level 5. The exceptions are with karelia or sorelia, who can innately interact with you, depending on the individual's abilities. But beware—both can capture your spirit and decide what to do with it.

To live again, you must find your body and respawn. Failure to do so means remaining undead. The longer you remain undead, the worse condition your corpse will be in when you find it. You may be presented with the option to respawn or to become a corporeal undead (i.e., you have regained your body, but it is still dead). If you choose corporeal undead, this choice is permanent, barring supernatural intervention (magic, the gods) to reverse this choice.

You gained (3) proficiency points!

You have (3) unassigned proficiency points!

"Well, *that's* interesting," he said aloud. Usually, once dead, you just found your body and respawned. Maybe you dropped an important item, a level, or something else happened. But you didn't get reassigned to a class of undead, with new abilities and the chance to remain that way. The idea of changing to another undead class later was interesting. Could he become a liche? Banshee? He needed to look into undead classes. If his actual life hadn't been on the line, he might've been more tempted to go that route, but he had lost the ability to interact with Siren. Or maybe anyone else. He had to find his corpse.

Something about the description suggested that this new "life" as a ghost meant he was in no danger of dying in the real world. He wasn't sure what that bit about the quests meant. Maybe if he had one to learn something, he could still could, but if he needed a body to do it, then not. His game time would be compromised in one sense—everything he did as a ghost would raise his level as undead, but if he regained his bard life, he would not have gained experience there. What mattered now was his class description, so he pulled it up.

Class: Ghost

Summary: Ghosts are non-corporeal undead who have not passed to an afterlife. The Lord of the Undead, Everett, is aware of your existence as one of his servants. The god may call upon you to serve; disobey at the risk of your immortal soul.

Your new abilities are summarized below. Experimentation is recommended.

Spectral hit points (SHP) have replaced your hit points (HP).

Spectral mana points (SMP) have replaced your mana points (MP).

Your senses are altered.

You have no taste or smell.

Your sight and hearing are enhanced.

You will not feel many sensations related to physical items, and other items that can affect you will do so in new ways. You can pass through most solid objects. All physical contact with the living (plants, animals, species) triggers your *Necrotic Touch* ability, but this can be suppressed at higher levels. Your movement speed has increased.

At higher levels, you can teleport between familiar locations or ones important to you, depending on the distance. You will gain increased chances of moving undetected. Since you were a magic user in life, you may gain the ability to perform magic with spectral mana. You have new innate skills that will improve with level advancement.

Others can detect you with their sixth sense, which is why your own sixth sense is now enhanced, for your protection.

Innate skills: Horrifying Visage (level 1), Necrotic Touch (level 1), Possession (level 1), Wail of Terror (level 1), Possession Speak (level 1).

His first thought was that the innate skills might help him gain his body, so he pulled up a few descriptions.

Ability Name: Necrotic Touch.

Description: This causes painful necrotic damage, up to 20 HP, to whichever part of a living being is touched. On initial contact, the wound radiates several inches in all directions. Without treatment, and at higher levels, the damage will continue to spread over the target's body at two inches per hour. The victim typically loses the ability to use the affected area, such as a limb. If the taint reaches the brain, heart, or lungs, death follows. At high levels, the taint can become contagious. At very high levels, there is a 10% chance the victim becomes a zombie or similar corporeal undead.

Cast time: Instant.

Duration: Until healed, or death.

Cooldown: 2 minutes.

SMP: 3.

Ability Name: Wail of Terror.

Description: You can emit a piercing scream that reduces everyone within hearing range to half their current HP unless they successfully resist. All nearby karelia and sorelia will instantly know of your nature, exact whereabouts, and gain increased ability to track your movements for ten minutes. They will also be unaffected at lower levels of this ability, and suffer less damage than others at higher levels.

Cast time: 3 seconds.

Duration: Instant.

Cooldown: 1 hour.

SMP: 3.

The descriptions confirmed his suspicion that his abilities would act like spells. To try one out, he moved to a nearby tree, floating across the ground so fast he almost passed it. He touched a branch with his ghostly hand and a frost-tinged blackness spread out. On withdrawing it, the damage remained. Would it remain indefinitely? Maybe he could leave a trail for himself when needed. Would other people spot it? To make it less noticeable, he tried a fingertip with the same result.

Wondering what else had changed, he looked over the screens available and noticed his appearance—translucent whiteness, brightest at his heart and face, which wore an expression of menace. No armor, just a simple tunic and leggings. Bare feet and hands were hardly visible. No appearance controls were onscreen, so he held his hands up and willed them to disappear. They faded, then brightened again. With more concentration, they vanished.

"That's a relief."

With practice, he made most of himself disappear. Confirming the results on the *Character Screen*, he discovered how to make just his hands appear, or head, or a disembodied torso. A notification appeared.

You are proficient in Invisibility!
Proficiency Type: Active.
Level: 1.

That was a good one. He still had three points to assign but held onto them until he had a better sense of what to do as a ghost. He looked over his stats.

Name: Maestro Max.
Species/Race: Human.
Class: Ghost, Level 1.
Reputation: 0—Unknown.
XP: 15.
SHP: 45/45.
SMP: 6/6.
Strength: 4.

Dexterity: 4.
Agility: 7.
Constitution: 5.
Intelligence: 5.
Wisdom: 6.
Charisma: 9.
Morale: 8.

Some stats surprised him, including the high spectral hit points, or SHP. That was three times his start as a bard. His morale had also risen, but most stats were worse than the starting bard ones, which had been at 6. The high charisma seemed out of place until remembering stories of ghosts enthralling the living. Could he charm someone? Not looking like a ghost, probably. He again experimented with appearance to look alive, which was the name of the proficiency he soon earned. Siren probably would've noticed that his eyes, nose, and mouth were a little too far apart, or big, or narrow, but he could fool a stranger—until he moved. The living didn't float. He'd have to work on that but not now. He had to get his body.

On surveying his surroundings, he saw the Florin Tower's top a half-mile away. It seemed southwest of him. He was closer to the mountains than before. He felt certain his direction sense was off, even when looking at the map. Nearby stood the cemetery gates, a wooden sign he couldn't read from this side atop two poles of black steel. He moved that way. Finding his body shouldn't take too long. The map showed the way. He continued around graves before remembering he could pass through objects, but when he tried, it didn't work and he gasped in pain. A -1 SHP floated up.

"I took damage?"

He touched it again, and it didn't hurt him. Curious, he tried to move through another one and took more damage. Eyeing the fence, which also glowed, he tried that but suffered the same fate.

"Can't pass through anything glowing, or at least, not if it's related to a burial site. The cemetery gates it is."

Fortunately, they were open. What if they were closed? He'd be stuck here? Maybe that had been the Dark Trio's plan to prevent him from respawning. But they hadn't done it. They could still be en route. It seemed an odd possibility because someone could trap tons of players in here. Maybe it wouldn't work, or there was some severe restriction on that.

He passed the gates as his SHP rose by one, confirming he'd regenerate. But could he heal himself? It didn't seem like it. What happened if he hit 0 SHP? He'd probably reappear in the graveyard again.

While the dirt road to Evator beckoned, he soared into the thin forest, a few inches off the ground. His sharper vision easily picked out wildlife, like the small animals scurrying away when he was still fifty feet from them, but anyone would've seen the birds hurtle into the sky. All wildlife vanished. It became deathly quiet. Would his presence make the air get cold, too? Maybe this wasn't a good idea. Someone might realize he was coming.

He stopped. The karelia. They could detect ghosts without trying. And a Karelian Guard existed in Evator, keeping watch in the woods south of town all night. But he was north. Did they not expect trouble from the town's own graveyard? Apparently not, because here Max was, unmolested and, as far as he knew, undetected. On a hunch that maybe karelia were guarding the road instead of the woods, he moved back toward there. He sensed something ahead but wasn't sure what it was. It didn't feel dangerous, nor comforting. Was it a person? An animal?

When he stopped, he sensed it moving toward him, as if aware of his location.

Max ensured he was invisible and kept still beside a row of bushes. And then he heard it—soft footsteps on grass from a single pair of feet. They seemed far away despite how clearly he heard them. And they moved without hesitation straight toward him. Either whatever it was didn't know a ghost was ahead or it did and felt no fear. From habit, he looked for an escape route before remembering he could pass through whatever he wanted, as long as it didn't glow white.

Just as the footsteps stopped twenty paces ahead, he was about to bolt for town, but hesitated. All he heard was faint, even breathing, not the labored breath of someone frightened. Max had chased away the wildlife himself. It had to be a person. A few seconds passed before a high-pitched, friendly voice addressed him.

CHAPTER TWENTY-THREE

he voice said, "It's okay. I know you're there. I am not here
to hurt you."

That's exactly what someone here to hurt me would say,
thought Max. He had seen a few karelia around town and heard
their voices. This sounded like one. His senses honed in through
the foliage. He saw two green eyes staring at him, faint green
lorenia lines around them brightening as he watched. And yet he
felt no peril. Then he remembered that the goddess of truth had
created karelia with the gods of courage, intuition, and vitality.
These traits enabled karelia to withstand supernatural terrors.
Was that the reason this one was so calm, or did it really not
intend to cause problems?

"What do you want?" Max asked.

"To guide you to an afterlife."

Max grimaced. His real-life situation made that sound worse.
But then maybe this was a way to wake up? It was too risky. "I
do not want to die."

Gently, the karelia said, "You already have."

"But I can respawn."

"Yes, but you can also complete your demise and achieve one of the Seven Fates, that of Daeijonen, where you are born anew into new flesh, your life truly reset with no memory of this one."

The "complete your demise" remark struck a nerve. This karelia was a threat to him after all, if it was going to persist with that idea.

Max's *World Lore* skilled popped up a message revealing that the gods of the yellow sphere, who had created the species of querra, had also invented Daeijonen afterlife. He'd caught wind of there being Seven Fates before and was now curious. What if one of these afterlife options was the way to wake up from this game?

"What are the other fates? Do I get to choose mine?"

The karelia moved a few steps closer and a notification appeared.

Name: Ardyn Nightstrider of Evator.
Type: NPC.
Class: Ghost Hunter.
Species: Karelia.
Level 15.

Max wondered how much better a karelia with the Ghost Hunter class was at finding someone like him. The karelia had likely been stationed outside the cemetery. Max pulled up more about the class.

Class: Ghost Hunter
Summary: Karelian (or sorelian) Ghost Hunters specialize in the tracking and capturing of non-corporeal undead of all kinds

(not just ghosts). Karelian hunters send the captured spirits to the Orb of Souls, colloquiality known as the Karelia's Sphere, in the karelian homeland. The spirits are cleansed of the torment that ties them to Llurien, so that they may achieve their destined afterlife. What a sorelian Ghost Hunter does with a captured soul varies by the sorelia but is seldom pleasant.

Answering his question, Ardyn answered, "You do not choose a fate. Solon, God of Fairness, judges those who perish."

Fuck that, thought Max.

"What are the other options? I'd like to know what else I would risk happening."

"For the most sinister, they are consigned to the oblivion of E'kainum, their soul ripped apart and unrecoverable by even the gods. They are forgotten, as if they had never been."

Damn. That's harsh.

"For those less evil," the karelia continued, "they spend eternity being tortured in Lochiare. And the least unsavory experience, Maeryndor, a never-ending boredom."

It sounded to Max like Lochiare was this world's version of hell. "I guess I can see why they're tiered like that."

Ardyn said, "Not everyone deserves the same fate, and the seven spheres of gods each had their own ideas. There are very few who are truly neutral at death, but they are given the least common of all fates, that of Myrradim. It is a rebirth as a supernatural chameleon and shapeshifter of human appearance, who tempts other humans to reveal their nature, so the myrradim can judge and punish or reward them. Many do not believe this fate truly exists, but I assure you it does."

"Are there three good fates, too?"

"Yes. The humans who are least good experience the rebirth of Daeijonen. Those who are more noble in spirit enjoy the everlasting pleasures of Leisiran."

That sounded like heaven to Max, who asked, "And the most good?"

"They ascend to Sorrairyn, the city of the gods, as supernatural beings who excelled so much at something in life that they become demigods of that trait."

Max perked up. "Ascension, huh? How good does one have to be at something?"

"The best who has ever lived."

Max's ambition as a musician popped into his head. He'd been killed for it, assuming he died in here. And he hadn't been all that ambitious to begin with. He'd just wanted to make a name for himself. A mark. Maybe leave something like his music behind when he... died. He hadn't done anything yet. Not really. The closest was building Kat, the axe-shaped guitar that helped get him attacked, but she was gone now, in pieces. What if he became a badass musician in here, one so good he ascended? What would that mean for him? He might have already died without leaving something behind, especially with Kat smashed to pieces. Maybe he could last in this game and not be forgotten.

But he supposed he'd already made an unintended mark— the first coma patient in a virtual reality game. He was famous for it. If others followed and this became some sort of medical and legal breakthrough, with new rights, this would never be forgotten. Was it enough? No. He wanted more. To make whatever came next more memorable. To not be known as a victim but someone who had thrived despite what happened Fuck this, it wasn't over. He would not die in this game, nor was this the only mark he would leave. The fame he apparently had suddenly irritated him.

Since the karelia didn't seem at all threatening, Max closed the distance between them. But he remained on guard. He was ten feet away when he stopped, seeing a member of the five-and-a-half-foot tall species before him. The karelia had delicate features on a heart-shaped face, where everything seemed pointed: ears, nose, even the chin. He seemed childlike despite the silver-etched black plate armor he wore, the sword and dagger on opposite hips, and the calm seriousness with which he faced a ghost. He also seemed like he was of Asian descent, even the eyes being a little slanted, the long straight hair black and tied in a ponytail. Those glowing eyes and the lorenia lines sweeping away from them on his cheeks and forehead had shone brighter as Max approached, but Max couldn't tell if his proximity had brightened them or if it just seemed so.

"If I ascend, do I become part of this... uh, environment?" Max asked, wondering if he could admit he was in a game. None of the NPCs had acted like it was.

Ardyn examined him, clearly able to see the invisible Max anyway. "Yes, your consciousness, or a likeness of it, remains here."

"As a, uh, person with freewill, or someone serving the environment's needs?" He tried to avoid saying player or NPC, but that was what he meant.

"A little of both, of course."

"What do you mean when you say that my consciousness remains?"

"I am unsure how to answer that, as it varies and is not my specialty."

Max frowned. He was wondering if ascending to Sorrairyn in the game would keep his consciousness around, even if his body died in the real world. But even if that was somehow true, and he didn't think it was, he had only a few days to achieve that. He snorted. That was impossible, unless his attorney succeeded in buying him more time. He'd pass the idea on to Siren. For now, he'd pretend that this self-assigned Ascension Quest, as he dubbed it, would happen.

Max said, "You said that the least good humans get Daeijonen. It's only for humans?"

"Yes."

"Why no one else?"

The karelia paused. "There are seven spheres of gods. Three nefarious. Three benevolent. One neutral. Each sphere has four deities, and each created a species that inherited their combined traits. This resulted in three good species—karelia, mandeans, querra. And three evil—daekais, riven, and jhaikan. And one neutral—kryll. Each of the seven species are uniform enough in disposition to have a predictable outlook—and after life. But after this, all twenty-eight gods created the humans, who are far more varied. As a result, they are assigned one of the Seven Fates created just for them."

"The other species have other fates?"

"Yes. Almost without exception, a karelia, for example, knows where one is headed upon death."

"Almost?"

"Yes. Exceptions are rare."

"What about reformed races of a species, like rhaikan, or a morkais? Or a corrupted one, like sorelia?"

"Let's just say it gets more complicated."

Max laughed and let it go. "So you just want to help me reach an afterlife, but I don't want to go. So what now? Are you going to let me walk away from you?"

Ardyn asked, "You intend to return to your previous life?"

"I do. I'm not intending to harm anyone, if that's your concern."

"It is. As part of the Divine Covenant, the gods tasked karelia with resolving supernatural disturbances on Llurien. You are now one such disturbance, and I am obligated to assist, though it is up to my discretion how to do so. One option is forcing your tormented spirit to the Orb of Souls, where is it cleansed of the anguish that keeps you here, so that Solon may judge you and assign your fate."

"I do not feel particularly anguished." As soon as he said it, Max knew that wasn't true. This Orb of Souls sounded like a kindness awaiting the undead, but he needed to avoid this. What if a karelia forced him to it? He asked.

The karelia replied, "Some karelia are more inclined to override what you want for yourself. I am not. If you can resolve your situation by yourself, that is best."

"I believe I can do so. I just need to find my body, right?"

"That is correct."

"I know where it is. I would like to go now, if it's alright with you." He didn't really want to ask permission, but he felt that being civil was better than tempting an altercation he was unlikely to win.

Ardyn nodded. "You seem sincere. I will return to my post near the cemetery. You will know where to find me should you need my help."

"Thank you. You've been very helpful. Maybe we'll see each other when I'm alive again. I'll buy you a drink."

The karelia smiled. "It is a karelian custom to buy a drink for those who've regained life."

Max liked that. "I will accept."

Ardyn let him go, Max focusing on his sense of the karelia so that he'd recognize what the presence of one felt like next time.

He needed to avoid any in town. Maybe they wouldn't be so kind. And then there was that sorelian bitch who'd helped kill him. She'd be able to sense him, but would she know it was Max? What if she was waiting near his body to do something to him that only sorelia or karelia could do? He cursed. He needed to scope the area out.

Pulling up the map, he saw the town and three arrows marking the Dark Trio. To his surprise, they entered the settlement from the nearby north gate. Had they just gone to the graveyard while he was in the trees talking to Ardyn? He liked knowing their position, and that of his body... except it wasn't on the map. Maybe he was looking in the wrong place. He zoomed out and moved the view around, but there was no icon for it anymore. The arrow pointing the way was gone, too.

"What the hell?" he muttered aloud. Was it a bug? He closed and reopened the map without change. A logout and reboot was annoyingly not an option. The Dark Trio's icons remained, moving down the main street in Evator. The last he'd seen of his was before leaving the graveyard.

Alarmed, Max hurtled through—literally—the sparse trees toward Evator, soon bursting into the open, rolling land. No one was out here. A hundred yards away stood the stone walls and north gate, which he didn't need. He soared at the wall, passing into it and unable to see until emerging from the other side into a narrow road hugging the wall's inside. Though he could pass through buildings, he mostly kept to the streets but cutting corners.

Max finally raced into the alley outside the tavern and hurried to the place of the attack, only to find nothing there. Not even blood. The pavement was wet, as if someone had washed it away. There was no sign a fight had occurred. But one missing element stood out more than the others.

His body was gone.

CHAPTER TWENTY-FOUR

Max had never seen this in a game. If you died, sometimes you dropped an item or a level, but your body remained. Were players able to move someone's corpse? That seemed like asking for trouble. How could the game designers let that happen? This had to be a mistake.

"That's fucking great," he said, laughing bitterly. "I can't get back into my actual body in the real world, and now I can't get into my game body."

The map showed the Dark Trio, who'd said something about preventing him from respawning. Had they moved his corpse out of town while he was talking to the karelia? Was he buried? He started moving the Dark Trio when their icons disappeared one by one.

"Fuckers logged out," he said. Now he couldn't even eavesdrop on them.

Max sensed a karelia south of him. It didn't appear to be moving toward him, but it was time to go. He took the road out the north gate, scanning for footprints, but there were too many, though Reaper left distinct marks. Few if any other rhaikan were here. But it looked like someone had obscured tracks by dragging something behind them. And it was too dark for this, especially the way grass merged in his vision and the moonlight was fading as dark clouds rolled in, as if a storm brewed.

He gave up and took the rolling dirt road toward the cemetery. On nearing, he sensed Ardyn. Then a wooden shack beside the road appeared, the karelia exiting it as if knowing he was coming. He stared at the still invisible Max, eyes and lorenia lines glowing brighter as the ghost neared.

"You were unsuccessful." Ardyn seemed unfazed by the realization.

Max tried to sense whether the karelia's helpful disposition had changed with that detail, but he didn't think so. "My body is gone. Did anyone come this way with it?"

"No one has been out here but you and I."

"I saw the three who killed me re-entering town from the north. Is there another graveyard?"

"None, but there is a Kryllan Burial tree. It lies further to the east from here. They would not have been able to pass by me unnoticed." He gestured at the overgrown dirt trail that continued past the graveyard. Max had wondered where it led on glimpsing it before.

Instead of relying on his *World Lore* skill, he asked, "What's a Kryllan Burial tree?"

"Kryll tie their deceased in tall trees reminiscent of their homeland in the Kryllan Forest. The bodies inevitably fall to the ground, where they remain undisturbed except by scavengers. Animals. Some such trees and their remains are guarded either by magic, gates, or the living. And sometimes the dead. This one is not."

As Ardyn had spoken, Max had increasingly sensed the tree off in the distance, and then a notification popped up.

New Quest: Find the Kryllan Burial Tree.

Objective: Outside Evator, discover the location of the Kryllan Burial Tree, where a unique item may be found by worthy players.

Class: Common.

Difficulty: Easy.

Rewards: 1 Unique Item.

Accept?

Intrigued, Max accepted the quest. Getting back to the reason he was talking to Ardyn, Max said, "I no longer see my body on my map."

The karelia cocked a thin eyebrow. "That is peculiar."

"What could have caused it?"

Ardyn appeared to be thinking aloud as he said, "It could have been destroyed, though this is unlikely. People do not take kindly to desecrating a corpse, even of those reviled. If someone attempted that in town, some would intervene. It was not so late when you died that the streets would've been empty."

Max grimaced. "I didn't see signs they'd done anything to my body, like burning it, at least not there." He glanced north as if expecting to see a column of smoke.

"That would've left bones, as well. So they must have moved it, but you would still be able to see it on your map. Unless..."

"What?"

"There are no spells to hide a body specifically, but some can hide things from the living, sometimes from the dead. But your remains would not be easily hidden from you."

"Is there a spell to reveal its location?"

Ardyn nodded. "I need something of yours to do it."

Max cursed. He had nothing. When he'd looked in his inventory, nothing physical had been in there. He assumed—or hoped—that when he reincarnated, it would all still be there, but that didn't help now.

"What about my blood? Would that do it?" Even as he asked, he knew there likely wasn't enough at the scene, but maybe one drop was all that was needed.

"Yes, but it must be pure."

"What do you mean?"

"It cannot be tainted with anything like dirt. If there is some on the ground there, it may not be useable."

Max asked, "Can you try to get it for me?"

Ardyn considered. "I am not to leave my post, so it must wait until morning." He glanced at the dark sky, where clouds were rolling in. "The weather may complicate matters."

Goddamn it. "I need to find them and eavesdrop. Any tips on staying undetected?"

The karelia frowned as if he didn't agree. "No one will see or sense you without a spell, but a sorelia can do both. If she is untrained, she may be unable to do more than that."

"And if she *is* trained?" Max knew that was unlikely, given that she couldn't have been in the game more than two days. But she could've assigned a proficiency point to a skill that would help. He had to hurry.

The karelia shrugged. "It depends on her innate skills and training. We're not all the same. Some of us can capture your soul, or repel it, or force you to the afterlife of your destiny."

As soft thunder rumbled, Max thanked Ardyn and headed for the Kryllan Burial tree. Floating past the cemetery, he paid more attention to it this time. Dotting the rolling land inside the gates were unmarked dirt mounds, stone markers with deity symbols on them, full-blown mausoleums, and statues, but nothing extravagant. He soared beyond into the dark wilderness, a sense muted foreboding leading him. It grew stronger as he neared a forest east of town. He'd flown over it before so that his map showed it as a few miles deep, but he didn't go far into it before stopping at oblong clearing. In the center loomed a lone, deciduous asyander tree like the others nearby, over 125 feet tall.

Around the tree's base lay a multitude of white bones, most picked clean, a few having bits of hair or mummified flesh. Maybe a hundred bodies rose in one pile up the trunk to 5 feet, spreading out a dozen yards and getting lower as if the corpses were dumped at the tree's base. Then, when they decayed too much, the loose bones tumbled down and outward. The kryllan population was too small to cause this many, so it must've gone back hundreds of years or more.

Max was becoming accustomed to the silence his ghostly presence caused in the wilderness, but he heard muffled squawks above, and the occasional ruffle of feathers. Far up in the tree, a nude kryllan male hung upside down from a rope tied about his ankles and over a thick branch. He swayed gently as a turkey-sized, bald bird with black feathers and a white underbelly pecked at the corpse.

Moragul. This large carrion bird is the boldest of them all, being so aggressive that it has even attacked the undead or ridden one's shoulder like a parrot, chomping away at its flesh. The corrosive vomit they can spit is best avoided but can be used in spells.

HP: 3/3

That explained why the moragul hadn't fled. The bird paused to gaze at him before resuming. He wondered who the body belonged to. He hadn't heard of any kryll being killed in the daekais attack. Would a kryllan player like Siren find herself here? He guessed not. His body wasn't—or hadn't been—in the graveyard. This corpse was probably an NPC.

As he stood there, the pitter patter of heavy rain drops striking leaves began. Noticing he wasn't getting wet, he held up a hand and made it visible. The drops passed right through it. But he wasn't ready to assume other elements of the physical world wouldn't affect him. Some already had. He needed to experiment.

Suddenly, something small and round fell from above to crash into the bone pile with an audible crack. As it bounced down and rolled near his feet, he recognized a skull. The pile had shifted from the impact, several bones sliding apart. He floated over to there, and when he looked at the point of impact, something caught his eye. The blow had created a small crater and his sixth sense more than his sight detected something. He moved closer and felt a tingling growing.

Making his entire right arm visible, Max reached toward the bones, but his hand passed through them. Picking up something was apparently not an option. And yet he still sensed an item in there and remembered what the quest said. He extended his arm shoulder deep in the pile. And then his finger struck an object. With little feeling in his ghostly body, he couldn't tell what it was and struggled to get a hold. But his hands finally closed over what felt like a straight bone. He started pulling, the item dislodging bones as he slid it out with a cringe for disturbing the site. It finally came free, and he straightened in surprise.

It appeared to be a lyre, but unlike one he'd ever seen, not that he had much experience. But anyone would've been startled by what he held. It was a humanoid skull with blood-red hair still flowing in long, silken strands. The top of the skull had been cut away. In its place was some sort of leather hide that had been stitched to the upper edge of the severed head like a drum. At the back of the skull, near the top, two curved horns from some animal extended to a connecting crossbar of bone, which he was holding. Tuning pegs of glowing silver metal had been drilled into the crossbar. Stretching from there over the leather to the skull's front were seven strings made of some kind of nylon.

"What the hell is this?" he asked aloud, amazed and creeped out. A notification appeared.

Item: Lyre of Murryn.

Description: Murryn was a kriserian kryll, and a gifted singer whose lover tricked her into removing her mask on the Night of Terror. The God of Fear and Patron of the Undead, Everett, saw her face and put his mark on her soul so that she became his undead minion upon death. And so it was that Murryn's lover damned her to walk the earth—until karelia finally captured her and sent her to the Orb of Souls and an afterlife. By then, she had fashioned her supernatural lyre and wrought havoc with her legions of ghosts, ash fiends, reanimators and more.

Only those who have died can play the unique Lyre of Murryn. She constructed the lyre from the hollow skull of a kryllan princess who had committed suicide. This skull is topped with banoth skin that is tanned with oil from a Sira void cat. The curved arms are from the black trunks of the predatory Linganore trees. A crossbar of bone from an undead sorelian sorcerer connects them. The tuning pegs of valentium steel are niquerran-made. The strings are from the gut of an undead moragul.

Bonuses: +5 Dexterity, +3 Charisma, +5 Singing Enthrallment.

Abilities: Can summon 1-5 undead of varying levels under your command for 10 minutes. Can create a 25-foot radius magic void. Can drain 1 HP per second from the living within a 25-foot radius. Spell songs performed on it can affect the undead instead of the living.

Max knew what some items in the lyre description were, but pulled up other explanations. Niquerra made the valentium steel, which held supernatural energy more efficiently and powerfully than anything else. The Sira void cat was a small feline that emitted an area where magic didn't work. It seemed counterproductive to have tanned the banoth leather with that, but then maybe it helped in some way he didn't understand. The predatory Linganore trees were found in a supernatural land called the Ever Pathways, and they devoured the soul of anyone they caught.

"This thing is creepy," said Max, eyeing the instrument, which had seven strings. He noticed those were color-coded like the seven spheres of gods. Did that matter? It couldn't be a coincidence. He knew nothing about playing this and might need to burn a proficiency. Asking Ardyn risked the karelia taking it. Wondering if it would fit in his inventory, he tried, and it went in.

Quest Complete: Find the Kryllan Burial Tree.
You found the Lyre of Murryn!

Deciding to go, Max attempted to move the bones back into position, but he couldn't until using the lyre to nudge them. Then his finger bumped a bone and moved it. Curious, he tried again, but his hand passed through. Long ago, he'd seen the movie *Ghost*, where spirits could move objects if they were upset and focused enough. He tried to feign annoyance and failed twice more before real annoyance kicked in and the bone moved an inch. Concentrating more, he picked it up and tossed it onto the pile.

You are proficient in Moving Objects!
Proficiency Type: Active.
Level: 1.

"Nice."

After realizing the body above would land there before long and jumble things again, he stopped and left. The darkness and pouring rain made the path impossible to follow, so he used his map to avoid both the graveyard and Ardyn on the far side. He passed two abandoned and overgrown houses, which prompted a desire to do reconnaissance. What else was out here? His body?

He stopped suddenly on realizing something.

CHAPTER TWENTY-FIVE

There had to a shallow grave or building Max's body had been left in. He had to look right now. And his ghostly speed would shorten the search.

Still north of town, he raced for and found the road, which he followed north. Maybe an obvious path from there had piqued the Dark Trio's interest and suggested a place to dispose of him. Where would three players hide a body in the short time they'd had? They could not have gone far.

Ahead, the land undulated over rolling hills, bursts of lightning illuminating small stands of trees as rain fell. He came across a burned-out building, only the masonry remaining. Nothing. They could've used this as a landmark, so he searched in widening concentric circles. Still nothing. After returning to the main road, he repeated this elsewhere. Two hours passed before he conceded defeat. He might have to try this again in daylight.

Unable to logout, respawn, or even sleep, Max had nothing to do, so he decided to learn as much as possible about the town and castle while he could go through walls. The keep was higher priority, partly because more karelia to avoid were likely in town. He bypassed it to the west, soaring over the cleared land. He skipped the Florin Tower for having been inside already and the fear of scaring the birds.

First, he went into his barracks. A quick search found only a stash of weapons and armor he hadn't known about, and a rack of scrolls he worried about disturbing. He moved through the kitchens, servant quarters, and other places before checking the dungeon, where Norus and Evanel, the niquerra he agreed to free, lay asleep. The guards came alert when Max, still invisible, flowed through the room.

"Sudden chill in the air," said one, shivering.

"It happens down here sometimes, but not usually like this."

Max raced through a stone wall so they wouldn't remember it long. What if people got to talking tomorrow, learning this had happened throughout the castle? Would the karelia realize what it meant? Maybe it didn't matter. One already knew, but Max didn't want to push his luck. Still, NPCs being asleep added urgency to do his now.

He accelerated, systematically checking floors, only pausing if all were asleep, which was most of the castle. In modern life, electricity salvaged nighttime, but not here. Only guards and a few others were awake after midnight. That made him wonder what would happen to him when the sun rose. Would daylight hurt him or restrict movement to inside? That would interfere with recovering his body or eavesdropping on the Dark Trio.

He stopped short. If they never returned, he might be screwed. He couldn't identify them to Siren, whom he couldn't communicate with anyway. She had no way of knowing to follow them to find his body. Right now, she didn't even know he'd been killed. He had to tell Ardyn to tell her. He should've thought of that sooner, but he had time and would do it once done with the castle. He had just sensed something supernatural above him in the castle's center and wanted to check it out. But the stairs were some distance away.

For the first time, he wondered if he could float up through the ceiling. He hadn't considered vertical movement and had been using stairs when he came upon them. His ghostly form hovered a few inches above the floor or ground, rising or falling by itself on steps. To experiment, he first tried to lower himself to be level with the elegant rug beneath him, but he couldn't see the result because he was invisible. He glanced around the empty room to double-check for witnesses and, seeing no one, changed that. He'd gone too far, his feet through the floor. Willing himself up, he rose but couldn't be sure he was really level until making his feet touch like when he'd moved the bones. Then he felt himself land, though he couldn't feel the carpet's texture or temperature.

Curious if it would work, he tried walking. The first thing he noticed was the slower speed, just like a living person, so he wouldn't want this unless trying to look like alive. But concentrating on touching the floor proved difficult until he did it long enough that he received a notification.

You are proficient in Spirit Walking!
Proficiency Type: Active.
Level: 1.

His next step made a sound of a bare foot on carpet and more easily kept contact with it. He tried stomping and heard the familiar thump that anyone below him might've heard. Maybe this was how ghost stories began. He turned his attention to the ceiling. To his surprise, he rose with little effort. He went through the floor above, following his sense of something supernatural awaiting, but nothing was there. He continued up, remembering to make himself invisible again. He'd gotten lucky just now that no one had been in this room.

When his eyes passed through the ceiling, he saw the wooden rafters, dusty stone blocks, and cobwebs in between floors before his head entered the stone and then into the room above. And he stopped there, peering around in surprise.

The forty-foot square room held only one entrance, a wooden door that stood closed and had two thick beams across it on this side. On either side of it stood burly guards in plate mail, swords at their hips. Their status notifications showed both were level 20 knights. He sensed that each wore magical armor and carried magic swords. On the stone walls beside them were axes, crossbows, and other weapons suitable for close combat, like maces and flails. Most were magical. A half-dozen empty wooden chairs with blue and tan cushions sat against other walls, which tapestries covered, each depicting scenes of royalty in and around Evator.

The clear glass ceiling stood twenty feet high. Max had seen this from above while on florin back, and from the Florin Tower. Each pane appeared to glow with a soft, white light. Moonlight filtered in despite the heavy raindrops splashing and pooling on the panes, acting like a prism to cascade the flickering light down into the room. No other illumination was apparent.

He had to remind himself that, as bright as it all seemed to him despite the stormy sky, his ghostly vision made everything seem lighter. The room was probably much darker than it seemed to him. Much of the grey stone floor lay bare, but a golden rug that reminded Max of a red carpet for its placement filled the entire space between the door and the lone object in the room's center.

Deciding it was safe to ascend all the way, he did so and avoided *Spirit Walking* so that his ghostly feet would make no sound. He drifted toward the source of that supernatural tug he felt, eyeing what appeared to be an empty, rectangular silver frame. About the size of a doorway wide enough for one person to use at a time, it looked like a standing mirror without the glass. Where that reflective surface should've been hung a softly moving, vertical wall of silvery liquid that reminded him of mercury. As he watched the subtle ripples, an image of a similarly guarded room appeared before fading back to the previous liquid-like state. A few seconds later, a different picture materialized, then vanished.

The frame's edges seemed to shimmer to his eyes, as if wisps of smoke curled around them. Two white diamonds in the shape of crescent moons adorned the top. On examining the frame, he saw seven different points on it, at the four corners, in the middle of the top, and the remaining two points two thirds of the way down either side. Each bore a color of the rainbow, which seemed to be a theme of this world's lore. Did these seven points have something to do with the seven spheres of gods, which were also color-coded? When he moved closer, a message appeared.

Warning: As a non-corporeal undead, it is not safe for you to enter a Moon Gate.

"Huh," muttered Max, curious about the name, which seemed to explain the crescent moons on it. He had suspected this was a magic portal and couldn't tell if the thing was actually on or not. He suspected it wasn't. The guards probably would've been more alert. They seemed bored. Did their presence mean something could come through without warning? Or were they here to stop anyone from entering this room and using the Moon Gate? They probably hadn't counted on a ghost coming up through the floor. Too bad he did not know how to use this thing or to where it led, though the images suggested nowhere fancy, just a similar room in what was likely another settlement. Did this only go to places in this kingdom or somewhere else, too?

He focused on the gate to get a notification.

Item: Moon Gates.

Description: Invented by karelia, a Moon Gate is a magic portal that allows someone to instantly travel between two different locations, even if a vast distance separates them. Except in rare instances, each location must have one. The gates are powered by moonlight, which the valenium steel from which they are made absorbs. The gates stand where this absorption can occur.

One of the creators of karelia, Scrylyn is the Goddess of Intuition, a trait that allows one to navigate life. She is therefore the goddess of navigation, and by extension, of the stars and moons. Her priests control access to many gates to ensure accurate travel and control; some gates only send travelers to one predetermined destination while others have several. Rarer gates are designed to go anywhere, while some items, and strong enough magic-users, can force any gate to go where they please. One-way gates exist, where only arrival or departure is possible. Solo gates that do not require a corresponding second gate are rare, as are moveable gates that are not in a fixed position.

Max eyed the ceiling, where moonlight shone through to bathe him and the gate. Was that why the gate's frame seemed to smoke? It was absorbing moonlight? This seemed like an obvious vulnerability one could exploit. The room had to be magically... He nodded. Perhaps that's why the ceiling glowed to his eyes. It was probably supernaturally guarded or strengthened.

Did people know a Moon Gate existed here? Anyone who flew over the castle, or climbed the Florin Tower, could see down into the room, though now that he thought about it, he'd been unable to see this gate when he'd looked. Maybe something hid it, the way a privacy screen on a laptop kept others from prying into what you were doing. He sensed that the area above the castle had been protected and thought it was for the obvious reasons, but inhibiting detection or entry to this room was likely another.

Had the daekais realized during their attack? They almost had to notice it, but had they known beforehand? Had it been a target? He didn't think so. The description didn't suggest the Moon Gate could be moved, unless it was one of the rare transportable ones, and the daekais hadn't come in enough numbers to occupy the castle. It had been a smash and grab.

After rescuing the princess during the daekais fight, Max's tour of the castle had not included this room. He'd have to learn more about this. Getting to Gitarna with Norus during a rescue would presumably be much easier if this Moon Gate went there and Max could learn how to control it. But he doubted it did or that he could anytime soon. The two places were enemies. Surely, more guards than these two would be here if the enemy could just enter the heart of the castle. He was going to need his body back first anyway, according to that warning he'd received.

Curious about the room's defenses, he eyed the guards, who exchanged a look as if sensing his presence. Their breath showed in the cold Max was causing. Was there a way to suppress that? He went past them through the normal door, where he found more beams blocking the room. Max floated down the curving stairs to a landing with more guards at attention, though more casually than those above. He recognized this location from his tour, his rescue of the princess having happened one floor down.

He soon found a magically sealed room he couldn't enter from any direction, and in the bowels of the castle, hidden rooms and a tunnel leading south under the river, it likely emerging in the woods. On sensing karelia, probably from the Karelian Guard, out there, he didn't follow it far. And he felt them sensed him, too. Figuring he should quit before something bad happened, he returned to Evator.

By then, his *Invisibility* skill had risen 2 levels, coming more naturally, faster, and needing less concentration. But it couldn't help against everyone. Floating down a street, he sensed a karelia inside an inn. Somehow, Max felt its attention turn toward him, and the subtle impression of aggression removed any doubt it wasn't Ardyn. He continued north, but he sensed another karelia ahead, this one approaching, so Max veered left through several buildings and into an alley. He held still there, aware that outrunning them was easy when they couldn't go through walls like him. But how far from him could they be and capture him?

He sensed both karelia closing in. Time to leave town. He headed for the western wall, passing through shops, most having living spaces above them. In one, a force suddenly began pulling him backward. Max struggled to turn around as he slid through walls. Around his waist, a tendril of black nothingness had wrapped itself. It drew him toward a dark, rectangular void that reminded him of a black hole, colors swirling around its edges as if everything would be sucked inside. But it wasn't much bigger than a hand. And that's when he noticed a small hand holding it.

Max's eyes darted to a purple glow to one side, the familiar sight of a karelia's lorenia lines brightly glowing on his captor's face. The color had always been green before. Two eyes shone in the dark room. Just before he was disappeared into the blackness, he remembered his *Wail of Terror* skill and screamed. The shriek shattered two crystal goblets and caused shouts outside, and when the unaffected karelia sneered, Max knew the truth.

And then he plummeted into the dark.

CHAPTER TWENTY-SIX

As if he hung in a painfully cold, starless outer space, Max saw nothing but his brightly glowing form and a rectangular window ten feet away. The entrance. Or exit. He'd been sucked through that. He tried to rush toward it, but nothing happened. Then he heard unfamiliar words that sounded karelian.

Suddenly, a force yanked him out into an unfamiliar room. His darting eyes found the figure standing before him, lorenia lines ablaze. In one small hand, it held the rectangular device, edges glowing silver to Max's eyes, like the Moon Gate. A tendril of inky black still encircled his waist. It felt like ice. The other end was attached to the item. Max eyed his abductor.

Name: Kiavalon of Ansini.
Type: NPC.
Class: Spirit Warrior.
Species: Sorelia.
Level 9.

Max groaned at his suspicion's confirmation. A sorelia, a corrupted race of karelia. This one didn't look any different, aside from the purple eyes and lorenia lines. These facial patterns differed on each karelia he'd seen, like a fingerprint, and Kiavalon's resembled outstretched bat wings. The sorelia wore black leather armor.

He pulled up the description of a Spirit Warrior.

Class: Spirit Warrior

Summary: Karelian (or sorelian) Spirit Warriors specialize in combat with non-corporeal undead. They are arguably the hardest class for such undead to fight, and they make great allies when facing souls. Spirit Warriors can undertake this role whether or not their own soul is in their body.

No wonder this guy had trapped him so easily. Max hadn't even sensed him, either, which was odd. Did Kiavalon have some way of suppressing Max's ability to detect him? Did the whole species? If so, that was a serious problem.

"Greetings, Maestro Max," said the sorelia.

Max frowned at the pleasantry. "Kiavalon. Something I can help you with?"

"Yes."

Wondering if the answer would be good news or bad, Max asked, "Can the karelia who were chasing me still sense me here?"

"No. I'm suppressing attempts at descrying our existence."

There was no telling what the karelia would've done with him, so Max wasn't sure if they would've rescued him or sent him to the Orb of Souls. "Is that why I didn't sense you?"

"Yes. Karelia don't take kindly to sorelia and can detect us without effort, so all sorelia learn to suppress the awareness of us, or make others sense us as a karelia instead."

Now Max wanted that skill. It would've kept him out of this trouble, at the least.

As the sorelia sat on a wicker chair, Max glanced around the small room, which had a tiny table, a lone chair, and a large chest that lay open, a few cloth items inside but mostly empty. In one corner lay a rickety bed sized for someone taller, like a human or a kryll. That suggested Kiavalon didn't live here long term. Max eyed the closed door.

"We are not where you captured me."

"Your scream made that unwise."

Max nodded. The karelia had likely descended quickly on that spot. If Kiavalon had taken damage, he might've healed himself by now. Max asked, "Your room at an inn? Is that where we are?"

"For now."

Nodding at the device that held him, Max asked, "What is this thing?"

"Your prison until I free you."

Max focused on the device.

Item: Black Mirror.

Description: Made from Ever Sand, this rare item can ensnare a nearby, disembodied soul.

Bonuses: +3 Necrotic Resistance, +5 Sixth Sense.

Max noticed the message didn't say how long he'd be captured. Asking a sorelia was unlikely to cause an honest answer. That he might need to do something before being allowed to escape seemed obvious. Mandatory quests were common in some games, especially in starter areas, where he figured he still was. Killing the sorelia was the clear move, but as a level 1 ghost, he likely would not succeed.

Max asked, "What do you want?"

The sorelia replied, "In a moment. First, I want to know why you're still here and not the afterlife."

Wondering if any harm would come from the truth, Max replied, "I'm not ready to die, but I can't find my body so I can live again."

With a smirk, Kiavalon asked, "How are you going to find it?"

Max shrugged. "Haunt the people who moved it and hope they reveal it."

"That is unlikely to work. I have a better way, but there is a price to pay."

Max sighed. He knew his approach was lame and had felt stupid admitting the plan, so maybe this was a blessing in disguise. He asked, "What is it?"

"A quest."

"Even more surprising," Max drawled. But a completed quest could help him level up as a ghost. "What do I have to do?"

"Journey to Sorrairyn, the City of the Gods, to rescue someone from Everett, the Lord of the Undead, and return her to me."

Max snorted. That was over-the-top. Maybe it was simpler than it sounded? But this Everett was a god, one who was technically Max's new master as an undead. There had to be a catch. He asked, "Why don't you do it yourself?"

"He would expect me to come."

Max rolled his eyes at himself. *The real answer is that I'm in a game and am supposed to do these things. Stupid question.*

He used his still functioning *World Lore* skill to pull up info on Everett.

Deity: Everett. God of fear, death, loss, darkness, cowardice.

Titles: Lord of the Undead, Undead King, the Shrouded One.

Patronage: Patron of the Undead.

Symbol: Tombstone.

Sphere: Orange. Co-creator of daekais and E'kainum afterlife.

Alignment: Nefarious.

Season/Element: Winter/Water.

Power Day: Orange Day, Water Week.

Court of Gods Month: 10.

Unique: If Everett puts his mark on someone's soul, they become undead once they die.

Max asked, "Who am I rescuing? What does Everett have them and what are they to you?"

"She is my beloved. She was to perform a service for Everett and failed to do so, so he keeps her imprisoned in his neighborhood."

Max hadn't expected the word. "Neighborhood? Sounds a little chummy."

Kiavalon looked at him flatly. "Sorrairyn is divided into seven districts, one for each of the Seven Spheres of gods. They are color-coded like the spheres. Everett, being in the Orange Sphere, is in the Orange District. Within each district are four neighborhoods, one for each god in that sphere. It is in Everett's neighborhood that you will find my beloved."

"Am I supposed to search this entire neighborhood?"

"No. She is a special prisoner in his castle. He makes an example of her, displaying her before those who approach his throne."

Max had a sudden image of a bunch of undead dressed in finery befitting a medieval court. What was he going to find? This quest didn't sound easy. "So what am I supposed to do? Just walk in there and ask for her?"

The sorelia shrugged. "You will bargain with Everett. How you do so, and what you offer, is your decision. All that matters to me is that you free her so that she may return to Llurien."

Max liked a game that left some choices up to him, but some guidance would've been helpful. Still, he had an idea. That Lyre of Murryn could control undead. Maybe he could use it to get to Everett, and then trade that for this sorelia, not that he wanted to part with it. But getting his game body back was more important.

"If I do this quest, you will let me go?"

A look of surprise disappeared as quickly as it came. "I will release you from the Black Mirror. I will tell you how to find your body. And I will gift you something for your service."

"What's stopping me from just disappearing once you send me on this quest?"

Kiavalon's eyes hardened as he rose. "The Black Mirror binds you to it until I release you. I can summon you from anywhere with this, now that it possesses you. Should you attempt to flee, I will send you back into it to suffer for eternity, if I choose."

Normally hard to intimidate, Max felt a chill come over him. "That sounds lovely."

"Do you accept this quest?"

"Do I have a choice?"

The sorelia held up the mirror as another option. "Yes."

New Quest: Rescue Kiavalon's Beloved from Everett.

Objective: The God of Fear, Everett, has captured Kiavalon's beloved for her refusal to perform the service she

promised. Journey to Sorrairyn to bargain with Everett for her freedom, so that she may return to Kiavalon's side on Llurien. You must secure her release to succeed.

Difficulty: High.

Rewards: 1 Rare Item. 1 Uncommon Song. 5,000 XP.

Accept?

Max cocked an eyebrow at the XP, which his ghost class would get. It was enough to raise him a level. That might help him deal with the Dark Trio. He eyed the Life Counter, wondering how long this was going to take. He probably needed to be back in his body by the time it ended if he wanted to wake up.

"So, how do I get to Sorrairyn to do this quest?" he asked.

The sorelia flashed an insincere smile. "Possess someone and force their body through the Moon Gate."

Chapter Twenty-Seven

Still floating before the sorelia in his ghostly form, Max feigned ignorance. "There's a Moon Gate that goes to this City of the Gods in Evator?"

The sorelia laughed condescendingly and sat, then settled back in his chair. "Certainly not. Most gates go to fixed locations. Some can be forced to go wherever someone wants with a spell. Neither of us are that powerful. But I have a Moon Pass. It will redirect a gate once. I acquired it at great cost. You will use this. But you will still need a Priest of Scrylyn."

Max remembered who Scrylyn was, but his *World Lore* skill popped up a reminder that she was the goddess of intuition, her priests controlling the gates. "So I'm to take this Moon Pass, possess one of these priests, and make them open the gate? And I change the destination and go through?"

"Correct. You will not need it to return. The gate keeper in Sorrairyn will set the destination to Castle Evator on your behalf."

Max couldn't argue that. "Why do I need to possess a priest to do this?"

"While a spirit can enter a Moon Gate, it is unlikely to come out the gate on the other side."

Max cocked an eyebrow. "What happens to it?"

The sorelia shrugged. "Torn apart. Lost. No one is really sure despite some theories. It isn't relevant to you because you won't be dumb enough to try it as a ghost. Moon Gates act on a physical body, so you'll need one. It's that simple. Many gates are also warded to prevent spirits from entering, but there's no safeguard against a possessed person. And you need a body to control one."

"And a Priest of Scrylyn can do that and get close without suspicion. I assume some are in town."

"Of course. However, there is a problem. Most people cannot control a Moon Gate until they're stronger. A Priest of Scrylyn can do so earlier. As a new ghost, you're too weak to possess such a priest. Even if you succeed, you may struggle to control them. And you are limited to possessing someone for thirty minutes per skill level."

Max muttered, "Well, that's great. How do I.... Oh, I get it. I need to get stronger."

"Yes. Your innate abilities provide you with easy ways to kill people."

Max scoffed at his blithe indifference to life. "You really are different from karelia."

"Thank you."

"It wasn't a compliment."

The sorelia smiled, apparently not insulted. "Come to me when you are ready to possess someone. I suggest staying away from karelia."

Easier said than done, Max thought.

The possession time limit meant struggling to reach the Moon Gate before it expired, and there was almost certainly no way he'd return to Llurien before that. That meant needing to possess someone in Sorrairyn to come back. Would he be able to get the same priest, who might return to Llurien before Max could? If that happened and Max possessed someone else, would the gate keeper Kiavalon mentioned do what the sorelia claimed—know to send Max back to Evator? And how many people of low enough level could there be in the City of the Gods for him to possess? It sounded like somewhere high-level players were far more likely to frequent.

Now he wanted to decline the quest. It was getting too complicated, though it seemed like he didn't have a choice, if that Black Mirror had control over him. And the idea of just waiting around for the Dark Trio to reappear and hopefully comment on his body's location was so passive and lame. He'd heard it said that hope is not a plan. He had too much to risk to just sit around waiting. Then he thought of something.

"Would the person I'm to rescue let me possess her to return?"

Kiavalon's brief look of surprise did little to reassure Max. "Certainly. A brief sacrifice to make for her savior." He smirked.

And Max felt suspicious. Maybe he could level up as a ghost and keep the priest. Two hours might do it. That meant reaching level four. He eyed his time remaining.

Life Counter: 4 Days, 3 Hours, 14 Minutes.

Time to get on with it.

Kiavalon said he was letting Max venture out to gain levels and do the quest. Max left by floating through a wall, the karelia pursuing earlier long gone. The sun was nearly rising, the black sky lightening to the east. While Max felt no physical need for sleep, his mind wanted rest, a luxury he didn't have. An idea for leveling without killing had him in an alley, where he spent a half hour manipulating doorknobs, picking things up, and carrying them. Sometimes he accidentally dropped items like a stone, bucket, or piece of wood, the audible clatter causing someone to peek out or yell for quiet. Was this how ghost stories spread? Max's *Moving Objects* skill rose 2 levels.

Mindful of karelia and still invisible, he swept through town and the castle courtyard, noting guards. Tomorrow, he was supposed to be one. Had anyone noticed his absence? Kari would be all over him for not showing up as expected. Into the keep he soared, seeing only a few servants up this early. He plunged through the floor's masonry to erupt into the guardroom, where two guards stopped their idle chatter and looked around, their breath visible in the suddenly cold air.

Max moved toward the nearest unlocked cell and, on the second try, swung the door until it creaked eerily. He began experimenting with how awful a sound he could cause. Unsure if they would hear him, he spoke menacing words and then noticed a small stool he violently kicked into the wall with a loud clatter. The concerned and fearful voices of the guards meant it was time for the finale.

Max raced down the corridor at them, making his head and outstretched, grasping hands glow brightly. His long hair flowed around him, his mouth agape in a silent scream. As he reached them, the men recoiled, one leaning toward the exit, but Max grabbed them by their throats. A red -13 HP floated up from one, Max's *Necrotic Touch* skill blackening the skin. But a burst of pain in his other hand made him curse and jump back, a -12 SHP floating away from himself. That guard took almost no damage.

Warning! You have touched someone protected by a god's blessing. Doing so will inflict damage on you.

Damn it!

Max screamed his anger and the guards bolted up the stairs, leaving the black iron keys as he'd hoped. So they could definitely hear him. What had he sounded like? They could definitely hear him. He grabbed the keys and used his *Appear Alive* skill to look like himself, then moved to Evanel's cell. Next to that was another prisoner, who roused along with the niquerra. On the second try, Max slid the key into Evanel's cell door, turned it, and shoved the door open.

The niquerra sat up, his hair matted, which Max's night vision helped him notice. No torches or lanterns burned. "I thought you had forgotten."

Unable to talk with him, Max shook his head, held up one finger to his lips for silence, and pointed toward freedom.

"Did you bring the querra clothes?" Evanel asked, rising.

Max shook his head again. Without access to his physical inventory, the items languished out of reach. He waved for the niquerra to get moving.

Evanel came toward him. "No matter. This deed will not be forgotten, Maestro Max. My jailers have niquerran-made, kryllan hand bracers they stole from me. They are yours."

Then Evanel race down the hall, his feet quieter than expected. With that kind of stealth, he might escape town. He thought the niquerra would need to get farther because the notification he received moments later.

Quest Complete: Free Evanel Soulcutter from Castle Evator. You earned 1,000 XP! You earned +1 Reputation among niquerra!

You received niquerran-forged kryllan hand bracers!

He immediately received another note.

Notice: You have completed a quest while dead and in non-corporeal form. You cannot accept one reward, a physical object. It has been placed into your inventory and will be available should you regain life.

He breathed a sigh of relief. For a second, he was about to get mad he'd cost himself an item by finishing the quest as undead. His calm didn't last.

Warning: Your actions have alerted nearby karelia (and sorelia) to your presence.

"Time to go," he said to himself. Then another notice appeared.

You achieved Level 2!
You gained 9 Spectral Hit Points!
You gained 2 Spectral Mana Points!
Class bonus: You gained Dexterity +1, Agility +1, Constitution +1.
You gained (2) proficiency points.
You have (5) unassigned proficiency points.

Max didn't waste time appreciating it now. He let out the other prisoner, who would hopefully cause a distraction for any reinforcements heading this way. Max hurried to reach Norus, who was standing near the cell door.

"Max, it's you." A look of concern appeared on the hunter's unshaven, bruised face. "What? Are you dead, my friend?"

Nodding, Max handed the keys to the hunter, who let himself out. Then Max raced ahead through stone and wood as Norus followed to and up the stairs. At the top, they saw that the other prisoner fought with two guards near the keep's main doors. Max headed further into the castle with Norus trailing along.

"You know where you're going?" the hunter whispered.

Max nodded as Norus grabbed a long sword from a decorative suit of armor on a stand. Max hadn't thought of that, or where to get the hunter's belongings from, but it was too late. They descended a wide stairway to a dim chamber, then through a warren of dark, damp halls and descending passages deep under the castle. No one was down here, the soft glow of Max the only light. More than once, he bypassed a locked door by floating through it and turning the latch from the other side. Their depth held an advantage he could use soon—no one would hear his *Wail of Terror*.

He motioned for quiet. At the end of a hall, a flickering, golden light illuminated a small room. Max indicated Norus should plug his ears before making himself invisible. Max slipped into the rectangular room. Two guards in plate mail stood to the right beside a barred door, daggers and short swords at their hips for fighting in tight quarters. Max knew the door led to the tunnel that passed under the castle walls, the river, and out into the forest south of town. Whether the tunnel's other end was guarded would be for Norus to deal with. Max needed stay away from the karelia there.

To one side, a golden bell disappeared into the stone ceiling. At the first sign of trouble, the guards pulled it, reinforcements pouring down. He needed speed. The two men were already exchanging a confused look, their breath white. Max shot past them, then willed himself visible. The guards hesitated in surprise, so Max emitted *Wail of Terror* and both men's health bars appeared halfway down, the shriek stunning them.

When the sound stopped, Norus charged them from the other side, his sword stabbing into one man's neck. The ghastly wound dropped the guard to his knees. Max grabbed the other guard by the hand, inflicting *Necrotic Touch*. Norus slashed at the other fast enough to keep him from drawing a weapon, killing him. Max finished off the other with another grip. It was over quick.

You achieved Level 3!

You gained 15 Spectral Hit Points!

You gained 6 Spectral Mana Points!

Class bonus: You gained Dexterity +1, Agility +1, Constitution +1.

You gained (2) proficiency points.

You have (7) unassigned proficiency points.

Max sighed in relief. Leveling was going faster than he had expected, but he still needed to reach level 4, at least.

"Think anyone heard that?" Norus asked, looking at the bell pull hole.

Hope not, thought Max, eyeing the door. *Doesn't matter, though.*

Hefting a key from one man, Norus unlocked the door, which swung into the dark tunnel. The hunter spoke a word and an orb of light appear floating in the air. He sent it ahead twenty feet before turning back to Max.

"I'd clasp your arm, but... I hope you regain your life. You have a friend in me and Gitarna, should you make it there. It is southwest, but the Karelian Guard is in these woods. Find your flesh and come to me. We will celebrate."

Max nodded, wishing he could say something. Norus had saved him from imprisonment, and now Max had freed him. The debt was paid. Norus closed the door and stepped into the tunnel.

Quest Complete: Free Norus Shadowmoon from the forces of Castle Evator.
You earned 1,500 XP!
You earned +1 Reputation in Karendi Kingdom (Gitarna)!
You received a Kriserian Amulet!

Max received a notification about the item going into his inventory until he had a body, as if he needed more incentives.

While he felt safe here, he fled through earth and stone in case reinforcements included karelia. He found an unexpected cave he briefly explored, but it appeared undiscovered and inaccessible by anything larger than a hand. It might be a good place to hide something. He soon passed beyond the castle to the east before rising to the surface into the sparse woods. He sensed no one around and pulled up his stats.

Name: Maestro Max.
Species/Race: Human.
Class: Ghost, Level 3.
Reputation: 0—Unknown.
XP: 2745.
SHP: 69/69.
SMP: 14/14.
Strength: 4.
Dexterity: 11.

Agility: 9.
Constitution: 7.
Intelligence: 5.
Wisdom: 6.
Charisma: 12.
Morale: 8.

The lyre had really helped his dexterity and charisma. But his reputation as unknown surprised him. It suggested he hadn't been identified as the ghost lurking in town. He worried what would happen if he did awful things and regained his body. Would he be identified, even captured and held accountable? The question had special importance right now because Max knew he needed at least one more level, and there was only one way left to gain it.

The time had come to kill other players.

Chapter Twenty-Eight

An invisible Max floated above the grassy ground a hundred yards outside Evator's west gate, the sun overheard on his fourth day in Llurien Online. He wasn't sure what day of the week it was in the real world. Had people been at work all day? Did that explain the limited players here until now? He'd been waiting for hours, the logout button still as grey and unyielding as a block of stone, the timer dropping.

Life Counter: 3 Days, 16 Hours, 24 Minutes.

His thoughts had drifted to what his distant parents likely thought of this. Would they give him an uncomfortable hug if he awoke? Was avoiding that the unconscious reason he couldn't logout? He'd chuckled for the hint of truth in it, but that made him try to lose the resentment he'd often felt toward them. It wasn't that they didn't care. They were just self-absorbed and preoccupied, but he supposed that had ended. Yes, they would hug him. And then once he was okay, maybe in another few days, they'd go back to ignoring him. He sighed, trying to let it go, but only because it might be the reason that damn button couldn't be clicked. Did he need to be more sincere? Probably.

He felt ambivalent about the murder and mayhem he was about to do. People assuming he was a jerk had landed him in here, and now he was going to make it a kind of self-fulfilling prophecy. Maybe they had it coming. The Dark Trio did, but probably not these players. But it was just a game in the end. And yet for him, it was his actual life on the line.

Yeah. Fuck 'em, he thought, trying to talk himself into it.

Max surveyed the field. The sounds of men and women exerting themselves filled the air as players trained with NPCs and each other. Swords clanged, bow strings thrummed, and maces struck wooden shields with an audible thwack. The next sound joining them would be a lot of screaming. The town sat behind them. So peaceful. Unaware of the impending massacre by an unseen force—Maestro Max, Death Singer, though what he was going to do was more of a scream.

Two karelian players had been practicing their sword fighting but finally left, neither detecting him. Maybe they weren't skilled enough or paying sufficient attention. Or Max had kept far enough away. He still wasn't sure how that worked. He needed to ask Siren to look into things for him.

Leery of priests, who could potentially detect or repel him, Max guessed that the mace-wielding players in the training area's center might be that class. The cliché of robed wizards and priests wasn't true in Llurien Online. He intended to start on one side with the archers, who might be delayed switching weapons. He pulled the creepy-looking Lyre of Murryn from inventory into his ghostly hands. He'd spent the morning experimenting with it far out of hearing range.

Here goes.

Max soared across the mostly flat earth toward the middle of the archers. Some spells had a radius of up to 25 feet, and he wanted as many affected as possible. On the way, he got a little too close to a staff-swinging human so that the weapon passed right through him. Since he took no damage, it must not have been magical, which didn't surprise him in a starter area.

He stopped amid people. With the lyre, Max plucked the undead-moragul gut strings. Soaring into the morning air came a dissonant melody that would've made Metallica proud for its creepy diminished fifth and flattened second scale steps.

"Do you hear music?" a level 2, querran druid asked, his eyes scanning the area.

"Yeah," answered the level 3 human fighter beside him. He let fly with an arrow that missed a square archery target. Max got the impression they were friends. "Sounds like death metal. Kinda my thing."

Max smiled. *Yes, death metal. Totally.*

"Liking it is not the point," replied the querra. "There has to be a reason it's play—"

Two skeletal hands erupted from the ground between them, one holding a sword. A skull followed as a skeleton climbed from the earth. Ten feet away, another hand shot into the sky, sending dirt and grass flying. But this hand had withered flesh. A matching hand appeared, then the head of rotting flesh and straggly long, grey hair. All-white eyes glared around as the zombie hoisted itself to the surface. Max had hoped for more than two, and both were only level 1, but it was a start. The spell cost him 5 SMP, leaving him with 9. And it came with a side-effect—everyone within its radius was stunned and lost a turn. As a result, the next move was still his.

For several seconds, Max emitted his innate *Wail of Terror* as loud as he could. The ear-splitting sound visibly startled every player in sight, including those at the far end. Some nearest him fell to the ground. Others crouched and held their ears. One vomited. A few staggered away in fear. Of the four-dozen people nearest, only fourteen were unaffected. The health bar of everyone else appeared, halfway down. The next notification muted Max's satisfaction.

Warning: Your actions have alerted nearby karelia (and sorelia) to your presence.

"No surprise," Max muttered. And then he saw several eyes turn to him in horror. "So much for being invisible."

The zombie turned to the human fighter with the bow and slammed both arms into his head, dealing 4 HP of necrotic damage and dropping him to 13 HP. The skeleton advanced and slashed with his sword on the same guy, dealing another 5 HP. Max wondered if that was a coincidence or if his hope that they should work together guided their attacks. The fighter dropped the bow, his sword quickly out and slicing across the zombie's chest, from where a shriveled and dried up heart fell out. The zombie's health fell to 17 HP.

A level 3 kryllan hunter smashed through several ribs of the skeleton with a jhaikan staff, bones flying, and dropped it to 8 HP. Max's minions would not last long, but he had another spell ready.

So did the querran druid, who held up one tiny hand, palm outward toward the zombie and skeleton, while he clutched a medallion with the other. He spoke a few words and a white glow lit his hand, but nothing else happened, and he frowned. Max wondered if he'd just tried to turn the undead and failed.

Max strummed the Lyre of Murryn and focused on draining the life from everyone near. The gasps of pain and so many "-1

HP" indications floating up showed it worked. Even as he put the lyre away, the spell continuing, all affected players dropped another 1 HP. If they didn't get away, they'd all be dead soon.

Several people swung at him, including the sword of a kryll, whose class was defender, in leather armor. The weapons passed through him without effect. So did several arrows and a throwing knife.

Idiots. Don't they know they need magic weapons to hurt me?

"Get magic weapons!" someone yelled before running away.

The kryllan hunter slammed the jhaikan staff into the zombie's stomach and dropped it to 12 HP, while the human fighter severed one of the skeleton's arms, the one without the sword, bringing it to 3 HP. But this was too late to save himself. Both zombie and skeleton struck the human fighter, who fell dead.

Your minion(s) has killed (1) Human Fighter, Level 3!
You gained 250 XP, half of the total!

Max grunted in relief. He'd been wondering how much XP he'd get. He wasn't prompted to loot the body. Was it because he was a ghost, because his minions had done it, or because he couldn't loot players?

Warning: You have killed another player as the aggressor. Continued actions of this nature may affect your reputation and gameplay.

Huh. Fair enough.

The Dark Trio had probably gotten a similar message for killing him. Or hiding his body. He'd have to see about tricking them into attacking him once he was alive again, so he didn't damage his standing more than necessary by striking first.

The querran druid had done little and quaffed a potion so to raise his 5 HP to 10. Max knew the guy was doomed and felt no remorse. The kryllan hunter charged him and swung the jhaikan staff, which passed right through Max's chest as if missing him, but he felt a searing pain as a -10 HP floated away. Max grasped him by the biceps and watched in satisfaction as a -20 HP of necrotic damage killed the player, who had already lost HP from the lyre's ongoing *Life Drain* spell.

You have killed (1) Kryllan Hunter, Level 3!
You gained 1500 XP!

The amount of XP surprised Max, but he'd gotten the impression that kryll were considered harder to kill. Maybe they were worth more. He received another notification, that he'd risen to level 4. He'd finish what he started, but the moment this attack went bad, he was leaving.

The skeleton raked the querran druid across the neck, dropping him to 5 HP, and the zombie leaped upon the screaming man to tear out the throat, finishing him. Yelling in anger, the human fighter swung his sword into the skeleton, which blew into pieces as it died. Only the zombie remained, but it and the kryllan defender traded blows until the undead perished. Max floated up behind the defender, who turned too late as Max grabbed his arm and killed him.

His satisfaction ended in a burst of pain as fire engulfed him from behind. He soared away, glancing at a notification that his fire resistance had reduced the damage by 50%. The human wizard behind it who stood near with both hands raised, but

Max saw three karelia sprint through the gate to Evator. He briefly weighed his options.

Damn it.

CHAPTER TWENTY-NINE

Time to go, Max thought.

He almost fled toward the distant trees as planned, but the wizard might get him with a range attack, so he raced to and plunged through the town wall as missiles struck nearby. Into buildings, objects, and people Max hurtled, his sixth sense alerting him to various karelia, none straight ahead. Ensuring he was invisible again, he kept going eve after passing out the eastern wall and into the woods.

Once far enough, he stopped and pulled up notifications. The most important was the level increase.

You achieved Level 4!

You gained 21 Spectral Hit Points!

You gained 6 Spectral Mana Points!

Class bonus: You gained Dexterity +1, Agility +1, Constitution +1.

You gained (2) proficiency points.

You have (9) unassigned proficiency points.

He felt rich in points but held off on assigning them. Instead, he looked up what effect the stats had on him as a ghost. A proficiency could compensate for them. The constitution boost improved his resistance to magical attacks, the agility made him faster, and the dexterity improved his ability to manipulate objects.

Both his Invisibility and *Appear Alive* skills had risen to 2. Usage could improve those, but he wasn't sure that was true the ones he'd begun with: *Possession, Possession Speak, Necrotic Touch, Wail of Terror*, and *Horrifying Visage*. The first was about to be crucial, so he poured 5 points into it to reach level 6. He added 2 for *Necrotic Touch* and 1 for *Wail of Terror*. He belatedly realized he should've done that before the attack. He had to play smarter.

On checking his reputation, he saw it now said "1—Suspected (Andra)." Normally, a charisma bonus came from reputation gains and made it easier to charm people. Would this ghostly reputation make it simpler to scare them? What effect would that have?

Laying low seemed wise now. He'd undoubtedly riled the karelia, making this a poor time to possess the Priest of Scrylyn he'd identified as a good target earlier. The guys he'd killed would be leaving the cemetery soon and might tell….

"Shit," Max cursed.

He hurtled toward the graveyard north of him, probably too late. He reached the southern fence and looked in vain for the players. Charging down the road toward Arydn, he came upon the last of them, the kryllan defender's glowing white form floating over the road. The player hadn't adjusted his appearance. The ghost whirled toward him, eyes widening in recognition.

"Stay away from me!" the player screamed.

Surprised he could understand the guy, Max stopped advancing. "Wait. Can you hear me?"

The ghost scowled. "Yeah, I can hear you, prick. You fucking killed me!"

"Yeah, sorry about that. Had to."

"Bullshit. You're a dick, man. I'm gonna find you and fuck you up."

Max felt a jolt of anger. "I wouldn't make threats right now if I were you." He pulled out the Lyre of Murryn and the kryll bolted, screaming for help.

Max frowned. "Crap. I need to get out of here. The karelia are a pain in the ass." He rushed back the way he'd come. Using the lyre and *Song of Gathering* to make them not tell Ardyn who'd done this to them had been a good idea.

Before attacking them, he'd scoped out the Shrine of Scrylyn on the town's east side and chosen a priest to possess, following the guy home. The target hadn't looked around suspiciously as if sensing Max, like some of the others, suggesting he was a better choice. And Max hadn't been surprised that crossing the shrine's threshold had done spectral damage to him.

With nothing else left to do before possessing the priest, Max went to Kiavalon and got the Moon Pass. The sorelia had heard about his exploits and knew Max was serious about the quest. He seemed amused, which made Max realized how much he disliked the guy.

The pass looked like a small smartphone and weighed about half the size of one. It had an etched, silver edge and shiny black surface. Kiavalon indicated it was already loaded with the spell that would take him to Sorrairyn instead of where the gate was opened to. He wouldn't need to do anything but have it in his hand. He slipped it into his inventory, where a note next to it showed it belonged to Kiavalon and was on loan. He wondered what would happen once it was spent. Remain his? Could it be recharged, or whatever it was called when spent magic items were loaded again?

Now Max waited near a priest's two-story wooden home, the first floor a pastry shop. That might've explained the guy's portliness. Like many buildings, each was right up against neighboring ones. He could only tell they were separate structures from paint changes, subtle differences in height, or being a foot or two closer or farther from the street than the adjacent building.

Twenty minutes passed before the balding priest, Kella Morningdew of Evator, approached in a dark green tunic with brown hems and matching leggings tucked into doeskin boots. Embroidered stars and moons in silver thread graced the breast, while a depiction of a Moon Gate lay over the heart. This was fancier than other clergy, maybe because Moon Gate controlling priests were the first people some visitors to Evator saw. On his neck lay a mark of an open green eye with a heart-shaped pupil.

Unfortunately, a cleric of Scrylyn walked beside Kella. Max wanted Kella indoors, alone, and out of sight. He moved closer and saw a prompt above the cleric's head, as he was closer.

Possess? Yes or No.

Max had been wondering how to do this and muttered, "Guess that answers that question."

With one hand on the door handle, Kella turned toward the cleric. "Did you say something?"

"I was going to ask you that," replied the cleric, looking around.

"It's chilly here. Let's go inside."

Max thought, *Huh. So the living can hear me at least a little. I've been wondering. I wonder what I sounded like. Have to watch that.*

As the men entered and closed the door, Max checked his sense for karelia or nearby magic. Nothing. He slipped inside the house through a wall and observed Kella handing the cleric a scroll before the visitor left alone.

Max had learned the three major roles in Llurien religions. Healers did adventuring and offensive spells, but mostly they prayed to a god and acted as a vessel of that god's divine power to heal someone. A cleric did clerical duties and seldom traveled. Both were technically priests, but that word usually meant those leading a church, giving sermons, and offering advice. All three could channel a god's power. But Max needed a specific type of priest, one able to control a Moon Gate. As he watched, Kella reached into a cupboard. Max revisited the guy's info.

Name: Kella Morningdew of Evator.
Type: NPC.
Class: Priest of Scrylyn.
Species: Human.
Level 5.

Kella shivered, his breath appearing.
Shit. His guard is about to go up.

Max approached and received the prompt, which he accepted. And an invisible force yanked him into Kella.

Sensations bombarded Max. The tunic fabric his belly strained against. The cold air he'd caused atop Kella's bald head. The weight on his feet inside the boots. His eyes seemed unfocused so that he blinked. He held up two pudgy hands and curled the fingers. His mortal ears heard fewer sounds. Was this guy a little hard of hearing or… no, Max's enhanced ghostly hearing had ended. And his sixth sense felt muted.

And he felt fear. But it wasn't his. Kella struggled against his control. Max saw the hands drop, but he hadn't done that. The body stepped toward the door. Max resisted, exerting his will, and they stopped. They teetered. Then a surge of determination filled Max. He *needed* this to work. He forced the body into a chair, which it did so heavily with a whimper.

Calm down, Max thought about the guy, feeling guilty.

"Who said that?" Kella asked through his mouth. "What do you want?"

That startled Max. He hadn't expected the guy to hear his thoughts. If they could communicate silently, no one would think Kella was insane, talking to himself.

Don't speak, he mentally commanded, hoping this would work. *Just think what you want to say.*

After a pause, Kella thought at him, *Please don't hurt me.*

Max cringed, then hardened his heart. *I'm not going to. I'm sorry about this, but I need to borrow you. If you understood, you might even want to help me.*

I can't imagine what would make you think that, replied Kella.

We need to do something to get my body back. Once done, I will release you. I do not intend to harm you.

You will forgive me if I do not trust you.

Max couldn't blame him. *Would it help if I told you?*

After a long pause, the priest said yes. And so Max explained being murdered, his body hidden, and a sorelia capturing him and promising that, as a reward for doing this quest, he'd get Max his body back. He didn't admit to where they were going.

You should not trust a sorelia, thought Kella.

I don't, but it's my best option.

There was probably another way, though I don't know what it is.

That makes two of us.

After a few minutes of reassurances, he sensed Kella relinquish control, to his relief. Was it always going to take that long? There might come a time when he'd need this to happen faster.

Warning: you have possessed a character. You can maintain control of this body for 30 minutes per your level as a non-corporeal undead. The host's ability to expel you can increase under certain circumstances, such as you putting them in grave danger, their HP becoming dangerously low, or them receiving help to expel you. If you enter a magic void, you will automatically be expelled unless you are stronger than the victim.

You have full access to this person's physical abilities. Their strength, agility, dexterity, and constitution scores are now yours. However, each has been impacted by your own numbers and your level in relation to theirs. Some of your heightened senses are no longer augmented and will remain muted until you leave this body.

You can make your victim perform spells they know, but you do not. You can also perform some of your own abilities.

You have full access to their inventory. You may not transfer items from theirs to yours and vice versa.

Max absorbed that. At least the sorelia hadn't lied to him about the duration issue. Curious what his stat sheet looked like, he pulled it up.

Name: Kella Morningdew of Evator (Possessed by Maestro Max)

Class: Priest of Scrylyn, Level 5

Reputation: 4—Good Standing
HP: 81/81
MP: 27/27
Strength: 6
Dexterity: 9
Agility: 8
Constitution: 7
Intelligence: 6
Wisdom: 11
Charisma: 11
Morale: 11

Nothing stood out except the reputation, which might take a hit from Max's activities, but maybe Kella could prove someone had possessed him for an unauthorized Moon Gate destination. The priest felt calm. Was he biding his time to expel Max? Only now did Max realize he had taken no damage from possessing Kella. Curious about the priest's inventory, he saw random coins, a pack of valend cards, and herbs. The robe was enchanted for a charisma boost, but the real find was a Mace of Truth +3, which caused mental clarity of several minutes for someone struck with it. The damage and strength bonuses were more helpful, but he imagined that if someone was full of shit, and that led an altercation, striking them with this might be entertaining.

Kella's spells were at his level when alive, but his were inaccessible unless Kella had them, too, and the priest had new options. These included *Cast Away* to teleport something away, and *Corrode* to ruin a metal weapon. Kella's *Stun* could replace his missing *Disarm* spell. *Raise Undead* surprised him at first, but evil priests existed. Kella only had few materials needed to cast spells, potentially limiting them.

Feeling ready, Max made the priest rise and walk toward the door. The control came more naturally as they passed through town to the grounds of Castle Evator, a few people greeting Kella along the way. When Max spoke, Kella's voice emerged. They soon ascended the stairs to the Moon Gate room.

Kella asked, *This is why you wanted me?*

Yes. We're going through the gate.

Will I ever return?

Of course. My body is here somewhere in or near Evator and the whole point is to get it back.

After a pause, the priest admitted, *I probably shouldn't tell you this, but while I control the gate for others, I do not pass through. You will arouse suspicion once you do.*

Max hadn't thought of that. Was Kella was telling him that to discourage him? *It won't matter because the gate will close and we'll be where they cannot follow.*

How can you be certain? They could come right behind unless I close it. And it is likely you will be apprehended on the other side.

You will see. Max felt Kella's frustration. Possessing the body made it harder for the priest to suppress feelings that Max would not detect. This was an advantage he hadn't expected.

Will I be in danger? Kella asked.

Max hesitated, not wanting to inspire a struggle for control by admitting the truth. Could Kella sense deceit? He thought, *I cannot be sure. I hope not. I do not intend to put either of us in danger.*

The priest didn't respond and Max suppressed him into silence as they reached the wide landing outside the Moon Gate room. The wooden door had been carved with scenes of a road traveling past a lake, forest, and between mountains. Beside it stood two level 15 knights in plate armor, swords and daggers at their hips.

"Greetings, Kella," one knight said, his face friendly. "You were not expected."

"Greetings," Max made Kella say, trying to speak like him. "It is a pleasant surprise, is it not? If you may be so kind," he added, gesturing at the exit.

The guards lifted the heavy beams off and called through the door for the same to occur there. Max heard the beams being moved. This was not a place to storm. Subterfuge was the way. The door creaked open, and he nodded thanks before going through, passing the even higher level knights inside. The room hadn't changed except for the sunlight. Behind him, the door shut, the beams going back in place with a scrape and thud. Ahead, the silver-framed Moon Gate gleamed in the sunlight, the edge not shimmering like before. An image of a destination sometimes briefly replaced the swirling, mercury-like sheet of liquid on its surface.

Max thought to Kella, *I need you to turn on the gate. I can force you to, but I'd rather you cooperate.*

I'll have to speak.

Don't try anything, like alerting the guards.

I will also need control of my hands.

One or both?

Just one.

Max relinquished his hold on the hands and Kella reached into his pocket. This felt weird to Max, like he'd lost command of his own limb. Never mind that it belonged to the priest. The fingers closed around a smooth, dime-sized metal and pulled it out. Max saw a silver piece, which Kella placed against the frame it matched. The priest held it there while speaking magic words. Max felt the energy gather inside the body.

"To vistas far, you lead the way. Bring us safely on this day."

A swelling energy preceded a tingle in the fingers touching the Moon Gate. Light filled colored gems at the doorway's four corners, along the sides, and at the top in the center. The two crescent shaped diamonds on either side of that also lit. As they brightened, the viscous silver liquid flowed into a flat, vertical sheet. An image of a similar room to this one appeared, guards snapping to attention, hands going to their swords.

Where does this lead? Max asked Kella.

The capital, Andra.

Max resumed control of the priest and retrieved the Moon Pass from inventory. Its surface had changed to resemble the Moon Gate's, except it showed an open square with stone buildings in the distance, forests and snow-capped mountains far away. The area just beyond the gate appeared clear of life, but he worried what might await them. Hoping for the best, he stepped through, a rainbow of colors flashing by.

CHAPTER THIRTY

Eric shielded himself and the unconscious Anna from the .

"Welcome to Sorrairyn, city of the gods," said a deep, soothing voice. "I am Kiseron Springhew, Keeper of the Gate. To where are you headed?"

Max blinked in confusion, trying to get his bearings. He hadn't expected to be addressed so soon and felt relief that the words were not the equivalent of "Roll initiative!" in AD&D, the infamous sign a battle was to begin.

He turned to see a handsome, dignified, middle-aged man with raven hair and calm black eyes regarding him. At nearly a foot taller than Max, well-built, and with a strong brow that made his gaze intense, he would've been intimidating were it not for the smile. His face looked human, with a square jaw, but he also reminded Max of kryll.

The man wore a tailored green tunic, black trousers, and black shoes, but he bore no weapon. Over his heart lay a symbol that looked like the pattern of seven colors Max had seen on the Moon Gate's frame—a vertical rectangle with a circle at the four corners, one at the top center, and another two circles two-thirds of the way down the sides. Max figured this was some sort of symbol of the collective deities, rather than of one in particular.

Max cast a quick glance around and saw that he stood in a wide, paved area with gardens, like a town square. He wasn't sure which direction was which, but a rectangular wall surrounded the square, and at four different points stood wide openings into what he assumed were the neighborhoods of the four gods of this district. He surmised it was the Red District from the color of awnings, flags, and little scarlet touches on structures. A dozen individuals, most of whom weren't looking his way, seemed intent on going about their business.

Max focused on the man in front of him.

Name: Kiseron Springhew of Sorrairyn.
Title: Keeper of the Gate.
Deity: Kriseri, Goddess of Peace.
Patronage: Patron of Hospitality.
Type: Sorrairyn, NPC.
Class: Herald.
Species: Hybrid (Human, Kryll).
Level 250.

Huh. That's the first hybrid I've seen. Maybe that explains this guy's height. Why didn't I see a hybrid in Evator? Then he realized he hadn't been checking everyone, so maybe he hadn't noticed.

The class designation also caught Max's attention. This was someone who had excelled at something to such a degree that he'd ascended to become the personification of that trait to all of Llurien. A sorrairyn was a demi-god. This one was level 250. Was that how high someone had to get to ascend? How long would *that* take? If Max wanted to do so, he'd never succeed before the Life Counter ended. He shrugged off his questions, having no time for that.

"I am here to see Lord Everett," he said, wondering what reaction that would get. Maybe he shouldn't have admitted it. Too late now. "Uh, can you tell me the way?"

"My pleasure. You must pass through the Red District, where you now stand, to the Orange District." Kiseron pointed across a wide stone square to a street bisecting two walls. "Once there, if you are worthy to find Everett's neighborhood, you shall."

Max cocked an eyebrow. "If I'm worthy? What does that mean? Is there a test?"

"That is for you to discover. You have made it here with your Moon Pass, so you do not lack for courage. And yet the gods often test those who seek them. I may not improve your chances with information that would help you. Or at least, not much." Kiseron smiled.

Having almost forgotten the pass he held in one of Kella's hands, Max returned it to his inventory. "So you will not stop me."

"No. Just be alert and trust your instincts. Not everything is what it seems."

Max nodded his half-assed thanks for the vague information. For someone so good at hospitality, Kiseron hadn't been terribly helpful. But it seemed that the gods were limiting his responses.

As Max walked away, Kella interrupted his thoughts, feelings of fear and indignation apparent.

You didn't say we were to see Everett!

And your upset response justifies not telling you.

Ha. Well, I suppose I cannot argue that.

Look, we're only going there to request he free someone.

And how were… you weren't planning to trade me, were you?

What? No, nothing like that.

He will require a trade!

I have a plan.

Max had expected a bargain with the Lord of the Undead, which the metal head in him thought sounded cool. But he didn't want to go through with the trade because he liked the item in question. He hoped another option would occur to him by then.

Realizing his map could help, Max pulled up the interface to see he had a new tab for Sorrairyn. The previous map's tab now said Antaria, the continent on the planet Llurien that the game was named after. The Antaria map mostly showed places he'd already been with only vague indications of other areas. But the Sorrairyn map showed the overall city plan.

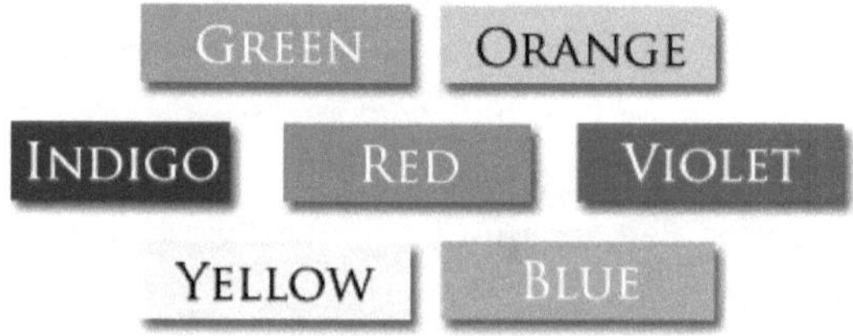

The seven districts were laid out in a pattern that matched an informational diagram he'd seen in the game notes. That picture had the three groups of benevolent gods—green, indigo, and yellow—on the left in a vertical line, and the three groups of nefarious gods—orange, violet, and blue—on the right in another line. Those two lines were sort of curled around the seventh, red group of neutral gods in the center, almost like those neutral gods acted as a buffer between the good deities on the left and the evil ones on the right.

The city was the same. In relation to the central red district, Max considered two districts to be northeast (orange) and northwest (green) of him, another two southeast (blue) and southwest (yellow), and two more due east (violet) and due west (indigo).

While the buffer-like arrangement made sense, he didn't understand why the three groups of evil gods were north to south as they were. Or the same with the good gods. Did the gods in a group, or district, have something in common? He pulled up the info diagram and saw that they did.

Each god was associated with a month of the year, and the order of the three spheres of good/evil gods matched this on the diagram. The start of season gods for months 1, 4, 7, and 10 were north, the end of season gods for months 3, 6, 9, and 12 were south, and the mid-season gods for months 2, 5, 8, and 11 were in the middle. Since there were only four neutral gods, each got an entire season, which also explained the central position of their Red District. Max doubted this would impact what happened here.

But the circular layout of each district would. All seven were the same. Each had a god of every season. The spring god had the northern neighborhood, which explained why Max saw blooming flowers north of his position in the Red District's town square. The other seasons went clockwise so that the summer neighborhood lay to the east, autumn stood to the south, and winter lay to the west. From this, Max now knew which way he was facing.

Where the winter god's neighborhood lay, he saw snow on the taller roofs, and a few inches blown into the square. Dried leaves rustled inside the area from the autumn neighborhood, while a waft of air brought a fresh sprinkling of pollen to the stones near the spring neighborhood. Only the summer one hadn't impacted the town square, that he could see.

The district was like a giant pizza that had been cut twice, resulting in four triangular neighborhoods. Four roads led from the district walls to the town square, like where Max stood. And the Moon Gate was right in the middle of the entire city of the gods. Did they use it to come and go as well? Was that the only way in or out?

Wilderness separated the seven districts of Sorrairyn. Max wasn't sure if the map was to scale, but he couldn't tell how many miles separated them. What would he find? Was that a place of lawlessness where no deity held sway? It seemed like it, given how everything else was strictly divided by jurisdiction.

From the diagram, Max saw Everett belonged to the orange sphere of gods, and therefore his neighborhood lay in the Orange District to the northeast. And since Everett, the God of Fear, was a winter god, that meant his neighborhood lay on the nearest or western side of the district, in between that of the spring Goddess of Deception to the north, and the autumn Goddess of Envy to the south. Directly across from Everett's neighborhood was that of the summer God of Greed. He wondered if, since those gods had invented daekais, whether he would find more of the race present there or near. And how high of a level would they be?

He activated his *Local Lore* skill.

Settlement: Sorrairyn, City of the Gods.

Location: Unknown. Surrounded by impassable mountains, the city has seven districts that the wilderness separates. Those who leave the Red District in the center do so at their own risk.

Population: No authority reigns supreme here, except in each neighborhood, where a deity has absolute authority. All

species can be found here, but higher concentrations of one will be found in the district of the gods who created them. This is not true of altered species such as morkais, sorelia, niquerra, rhaikan, and more, as the deities who created their species are usually not pleased that they exist; they therefore appear more frequently in other districts, especially the neutral red one.

Recent Events: None acknowledged.

Important Features in Town: There are too many significant places to list, but the Moon Gate at the Red District's center provides the only entrance. The Solon Tower is where wayward gods are imprisoned for breaking covenants.

A ten-foot-high stone wall surrounded the wide Species Square where Max stood. Four open gates led into the neighborhoods. Four additional open gates led onto wide avenues leading out of the district, each lined with trees, bushes, and flowers. The road cleaving between the spring and summer neighborhoods had leafy green trees, whereas the one between summer and autumn had colorful leaves ready to fall. The road between autumn and winter had bare trees, some covered in snow and ice. And the road between winter and spring showed trees with buds. Getting his bearings like this could be useful.

Max headed for the northeastern gate, Kella not fighting his command. Despite the name of the Red District, everything was normally colored except for the prevalence of red on decorations and on inhabitants' clothing. All around, miles off in the distance, snow-topped mountains loomed as if the city of the gods lay in a valley. He didn't know if the settlement was on the surface of Llurien or another plane.

Nearby, in the neighborhood of the god of fairness, a tower topped with a minaret soared hundreds of feet into the sky, a rainbow of hues swirling around its surface down to the pavement below it. Elsewhere, several kais and even great birds flew through a sunny sky. Max had only seen a few people in the town square. He couldn't tell if they were residents or visitors like himself, and none were close enough to examine. He assumed they were a far higher level and might be trouble. No karelia—able to detect he possessed someone—were among them.

As he walked, Max looked in Kella's inventory and swapped out the priest's clergy attire for another tunic and trousers, neither adorned. Both were a dark green that might help him blend into the woods. He didn't want to advertise the class, or more specifically, that this priest worshipped a different god than the one Max sought.

When the road reached the stone archway at the district edge, Max hesitated. Exterior walls topped with red banners on either side curved away. The road split, one path heading right toward the Violet District, another left to the Green District, and one ahead to the Orange. Whereas the Red District had been flat, he saw a marble path cleaving between the rolling hills into a dark forest. Standing a few miles beyond was the Orange District, with menacing architecture of dark stone. He hadn't seen a place more uninviting... until he walked far enough to see the Violet District due east. A multitude of towers seemed like knife points jabbing at the sky. He pulled up the diagram to see which deities called it home: the gods of haste, hate, cynicism, and sloth, the ones who'd created riven and the Maeryndor afterlife of eternal boredom.

As he continued, a dark-haired woman stepped from behind a tree to face him. She carried a bow and arrow-filled quiver, both adorned with a lily. Her green and brown leather neatly camouflaged her. She seemed at home and was human, her brown eyes bright with intelligence, depth, and alertness. Her overall demeanor seemed wary but relaxed and unthreatening, which was just as well once he examined her.

Name: Tessium Lightfoot of Sorrairyn.
Title: Mistress of the Hunt.
Deity: Adarra, Goddess of Aspiration.
Patronage: Patron of Hunters.
Type: Sorrairyn, NPC.
Class: Hunter.
Species: Human.
Level 300.

Max thought, *I won't stand a chance if I run into an evil sorrairyn who works for a hostile god. Are they allowed to attack visitors? Would anyone, like another sorrairyn, come to my defense?*

"Follow the stars to find your way," Tessium said, her voice a stirring alto. She glanced up and then over one shoulder toward his destination.

Max looked up and saw that the sky had darkened to reveal stars, two moons, and dark constellations of interstellar gases, a violet and orange against the deeper blackness of space. It had just been daytime in the Red District. Had the change just occurred, or was he so preoccupied he hadn't noticed the sky altering? Did time pass normally here? He suspected nothing was what it seemed. His Life Counter was progressing normally.

"I can't just follow the path to where it leads?" he asked, hoping she'd be more helpful that the Keeper of the Gate.

Terssium shook her head. "Your eyes will deceive you. The trees move. The path disappears. This road leads to Moiryn, the Goddess of Deception. In his greed, Neistrum will assume you come for what belongs to him. And Ronkainen is jealous of all, even one as lowly as yourself, though she is a goddess. Everett wants you to be afraid. All will test you."

Shrugging off the comment about him being lowly, Max asked with a smirk, "Any advice?"

"Turn back."

Not what he wanted to hear. "I can't do that."

"Then may Adarra bless you." The huntress stepped off the path and into the wilderness, disappearing sooner than he would have expected. Being level 300 undoubtedly helped her.

Kella interrupted his thoughts. *I may be of assistance.*

How?

My Detect Truth spell could help us avoid being misled. On-ly…

What?

The spell has two versions, one by Tarrera, Goddess of Truth, and one by her sister Moiryn, Goddess of Deception, to whose district we are going.

Not sure what he was getting at, Max speculated, *You think Moiryn may have a counter for it?*

Something like that. Direction Sense is probably better.

Who created that? Scrylyn?

Of course.

And given that Kella was one of her priests, that seemed a safe bet. He pulled up *Direction Sense* to see it cost 0 MP because it was a valender, those simple spells even non-wizards could do. It would last an hour and had a short enough cooldown to do it on the way back, too. He also noticed the priest had *Orb of Doom*, so Max added it and *Halt* to the hot list. Before resuming, Max and Kella cast *Tarreran Sight*, which let him see hidden objects. To his surprise, several appeared nearby, including an alternate path winding into the trees.

He asked Kella, Do you think that way is a good idea or a bad one?

I was wondering the same. I honestly have no idea.

I'm inclined to take it.

What is your rationale?

That it being hidden, it is less likely to be traveled and we are less likely to be expected.

True. Also true is that anything able to see that path is more advanced, and therefore any danger is likely to be more serious.

So our choice is to take the hidden path and be less likely to encounter danger, but it will be more serious if we do, or to take the more obvious path and have a greater chance of danger, that will at least be less formidable.

That would seem to be the case.

Max already felt out of his league and decided against the hidden path. He looked over the spell list again, trying to find something to hide them. Instead, he noticed the teleportation spell, *Cast Away*, that could either get him out of trouble or cast away the threat. But he wondered—would the level of the creature prevent it from working on them? Removing himself seemed more guaranteed. *The Flock* could summon animals to protect him, but *Animal Shapeshift* suggested he might escape attention with the right option. Kella's lack of materials stopped Max from using the latter, which required something from the animal. He only had daekais feathers, talons, and Antarian sparrow feathers in his inaccessible inventory.

They set off, eyes alert for dangers and an animal to kill and change himself into, but small creatures were heard in the underbrush. Max cast the version of *Detect Truth* that the goddess of deception had invented, since *Tarreran Sight* only showed hidden items. Now his left eye saw illusions while his right didn't. To his surprise, he was already heading the wrong way, south instead of northeast.

Should've cast that sooner, he thought. *I don't have time for this shit.*

He began jogging, which now felt natural after possessing Kella for over twenty minutes. Every fifty feet, he stopped and listened intently. He made it a half mile before a squawk above and to one side made him duck behind a tree. A moragul flapped its black wings as it soared over the path toward him and the Red District. Then it banked to make a U-turn and follow the path back toward the Orange District. Max followed and thought the bird was looking for carrion to consume. That didn't comfort him.

For a moment, he was confused about it following the actual path, unless it, too, could tell what was real and what wasn't, but then he noticed that the illusion didn't exist. The correct and wrong paths were the same. Or had his spell worn off? He checked and saw it had. It only lasted ten minutes, so he cast it again. The moragul was out of sight by the time he finished.

Max continued and soon stopped to peer over a hill before cresting it. A human woman in a red tunic and black leggings strode in his direction. Max saw nowhere to hide that might actually work. He braced himself for battle.

CHAPTER THIRTY-ONE

As the woman neared, Max realized she didn't seem threatening, having only a dagger on her waist. But she could've been a wizard. One braid of her long blonde hair fell over a modest bosom, where generous cleavage drew his eye. The ale maiden's high cheekbones and long lashes gave her a sultry look that made him stare.

Name: Nia Springhollow of Illiandor.
Type: NPC.
Class: Ale Maiden.
Species: Human.
Level 17.

What was a level 17 ale maiden doing here? Was there a tavern near? Her class suggested she was no threat, and she seemed unmindful of peril, maybe because NPC didn't kill each other? Maybe she had information. He noticed that both of his eyes showed the same thing, so she wasn't an illusion.

Knowing he could not evade her, Max leaned against a tree with a non-threatening demeanor and waited for her to crest the hill and see him. It didn't long, and she met his gaze, worried brown eyes turning hopeful. She stopped a few paces from him, one hand going to her heart.

"Greetings, traveler," Nia began, "have you seen my pet mosk?"

Max's *World Lore* skill told him this was a large canine. "I have not."

"Would you help find him? I don't know how I will survive alone."

Before he could respond, a notification appeared.

New Quest: Find and return Nia's pet mosk.

Objective: Nia's pet mosk has escaped! Help find and return him to her.

Difficulty: Medium.

Rewards: 1 Uncommon Item. 1000 XP.

Accept?

Max declined the quest. He didn't have time, and it wasn't worth the trouble, especially given the supernatural forest. Dragging Kella into unnecessary tasks was risky to his possession, too. He figured Nia would just pout or plead, then walk on, but she glared, brown eyes dazzling with anger, and pulled out her dagger.

"What kind of awful man won't fetch my beloved mosk?" she yelled before charging.

"Seriously?" Max backed up to give himself room. "Gather air!"

He felt the *Orb of Doom* fill Kella's hand as if it was his own. With Nia almost upon he him, he threw it straight into her chest. She flew backwards with a sickening crunch as a red -24 HP floated away, another few HP being lost when she crashed into the ground with a thud. She dropped the dagger on impact. A red health bar appeared. She apparently didn't have that many HPs, but then she was an NPC without a gaming sort of class, like fighter or wizard. Such NPCs presumably gained little in stats or anything when they leveled.

"Stupid bitch," Max muttered, as he picked up her blade and went to stab her.

No wait! came Kella's thought. But Max finished her with two blows. This was the first quest he'd refused. Would an offering NPC always attack like that on declining? It was messed up, if so.

You have killed (1) Ale Maiden, Level 17!
You gained 2250 XP!
Loot corpse?

From the body, Max got some junk, a decent haul of both metal and gem coins, and a golden *Mug of Quenching*. Regardless of what liquid he drank from it, it restored 25% of his HP if he consumed the whole thing, or 50% if he imbibed ale. So he'd either end up needing to pee really badly or get half drunk. Would he have gotten it if he'd found her dog? Or would it have been something else? He got 2250 XP for killing her instead of the quest's 1000 XP, so it almost like a good idea to kill NPCs who offered him a quest.

He pulled up a notification.

You achieved Level 5!
You gained 28 Spectral Hit Points!
You gained 7 Spectral Mana Points!
Class bonus: You gained Dexterity +1, Agility +1, Constitution +1.

You gained (2) proficiency points.
You have (2) unassigned proficiency points.
You have gained the Blind Descryer ability, level 1!

Max perked up at the last part and pulled up the description, hoping it was what he thought.

Ability Name: Blind Descryer.

Description: This ability prevents karelia, sorelia, or those with a spell that can detect the supernatural from sensing your presence, whether your spirit is inside another body, your body, or roaming free. In the latter case, you can still be visually seen. Those whose detection abilities are stronger than your *Blind Descryer* ability are more likely to still sense you, either with diminished accuracy or no reduction in skill.

If you use the *Appear Alive* ability at the same time, those who physically see you, and could normally sense a soul there, will sense no spirit and may think you are either an illusion, a body without a spirit, or realize you're a spirit using the *Blind Descryer* ability.

Cast time: Instant.
Duration: 15 minutes.
Cooldown: 20 minutes.
SMP: 5.

Max sighed in relief. *It's about damn time.*

He assigned the proficiency points to his new *Blind Descryer* ability, raising it to level 3. He checked the HUD to see he'd gained another 30 minutes of possessing Kella, who wondered to him why they were just standing there. Apparently he couldn't see Max's HUD or notifications. Maybe he didn't know about any of that.

A growl interrupted his thoughts. Max turned. A black dog as tall as his waist was snarling at him from within the underbrush. It had big jowls and floppy ears, a line of drool falling to the green grass.

"Guess I found the mosk," Max said. Had it been there all that time? He doubted it. The quest wouldn't have been worth that much if it was that easy. Maybe the moment the ale maiden attacked, the game moved the dog near. He focused on it.

Mosk, Tamed. This large canine is a lovable and loyal companion if bred in captivity, and is often used as a guard dog. Even the appearance of a threat to their master may cause an attack. In the wild, they travel in packs that can be very dangerous, especially when food is scarce.

HP: 4/5

It had lost a hit point. What had it been doing? Had something around here done that or had the dog hurt itself?

"Feel the touch of Krairon," Max whispered. The mosk continued snarling but stayed still. Max sent the magical hand into the underbrush off to one side and came at the canine sideways so it wouldn't see this. It worked. The mosk whimpered, a -5 HP floating up as it fell dead into a leafy green bush.

You have killed (1) Mosk!
You gained 10 XP!
Loot corpse?

Max looted it and came away with two teeth, one entire paw, two nails, and a handful of fur. He considered morphing into the dog, but on seeing the moragul circling above, Max dragged the mosk onto the path and moved away, giving the bird the impression it was safe to land. It took the bait and descended to alight on the mosk. It looked around for almost a minute before pecking at the beast.

Max whispered, "Feel the touch of Krairon."

It was almost too easy. The moragul died, never seeing the hand of death. Max looted the body for the feathers, some moragul spit, and two talons. Now he could turn himself into one and fly the rest of the way, though something could shoot him from the sky. And the gods who'd created daekais were in the district ahead, making their presence more likely. But he only needed it get beyond the forest.

He recast the detection spell. Then Kella helped him cast *Animal Shapeshift* using one of the moragul feathers. Max hadn't expected the transformation to hurt as Kella's body shrank to half its size and everything from bones to muscle contorted. Max thought he might lose control of Kella, but the priest seemed too preoccupied with the agony.

Once the pain stopped, Max saw the world differently, little motions in the forest attracting his attention as if prey caused them. The smell of blood from the three bodies was sweet and attractive. An urge to hop over to the dead mosk and chomp into its belly for entrails didn't make him sick. He actually felt hungry. Stretching out the wings, he expected them to feel odd, but they didn't. He sensed he knew how to fly.

With a few powerful thrusts of black wings, Max—and Kella—launched into the air. They soon crested the treetops, where confiners and deciduous trees fell below them. Just like when Max flew atop the florin bird, he felt the rush of air in his face, but also in his rustling feathers on his belly and wings. The pleasant sensation soothed him. To reduce noise, Max tried to glide when able while staying low and near the path, which forked more than once, sometimes in three directions, one often an illusion. He saw clearings, large hills, and small buildings. Ahead stood the Orange District, while the Violet lay right, and the Green left and behind. He saw the tops of others beyond the Red District directly behind him.

As he neared the destination, more illusionary buildings and path appeared. Had the goddess of deception ramped up her game here? He spied a group of twenty daekais flying toward him, but out of only one eye. They weren't real. They finally passed beyond the forest's edge and landed behind a few trees just past it.

You don't think we should fly over the walls? Kella thought at him.

I'm afraid to, to be honest.

Good. I'm glad you're being careful with my body.

You would do the same.

Max peeked at the Orange District's gates. One eye showed they were closed, locked, and a group of mercenaries stood in front of them. The other showed them open and no one there. Above the district, a few real daekais flew in their haphazard way on some business or another.

He mentally asked Kella, *What happens if I know something is an illusion? Does it just have no effect on me?*

Yes. The guards will try to stop you because they don't know you're aware of their nature, but your awareness means they cannot impact you.

Okay. I'll let you transform us again.

Kella did the deed, and they experienced a similarly painful change back into the priest's body. Max used his new *Blind Descryer* skill and checked his HUD, which showed an icon of a blindfolded and seemingly karelian head with pointed ears and lorenia lines on the face. Max stepped out from behind the trees to the now cobblestone road, passing a few boulders and an abandoned wagon. He wondered how many visitors this place received.

At fifty feet high, and with orange pennants flying at regular intervals, the grey stone walls were much higher than the Red District and suggested they expected trouble. Or was it for show? The god of greed was here. Did he just want bigger walls? Max saw no one atop them. Surely a large force never materialized in Sorrairyn? The situation seemed ripe for sneaking over the wall. Maybe they'd fly out of here once they knew what they were up against.

The illusionary guards commanded Max to halt, but he walked right through them, and they vanished. He strode through the image of the closed gates, finding himself on a road to the town square. He had arrived inside the Orange District.

CHAPTER THIRTY-TWO

Ahead of Max, the main road into the Orange District separated two walls parallel to it. He thought the left was Everett's neighborhood and the right that of Ronkainen, the Goddess of Envy, but both had skeletons, skulls, and grave markings embedded in them. The still-active *Detect Truth* spell revealed the right one as an illusion by Moiryn, the Goddess of Deception, as the wall was actually ornately decorated and yet crumbling. Unlike the Red District, there appeared to be no openings or doors on either wall except for where the right one had fallen altogether. He would have to reach the town square to enter Everett's neighborhood, so he began jogging. He'd already used forty-five minutes of his now 2.5 hours possessing Kella.

So what's the plan? Kella asked. *You do have one, I hope.*

Yes. I'm hoping to figure out where this sorelia is and escape with her.

Kella snorted strong enough that, even though Max controlled the body, it still sounded aloud. He asked, *You're going to run all the way back through that forest? I mean no disrespect, but are you insane?*

Max sighed. *I said I was hoping to do that. I don't think it's going to work.*

I can almost guarantee it won't.

A little optimism would be nice.

So would a lot less foolishness.

You know, for a priest, you're a little snarky.

Maybe it's a side effect of having my body possessed, forced through a Moon Gate to the city of the gods, dragged through or flown over a hazardous forest, and being marched straight into the home of the Lord of the Undead, all by a ghost.

Max tried not to laugh. *Well, when you put it that way… look, if I can sneak her out, it may not be so bad.*

Did you bring a disguise at least?

No. You didn't have one in your inventory.

I suppose it's my fault then.

Max suppressed a smile. *Yes. Listen, it's the least dangerous way, and I promised not to get you hurt.*

I would comment on the likelihood of that, but I wouldn't want to be seen as negative again.

I appreciate that.

Was there another plan?

Yes, I have a lyre that I can trade for her. It controls the undead. I think Everett would like giving it back to the woman who created it. He is her master.

And yours. You know she'll just wreak havoc on Llurien with it.

One problem at a time. I don't really want to give up this lyre, though, so we'll see what happens. Now be quiet unless you have something helpful to add. I need to concentrate.

By now, they had passed a human and kryll who were headed the other way. Both were high-level players who eyed him more curiously than suspiciously. Max wasn't outwardly armed and probably didn't seem threatening. He slowed on nearing the road's end, Kella's lungs huffing from the effort. He tried to waltz into the town square like he knew what he was doing.

He saw a dozen daekais on the cobblestones, in three groups. One seemed drunk from their loud joking and stumbling. Another group was tossing stones into a target with seven color-coded circles, hooting and hollering about their performance. The last appeared to be playing valend cards and getting upset with each other over a winning hand. Elsewhere, a few humans, kryll, and what Max assumed were sorelia instead of karelia went about their business. Not all were real, but even some of those who were wore an illusion of a friendly expression that hid their sinister way appraising of people. Max played along and smiled pleasantly.

Max had assumed the only Moon Gate in Sorrairyn was the one he'd arrived through, but another stood in this town square's center. Could he really just leave from here? It would shave at least thirty minutes off his time possessing Kella. He wanted to investigate but wasn't sure it was wise, given the people near it possibly questioning him.

Do you know anything about that Moon Gate? He asked Kella.

Not specifically.

What does that mean?

There is another in the Green District, where my god, Scrylyn, dwells, so one more existing in a different district does not surprise me.

What is that one for?

I know only that it is a one-way gate, for use from Sorrairyn. One cannot enter the city of the gods except through the way we did.

Supposedly. Can you leave through another one?

I believe so, yes, but controlling your arrival on Llurien is less certain, especially with Moiryn and her many illusions here. She could make the gate show a destination different from where you will actually arrive.

Yeah, she's a pain in the ass. But in a pinch, we might get back to Llurien this way but be far away from my body.

It is a possibility. I would also be far from home, presumably.

Okay, let's only try that as a last resort.

Agreed. I would much rather be lost on Llurien than in Sorrairyn, mostly because it is far more dangerous here.

Not until Kella thought this did Max realize he'd definitely left the game's starter area. Another reason not to dawdle.

He reached the entrance to Everett's neighborhood, where the tall gates stood open, skeletons impaled by the black metal bars. He assumed they were decorations until the head of one turned in his direction and cackled.

"Welcome!" it said. "May you find your soul mate, unless you already have!"

A skull on the other side said, "Having two souls to rely on is always better than one!"

"Or none!" the first added.

Max looked sideways at them. Could they tell he was possessing Kella? The jokes seemed too coincidental. He examined them and saw that both were level 20. He shrugged it off. They couldn't do anything if so, being impaled as they were.

"Stick around, guys," he said, and they hooted.

As Max stepped over the threshold, he received a notification that his powers as undead were enhanced, though the message wasn't specific. Would a similar message happen in other neighborhoods if he aligned with that deity? Or instead of a buff, he might get nerfed. He needed to expect the latter, which was more important.

His breath appeared in the cold air, a subtle breeze cutting through his clothing. While snow had amassed on rooftops, and wicked icicles hung from seemingly everywhere, someone had partially cleared the stone paths of precipitation. The layout left little doubt where he'd find Everett. Each neighborhood here had a castle, though this hadn't been true in the Red District. Standing in the rear against the district's far wall, Everett's looked to be made of obsidian, the black glass foreboding, jagged spires of blue ice topping the minarets.

All of the black, grey, or marble buildings looked like a church, mausoleum, or tomb. Where a garden might've been, tombstones were planted instead. The sky remained dark as if night had fallen, a band of interstellar gas running across it with a multitude of stars within. With Everett the God of Night, among other traits, it seemed he controlled how the sky looked here.

As he went, Max tried not to engage the undead all around, but they watched him pass. He saw zombies carrying a coffin, and two wights dragging a black bag—with someone or something struggling inside—across the road. A legless ash fiend hovered in a doorway, two glowing, orange eyes observing him, its black, sooty form rustling quietly when it moved an arm. The skeletons were the most abundant, some catcalling him while others rolled dice or played valend cards in groups.

Max saw a piece of parchment hanging on a wall. It looked like a faded sign, the paper ripped at one corner. The spell he wanted to use it with would take an uncomfortable minute to complete, but when done, a hopefully accurate map of Everett's home would be scrawled in black ink on in. Max forced Kella to cast *Map Structure* for 3 SMP. He studied it for a minute and then had a thought. Pulling up his digital maps, he saw it was there now, too, and he didn't need the physical paper, so he put it away. He'd have to use that spell more often; it was on his list, too.

"What brings you to Everett?" said a hollow voice on his left.

Max turned to see burning, orange eyes regarding him. The creature gave off a subtle wave of heat, embers sometimes glowing amber at the edges of its otherwise smokey form. It didn't seem to have a face, or at least, one that remained in place, its form shifting.

Ash Fiend. Created from the charred ashes of corpses, ash fiends are formidable opponents that cannot be hurt by physical weapons.

Level: 37.

HP: 540/540.

Max realized he wasn't seeing smoke, but ash, and when the creature moved its arms, it was as if the ash on the edges briefly turned back to a fiery cinder. "I, uh, have come to, uh, pay tribute to Everett."

"As a priest of Scrylyn?" A black opening that vaguely resembled a mouth moved when the thing spoke.

The question surprised Max. He had removed all identifying attire. "How did...?"

"The tattoo beneath your ear."

Shit. I forget about that. Max had seen the mark of an open green eye with a heart-shaped pupil on Kella's neck but had paid little attention to it. And all this time, he thought no one knew Kella's class and deity. He felt like a schmuck, but thought of a lie.

"I am no longer a priest of Scrylyn. I wish to dedicate myself to Everett."

"You can do that without coming here."

Max was getting frustrated with smart NPCs. Why couldn't they be easier to lie to? "I wanted his blessing."

The ash fiend waved one arm toward the castle, his black, sooty face unreadable. His entire body shifted as if subtly moved by a breeze. "Then I shall escort you."

Shit. The last thing I want is a chaperone. How do I ditch this guy? He said, "I'm not sure that is necessary. I don't want to trouble you."

"I must insist."

Max stifled a sigh and nodded. So much for sneaking around. He wouldn't be finding the sorelia and escaping with her, but bargaining for her release and likely trading in the Lyre of Murryn.

He followed, the ash fiend's heat almost pleasant in the cold air. It sailed a few inches from the ground, a little trail or tail of ash dragging the ground. Though it seemed to go forward, the eyes suddenly appeared in the back to scrutinize him. He had the impression it didn't need to turn around to, well, turn around. The eyes seemingly returned to the front. Max had to watch that if ever fighting one. There would be no real sneaking up on one if they effectively didn't have a rear side.

After a few turns, they approached a castle bailey, courtyard, and then the keep, where towers rose into the night sky. More undead jeered him. He never would've have made it through here unnoticed or unmolested. Two death knights in silver and black plate armor stood beside the gates, swords and daggers on their hips. Twin pinpoints of orange light glowed in the black eye sockets of each, but they ignored him.

A few steps into the keep, the doors boomed shut behind Max. Only darkness lay ahead. The air smelled musty with decay. They hadn't gone twenty paces when dim torchlight lit the dusty stairs of smooth glass they ascended. This ended in a tall room, where Max saw stacks of piled bones from every species, rows and columns of them holding up the ceiling. Skeletal decorations ranged from the humorous to the mundane and sexual.

Max pulled up information on Everett to remind himself who he was facing.

Deity: Everett. God of fear, death, loss, darkness, cowardice.

Titles: Lord of the Undead, Undead King, the Shrouded One, the Night Lord.

Patronage: Patron of the Undead.

Symbol: Tombstone.

Sphere: Orange. Co-creator of daekais and E'kainum afterlife.

Alignment: Nefarious.

Season/Element: Winter/Water.

Power Day: Orange Day, Water Week.

Court of Gods Month: 10.

Unique: If Everett puts his mark on someone's soul, they become undead once they die.

They descended more staircases of bones, each spiraling into creepy dark spaces where voices whispered. In the cavernous chambers, cobwebs hung and burning torches or pits of fiery liquid dotted the way. Creatures huddled in corners, by the steps, or hung from the ceiling. Max saw other ash fiends, wraiths, and more mundane undead, plus creatures he'd never heard of. The idea of sneaking in or out seemed more laughable by the moment.

They finally reached a large hall with more columns of bone and sinew holding up the rafters. Gossamer tapestries of humanoid hair hung from black walls, depictions of undead debauchery adorning them. Somehow, the ceiling was the night sky, pale moonlight shining down on the scene. A waterfall of blood splashed from the nearer right corner and ran like a river through the room's center, several bridges on the obsidian floor traversing it. In the nearby left corner lay a graveyard, white light shining from within a pale mausoleum onto an orgy of writhing flesh and bone in the dirt among the headstones. And against the farthest wall, from the floor to where a ceiling would have been, stood cage upon cage. Some had wicked-looking monsters that either lay peacefully or thrashed in fury. In others, Max could make out no one.

To one side on a wide dais, an ash fiend conducted an orchestra full of skeletons, zombies, and ghosts who were performing a raucous symphony of some of the evil sounding music Max had ever heard. In the room's center, other undead danced as if drunk or mocking the elegant dances of 18th century England. They stumbled, laughed, and ripped off body parts before playing "key away" with a fellow jester. Two fell into the blood river with a laugh, cackling as it swept them away.

Death knights to the other side were jousting on black horses with flaming hooves, manes, and eyes. Elsewhere, a wraith drank a silvery liquid from a fountain, its form becoming almost blinding white as it shrieked and raced from the room into dark tunnels as if it had gone mad. And a trio of women in evening gowns stood sipping blood from golden goblets, rivulets of red dripping down their chins. They leered at Max.

At the hall's far end sat a giant obsidian throne of shiny glass, spirits swirling within. Everett, God of Death, sat upon it, his black eyes deep and despairing. Long black hair flowed out from beneath the hood of his matching robe. A straight nose, high cheekbones, and powerful jaw made him masculine but refined, as if the horrors he visited upon others ranged from the physical and ghastly to subtle mind games. He was both attractive and repulsive. Max stared into the dark void of his eyes with an unexpected mixture of longing and fear.

"Welcome to the Grand Hall of the Night Lord and God of Darkness, the master of undead, and therefore yours." The ash fiend's voice pulled Max's attention away, and a moment passed before he realized something.

"What? How—oh shit."

They know! Kella's panicked thought shot into his mind.

The ash fiend's ember-like eyes grew hotter, a wave of heat striking Max.

"Seize him!"

Chapter Thirty-Three

Max stepped back, a wave of cold from behind preceding two frozen hands gripping his upper arms. He stifled a howl of pain that Kella did for them. His head whipped around to see two orange pinpricks of light in a skeletal face, frosty mist rising from a death knight's plate armor. Another one stood on his other side. He hadn't noticed them before. His arms were going numb and his body shook.

From across the cavernous hall, Everett spoke in a deep, booming voice, hollow like a sepulcher. "Bring them to me."

Max felt his feet leave the floor as the death knights carried him by the arms. The orchestra began a march. Undead fell in beside them, the clacking of bony feet punctuating their steps until they reached the center bridge over the river of blood. They stayed behind as the knights carried him onward. It wasn't until they neared the god that Max realized Everett was over ten feet tall, or at least, he appeared as if he was.

The death knights stopped and released him fifteen feet from the obsidian throne. They stepped back two paces, leaving Max by himself. He shook and rubbed his arms, unsure of what to say. Was he supposed to speak first? What was the etiquette?

"Welcome to my humble abode," said Everett, eyes boring into his.

Max bowed his head briefly. "Thank you. How should I address you?"

"As master. And to whom do I have the pleasure of speaking?"

"Maestro Max, Master Everett."

"Is that all?" The god seemed slightly amused.

Max wasn't sure what to admit and hesitated. It seemed obvious the deity knew he was possessing Kella. Before he could decide, Everett continued.

"You cannot fool me, boy. I know you are a ghost and belong to me. And you possess that Priest of Scrylyn." Everett leered at him. "Or you *did*."

Max's face fell as the god raised one hand, from which a shockwave-like pulse hurtled toward him. He felt himself somersaulting backwards, the room spinning wildly before he regained equilibrium. Noe he was floating ten steps from where he'd been.

Alert! You have been expelled from your host!

Warning! You have been stunned!

Max's ghostly senses returned. He held up both glowing hands to confirm he had been ejected from his only way home. Kella lay unmoving on the obsidian floor, eyes staring unseeing at the night sky as if his last gaze had been toward Scrylyn, his goddess of the stars and moons.

Max's eyes locked with Everett. Around him, the assembled undead began shrieking, laughing, and dancing.

"One of us! One of us! One of us!"

With a hand wave, Everett silenced them into standing still. "You were not forthcoming with me, and so I will send you to think on how you might better serve me with the truth, should we speak again. Into the tomb."

Everett made a dismissive backhand gesture, and Max floated inside a rectangular room of white marble with no way out. The room was barely taller than him and about as long. He tried to press his hand through but, like any structures from the graveyard near Evator, he couldn't pass into it. He knew better than to try it at higher speed and take damage. For all he knew, he might not regenerate while here.

Sighing at how dismally this had gone, he settled into wait, pulling up the timer.

Life Counter: 3 Days, 14 Hours, 46 Minutes.

It almost didn't matter. Without Kella, he saw no way back to Llurien. He hadn't seen anyone nearly low enough in level to possess. He was getting tired. Not physically, but mentally. Emotionally. The game's distractions had vanished. The hours disappeared with agonizing slowness.

He wondered about his legal case. Had the lawyer filed something? An extension would give him time to wake up and for a judge to rule on the bigger issues. But that sometimes took years. He didn't want to stay in a coma that long, though it would give him time to ascend into the game if it became possible.

The logout button remained greyed out without explanation. The game wasn't so entertaining that he wanted to remain, especially when he could always log back in like normal people. Was his life not fulfilling enough to return? Sort of. He'd been content with his plans to finish college, maybe take a year off before a master's degree and doctorate, and aim for a life as a college professor and performing classical musician and composer. But it was a backup plan to making a name for himself as a rock guitarist.

The band wasn't doing well because people wanted to see him fail, and that meant his band failing. Had the guys replaced him? They had shows lined up and had to cancel if not. Were they relieved he was gone? He didn't think so, but they had to know some people wouldn't support Burp the Worm just because Max was in it. Getting away from the nasty attitudes was something he'd often thought about. Maybe that was the reason he stayed in here. This was an escape, except it sort of wasn't, since that had put him here.

He wondered if Siren had come looking for him. Did the *Party Screen* show he was dead? Would she know he was a ghost and try to communicate? If she told her father, maybe someone could restore communication. Would it even work while he was in this tomb?

Without warning, Max reappeared before Everett as if he had never left, except he was closer, where Kella had been before the god expelled Max. The last he'd looked at the Life Counter, most of the night had passed so that he was almost down to three full days. The throne room had changed, with most of the undead gone. To his surprise, Kella sat in a bone chair, looking alive except for his pale face. He once again wore his priestly garb. Max wasn't sure he should speak to him, but the priest's haunted eyes met his and he couldn't help it.

"Are you...?"

"Alive?" the priest answered weakly. "Yes."

Max relaxed and turned back to the god, who regarded him with a subtle smirk. Time to bargain and seem like that's not what he was doing. While Everett wanted information, Max needed intel, too. "Master," he began, "I apologize for hesitating to tell you everything. I will do better if you give me a second chance."

"As my servant, that is wise."

Max bowed, the deferential display unnatural. "I understand."

"So tell me, why come to me in possession of this priest?"

"I could not make it through the Moon Gate to Sorraiyrn without a body."

"Yes, but you don't need him now that you're here. You intended to use him to leave as well."

Max caught the hint of displeasure that he hadn't intended to stay, though the game could not have expected a player to sit in one spot, so he admitted, "I was hoping to return to Llurien, yes."

Everett leaned forward, glittering black eyes hard. "For what purpose?"

A little flattery couldn't hurt. "To wreak more havoc on your behalf."

The god laughed, the sound rumbling so that the floor vibrated. "A worthy answer! But if that is what you wanted, you should still be there now. Why did you come?"

"I am on an errand. If I fail, I can do no more work for you."

Everett cocked an eyebrow. "Explain."

Max had the impression the god was bothered that his servant had been interfered with, so he hoped to use that. "I was captured by a sorelia using a Black Mirror. He has forced me on a quest before he frees me."

The god looked puzzled. "But he already has, or you would not be here."

Now Max felt confused. "Pardon, Master Everett, but he said he can pull me back to the mirror at any time, from anywhere, and I am only free to do this." Even as he finished it, Max realized it didn't seem believable.

"You fool," said Everett. "A Black Mirror does not have such power. Never trust a sorelia."

Goddamn it. Max flushed and didn't have to fake hanging his head in shame. But this revelation was good news. He wasn't beholden to this now. If he failed, that only meant Kiavalon didn't help him find his body. But then maybe that had been a lie. If so, this quest was a waste of valuable hours. And he was about to lose the Lyre of Murryn for nothing, as he doubted he could just turn away now. His anger grew. Time to get on with this.

"The sorelia is named Kiavalon."

At this, Everett sat up taller, eyes narrowing. "I know that name and what he wants."

Max nodded. "He is hoping I can gain his beloved's freedom and return her to Llurien."

"Unacceptable. She failed me."

Reluctantly pulling the lyre from his inventory, Max held it aloft. "I have found this and hoped to trade it for her."

Everett's eyes flashed in recognition. "Ah. A worthy item, to be sure." He made a rising gesture and it lifted from Max's hands, floating over to the god. "I will take it as your apology and let you leave."

Max stared. *Seriously? The asshole is just going to take it?*

Everett's booming laughter filled the room. "You do not like my offer?"

Only then did Max realize his anger had been apparent. But he suddenly didn't care. "No, I do not." Then something occurred to him, and he said it before thinking it through. "I understand she was to do a quest and failed. I would like to do her quest, and the lyre would've helped me succeed, so I am not happy. Will you let me do her failed quest, to show you I am worthy of you? And if I succeed, let me take her?"

Everett sat back, cold eyes appraising him. "A bold offer. Are you not curious what the quest is before volunteering?"

The game wouldn't offer it if it was impossible. I hope. "I will faithfully attempt it regardless."

Everett snorted. "Ambitious, reckless, loyal, or foolish. I cannot tell which. Very well. The quest is to steal a Linganore Staff from Krairon and return it to me, or failing that, to destroy it."

Max's *World Lore* skilled popped a message.

Deity: Krairon. God of domination, authority, conquest, and oppression.

Titles: Lord of the Dead.

Patronage: Patron of the Dead.

Symbol: Crowned skull.

Sphere: Blue. Co-creator of jhaikan species and Lochiare afterlife.

Alignment: Nefarious.

Season/Element: Winter/Water.

Power Day: Blue Day, Water Week.

Court of Gods Month: 12.

Stealing something from another god didn't sound good, unless he thought of a good plan. That required info. The sphere color told him where the Blue District was—southeast of the Red District, past the Violet District he'd already seen. That meant there were two ways of getting there. He could retrace his steps into the Red District before existing the southeast gate there and into what he presumed would be another wilderness area. Or he could stay in the wilderness throughout, skirting between the Violet and Red Districts. The settlements seemed safer, or at least the Red District had, but he would need to think about this more.

He wondered how these two deities were related, with Everett being Lord of the Undead and Krairon, the Lord of the Dead. Was this a turf war?

But what he asked was, "Can I ask what this staff does?"

Everett's eyes hardened. "It allows the wielder to control the undead, the most powerful of which can only be controlled by such a staff, or by me."

That there were undead that strong seemed a distant concern, unless one of them was around here. Max avoided glancing over one shoulder, but his eyes darted to the wall of cages behind the god. And among them, he felt certain he saw a sorelia or karelia. Was that the one he was here to retrieve?

He said, "I can see how that staff would be undesirable in the wrong hands."

"Krairon believes all the dead are to call him their master. This has led my brother to decide that I have stolen them by turning some into undead, who worship me instead. Some say he is right, but it matters not. They belong to me. Most will eventually fall and return to my brother's embrace. What concern is it that should I borrow them for eons first? He has so *many.*"

Trying to look sympathetic, Max asked, "What does he use the staff for?"

"He commands the undead he encounters to obey him. This has thwarted some of my plans."

Max was sure getting between these two was foolish, but felt the need to get stronger as a ghost. It might help him find his body if for no other reason than doing things to the Dark Trio to make them talk. He asked, "Are these staves rare?"

"Extremely. They are made from the trunk of Linganore Trees, which are only found in the Ever Pathways. Few can find their way there, and far fewer return. The Black Grove within is the only place the trees are found, guarding the tower where the Ever Fiend dwells. Only the bravest can reach or escape that place, for the sentient Linganore trees will let travelers pass only to ensnare them and drain their blood. They are not known to willingly part with a branch."

Sounds like a good place for a summer home, Max inwardly joked. "Where is this Linganore Staff? Krairon's home?"

"Unless he or one of his lackeys presently has it with them, yes. You will find his castle heavily fortified."

Given Krairon's traits, Max thought the god sounded militant, but the comment about a lackey having it gave him an idea. Stealing it from someone like that was undoubtedly easier than from a deity. "If I go as a ghost instead of with my body, someone could control me with the staff."

"Yes. And he is expecting me to send undead, though I have living devotees. Even possessing that priest again would not get you by anyone because he would expect this deceit. Sentries would detect a second spirit within."

"Now that you have expelled me from Kella, I have also lost my means to return to Llurien." Max was going to say more, but Everett interrupted.

"If you succeed, I shall let you repossess him."

Max bowed. "Thank you, master. I wonder if my mission to Krairon's might be more successful if I possessed him now? It would give me access to his skills, which proved useful on my trip here."

"Very well."

Max glanced over at the priest, who looked caught between dread and relief. He had to be worried about the mission, as

Max was, but maybe he wanted to get out of this creepy castle as soon as possible. Max couldn't blame him.

It might not matter, but Max asked, "I saw a Moon Gate here, in the Orange District. Is it possible for me to return to Llurien through it upon completing the quest?"

"Yes. I might even allow it."

Max bowed. "I hope to impress you enough to earn your favor."

Everett ignored that. "When you entered my neighborhood, you received a bonus to your undead abilities. This will not only end when you leave here, but on entering my brother's domain, your powers will be diminished. This has been true for millennia, long before he possessed the Linganore Staff."

"Thank you for telling me."

"Do you accept the quest?"

New Quest: Retrieve the Linganore Staff from Krairon, the Lord of the Dead.

Objective: The God of Domination, Krairon, has acquired a Linganore Staff he uses to command and control undead, interfering with the work of his brother, Everett, the Lord of the Undead. Re-acquire this powerful artifact and return it to Everett, or destroy it.

Difficulty: Very High.

Rewards: 1 Unique Item. +5 Reputation with Everett. 10,000 XP.

Accept?

Max's eyes bugged out at the XP, which could raise him more than one level, but it spoke volumes about how hard this would be. Convincing Everett to hand over the sorelian woman was a "high" difficulty quest, but at least for that, Max had brought something to bargain with in the Lyre of Murryn. He had nothing to give Krairon, who would never part with the staff and could command him with it. And he was essentially expected. No wonder the sorelian woman had failed to do it, or had she not even tried?

But a few things had occurred to Max, and a glimmer of hope made him straighten.

"I accept," he began, trying to look more eager than he felt. "I have a plan. To ensure I succeed, would you consider loaning me some of your undead for my assault on your brother's home?"

An evil leer spread across Everett's face.

CHAPTER THIRTY-FOUR

Having repossessed Kella, Max picked a leaf from a tree and tucked it in Kella's pocket as he eyed the open gates to the Blue District. Somewhere in there, presumably inside Krairon's neighborhood, lay the Linganore Staff he'd come to steal. And theft it would be. He had ruled out the possibility of an exchange. He felt determined and confident, Everett having approved the plan. So had Moiryn, who had briefly appeared in Everett's throne room and cackled like a crazy ex-girlfriend on hearing it. Sexy in all sleek black leather and wickedness, she had purred how much she liked Max.

He turned his attention to the two ash fiends who had accompanied him as bodyguards. Neither was in disguise. The intent was to frighten anyone who thought about screwing with Max to think twice about that. And so two level 120 ash fiends had been floating beside him all the way from the Orange District through the wilderness that lay between the Red and Violet Districts. They had encountered some riven, whom the gods of the Violent District had created. Apparently, they weren't smart enough to realize they should run away and had promptly been killed. Since both Everett and Moiryn were in on Max's plan, the gods had also sent two dozen daekais flying overhead. As intended, this result in a simple walk to the walls of the Blue District. He'd earned 2,000 XP from others killing on his behalf.

Max had half-expected trouble from jhaikan, whom the blue sphere gods had created, but aside from one or two who had briefly followed and been killed, no attack had come. He knew why, because he'd caused them to be absent on purpose. Now the interesting part started.

He had multiple undead in his *Party Screen*, allowing him to communicate with them. This was critical, given that most of his forces were far away and out of sight. The timing was important because he wouldn't have much time to evade detection as a ghost possessing a priest of Scrylyn. Once that was known, he was doomed. The trick was a distraction.

Two wights in his party had just entered the Blue District, striding along ahead of them. They looked like zombies, though each had ice-blue eyes and long white hair, as opposed to the varied and unpredictable appearance of zombies. But Max had learned the actual difference lay in their capacity. Zombies were relatively mindless. The wights were closer to intelligent beings, able to follow multi-step plans, think for themselves, and even perform magic. That's why they had been offered to Max. They had walked ahead of him by up to fifty yards all the way here, as if fleeing, which was the impression he wanted to create.

They were decoys, a ruse, willing sacrifices who knew their role and that Everett would revive them. Max now told the ash fiends to remain behind and out of sight until his return. In the guise of Kella, a Priest of Scrylrn, he stepped into the Blue District, acting like he was pursuing the wights. He jogged along behind his fake prey, who looked back as if worried about what Max would do to them if catching them.

On his right, storms swirled above the neighborhood of Okier, the God of Wrath. The buildings beyond the cracked wall showed signs of earthquake and hail damage, seeming like they would collapse at any moment. The ground rumbled as Max jogged, a flash of lightning unleashing a boom of thunder an instant later, as if it had been right atop him. He'd thought Everett's neighborhood was dangerous, but it seemed placid by contrast.

To Max's left, barbed wire, spikes, and vines that his *World Lore* skill identified as poisonous adorned the walls of another neighborhood. Loiria, the Goddess of Malice, lived within. Many of the spires he saw looked razor sharp and clearly had someone impaled atop them, rivulets of blood staining the stone. The occasional scream split the air. Some structures reminded him of torture devices in their design. And as if to remove any doubt, on the exterior of the wall beside him, the random body had been stretched to the point of snapping, the victim delirious, drooling, or babbling nonsense.

With an effort, Max ignored the gruesome sights and sounds. In case anyone was watching, and he was sure that someone was, the wights ahead continued to pretend they were worried about Max. All three continued down the path toward the Blue District's town square, no one on this road leading in but them. When Max reached the center, the wights twenty yards ahead, he saw what he now thought of as the usual denizens of Sorrairyn—locals, adventurers or players, and NPCs of various species and races, mostly jhaikan. Only a few were present and were far enough away to not matter, including the two lounging beside a Moon Gate in the square, sitting on thrones of skulls and other bones.

The wights ran toward Krairon's neighborhood. A few people present watched but made no movement to intervene. A jhaikan pointed and seemed to laugh as two others followed his pointing arm. Did they know why the wights were here and expect them to be destroyed at Krairon's gates? That was exactly what Max intended, but it would not go how anyone likely thought.

Are you ready? Kella thought at him.

Sure, Max lied. He honestly didn't know what was going to happen if this didn't work.

I bear you no ill will.

That surprised Max. It also created the impression that they were going to die in a few minutes, and this was a farewell. *Why not?*

I have been with you long enough to know you are only trying to regain your life and have good intentions. Despite some of your actions, I forgive you.

Max wasn't sure what to say about that. It was premature, given that both of them might be headed for unending damnation. He felt the genuineness of Kella's sentiment. Being able to accurately read someone was one benefit of having possessed their body.

For what it's worth, I'm sorry for dragging you into this. I didn't think it would go this way.

Your plan is solid. Impressive even.

Stroke my ego when it works.

Fair enough! You have my support.

I'm going to need it in about twenty seconds.

I know. I'm ready.

The wights looked back. Max broken into a run. He'd fallen too far behind and now rapidly gained. Ahead, the walls of Krairon's neighborhood left little doubt the God of Domination lived here. The fortifications suggested an assault was always expected. Archery towers rose every fifty yards. Mostly human knights in black and silver armor stood beside the steel gates. A wooden drawbridge lay over a mote with who knows what in the waters. Beyond it, the buildings were foreboding, dark, menacing, brooding, and oppressive, snow and icicles apparent. The upper levels leaned over the lower ones and into streets, as if to intentionally block out the sky and make someone feel small and insignificant. This was no open and welcoming place, but one to avoid, and that made the defenses seemed superfluous. Who would want to overthrow an area that had been conquered from within?

As the wights neared the drawbridge, archers opened fire, striking a few blows but not stopping them. Max had to be the one to destroy them or his plan ended right here.

"Stop in the name of Scrylyn!" he called, having not thought of something better to say for this moment.

The wights whirled to face him, looked back once at the for-tifications, and seemed to decide they stood a better chance against him. They charged, the onlookers unable to know they were in Max's party and wouldn't actually hurt him.

Now! he thought at the priest. He then ceded control.

Kella began murmuring words of great need to his goddess, one hand on his medallion and the other stretched forth in a halting gesture, palm out, fingers up. A wide arc of moonlight shot from the priest's hand to engulf the wights, who writhed in agony before bursting into flames with a shriek. They ran away but collapsed into burning piles of flesh and bone after a few steps.

To Max's surprise, he received no XP for the kills, but maybe it's because they were in his party. They wouldn't have been worth much anyway, since both were only level 1. That had been required because Kella was level 5 and had to be more powerful than them to turn the wights, who otherwise would've just fled. Max had wanted a show of willingness to destroy the undead, partly to disguise the fact that he was one of them. Without earning the trust of those who'd been watching, he stood little chance of getting inside.

As the bodies burned, Max resumed control and approached the drawbridge. Several archers point their bows at him. He held up both hands. He hadn't been sure what to expect of the residents. Would they be alive or dead? If dead and still moving, weren't they really undead? And given Krairon's anger toward Everett, undead in Krairon's forces would be unexpected.

But he saw some undead there. This didn't seem to make sense, but maybe it was different here than on Llurien. In mythologies, the afterlife had people still walking around, which could have them viewed as undead, but they were considered dead. Someone was only undead if they were among the living, on Earth, or in this case, Llurien. In Sorrairyn, the line between dead and undead appeared to be blurred. Whatever the cause, Max saw both dead and living people among those in Krairon's neighborhood.

He stopped at the gates in front of the knights, both of whom seemed alive. "I understand the undead are an affront to your master. Please convey my pleasure in returning two of the dead to his command."

The archers lowered their bows, so Max stepped onto the drawbridge, booted feet clonking on the boards unless he stepped on the ropes holding them together. He crept his way across without seeing threatening gestures. Both knights were level 75. He received a message from the death knight in his party that their assault was beginning.

"Greetings," he said, hoping to keep this short.

"What do you want?" one of the human knights asked.

"I followed those two wights from near the Orange District. I don't know if they were headed here all along or if I accidentally drove them here with my pursuit."

"It matters not. They are dead."

"Yes, but I wanted to apologize if so. Please convey my regrets to Krairon."

"He is not here and would not care."

Well, that was a relief. At least Max wouldn't need to contend with another god, but if Krairon had taken the Linganore Staff with him, Max was screwed. "Fair enough. Do you mind if I ask where he went?"

"Yes."

Max stifled a smile at his stupid question. He was about to try something else to extend the conversation when the need to do so ended. A deep toll sounded from within Krairon's neighborhood, somewhere off to the right. The knights snapped to attention as shouting rang from within, the bell booming again.

"You must leave," one informed him, a hand going to the sword at the waist.

Max feigned ignorance. "What is happening?"

"An attack on our northern wall. Step off the drawbridge." He jutted his chin to suggest Max get off the far side, but Max needed to come in, so he didn't move.

"An attack? Who would dare?"

The knight smirked. "Can you not guess?"

"No. Faster if I come in, I think."

The knight frowned but didn't stop him as the drawbridge rose. He had made it inside, a chill wind whipping past him. He'd already felt and seen a notification about his buffs from Everett going away on leaving that neighborhood. Now, as he stepped into Krairon's, he felt the nerfing of his abilities. The bell continued tolling.

"Who would dare to attack the Lord of the Dead's home?" he asked.

"Everett, the Thief of the Dead."

Max hadn't heard that title and suspected it wasn't a real one to anyone but Krairon's followers. "Are you saying undead are attacking the north wall?"

"Precisely."

"I have spells that your priests may not have. Maybe I can help?"

The knight snorted. "Unlikely, but you may go as you please. Perhaps you will get yourself killed and become our master's plaything."

How charming, Max thought. "Which way?"

The knight pointed, and Max took off at a run, not wanting to dawdle. He knew roughly where his hundred undead were attacking. He'd sent them through the Red District, but not attracting too attention had required going in small groups and through two different entrances. And disguises. Moiryn, who had made getting to the Orange District such a pain in the ass, had been delighted to provide them, whether magical or mundane. Max had approved of their appearance. They looked like random adventurers, mostly fighters, a few rogues, a handful of wizards, and a few bards in recognition of Max's true class when alive.

He'd also sent a few seemingly living people through the Red District ahead of the rest. Their mission had been to reach the Blue District from the northwest gate Max had wanted to use for himself, or get as close as any jhaikan would let them. They had told the jhaikan that a horde of undead was approaching in disguise from the Red District and would be there any minute. This had drawn most of the jhaikan in the wilderness north of the Blue District away from the gate where Max had entered. That had kept him, his ash fiends, and the wights he'd pretended to follow from encountering more jhaikan before entering this district. But now the real gambit began. His undead horde had begun their assault.

Max raced through the shadowy streets, the winter wind tugging at Kella's priestly robe. Passing the first of several small graveyards, he wondered how to find the way until he saw jhaikan ahead and hurrying in the same direction. Would he be seen as a friend while inside the defenses? He ducked into a side street to a parallel one and then followed the commotion from there. Anyone else he saw was human or kryllan, only some heading the same way. Others went about their business, some tending to still more graveyards, which were so common that Max had another idea. The worn streets smelled of death more than in Everett's neighborhood, but after the twisting streets brought him closer to the jhaikan than he wanted, he emerged to a tense sight.

Chapter Thirty-Five

Through Kella's eyes, Max saw a short field that looked like a now-trampled garden. Two dark statues of a crowned figure towered over the throng of armored warriors, some of whom stood in neat rows. Nearly half were alive, the others not so much. Most seemed human, with a few kryll and jhaikan. All wore chainmail or plate mail decorated with skulls and bones, or actual bone mail. Beyond them loomed the district's outer wall, curving inward. Archers with flaming arrows stood atop it, firing down into an unseen threat, from where shouted commands and groans came. A few knights strode the walls, issuing commands Max could not hear. He didn't care about what happened there, only that it drew their attention.

Back toward Krairon's bleak and black castle he moved, the widest road from there beckoning him. The leaders of Krairon's forces should be near there. He assumed the Linganore Staff was inside the castle, and someone had to be bringing it to the commanders. The staff could take control of the undead horde, which Max had sent as a distraction to help him gain entry. And now it served another purpose. Why infiltrate this place any more than necessary when he could trick someone into bringing the staff right to him? This was a lot easier than trying to gain access to it wherever it was kept.

From the death knight leading his horde beyond the walls, Max received a message that they would soon reach the top. They were climbing upon each other's backs, a siege engine not being feasible. The jhaikan drawn to outside the walls by Max's messengers had slightly damaged the horde before being killed.

Near the widest road from the castle, he spied a half-dozen people who seemed more important from their bearing, resplendent armor, and the way others hung around them as if awaiting commands. Two priests and a few archers were among them, but no wizards, who were by the warriors at the wall. Max approached and focused on a living, human knight in black armor, his blue eyes intense beneath a strong brow and above a chiseled jaw.

Name: Amant Kinkiller of Sorrairyn.
Title: Warlord of the Dead.
Deity: Krairon, God of Domination.
Patronage: Patron of Warlords.
Type: Sorrairyn, NPC.
Class: Knight.
Species: Human.
Level 250.

At a higher level than the others, Amant barked at people who scurried away to comply. If someone brought the staff to this guy, Max would never get it away from him, but he'd figured this might happen. Now it was time to make them ignore him by getting their attention first. If he skulked about, someone might wonder what he was doing there, but if they already knew, they would pay less attention. That was his theory, anyway.

"Excuse me, my lords," Max said, stopping at the building's stairway, the commanders ten steps above while surveying the impending battle.

Amant sneered down at him. "What is one of Scrylyn's priests doing here? Go back to your mistress."

He bowed his head. "I followed two undead through the district and destroyed them at the gates. I came to help here."

"Stay out of the way." The knight turned toward the street leading toward the castle, dismissing him. "What is taking that fool so long?"

Max followed his gaze but saw only people going about their business farther away. This was the likely direction someone bringing the staff might come from. Everett had said he'd feel its presence, but his sixth sense didn't detect it, though with him being nerfed, maybe that meant nothing.

With a glance at Amant and other leaders, Max headed down the street as if following the knight's order. Behind him, the first undead topped the wall, a roar of anticipation from Krairon's forces greeting this. He stepped off the road and between open cemetery gates and past gravestones, hurrying out of sight behind a church.

"Okay Kella," he murmured, glad Everett had loaned him the Lyre of Murryn, "a slight addition to our plan. I want you to cast *Raise Undead*. I feel like we need more than what the lyre will summon."

I suspected you would want this when you brought materials for it. I've never cast this.

Life and death are full of surprises.

Max ceded control. Kella reached into one pocket to retrieve a pinch of bone dust from a tiny box, a small vial of blood, and a dried piece of skin. With a rising motion of his hands, he crushed them together and spoke an incantation that didn't last long, like most spells Max had observed so far. The ground beside a headstone parted, and a mummified hand appeared. It didn't take long for the zombie to climb from the earth and stand before them, dirt still falling from its emaciated body. Two glowing blue eyes silently regarded them.

"My turn," said Max, resuming control. He retrieved the lyre from inventory and quietly summoned two zombies, though he had no control over their form. He had hoped for more, but with his abilities nerfed, this might've been all he could get. Pulling cloaks out for all three to wear, he glanced around, listening to the commotion as the battle intensity rose.

"Again, Kella," he said, as the cooldown for *Raise Undead* completed. The priest did it once more, this time gaining a skeleton, and Max then repeated his use of the lyre to gain another skeleton and two zombies. But he only had one more cloak and decided the skeletons would go without. It wasn't like someone couldn't tell what they were at once. No cloak was going to help that.

He eyed his group of seven undead—two skeletons, four cloaked zombies, and one uncloaked zombie. Max commanded one skeleton to sneak down the road toward the castle by staying behind the buildings. Time for more subterfuge. He knew the ones he had summoned would obey mental commands and didn't need to be in his party for communication. The other skeleton was to hang back here with the uncloaked zombie. He was about to cautiously return to the road with the four cloak-wearing zombies to find an inconspicuous place to watch. But then running footsteps sounded from the direction he expected someone to bring the Linganore Staff from. He now sensed it and realized he had for a half minute.

Max strode toward the street with his disguised zombies behind. Acting casual, he eyed those he sought and cursed. A black-haired woman in a blue robe held the staff. A level 21 wizard, she was running in his direction, already closer than he wanted. Two warriors in silver chainmail, both level 15, were right behind. All were alive and their levels suggested Max could not change that, not that he needed to. He'd expected being outmatched, his undead evening the odds. A new plan forming, Max retreated but commanded the undead to the road's other side.

Nearby, the undead attacking the Blue District's outer wall were increasingly reaching the top and dropping to the ground to engage Krairon's forces. The screams, shouts, and clang of metal and bone rang out. The occasional whoosh of fire preceded screams. As Max looked, Amant snapped his head toward the woman bringing the staff and leered in triumph. Max intended to wipe that expression from his face.

Standing hidden behind the church wall, Max pulled out the Lyre of Murryn.

What are you going to do? Kella asked.

The lyre can create a magic void, 25-foot radius. It's the only way to keep the wizard from destroying all of us in a few seconds. She won't be able to cast.

Probably true, but it will destroy the undead, too.

What? Why?

If undead enter a magic void, they fall unconscious and will quickly perish if no one removes them.

Shit. Then we're doomed.

Not necessarily. Tell them to attack the warriors and let the woman keep running toward us. This will separate them and—

I get it.

Grateful for the tip, Max gave the command and the skeleton that stood off to one side down the road ran into the street. The wizard looked surprised and dodged sideways as she continued. The skeleton barreled into one warrior behind her and both went down in a heap. The other warrior stopped and pulled out a sword. It only took two quick blows to destroy the skeleton.

But Max sent the cloaked zombies running there to keep the warriors occupied. As the fallen warrior rose, the zombies attacked in a snarling rampage of flailing arms and gnashing teeth, screams splitting the air. The wizard stopped, clearly thinking to help them. She glanced at Amant, whose intense gaze was impatient.

Max quickly cast the lyre's magic void spell at the wizard but couldn't tell if it worked, though a look of confusion came over her. Was she wearing magic items that had just stopped working? Frowning, the wizard turned to help the warriors. In one raised hand, she held the four foot long, gnarled, black Linganore Staff, which wasn't straight like a weapon, but twisted and curled as if the tree itself had lived a tortured existence that warped its growth. Max pulled out Kella's Mace of Truth +3.

Shit, he thought on realizing something. The wizard made a gesture, but nothing happened.

What? Kella asked.

I was going to run out there and club her, but if I step into the void, I'll be expelled from you, won't I?

Yes! Wait until she leaves it.

Two of the zombies had fallen, but the others continued slashing at the warriors, who were cut and bleeding but still a threat. The wizard once again gestured with both hands. It did not appear as though the second effort produced a result.

But she'll have magic again when she's out of the void, Max thought.

She may not know that until you're upon her and it is too late.

Max was going to say more, but then the wizard gave up on helping the warriors and ran toward Amant. Max sent his remaining skeleton and zombie running at her with instructions to let her pass, but slow her. If she stopped inside the void, Max couldn't reach her.

Seeing them, the wizard hesitated, but then from her expression she seemed to realize that they were outside the magic void or they would've fallen. Maybe that meant she was outside of it, too. Max hadn't thought of that. This was all too complicated. Even as she raised an arm to try something, Max ran out, eyes focused on the undead as if they were his target. The wizard's gaze shifted to him.

"Stand back if you cannot cast!" he yelled, raising the hand without the mace. Then he thought of something better to suggest. "Run to Amant!"

"My thanks, priest!" she replied, taking off again. Max saw the warriors finish the other zombies, so he sent the skeleton to intercept. Since the zombie was the fastest, he sent it ahead of the wizard to stop her this time. She could destroy it in a second, but that would not matter. Her standing still with her back turned to Max was the goal.

After several strides, the zombie got in front of the wizard, who wasn't quick. She halted, raising the staff even as the zombie swung.

"Perish!" she commanded. The zombie burst into dust with a quiet whump.

Max swung the Mace of Truth +3 as hard as he dared into her back, a sickening crunch making him wince. The wizard gasped as she fell face first to the ground, the Linganore Staff tumbling over the cobblestones with a clatter. A red -32 HP floated up, surprising Max with the damage until he saw the system messages explaining it.

Critical Hit!
Stealth Attack!

Behind him, Max heard the skeleton's bones tumble across the ground. He and Kella had no help now. Max emitted *Wail of Terror* to gain time, unsure if it would work while he possessed someone. To his relief, the wizard and both warriors took 50% damage and became stunned. Ahead, an enraged and unaffected Amant drew his sword.

"Time to get out of here."

Max picked up the Linganore Staff and ignored a message that he wasn't high enough level to use it, as he ceded control of the body to Kella. Being in on the plan, the Priest of Scrylyn knew what to do.

"From here to far cast me away, take me to where my visions lay."

Then they vanished.

Chapter Thirty-Six

Cast Away deposited Max outside the Blue District's northeastern gate, where he had entered. The spell had a distance limit that Kella's level determined, but this had been enough. He just had to make it through the wilderness to the Orange District, but that was the easy part now. He wasn't planning to walk the whole way, either.

He took a moment to enjoy his relief. Then he laughed that the plan had worked. Through the *Party Screen*, he told his death knight to fall back and return through the Red District. That could convince anyone wondering where Max had gone that he went that way.

The two ash fiends he'd left here now returned from within the dark forest, their shifting, sooty appearance no less disturbing. Max healed himself and started for Everett's, noticing that the nerfs from being in Krairon's neighborhood had ended. Then a jingle of metal made him turn.

And there stood Amant, the Warlord of the Dead, a sinister black sword in one hand. He was alone at least, having arrived by magical means, as far as Max could tell.

Kella thought at him, *How did he—*

Cast us away.

But—

Just do it! Toward Everett!

Max sent the ash fiends to intercept Amant before ceding control. He'd already sent so many undead to their "death" to today. What was two more?

Kella cast the spell, and they vanished, reappearing farther north in the wilderness between the Red and Violet Districts, a few feet from the trail. Max took control again and ducked behind some bushes, listening intently.

Won't he just follow again? Kella asked.

I really hope not. His class is knight, not paladin. That means he's not a wizard. Someone sent him after us, like maybe the wizard I struck.

Unless he has a magic item that's letting him follow.

Why do you think we're hiding in the bushes?

Several minutes passed without Amant appearing. By then, his death knight revealed that all the undead back in the Blue District had been destroyed. So were most of those outside the walls. The death knight was among only three returning. Max didn't know what had happened to the ash fiends he had just left behind, but he presumed they were gone. He and Kella were alone in the wilderness.

I think it's safe to cast again, Max thought. Kella's mana regenerated quickly out of combat, like his.

I must applaud your foresight in gathering the materials as we journeyed there.

Thanks.

The spell needed something from the destination. On the way here, Max had picked numerous leaves during their journey. The trick was grabbing the right one when he cast the spell, but the inventory helped with that.

It took two more times before they arrived outside the gates to the Orange District. The illusions there didn't pester them as they went in. By the time they reached Everett's neighborhood with the Linganore Staff in one hand, a kind of honor guard of undead stood at the gates. Several death knights stood at attention but didn't include the one who'd led the assault, as that one was presumably still making his way here. Rows of skeletons, zombies, and more powerful undead had gathered to welcome him. This was so unlike the last time that he stifled a laugh. He hadn't expected gratitude or respect.

Two knights led the way, a growing crowd of supporters following. Word spread long before he arrived back in Everett's hall, where the orchestra began a celebratory march until he stopped before the Lord of the Undead, whose eyes blazed. Max couldn't tell if it was excitement, disbelief, amazement, or what, but the gaze was not threatening so much as lust-filled for the staff. Max held it up just as the orchestra stopped on a triumphant brass fanfare that shook the room.

"Behold!" he said, feeling silly for using the word. "The Linganore Staff, stolen from Krairon, Lord of the Dead, and presented to its rightful owner, Everett, Lord of the Undead!"

A cheer filled the crowded room. At a gesture from the god, the staff lifted out of his hand and floated to him, settling comfortably in his hands. The god caressed the staff and stared at Max. He smiled.

Quest Complete: Retrieve the Linganore Staff from Krairon, the Lord of the Dead.

You earned 10,000 XP!

You earned +5 Reputation with Everett!

You achieved Level 6!

You gained 23 Spectral Hit Points!
You gained 5 Spectral Mana Points!
Class bonus: You gained Dexterity +1, Agility +1, Constitution +1.
You gained (2) proficiency points.
You have (2) unassigned proficiency points.

The god said, "I observed you through the eyes of my undead. Most impressive, Maestro Max."

Max bowed before straightening. "It was my pleasure, master."

"You show little fear, great cunning, and quick thinking. I am pleased to have you in my service, but I understand that regaining your life is valuable to you. I must honor this."

"Thank you."

"So if you return to life, I must wait for you to die to serve me, but this I do not wish. Perhaps there is a way we can both have what we want. Are you familiar with kajina?"

"Kajina? I am not."

"It is the name karelia and sorelia use for their ability to separate their soul from their bodies and remain alive. Not all of them can do it. They must be trained. There are limits, as well, such as how long they can do this, and how far apart body and spirit can be. It is wise to leave the body somewhere safe, preferably under protection."

Max asked, "Why do they have this ability? Sorelia I can understand, if they want to cause problems, but karelia?"

"We granted them this long ago as part of the Divine Covenant. Spirits were to be let loose on Llurien, which naturally pleased me. But many of my brothers and sisters did not want this due to the damage the spirits could cause the living. We compromised and gave the karelia augmented supernatural traits so they could resolve spiritual disturbances that were thus created. Kajina is one of these."

As Everett had spoken, his *World Lore* skill had popped up a message he ignored.

"I have a gift for you, Maestro Max," said Everett, breaking his thoughts. He held up his hand, in which a black and silver ring lay.

Item: Kajina Ring

Description: Named for the karelian ability, this kajina ring lets the wearer separate soul from body, just like karelia and sorelia. The body will not die and can move independently of the spirit, which can travel up to a half mile away; the ability to control both is nonetheless difficult to master.

When the ring is activated, the wearer becomes dual-classed. The body retains its current class. The spirit has the class that it last used in death, but this must be spiritual and not corporeal undead, like a zombie.

Cooldown: 1 day.

Duration: 10 minutes per undead level.

Bonuses: +3 Intelligence, +3 Wisdom, +3 Morale, +3 Strength (as Undead Only).

Special: This item is soul bound.

Holy shit, Max thought, excited. He no longer resented all the time spent trying to get his body back. He'd be able to use his ghostly skills once a day without dying first, though there was still the threat of someone capturing his spirit. He'd have to work on protecting himself. But this was an amazing reward. The item being soul bound meant he could never lose it by being killed in the game. The ring floated over to him, and as he held up one hand to grasp it, it entered his inventory instead.

Notice: You have completed a quest while dead and in non-corporeal form. You cannot accept one reward, a physical object. It has been placed into your inventory and will be available should you regain life.

"There is something I require of you," began Everett.

Max stifled a sigh, not wanting yet another task. "Yes, master."

The god raised one hand, palm outward. A brief orange glow surrounded it and Max gasped in pain as something seared his chest over his heart. He looked down and saw a glowing sigil of swirling lines he didn't understand fading from view.

"I have marked you," said Everett, as if it was no big deal. "Even if you regain life, you shall always be my minion in death. I have accepted your soul's allegiance, and now it is binding."

This time when his *World Lore* skilled popped up, Max read it at once.

Info: Everett's Mark
Summary: The God of Fear, Everett, may mark someone's soul so that when they die, they become undead. Some karelia and sorelia can sense this mark, which cannot be removed. It is among the most feared fates and results in the Great Masquerade on the Night of Terror—the annual day when Everett is at his strongest influence on Llurien, where a worldwide masquerade takes place to hide one's face from him, lest he place his mark.

Wryly, Max thought he wouldn't have to worry about that masquerade now that he was already marked. He wasn't sure any of this mattered. The game was based on a book series where this was considered real. In the game, it likely figured less, given that everyone died eventually and became undead long enough to respawn. Maybe this was nothing to worry over. But if karelia or sorelia could sense it, that might cause trouble.

In the real world, assuming such a thing as an Everett or Satan existed, it likely meant never achieving an afterlife like heaven. Did that mean he couldn't ascend in the game to live forever? That was his backup plan if he couldn't regain consciousness and his lawyer bought him more time. He could never achieve Sorrairyn, becoming a permanent part of the game as a demi-god of something… unless it was as undead?

He smirked. That was very "metal" of him. What if he became the ultimate undead like the King of All Ash Fiends? He'd have to become an ash fiend first in that case, of course, but maybe this development was good. He'd already impressed one god, and a deity likely had to cause his ascension, so maybe this was the path to follow.

Everett interrupted his thoughts again. "Your plan was so dastardly that my sister, Moiryn, devised an additional gift for you."

Max's eyebrows shot up, but something occurred to him. "That's great. Is there a price for it?"

Everett laughed. "You are wise. But there is not. She has, however, taken an interest in you and may call upon you for assistance."

Max bowed, wondering if he'd be required to do evil things between the two of them, as if he hadn't already started to. "I would be honored."

"To aid this, she is gifting you this ring, which will improve your ability to manipulate others and objects more deftly. It will also allow her followers to realize you are friend and not foe, so that they may trust you more readily. They will also know that you can be called upon to help if needed. Fear not, as she is the Mistress of Illusions, most will not realize the ring signifies this."

"That's great, master. I am relieved to hear of her wisdom on this."

Like the other items, the ring floated toward him, this time from the arm of Everett's obsidian throne. It once again deposited itself into his inventory, so he barely had time to examine it. It looked like a silver band with two gemstones on it, one green, one orange. He read the description.

Item: Friend of Moiryn Ring.

Description: This ring will identify you as an ally of the Goddess of Deception, Moiryn, but only to her followers. You and they will see two colored gems, orange and green, but all others will see two green gems, falsely showing you are an ally of Tarerra, the Goddess of Truth. The ring will also allow the wearer to see many illusions for what they are, especially spells Moiryn herself designed.

Bonuses: +3 Dexterity, +3 Charisma.

He wasn't sure if he should trust the idea that only the intended people could divine the ring's true nature, but since a god made it, maybe it was okay. In the back of his mind, he knew he'd always wonder if someone saw the truth. None of it would matter if he didn't get his body back, which reminded him of something very important.

"If you recall, my primary reason for coming here was to free Kiavalon's beloved from you and return her to Llurien. We agreed you would let me take her if I performed the quest that she failed to do."

"Tiardyn is yours." Everett waved a hand and something metal clattered behind him. Max's eyes darted to a chain falling away from cell at the wall, a door on the second level swinging open. A short figure stepped onto the stone landing, walked to one side, and descended stairs to the floor, her bearing upright. Even from here, Max thought she seemed at ease.

An important notification had popped up as he watched her gather belongings from a skeleton guarding a treasure trove of gear. Max glanced at the notice.

Quest Complete: Rescue Kiavalon's Beloved from Everett.
You earned 5,000 XP!
You received 1 Uncommon Song: Don't Tread on Me.
You received 1 Rare Item: Namaerian Chain Mail +3.

You achieved Level 7!
You gained 40 Spectral Hit Points!
You gained 6 Spectral Mana Points!
Class bonus: You gained Dexterity +1, Agility +1, Constitution +1. You gained Speak with Living (level 1).
You gained (2) proficiency points.
You have (4) unassigned proficiency points.

Since Max still had the leather armor from killing the guy the day he met Norus, the armor upgrade caught his attention. He dimly recalled having the niquerran-made kryllan bracers he'd barely gotten to wear before being killed, but he wasn't sure what namaerian was and used his *World Lore* skill to find out.

Info: Namaerian Steel
Summary: Made from niquerrium ore, niquerran steel is the strongest known metal. Valenium ore has properties that augment the supernatural, but results in valentium steel, a soft, lightweight metal unsuitable for weapons and armor. By

combining niquerrium and valenium, those on the continent Namaera invented a hybrid that is both stronger than all but niquerran steel and has the augmented supernatural properties of valentium—namaerian steel, the rarest of metals. And the only kind that can wound a god.

That last part was interesting. If a god could take damage, in theory one could be killed. But he couldn't imagine how much damage that would really take.

Seeing the sorelian woman Tiardyn approaching, Max looked up the spell he'd received.

Spell Song: Don't Tread on Me
Key: F Minor
Time: 4/4
Description: Rhythmically repeating this powerful chord in short bursts over five seconds will cause all enemies with a ten-foot radius to be violently knocked back twenty feet. They will also be stunned for several seconds and suffer burn damage of 3-5 HP per caster level.
Duration: Instant.
Level: 2.
Cooldown: 30 Seconds.
Lyrics: None.
MP: 3.

With the Metallica song of the same name stuck in his head, Max felt good about this acquisition. It could be a great first action, buying time while dealing damage to multiple targets. If he combined it with *Wail of Terror*, which also made people lose a turn, and did a lot of damage to multiple targets, he had a great start to fights. Of course, he had to separate his soul from his body or be dead to do that, so maybe he'd never be able to do both in a row that way.

Everett said, "While you were contemplating your obedience to me earlier today, I questioned the priest you inhabit. He told me your story, that three enemies killed you and hid your body so you cannot regain it. Is this true?"

Tiardyn had stopped a few feet from Max, a calculating look in her slanted violet eyes as she regarded him disdainfully.

He said, "Yes, it is. They were enemies in another life and followed me here to resume their interference with me."

"They will continue to do so should you regain your body."

Max noticed it was a statement, not a question. "I would assume so, yes."

"I do not wish this. You have proven loyal and resourceful. And entertaining. I will let you go about your business until I have need of you, but when I call upon you, I cannot have someone sabotaging our work. What do you intend to do regarding them?"

Max met his gaze and thought he saw an expectation of revenge in them, so he admitted the intention that had already been there. "I plan to hunt them down and destroy them."

CHAPTER THIRTY-SEVEN

Eyes gleaming, Everett said, "When you kill those who murdered you, take control of them and send them to a karelia for judgment. They will be out of your way, and mine."

Max perked up. "Does that mean you'll let me keep the Lyre of Murryn?"

"Yes. You are a skilled performer on it."

Max smiled. Having Everett for his god was reaping more benefits than he would've guessed, and the metal head in him felt this was the deity for him. They seemed of like mind.

New Quest: Kill Your Enemies and Deliver Their Spirits to a Karelia.

Objective: Why only kill your enemies when you can deliver their souls to a karelia, who may send them to an afterlife that keeps them from interfering with your plans? Kill and deliver your target(s): Reaper, Vixen, and Iron Heart.

Difficulty: Medium.

Rewards: +1 Reputation with Everett. 1,000 XP Per Enemy (3).

Accept?

And here I thought doing that would be its own reward. Max accepted the quest.

He turned to Tiardyn. He hadn't seen many female karelia up close except the Dark Trio's Vixen, who'd been in darkness. This one didn't look much different from males except for even more delicate features. The heart-shaped face and high cheekbones reminded him of a Japanese anime girl, black hair matching her black chainmail. The lorenia lines on her cheeks and forehead were more feminine but not glowing; she must've been suppressing that. Tiardyn's expression bore no gratitude or admiration. If the bold, frank, flat stare was her friendly vibe, Max didn't know what Kiavalon saw in her, though she was beautiful in a creepy way. His gut told him she was trouble. She didn't seem resentful of him for succeeding with her quest, when she had not. He pulled up her info.

Name: Tiardyn of Ansini.
Type: NPC.
Class: Ghost Hunter.
Species: Sorelia.
Level 8.

Her class designation seemed self-explanatory and differed from Kiavalon's spirit warrior. Since she wasn't saying anything, he introduced himself.

"Kiavalon says hi," he joked, not expecting a reaction.

Ignoring him, she turned to Everett. "Does this mean I am free to go?"

The god looked sideways at her and frowned before looking at Max. "Take her out of here."

Max bowed. "Yes, master." He turned to go, not checking to see if she was following. He didn't need her anymore. Not really. The quest was done, though she had to make it back to Llurien.

Kella's thoughts intruded on his. *I don't trust her.*

Neither do I, but I don't see what I need her for. Let's just get out of here. I'd like to get you back to your life, and me to mine.

Agreed.

As Max left Everett's neighborhood, he felt the buffs go away. Tiardyn kept a few paces behind and didn't move toward the Moon Gate. He'd forgotten to ask Everett about it, but the deity had increased the time limit on possessing someone until Max returned to Llurien, so he didn't need to rush. But something else kept him moving quickly.

Life Counter: 2 Days, 20 Hours, 26 Minutes.

Max figured that the mission to Krairon's had happened in the early pre-dawn. He surmised it was now about 12:26 PM and felt reasonably safe exiting the Orange District and through the illusions there. He couldn't use Kella's *Cast Away* spell because he'd have to leave Tiardyn. Would she even help if they ran into trouble? She'd probably run off.

As they entered the wilderness, Max heard Tiardyn speak behind him.

"Expel the thief where two are one," she began, "wrest this power, let it be done!"

Even as Max glanced back to see her extend one palm toward him, he violently flew forward, tumbling in the air. Everett had done this to him once, too. She'd expelled him from Kella, his only way through the Moon Gate!

His haphazard motion stopped, and he righted himself.

Alert! You have been expelled from your host!

Warning! You have been stunned!

Kella lay on the ground, seeming as dazed as Max felt. Tiardyn stood above the priest, the lorenia lines as bright as the triumph in her fierce eyes.

"Don't follow," she warned. "I can do things to you that you wouldn't like." She ran past him into the woods, toward the Red District's Moon Gate.

By the time Max felt able to move again, she was out of sight on the twisting path. As a ghost, he was faster, but rushing through this treacherous forest wasn't smart. Maybe the bitch would run into her own troubles.

"What are you going to do?" Kella asked him, worry on his face as he dusted himself off and rose with a groan.

The concern for Max surprised him. "I don't need her, really, though it would be nice to intercept—" He stopped, then pulled up his *Party Screen* chat. The death knight who'd led the attack on Krairon's neighborhood could still be coming this way through the Red District.

Max: Lord Kylon, where are you?
Lord Kylon: We have left the Red District and are halfway to the Orange, in the woods.
Max: Perfect! Listen, I want you to intercept a sorelia named Tiardyn. She is coming your way from Everett's, probably at a run. I will be pursuing.
Lord Kylon: Is she to be killed?
Max. No, captured. And feel free to be rough about it.
Lord Kylon: With pleasure.
Max. Contact me when you have her. I am on the way.

He exited the chat and smiled at Kella. "I'll explain as we go."

They both cast spells to help see through illusions and prevent misdirection. Beside the path, they soon found the corpse of a mynx, a horse-sized feline with stab wounds to the neck and chest. Had Tiardyn done it? A short time later, Max received notification that Lord Kylon and the two undead with him had captured Tiardyn after a brief fight. He wasn't surprised, given the disparity between their levels. He and Kella slowed and soon found them by the roadside. With bruises on her face and a bloody gash on her ribs, the sorelia knelt with hands bound behind her. The glowering expression triggered Max's anger. He grabbed her biceps, and she gasped at the *Necrotic Touch* damage that darkened her arm.

"What did you do that for?" he snapped, letting go. "Why expel me from the priest?"

Tiardyn sneered up at him. "Revenge."

Max scowled. "For what? I rescued you, you stupid bitch!"

Her expressed turned withering. "Not you, moron. Everett."

That brought Max up short. Maybe he shouldn't have been surprised by that answer, but it made him wonder something. "How long were you in there?"

She growled, "Fourteen months."

Max's eyebrows shot up. No wonder she was mad. But still. "How does being mad at him lead to forcing me from the priest so I can't return? You should be grateful I got you out of there. Why punish me for something Everett did to you?"

She gave him a withering look. "Didn't you hear him back there? You're his new favorite undead. He wants you to do all sorts of things for him. Trapping you in Sorrairyn, even if only temporarily, is the closest thing to revenge on him I can get."

Max's gaze hardened at her logic. It made sense, but he liked being screwed over even less when it had nothing to do with him. She'd waited until they were far enough from the Orange District for Everett or his minions to not see her do it. That explained the smirk she'd worn.

He asked, "What did you really do to get imprisoned? Did you even try the quest?"

"Of course not. No one could…"

He frowned. "I did. That another reason? You jealous? Just like all the little shits who put me into this world. I should march your ass right back to Everett and tell him what you've done. And why. My friends here will tell Everett what you attempted unless I tell them not to. If you pull one more stunt between here and that Moon Gate, you will never see Llurien again. That will be the least of your problems."

The defiance drained from her demeanor. He moved toward Kella and received the prompt to possess him again, but it was greyed out due to the cooldown. That prompted him to check his logout button, where nothing had changed.

With a new plan forming, Max left for the Red District with the undead escorting him, Kella, and Tiardyn. After consulting with the priest, he entered the neighborhood of Solon, the God of Justice, to whose followers he told a half-truth—that the sorelia was wanted for supernatural crimes in Andra Kindgom and Karendi Kindgom, and he would turn her in at Castle Evator to stand trial. He had surmised the first part, which reminded him of the peril he faced for the same. They had questioned his ghostly presence until Kella lied and said he'd let Max hitch a ride here and would do again on the way back. Then they let the group wait in the first floor of a building.

At his behest, Kella blindfolded a kneeling Tiardyn, who had set in motion hours of wasted time, during which every attempt to get a successful prompt to possess Kella failed. Max chafed. To distract himself, he practiced his skills like *Spirit Walking, Moving Objects*, and *Invisibility*, raising each to level 3. His *Possession* skill was already up to 8, having risen two levels since arriving here, while *Possession Speak* was up to level 6. After four hours, he finally got the prompt, which he silently declined in agreement with the priest.

Instead, Max moved behind Tiardyn and, without warning, possessed her. She fought but was only one level above Max, who was strong in this skill, prepared, and determined. If she expelled him, Max had another four hours of waiting. And so he clamped down and seized tenuous control. Kella unbound her wrists and Max removed the blindfold. He wouldn't be able to keep this up for long and realized Kella had submitted more fully than he'd known. Tiardyn put up such a continuous fight that her struggles caused Max to walk with a weird, halting gait as they left. Did being sorelian help her?

He ignored the tirade of cursing she unleashed all the way to the nearby Moon Gate, which hadn't changed. A group of assorted adventurers over level 40 stood near, watching him with raised eyebrows, either from his body language or the undead. They moved aside. Kiseron, the Keeper of the Gate, eyed them with amusement. As Max came with paces of the magic doorway, which was already on, Kiseron touched it and an image of the gate room in Castle Evator replaced the silvery surface. Tiardyn gave a last burst of resistance.

Feeling his control slipping, Max shouted, "Shove me through!"

A pair of ice-cold hands gripped him by the arms. A warning about necrotic damage flashed past Max's eyes. Then he fell toward the shimmering surface as Tiardyn shrieked.

CHAPTER THIRTY-EIGHT

Eric shielded himself and the unconscious Anna from the .

A rainbow of colors raced past Max's vision before an image stabilized—Castle Evator's gate room, its golden carpet rushing up at his face. He landed hard on his stomach, the stones beneath knocking breath from Tiardyn's body. At that moment, the sorelia overcame his control.

Alert! You have been expelled from your host!

Warning! You have been stunned!

Max tumbled through the air like usual—he was almost getting used to it. He caught sight of at least two knights with their swords drawn. Several robed figures that could've been wizards or priests were present. Then Kella stepped through the gate. Max finally righted himself and took in the scene more clearly while resisting the urge to just rush away through a wall. He needed to see what was happening, however briefly.

One knight had a sword tip to Kella's neck and yanked him away from the gate by one arm, as if clearing the way for anyone else coming through. The other knight jabbed a blade into the back of Tiardyn, who lay face down. Two other Priests of Scrylyn were present, judging by their attire, and a wizard in a tan robe had both hands up as if to cast something. Max didn't see a karelia or sense one near, to his relief. But one priest looked right at him, then another, and he looked down to discover that he wasn't invisible. He'd forgotten in the chaos. He changed that as more eyes turned to him. Sensing that he was no longer stunned, he descended through the floor.

"Goodbye, bitch," he said to Tiardyn, who glared at him in fury.

Max raced away, still searching with his senses for whether karelia were near. He activated his new *Blind Descryer* skill. First, he wanted to regroup, so he headed deep into the castle to the empty cavern he'd found before. Once there, he looked around to verify nothing dangerous was present and then tried to relax, eyeing the countdown.

Life Counter: 2 Days, 15 Hours, 46 Minutes.

The logout button hadn't changed. He was feeling a little hopeless and defeated about it, but he was also getting used to shrugging it off.

Thinking about what had just happened, he'd planned to end his possession of Tiardyn as soon as they arrived on Llurien anyway, so her expelling him had only been an issue for stunning him into being vulnerable. Kella had surmised that unless they returned weeks from now, an increased presence would await. They'd foreseen both Kella and Tiardyn being apprehended.

Max had intended to stun the sorelia by vacating her, but this had worked just as well. This was one reason he hadn't possessed Kella again, the other being to give the guy a break. Never mind the priest just being part of a game. The realness of it often made Max forget, despite this ghost business being so unlike real life.

Now that he'd regrouped, his thoughts turned to Tiardyn, who hopefully had no way to contact Kiavalon to hint that Max was coming for him. Max had a plan, and the time had come to get his body back and finish this.

—— • : • ——

Max waited on the first floor of a weapons shop that was closed for the night. He'd watched the owners leave, slapping each other on the back over some joke while heading to a near-by watering hole. No one was upstairs in the living areas. It was around 7 PM now, the sky darkening as the sun fell below the horizon.

He felt nervous about Kiavalon's ability to detect him even with *Blind Descryer* on, so he was a block away from the sorelia's rooms. He reasoned Kiavalon was in the same place as when they'd met, because this was a game and NPCs who gave a quest rarely went somewhere while you were doing it, if you were expected to return to them. Karelia might also detect the sore-lia's true nature if Kiavalon ventured out.

The lovers' big reunion had been put on hold. Tiardyn was probably sitting in chains beneath Castle Evator, an interrogation under way. She wouldn't reveal anything easily, he imagined, unless she wanted to. Would she say anything about Max that would come back to haunt him? Kella could also reveal Max's identity, but the priest had been so helpful that he might not. Would anyone believe a claim that Kella didn't know who had been possessing him? Even if Kella didn't "out" Max, he would likely admit that Kiavalon was in town, and that would trigger a karelian search. Max cursed himself for not realizing it sooner.

Better get on with this.

Max wasn't sure how to pray to Everett. He didn't have a talisman or something, but he gave it his best shot.

"Everett," he whispered, "I need a favor, so I can better serve you in life and in death. I'm about to summon undead and it would be best for them to be corporeal. Otherwise, Kiavalon's Black Mirror could trap them as it did me. Please grant me this."

He waited a few moments, unsure if he'd get a response, or what form it would take, but none came. Pulling out the Lute of Murryn, he summoned undead and got the maximum of five, all with bodies. Even better was their type and levels—two level 2 zombies with almost 40 HP each, one level 1 zombie with 24 HP, one level 2 skeleton with 20 HP, and a level 1 wight with 45 HP. The total of Max's undead HP probably surpassed the sorelia even without considering Max, who intended to avoid fighting or being seen. While he'd gone up in level since the last time he'd done this, there was no question Everett had answered his prayer. He apparently wanted to be certain Max succeeded, whether that was a pro-Max thing or an anti-Kiavalon and Tiardyn one.

He gave his undead orders to look for the Black Mirror and separate the sorelia from it, if possible. Then he opened the door and led them down the street at a sprint. There'd be no disguising this, and he knew the karelia weren't close enough to do anything at first. Everyone else who saw them would likely run away.

And that was exactly what happened with the few players and NPCs they passed before his lead zombie slammed open Kiavalon's door, knocking it from the hinges. They charged up the stairs while Max stayed below, feeling tense. A notification appeared.

Warning: Your actions have alerted nearby karelia (and sorelia) to your presence.

Max had thought that would take longer. The sorelia's startled voice and shouts turned to words of magic and a whoosh of fire that set the building afire. Notifications filled Max's vision. His undead were taking damage. But then came the screams, thuds, scrapes, and enough banging to know even without the notices confirming it that his minions were pummeling Kiavalon. Hoping to speed up this, Max emitted *Wail of Terror*. Shouts of pain and confusion sounded from nearby houses.

Warning: Your actions have alerted nearby karelia (and sorelia) to your presence.

Amid his notifications was one that the wail hadn't worked on the sorelia, but Max's enemy was close to death and the sounds of fighting stopped moments later. Max floated up through the ceiling to find Kiavalon on his back, blood flowing from many wounds on his black leggings and shirt. He hadn't expected company, clearly, not to mention this kind. His leather armor was elsewhere. None of the undead had perished, but one still burned silently, calmly patting at the flames on his torso with one emaciated hand. Kiavalon had 5 of his original 100+ HP left. Furious, pain-filled eyes glared at Max.

"You! How did... Where is Tiardyn?"

"Imprisoned in the castle," Max replied. He'd reminded himself that the sorelia didn't know Max knew the truth about the mirror not controlling him anymore. "Maybe you'll join her in a minute, but I'm pretty sure you won't release me from the Black Mirror, so I'll have to kill you."

Kiavalon's eyes darted to a chest on one side. The mirror undoubtedly lay there. Either that, or it was a trap, but Max would have one of his undead do the honors of opening it to find out.

Knowing forces were on their way, Max sent two zombies out and into the street and told them to run toward the castle and fight for their survival, and to make as much noise as possible. That would hopefully keep trouble away from here. For good measure, he sent the skeleton and remaining zombie to guard the entrance to this building from inside, but he kept the wight with him to hold down his enemy.

Max didn't much care what happened to them and felt a little bad about that. Was his cavalier attitude because they were already dead? He supposed so. But he felt like he should probably show them more loyalty or something. But he knew they had nowhere to go once they were done serving his needs. It wasn't like Max could keep them around and have no one troubled by that. Every undead he ever summoned was destined to be destroyed.

As the sorelia lay dying, Max saw a chance to find his remains slipping away. "I will spare you if you tell me how to find my body."

Kiavalon sneered. "I do not fear death."

"You should. In moments, I will have your Black Mirror, kill you, and ensnare your soul as you did mine."

"Without your body, you can't use it."

Shit. He's got me there.

As fighting and shouting began outside, sudden anger filled an impatient Max, who sensed karelia closing in. He grabbed Kiavalon's head and slammed it into the floor, doing several HP of necrotic damage. Apparently, he was getting better at moving objects. "Tell me how to find it!"

The sorelia laughed, and an enraged Max conceded defeat. He'd have to get the intel from the Dark Trio instead, and he knew just how to kill them now. He wrapped both ghostly hands around Kiavalon's neck, the black decay covering the sorelia's entire head until the eyes went dark, a look of agony on his delicate face. Several damage notifications came and went without him looking at them. A final breath escaped Kiavalon before Max let go.

You have killed (1) Sorelian Spirit Warrior, Level 9!
You gained 1500 XP, half of the total!
Loot corpse?

Letting his minions fight someone was safer but cost him a lot of XP. He'd have to reserve that for when it was most needed. Gaining XP certainly wasn't everything.

Max ordered the wight to open the chest. Nothing like a trap happened. The wight shuffled the contents, a book and vials amid the clothes. It straightened with the sought item.

"Bring it to me."

The wight obeyed, presenting the Black Mirror with bowed head and arm outstretched. Max took the item, which didn't cause any discomfort, and it went into his inventory as he brushed aside a message that he couldn't use it while a ghost. At the least, no one would use it on him again. The commotion outside was dying down and the karelia were moving in, so he told the wight to join the fight. Then Max quickly looted the chest and Kiavalon's corpse. But he didn't look over the items.

The warnings he'd received suggested that *Blind Descryer* had expired or been nullified with his actions. His HUD confirmed it, the little blindfold icon was missing. Max raced down and away through buildings and the wall west of town, into the wilderness, leaving everyone behind. He received another notification of the wight killing someone before being destroyed. If anyone found out he was behind these actions, he was probably in trouble. Only Kella and maybe some dead players and NPCs knew, but he was not killing the priest to keep him quiet.

He found a secluded area between two hills and stopped to check his notifications. His undead had killed three others in town, and since the last time he'd looked, Max's reputation as a ghost had risen, along with quite a few other stats.

Name: Maestro Max.
Species/Race: Human.
Class: Ghost, Level 7.
Reputation: 3—Feared.
XP: 26925.
SHP: 181/181.
SMP: 38/38.
Strength: 7.
Dexterity: 15.
Agility: 13.
Constitution: 11.
Intelligence: 8.
Wisdom: 9.
Charisma: 12.
Morale: 11.

That kajina ring gave him all of his undead boosts and kept him from becoming too lopsided. From Kiavalon's loot, he'd received a strong healing potion and a vial of moragul blood. The book had notes on random subjects that must have caught Kiavalon's fancy, and possibly Tiarydn's, as some of the handwriting was more feminine. Max scanned entries about Moon

Gates in various locations and a list of where they led to. Another list noted the location of magic voids in various places the two had traveled. Some notes were written in a kind of code Max would need to decipher.

He also received more money than ever before, over $1500 in silver, gold, rubies, sapphires, and a diamond. He now had more than $2000, not that he could do anything with while dead.

The last time he'd had time to think on anything had been when Everett trapped him in that tomb, or whatever it had been. Much had changed in the game, but that was all. Max increasingly wondered if resurrecting himself in Llurien Online would make him wake up, a desire that was growing stronger and more desperate. The idea of playing the game to help himself awaken had seemed to have merit, even if it was pure guesswork, but he was really questioning the decision now.

Needing to find the Dark Trio, he checked his map to see if they were in the game, and where, but their icons were missing.

But a far more important icon was present.

Chapter Thirty-Nine

Eric shielded himself and the unconscious Anna from the .

"What the hell?" Max said. For a moment, his disbelief was stronger than any excitement at seeing the arrow pointing to his body. "Are you serious? It's just there on my map now?"

Adrenaline pounding, he raced over hills and through trees to the north of Evator, wondering how this could be, wildlife scattering at his approach. His first guess was that the death of Kiavalon had somehow revealed his corpse. But he knew the Dark Trio had hidden him. Had the magic to do it somehow come from the sorelia? He'd been thinking the whole quest to Sorrairyn had been a waste of extremely valuable time if his body was just going to reappear by itself. But he'd come back stronger than ever and with great abilities. He told himself this was how it was meant to be, because believing it was random aggravated him.

Before relief could even start, he was halfway to the destination when he slowed. What if this was a trap? This was the obvious way to lure him somewhere, maybe to do something like what Kiavalon did with the Black Mirror. He abruptly changed directions to close in on the spot by circling it tighter and tighter.

Max had stumbled into too many problems. He needed to be smarter, less trusting. Naïve. He ensured he was invisible and moved away from the foliage so scurrying animals would not betray his presence.

Max kept his senses keen as he began encircling the spot, which lay north of a stand of trees he now passed right into. He sensed no one out here. His night vision made everything bright. He sometimes picked up a rock and threw it far away into some bushes, his eyes watching to see if anything nearby looked out from behind a tree or bush. Nothing.

The map didn't show the Dark Trio. Did they know he'd be able to tell if they were here? Could they do a *Blind Descryer* skill or spell? A magic trap could be here, but he could sense magic better as a ghost, since it could hurt him, and he felt nothing. But he had another way to keep himself safe.

Using the Lyre of Murryn, he summoned undead, getting a zombie, a spirit, and a wight, their levels unimportant. He sent them right for his body, figuring they'd trigger any traps. Still invisible, Max moved off to one side because the undead were making a straight line from him to there.

His body lay under some shrubs. The undead reached there without trouble. He made them move around the area, but they encountered nothing and no one, so he closed in. He had been out in this general area before but had not seen anything.

Now on top of the spot, he saw that the ground under the bushes had been disturbed. The Dark Trio had dug up the shrubs, buried him under, and put the plants back. He made the zombie and wight move the plants and dig before he had a better idea to verify this. He lowered himself through the ground horizontally. He only had to go two feet before finding himself, the clothes familiar, his severed arm tossed beside him as unceremoniously as the rest. They hadn't looted him, to his surprise. Maybe it wasn't possible to do that to players. The shallow grave didn't surprise him. Climbing out would be easy enough, but he'd get his undead to dig him free. Before he could, he received the message he'd been desperate for since being killed.

Respawn? Or become corporeal undead?

Vastly relieved by the first option and ignoring the second, Max decided to just do it now and clicked *Respawn*.

Warning: Unable to Respawn. You have been dead too long. A karelia may be able to help you, or a priest can resurrect you.
Quest: Find someone to bring you back to life.
Reward: Life! Oh, and 1000 XP.
Accept?

Goddamnit! Max rose out of the ground and let out a piercing scream. Scores of birds flew into the night air from nearby trees. *Like any fucking karelia is going to help me now!*

He floated back and forth, clenching his fists, his undead watching silently. He made them put the bushes back before his control of them ended. What happened to them then? He'd never found out because they were always destroyed. He assumed they wouldn't go after him, but just to be sure, he moved away. After they finished, he made them enter nearby trees because he had a suspicion of what was going to happen to the wight and zombie. When the time came, both of them fell where they stood. The ghost faded from view.

Max needed a plan. And a priest to resurrect himself. They were all in town, where he couldn't go. Not now. Karela had to be swarming the place looking for him. This was unlikely to change for days, but he couldn't wait that long. He couldn't go to Ardyn, the karelia who'd helped him outside the graveyard. Ardyn had warned Max not to do exactly the kinds of things he'd been doing. The karelia couldn't be trusted. Too risky. While his undead were the ones who'd been seen in town tonight, karelia had sensed him. He was sure. He had to assume they knew a ghost was around. Kiavalon's corpse and the necrotic damage Max had done probably left no doubt. Max was never getting inside Evator while a ghost. Possessing someone wasn't likely to work. Some karelia were better at sensing a second spirit inside a body and it would be just his luck to encounter one.

Someone had to come to him. Even if he got a message to a priest who could do it—and Kella could not—that priest was likely to know Max was the culprit and bring karelia instead. It had to be Siren, who was the only one he could trust. She would have to bring a priest out here. Even carrying Max's body back to town wouldn't work because Max would still have to enter Evator as a ghost... unless he came up through the ground with *Blind Descryer* on and the priest resurrected him at once. Or could he be resurrected while his ghost was out here? What was the distance requirement between body and soul? Maybe there wasn't one. In theory, people were resurrected while the spirit was in heaven or hell, according to lore on Earth, so this small distance wouldn't matter?

But he had no way to message Siren. He could communicate with the living now, but he had to be near, just like in life. He needed a messenger. Someone out here who could be sent into town to find her. Another player or an NPC. One had to come by, which subjected Max to waiting.

But wouldn't they be able to tell he was a spirit? He could use his *Appear Alive* skill, but in theory, anyone who focused on him would see his actual class as a ghost. That gave him a thought. That skill would be pointless unless it changed your class description from ghost to whatever. He activated the skill and then checked his *Character Screen* to see how his stats appeared to others. To his relief, it now said "fighter" instead of ghost. His class was really bard, but before arriving in Evator, he'd changed it to fighter and hadn't altered it back. It appeared to default to his previous customization. It also still said he was of Rook, not Evator. He probably should've changed various things about it before now, to evade identification during his undead escapades, but too late now.

A plan was forming, but he needed a good story to tell whoever came along the road. They would also need incentive, but he would just offer money. It was too bad he couldn't make it an official quest, but he was pretty sure players couldn't give those. He'd never heard of that. He would have to tell them to find Siren by name. But they would want to know why he didn't get her himself. It took him a few minutes to think of a decent story, but once he was satisfied he'd anticipated most questions, he moved to the road. He waited a few hundred yards closer to Evator than where his body was, just in case something happened and someone searched the immediate area and found the grave.

Thirty minutes passed before he heard someone coming from the north, as if headed toward Evator, and he activated *Appear Alive*. He would need to keep this conversation short so the skill didn't end while they were in sight of each other.

A muscular figure almost his height strode down the road, putting one hand on a sword hilt at his waist on seeing Max. His pace slowed, his head moving back and forth, so Max tried to seem unthreatening, even waving, though it made him feel like a dork. Once the figure was close enough, he got the info on him.

Name: Death Strike.
Type: Player.
Class: Fighter.
Species: Human.
Level 2.
HP: 21/21.

Death Strike wore the sort of cheap leather armor lower-level players acquired soon after starting, but he still wore plain shoes and didn't seem to have much. Offering him a reward might be appreciated. His face had a scar on one cheek and blue war paint on the other, a heavy brow making his dark eyes seem menacing. The long, braided, brown hair down his back contrasted with the shaved sides of his head. He looked like a biker transported to the medieval ages.

"Hey man," Max began as the player came within a few feet, "how's it going?"

Death Strike stopped, his expression even. "Good. You're not gonna attack me, are you?"

Max feigned surprise. "What? No. Actually, I was hoping you'd do me a favor."

"Oh." The guy laughed, revealing stained teeth, one of them missing. His demeanor now turned jovial and, like the appearance, didn't fit his personality. "Sorry, you're just a few levels above me."

"Yeah. Gotta watch out for player killers."

"No doubt. Those people suck."

"Yeah. So listen, you're headed to Evator?"

"Dunno. Is that where this road leads?" Death Strike nodded down the path.

"Yeah. You're almost there. The way is clear. I mean, you're close enough that there aren't monsters or other shit out here."

"That's good. Thanks for the tip."

"Yeah, no worries. Listen, I was hoping you could look for someone there and tell her to come out here to meet me."

Death Strike shrugged. "Sure, but why don't you just do it?"

"I'm waiting for someone, unfortunately. My girlfriend. She's gonna be pissed if I'm not here when she logs back in."

The guy laughed. "Yeah, I get that. But won't she be pissed you're meeting some other girl?"

Max smiled and thought quickly. "Nah, it's her sister."

"Is she cute?" Death Strike smiled, and Max inwardly cringed. With this low-life appearance, this dude was nuts if he thought any girl would be interested.

"Yeah, but she's a hard ass. Her name's Siren. I can give you some game money for the trouble."

"Cool, cool. Need some money for sure. What if I can't find her?"

"Maybe you can keep me posted? I'll give you more each time you come out here."

Death Strike considered and asked, "What if we form a party? That way, I can tell you if I find her without coming back out here."

As undead, Max couldn't accept a living person into his party. "Um, my party is full at the moment," he lied, "but that was a great idea."

"Alright, man. I'll tell her. Report back if I can't find her." He held out a hand and Max retrieved a silver coin from his inventory, placing it in the guy's palm. Then he gave a description and Death Strike walked off.

Max wasn't sure if he could really trust the guy, who gave off a selfish and indifferent vibe. Maybe Max should've thought of a more sympathetic story. Or waited for someone else. But the clock was ticking. Once Death Strike was gone, Max made himself invisible and hunkered down by the road to wait.

Only fifteen minutes passed before he saw four people coming down the road once more, this time from Evator. He figured it wasn't Death Strike, but was wrong. The others with the fighter were a level 2 human wizard, a level 2 kryllan hunter, and a level 1 querran priest. Max's instinct told him something nefarious was underway. Was he getting wiser or just more suspicious? Was that the same thing? He moved further away in case either the priest of wizard could detect him with a spell, though they almost certainly weren't looking for a ghost.

"How much farther?" the wizard asked as they neared.

Death Strike looked around and stopped close to the right spot. "I think he was right here."

"You *think*?" The hunter sounded annoyed. Death Strike shot him an irritable look.

The priest asked, "Are we sure this is a good idea? I still don't think we should kill another player."

Max's eyebrows rose. *That little fucker.*

"Look," began Death Strike, "we need loot, and he's got it. Money and other shit. It's four on one, an easy kill."

The priest shook his head. "I'm pretty sure we only get XP, split four ways, which hardly makes it worth it. We might get something like 25% of the money, maybe some spell components. That kind of thing. We can't take weapons, armor, or any of the cool stuff because people hate that and the game designers limit it."

Death Strike said, "Yeah, well, we'll see about that. And after we kill him and his girlfriend shows up, we'll do her, too. Hell, maybe I'll even lure the Siren girl out here, with all of you waiting for us. I'll act like I don't know you and I'm with her, then stab her in the back, getting a stealth bonus and critical hit. Lights out."

Max clenched his fists. Maybe he'd spare the priest, but the others were in for a surprise. Max was sick and tired of people fucking with him. It was time for some fun of his own. He moved behind a nearby tree and made himself visible. Then he used both *Appear Alive* and *Spirit Walking* before he moved toward them over the grass.

Feigning relief and ignorance, Max pulled out the Lyre of Murryn and strummed a few notes on it, as if feeling carefree. "Ah, there you are. I'm guessing you didn't find her?"

Death Strike's smile might've been genuine. "No. Looked around. I found these three and told them of our deal. They want to help."

"That's great!" Max stopped closer to them than was wise— if he'd been alive. There was almost no chance level 1 and 2 players had magical weapons that would actually hurt him. The priest and the wizard were the only threats. Malice grew in his heart.

Death Strike moved to one side and the hunter and wizard took their cues to surround him, while the priest frowned. "Well, it's great for us. I meant that they were here to help me, not you."

Max feigned concern and made a show of fearfully watching them encircle him. "What do you mean?"

"Was thinking if you paid all of us, we wouldn't kill you."

Max gasped. That almost made him laugh. "You're player killers?"

"Damn right. You'll give us all your loot, too, like that harp."

Max dropped the ruse. "It's a lyre, asshole, just like you."

Death Strike yanked out his sword and put it toward Max's neck. Max heard the hunter behind him draw a weapon. To one side, the wizard raised both hands. Only the priest made no move.

"Give us your shit now."

"Can I sing a song for your first?"

Death Strike scowled. "I'm gonna stick you with this sword until you scream."

"Funny, I was thinking about screaming any second now."

"Screaming for help won't save you."

Max laughed. "Wanna bet?"

"I've had enough."

Death Strike pulled back his sword and swung it at Max's torso. The blade sailed right through. Since he'd expected to make contact, this threw him off balance. The others gasped in surprise.

"An illusion!"

"No. A ghost?"

"Oh fuck."

Max drawled, "You know, it's funny that your name is Death Strike, because I nicknamed myself Death Singer a while ago. Let me show you."

As the wizard began muttering a spell, Max emitted *Wail of Terror*. He watched in pleasure as all four of them lost half their HP and their next turn, stumbling back, satisfying looks of horror on their faces. Feeling jovial and sinister, he used the lyre to summon undead, who climbed from the earth around all of them faster than the first time he did this. That appeared to be one side effect of gaining levels. He got a wight, two skeletons, and a zombie, all but one skeleton being level two.

"Subdue the priest, kill the wizard, then the other, and leave the fighter for me."

Death Strike stepped back and Max lunged, grabbing his shoulder and watching the *Necrotic Touch* blacken the skin. A red -12 HP floated away as a health bar appeared deep in the red. But Max didn't want him dead yet. He turned to the battle and saw the wight finish the wizard with a rake of his throat. The hunter killed the lower level skeleton while the other and the zombie had the priest on his back, health bar in the red. Max raced over to the hunter, who uselessly swung a sword right through him. Activating *Horrifying Visage*, Max permanently aged him by two dozen years, leaving him stunned for a turn. The wight finished him as Max turned back to see Death Strike running down the road.

"Coward," he muttered before racing after. His speed as a ghost was far faster, and he easily caught up with the guy, getting in front so that Death Strike stopped, huffing and puffing.

"Please…"

"Going somewhere?" Then Max thought of something that wasn't really important but annoyed him all the same. "I believe you owe me a coin."

Death Strike fumbled for it and dropped it on the ground. "There."

"Give me the rest or I will kill you, or worse."

"What? I…"

"I believe in an eye-for-an-eye justice," Max admitted, glancing back over Death Strike's shoulder to see the other undead still holding down the priest. "My turn to make that demand. Give me everything. Or die."

Death Strike fumbled for his coins and began leaving them and everything else on the ground in a heap as Max made him practically strip naked. Max took it all into his inventory – sword, leather armor, and the rest.

"Are you going to let me go?"

"I'm going to give you a piece of advice. First, don't go around killing players. Your priest friend was right. It's not worth it. Brings trouble down on your head. I would know. Second, I wouldn't come back out here soon. I'll still be here, since you didn't find my friend for me." Then he thought of something else and added, "Don't even think about telling the karelia in Evator that I'm out here."

Death Strike's face fell. "You're the one they're looking for."

Max bowed. "At your service. How did you learn that so fast? You'd only just arrived."

"My friends told me."

"I suppose that explains it. Well, time to die."

"No, wait!"

Max grabbed him by the throat again and killed him, only glancing at the notification and paltry XP award of 200. After awaking in the graveyard, hopefully these fools went straight into Evator, thinking they'd get Max captured by bringing karelia here, when it would be them that the karelia would ensnare. He didn't much care, so long as they went through even a fraction of the bullshit he'd gone through since dying in here.

Max went back to the captured priest, who held up his hands when Max loomed over him, hard eyes boring into the priest's worried ones.

"I'm sorry. They made me do it!"

"That's the only reason you're not already dead. You seem like a decent guy."

"I am. I swear. I don't like player killers. But they had it coming, so I don't blame you for doing to them what they were going to do to you. Are... are you going to let me go?"

Max considered. "I was going to, but I can't risk you going back to town and telling anyone about this."

"I won't say anything."

Max nodded, reminded of countless movie scenes he was about to replicate in his own way." Yeah, sorry, can't trust you. There's only one way to keep you from saying anything."

CHAPTER FORTY

The priest said, "Come on, man. My friends made me do it."

He leaned over the guy. "You need better friends."

"I said I was sorry! I didn't even attack you or fight back."

Max smiled grimly as he grabbed the arm, the necrotic damage rapidly spreading up to the head. "You're sorry. I'm sorry. And now we're both dead."

He straightened and sighed, his anger fading. Was he becoming a bad guy? These players had deserved it, except this priest, who he really could've let live. He wasn't worth much in XP. Neither were the others, except the kryll, who were always worth more for being better fighters. But letting this one walk back seemed like it would bring karelia here sooner. He had to think of himself.

Don't get soft, he thought. *Just wake the fuck up and do whatever you have to.*

He checked the logout button. No change.

He looked at the undead standing idly by. They had only minutes before perishing. He made them move the bodies off the road, throw them behind some bushes, and walk off into the forest. The wight was strongest and dragged away two by their ankles. They barely got Death Strike out of sight before they perished. Max was alone again in the wilderness.

Was it worth trying this again? The plan was solid. The flaw had been his choice of messenger. He needed to do it again, but not here, even though his body was near. The time it would take Death Strike and his friends to tell karelia, who would come out here en masse, was probably similar to the time to find another messenger who could find Siren and she reach him. But he felt like a sitting duck whose identity and location were now known. There seemed only one obvious alternative.

Max raced south through the wilderness, passing Evator a mile to his left, going through farmlands. No sense in getting too close. He found the other major road leading from town, this time toward Rook, the place he'd pretended to be from at the suggestion of Norus so long ago. Daekais had attacked the caravan here, but closer. Finding a small hill that let him see a traveler coming, he settled in to wait.

The impending resurrection, assuming he achieved it, increasingly made him wonder if he'd come out of the coma when it happened. It seemed plausible. Could the symbolism do the trick? He badly wanted to achieve both. But it seemed like desire was not enough or it would've happened. Did he not want it enough? Because he felt like he did.

Was there something about this world that made him want to stay here, or was something in the real world making him not want to return? That his subconscious might override his will frustrated him, but he knew people had demons. Those controlled them, made them do stupid or foolish things, or just gave them a hang up they rarely understood. He'd done some of it. But figuring out what might keep him here was a process that he was running out of time for. Like many people his age, he spent far more time doing things than being introspective. Was it going to kill him?

He still thought Siren was right, that playing Llurien Online could help him figure it out. It just wasn't working. Or was it? He'd ruled out a few things. Death in the game did not mean death in real life. Or waking up. This resurrection would answer whether that would help. Did he have to go down some list of possibilities before finding the one, eliminating the wrong options one by one? It was like looking for a lost item and a question his mother had once asked—why it is always in the last place you look? The obvious answer is that you don't keep looking after you find it.

So Max had to keep looking. The problem was that he didn't have a list of places to check. Where did he look inside himself when, as far as he knew, his mind and heart had already given an answer about what he wanted?

The sound of someone walking on the road caught his attention. Still invisible, he looked over the grassy hill to see a woman approaching Evator alone. Only her bosom made the gender clear, as his night vision didn't provide more detail from this distance. She wore leather armor and a cloak, a staff thumping on the ground as she came. He moved down the opposite side of the hill and made himself look alive. He really needed this to work and adopted his most unthreatening demeanor, since it was a woman. The thought made him realize the player might still be a guy, so he toned down the "I'm a super nice, harmless guy" vibe he was about to adopt. He turned himself sideways to pretend he wasn't waiting for her like a creep.

The woman topped the small hill, which he observed from the corner of one eye. He let her take a few steps before he turned, as if surprised by her. Before saying anything, he pulled up her stats.

Name: Lara the Fair.
Type: Player.
Class: Druid.
Species: Querra.
Level 3.
HP: 37/37.

She had chosen a benevolent class, at least. Was her player name about her appearance or attitude? Time to find out.

"Good evening," Max began as he turned toward her.

"Hi," Lara said, keeping fifteen feet away and stopping. She had braided her shoulder length brown hair to hang over one shoulder. A medallion of the goddess Kriseri, the one who had a statue south of Castle Evator, lay around her neck, depicting a tree. With blue eyes and a sweet smile, she was pretty, but that didn't surprise him when anyone in these games could change their appearance.

Trying to act encouraging, he said, "You're almost to Evator."

"I know. Been there already." She squinted at him then, and gasped. "Maestro Max! I knew I recognized you! You're the guy in a coma!"

Shit. Wasn't expecting that. Unsure what lie he'd say instead, he took a chance. "Yeah, that's me."

She rushed forward. "Oh my God. I'm so sorry about what happened to you. Are you okay? Do you need anything? Can I help you?"

Max blinked in surprise. "Um, yeah, actually, I need a favor, now that you—"

"Oh! Anything! I would *love* to help you. What can I do?"

Charmed by her enthusiasm and empathy, Max explained about needing to stay here while she searched Evator for Siren and told her where to find him. Lara didn't even ask why he didn't do it himself. While he wasn't feeling the least bit trusting after the bullshit with Death Strike, she had a kind of earnestness that had him trusting her anyway.

He added, "Just don't mention my name to anyone but her."

"Sure! And I'll search until I find her and come right back if I can't."

She sprinted away, leaving Max feeling hopeful. He made himself invisible and followed a short way. A desire to protect Lara had risen. It wasn't just that she was his messenger, but she'd been kind. That had made an impression. He wasn't used to it. Sure, Siren was in here playing with him, but she wasn't exactly all feminine and mushy about it. That didn't matter, really, but while he could tell Siren cared what happened to him, she had the same distant sarcasm that he did. Was it off-putting? Not really. He liked it. But the sweetness of Lara had made him feel like this was what was missing from his life—and like she reflected the innocence he'd long ago lost.

Was that what kept him here? That only a cold life awaited him world? It wasn't exactly all warmth and hugs here. The emptiness of his life struck him then. What was there to go back to, really? No one sweet like Lara. Surely if he'd been in love with someone who loved him, that would add greater urgency to awaken, wouldn't it? But it wasn't like he was going to find true love or some shit in here. And if he did, wouldn't that just backfire and make him want to stay?

That he had fame for being the first coma patient contacted in VR bugged him despite him having thought he wanted fame. What he really wanted was to be appreciated and respected. He'd assumed that would be as a musician. Instead, he'd been hated. And now he was likely pitied. He'd always be "that guy in a coma," like Lara had said.

Was being ticked off about that keeping him here? He did feel robbed of a chance at respect, like a door had been closed. And so maybe he refused to come out? That Lara had shown empathy and compassion, rather than pity, didn't mean others would do the same. But her respect made him realize his desire for it—and a bitterness that he might never get it now. Maybe what he really needed was to stop caring what anyone thought. That struck him as the truth, and he knew why he cared—people being rude to him because of what they thought of him. Maybe with just one Lara in his life, he'd find it easier to not care. He didn't know where that left him. The logout button was still greyed out when he checked. But he felt better and like he'd had an epiphany. It apparently wasn't the one to wake his ass up.

He was still in a good mood when, an hour later, Lara returned... with Siren striding ahead of her. He made himself visible, not caring that Lara would realize he was a ghost. Siren didn't react, but Lara looked startled and faltered before rushing to keep up. Max smiled reassuringly before turning to Siren, who stopped before him, eyes intense and face serious.

"Hey," he began, "I'm back. Sorry to—"

"Yeah, where the hell have you been? I've been looking all over for you!"

"I know. Or I figured. I had a bunch of problems."

She snorted, then chuckled. "You've created a metric shit ton of them, too. I thought I told you to keep a low profile? You're famous as shit in Evator, and not in a good way. You can never set foot in there again. You know that, right? I guess you have *some* idea, since you sent her to find me."

Max nodded. "Yeah. I have a good explanation. You wouldn't believe the shit that's happened since the last time I saw you."

"Some of it I know, figured out, or heard."

"Like what?"

"I knew you were killed. Got a message that a party member had died and I wouldn't be able to talk to you through the *Party Screen* until you were alive again. I was out of the game and hours had passed, and yet you hadn't respawned." She shook her head. "I was wondering what the hell happened until I went looking around and ran into this karelia outside the cemetery."

"Ardyn."

"Yeah. He told me your body was missing. I looked into that."

"Okay, but tell me about it later. We need to get moving."

She glanced around. "To where?

"My body. Finally found it. It's probably putrid, just as you like."

Siren rolled her eyes. "It's good to see you, too, Max. Lead the way." She glanced at Lara. "What do you want to do with her?"

At the question, the druid's eyes widened, so Max quickly turned to her. "I can't thank you enough for finding Siren and bringing her here. I'd like to give you something and—"

"It's no trouble," Lara interrupted, looking relieved. "I'm so glad I could help. You don't need to give me anything. Although..."

Curiosity piqued, Max asked, "Let's hear it."

"Well, I was wondering if I could tag along a little? Until you get your body back?"

Max wasn't sure what to say. He didn't see a pro or con to that.

Siren arched an eyebrow. "Your call."

"It might not be a bad idea. You could need help."

"Okay then," Siren said. "Let's go."

Max led them back north through the wilderness west of town toward his grave, exchanging info with Siren. They asked

Lara to keep back, unsure she should overhear everything. The druid didn't take offense and agreed.

Max learned that Sergeant Kari had questioned Siren. At the time, Max had been wanted for dereliction of duty, but after his attack at the training grounds, he'd been identified. He was suspected as the one causing disturbances around town, and the freeing of two prisoners had been assumed to be him, even though he'd brought Norus in. For Kari, this had virtually confirmed Max was never who he'd claimed to be. The messenger she'd sent to Rook to learn of his origins had returned with word that no one had any idea who he was. This has led to a harsher interrogation of Siren.

"I told her we'd only met here in town," she said, "which had the advantage of being true."

"Has she left you alone?"

"Not really. Been following me a bit. Not her personally. Some of her guards. Had to ditch them to come out here."

Max sighed. "Great. I was going to have you dig up my body and carry it in to be resurrected, but if they're watching you, they'll intervene."

"Why can't you just respawn?"

"Been dead too long."

"Huh. That's a new one. So you need a priest to resurrect you?"

"Yes. The two options are you bring my body to one, or you convince one to come out and do it."

"Neither is that great."

"Why? I'm thinking you bringing me in is no good now, but you don't think a priest will come out?"

She frowned. "Shit storm, Max. You unleashed one tonight. Word is all over town that you killed people in training, you scared some of their spirits at the cemetery after, and you freed two prisoners and attacked and killed guards. Plus, you wander-ing around town at various times. The karelia are assuming all of that was you. There's a rumor about you possessing a priest and forcing him through a Moon Gate, and then you coming back with that priest and a sorelia you were possessing. They locked her up. And then there's this thing with you killing some other sorelia in town with a bunch of undead you were controlling."

Max laughed despite the trouble this was causing him. "It sounds bad when you sum it all up like that. Part of me is sur-prised they know it's all me, but maybe I shouldn't be."

"What the hell were you thinking?"

"In a minute. I want to focus on getting my body back. Let's just say I had to do all of that to get to this point, and now I need help."

She shook her head. "A priest won't come out to resurrect you because you're infamous. If they know the resurrection is for you, they won't come. If I bring you in, they'll know."

Max looked behind them at Lara, then met Siren's gaze. "She could do it."

Siren nodded thoughtfully. "We still might need to disguise you a little."

"Not sure how to do that, but it could help if she brings me to the gate you just left instead of this one." He smiled ruefully. "I killed more people out here."

"Seriously?"

He laughed and explained why and that the karelia might be on the way even now, which was why they weren't on the road.

"Bunch of assholes deserved it," she said when he finished. "How much farther?"

"Almost there."

Max cast *Blind Descryer* more than once as they went, as he'd sensed karelia not far away on the road leading north. Being a ghost had stopped entertaining a while ago. All the hiding. Feeling hunted. Being an outcast, which seemed a little too familiar.

He motioned Lara to catch up and then asked Siren, "Do you remember the Dark Trio? They were the ones who killed me in the game."

Siren asked, "What for? You can get a bad rep doing that."

"You're not going to believe this, but they were the three people who attacked me in Baltimore. They came looking for me in Llurien Online."

Siren stopped. "Are you shitting me?"

"No. Let's keep moving. They admitted it before killing me. They assumed I remembered the attack and would identify them to police, so they killed me to keep me from respawning and talking."

Siren looked too appalled to speak, but Lara gushed, "Oh my God! That's horrible!"

"Yeah. They were the reason I haven't been able to respawn. They found some way to hide my body, so it didn't show on my map. A bunch of other things happened, but a while ago, whatever spell was hiding me ended. I saw my body on the map and found it, but when I tried to respawn, it said I've been dead too long."

"Got it," said Siren. "Attacking you means game logs. My father can get those and arrest their asses."

Max perked up. "Never thought of that. That could keep them from screwing with me anymore."

"Yeah, the company will probably freeze their accounts, too. Any idea why she could no longer hide your body on your map?"

"I can only guess. I've been wondering if the spell had something to do with the other sorelia I killed, and with him dead, it stopped working. Either that, or she had to log out, and it still worked while she was gone. Maybe it only lasted so long, and she didn't log back in in time."

Looking around warily. "Yeah, maybe."

Max noticed her gaze and asked, "Are you thinking it was a trap? They're still in town right now."

"Yeah. I don't like this shit. I can't believe those assholes. I'm gonna kill them. I'm tempted to log out right now and tell my dad."

He shook his head. "Let's get me back in my body first. The karelia are really becoming a problem. I just want to get the hell out of here." And he meant it. Whether it was Evator or this game, he needed a fresh start.

A few minutes later, they reached his burial spot. Lara dug up the body so Siren could logout for a while to tell her father the news. She returned not long after, saying she hadn't reached him but left a detailed message. Max felt a little better already, but more so when they helped Lara pick up his body and put it over one shoulder. They stuck his severed arm into a bag she had. Lara tried to sound positive but admitted the weight was a bit much. Her character had a low strength score, and she wasn't sure she'd make it to town. Or she would, but would struggle so much that someone might offer to help and discover Max's identity.

"It just says 'corpse,' not Maestro Max," Siren observed, "but I think you're right."

"You can change your name," Max observed to her, "so that could buy you time before anyone identifies you."

"I think I might need to. Hold on."

They discussed a few arrangements, including Max handing money to Siren if she needed to pay for his resurrection. Then Lara and Siren began carrying his corpse back to Evator. Max didn't really want them to go without him. He'd been through so much to find his body, only to watch them carry it away. But he shrugged it off and headed back toward where he had met Lara. They all believed he would be pulled from wherever he was for the resurrection, but if not, they would meet up there. He was out of communication once again, lurking in the countryside's rolling hills and sparse vegetation.

After an hour there, during which he wondered if something had gone wrong, he suddenly felt an odd tingling sensation. His sixth sense hadn't alerted him to anyone—or anything—nearby, but he scanned the area visually and with his feelings. No one. The sensation grew stronger, reminding him of when his arm fell asleep, and blood flowed back into it. This was getting uncomfortable. He moved off the road, fearing he'd become visible in his growing distraction.

His sight darkened so that, for the first time since dying in the game, the night sky no longer shone so brightly. His enhanced sixth sense faded. A white glow from him lit the grass before him and to both sides, and presumably behind. Holding up his arms, he saw he was no longer invisible but looked like his first appearance as a ghost—all shimmering white spirit. He received a prompt.

Warning: Someone is attempting to resurrect you. Rejoice or Resist?

Max slammed the *Rejoice* button and tried not to laugh at the choices.

And then another image began to materialize before him, blurry and indistinct. Two parallel rows of something dark, the space between them lighter. An oblong shape was on either side, narrower at one end. They moved slightly. It all disappeared in a bright light that blinded him before it vanished, leaving him seeing spots and blinking at darkness that began to clear.

You have been resurrected!

As you are under level 10, you will not suffer Daeijonen sickness.

Max dismissed the messages. When his sight returned, he realized he was lying on his back, looking at a raftered ceiling. An intense-looking Siren was leaning over him from one side, as was a yellow-robed human man he didn't recognize on the other. These were the shapes he'd seen as his spirit rejoined his body. He attempted to speak and realized his throat was parched. Dirt was in his mouth, too. He tried to spit it out but couldn't. Then a hand lifted his head, and a goblet touched his lips, water pouring into his mouth and out again across his cheeks and to his neck. He resisted the urge to swallow and instead leaned to one side with an effort and spat it out. A puddle with dark earth pieces in it formed. He wiped his lips, then grabbed the goblet from the man—a priest—with his right hand and gulped it down before flopping onto his back again.

"More," he croaked. The priest rose, taking the goblet as he moved away, and Max turned to Siren. "You did it. Thank you."

"How do you feel?"

He sat up with an assist from her, then saw Lara at his feet, looking concerned but smiling. They were in a small, sparse room with a cot in one corner, a stool, and a small table, plus the mat he was lying on.

He said, "A little sore. Stiff. Thirsty. Hungry."

"You will require some rest," said the priest from behind him, approaching with a full goblet.

Max took the drink with his right hand again and drank more slowly, noticing how dirty he was. Then he looked at the other hand and lifted it. His arm had been re-attached. He sighed in relief.

"You need a bath," remarked Siren.

"Yeah. I've got earth up my butt. I can feel it now."

"TMI, dude."

He smiled. "I look like I've been buried, don't I?"

"Yes. You'll attract attention. We need to get you cleaned up."

The priest said, "I will have a bath drawn for you. Some may find it uncomfortable if they know you've risen from the dead. I would not speak of this to others unless you know their views on such matters. I'll have some food brought as well." The priest left them alone.

Max fixed his gaze on Lara, feeling gratitude. He'd already discussed his arrangements with Siren, regarding her helping him, but not the druid. An offer popped into his head.

He asked, "Would you like to join our party? I can't promise you anything, and I might be a world of trouble for you when I'm really trying to thank you."

She beamed. "I would love to! This is so much better than just playing a game, being able to help you."

Siren gave him a warning look that suggested it was his call, but she didn't like it. Since Max could always expel Lara if needed, he let her in for now. Lara hadn't been in a party in this game yet, and while Siren gave her some pointers, Max took a moment to himself.

He had been distracted enough by the resurrection experience to have not really noticed that he was alive in Llurien Online again, but hadn't awoken in real life. Not automatically, anyway. He checked the logout button. No change. But he didn't let that dampen his positive mood. Some of his angst had faded. The pair of worries—that the karelia would nab him or he'd never get his game body back—had ended. A new worry came up—how to get out of Evator.

CHAPTER FORTY-ONE

Life Counter: 2 Days, 11 Hours, 23 Minutes.

When Max devoured the hart meat, Siaran wingfish, and noodles that the priest returned with, he felt much better. He took a moment to look up more info using his *World Lore* skill.

Info: Daeijonen Sickness

Summary: Those who have died and been reborn typically suffer ill health effects for a time that their level determines; characters below level 10 are unaffected.

The gods of the Yellow Sphere conceived of Daeijonen, which is one of the afterlife possibilities; therefore, any debuffs do not affect elements of their origin or influence. For example, their spells cast as normal during the sickness and items of theirs work at full strength.

Max had been wondering about the consequence of players dying in the game. That he hadn't dropped an item or a level was a relief. He could live with temporary debuffs. Some games had other negatives, but in this one, the potential of karelia or sorelia messing with him while dead was a big one.

His body restored itself faster as he ate, but the bath made him feel normal but sleepy, his fatigue debuffs not disappearing. Was it being fed, clean, recently resurrected, or the stress he'd been under fading? With no body, he hadn't felt tired since being killed, and now it was nearly bedtime. He had played far more than 24 hours straight while a spirit. After donning a tunic, he invited Siren and Lara in. They had been in the next room, removing the dirt from everything he'd been wearing.

"Based on the Life Counter," he began, "I probably can't reach another settlement like Gitarna before it runs out."

Leaning against the wall, Siren said, "Not unless you stole a florin bird, but you'll never get into the castle to get one."

"What level spells do you have?" Lara asked. "I think there's one that lets you change your appearance."

"Is there?" Max pulled up his spells and soon found it.

Spell: Body Morph.

Level 2 Transmutation.

Description: Changes the caster's body, whether cosmetically or to a deeper level, including species/race and gender. Note that neither mental nor physical attributes or abilities of another species are acquired.

Components: Verbal—"Change my form but not my soul, hiding truth is my new goal."

Cast time: Instant.

Duration: 1 hour.

Cooldown: 2 hours.

Sphere, Deity and Boost: Orange, Moiryn (Goddess of Deception), Longer Duration and Shorter Cooldown.

MP: 3.

"Based on this," Max began, dismissing his HUD, "I could hide in plain sight for an hour. This certainly makes leaving easier, but I don't see getting to a bird."

"Why not?" Lara asked.

"I had access as a guard before. Now I wouldn't."

Siren advised, "Forget the bird. You just need to leave and change your name when you do. A horse will do. We need to figure out where you can go and be safe for a while. Why don't I logout and look online for ideas?"

"Okay, but first, do you have any updates on the legal stuff?" It had been days since he'd heard anything and he felt out of the loop.

"Yeah, your attorney has filed something with the courts to see about getting you extra time while this idea of yours, that your situation is unprecedented and needs consideration, gets a ruling. But there's no word on the result yet. They are pushing hard for speed, and this is a public battle. Your fame grows by the day."

Max frowned. "Another reason to leave Evator. I wonder how many people know I'm here or that I'm the one behind the spiritual stuff going on lately."

She said, "Many know you're here, but the designers put a cap on those who can start here partly to reduce the trouble to you."

"That's going to be another problem when I leave Evator, isn't it? No more starter area."

"It's a risk."

Lara soon logged out, but he asked Siren to stay so he could tell her everything she'd missed. It took a while. She mostly seemed impressed and had a host of questions about his abilities and magic items. Only then did he remember he had a few he hadn't been able to put on yet. He showed her the Black Mirror but received a message the moment it was in his hand.

Warning: you are not powerful enough in magic to use this item.

He'd have to check that with ever level. Siren excused herself for the night while he played with his stash. She would re-enter the game before dawn and awaken him so he could sneak out of town when fewer people were around.

Next, he pulled out the physical items he received for freeing Norus and Evanel, respectively.

Item: Kriserian Amulet

Description: Blessed by Priests of Kriseri, the Goddess of Peace and the Wilderness, this amulet inspires friendliness from all wild creatures within 50 yards. The effect is lessened on tamed animals. The amulet's wood is from a sacred Evenorr Tree, while the golden strands of Kriseri's hair fashion the necklace.

Bonuses: +2 Charisma.

Item: Niquerran-Forged Kryllan Hands

Description: Rivaling the bracers made by kryll, these kryllan hands of steel were forged by niquerra, making them among the most durable available. Unlike most such items, the wearer needs no verbal or even mental command to make the magical gloves extend from within to cover the hands, or retract. They will appear and disappear instantly in dangerous or calm moments.

Bonuses: +5 HP, +3 Damage, +3 Attack.

Max immediately donned both.

The amulet hung from what seemed like a golden cord of intertwined silk. The pendant was a smooth, light-colored circle with the tree silhouette inside. It didn't look the least bit valuable except that it gave off a sense of comfort once Max had slipped it over his head. The cord was long enough that no one would see the amulet itself after he tucked it under his tunic.

The bracers were a silver steel with etchings of a wooden path leading to a mountain with a cave opening. His arms slid into the wider end and out the smaller with ease, after which they seemingly shrank themselves to fit snugly without impeding his arms' mobility. With a thought, he made the fine chainmail glove extend from his wrist to cover each hand. It felt almost like he wasn't wearing them, except that his sense of touch was impacted as expected. He'd have to see if he could wield a sword or knife without being impeded. The gloves disappeared back into the gauntlets with similar speed.

On one hand, he still had the kajina ring, which boosted his intelligence, wisdom, and morale by 3. The other bore the Ring of Coiryn with its +5 morale boost in a ten-foot radius. The Friend of Moiryn Ring boosting both his dexterity and charisma by 3. He possessed the Namaerian Chain Mail that raised his HP by 5 and gave him 10% resistance to magic. He felt much better outfitted than before and just needed a magic weapon besides the kryllan bracers, the Atorin short bow, or winged rider dagger. Those were good, but all hand-to-hand or range. He needed a more standard one like a sword. But he wasn't complaining. He was undoubtedly better situated than anyone in town, and it was time to leave for that reason, besides being a hunted man. He'd outgrown Evator.

It had been a while since he'd seen his living stats, so he pulled them up.

Name: Maestro Max
Species/Race: Human.
Class: Bard, Level 5
Reputation: -4—Accused (Andra), 1—Accepted (Karendi)
XP: 10,685
HP: 79/79
MP: 27/27
Strength: 9
Dexterity: 10
Agility: 8
Constitution: 7
Intelligence: 13
Wisdom: 12
Charisma: 12
Morale: 13

His reputation caught his eye. The last time he'd looked, it had been at 4—Good Standing. Now it was -4. The thought made him glad he'd changed his name before Lara had brought his body in here. The priest would have refused to resurrect him, most likely. He was safe for now, as long as he didn't leave just yet.

Before going to sleep, Max checked the door to see if it could be locked, but no luck. He put the chair and table against it to slow down any intruder and went to sleep with a dagger next to the cot.

⸺ ◆ ◆ ⸺

Max woke to the sound of Siren calling his name. He struggled to open his eyes and get his bearings to sit up. The lone window showed darkness outside. She hadn't gotten in through the door, which was still barricaded, but because this was where she'd been when logging out. She'd simply reappeared here. He hadn't thought of that, not that he was trying to keep her out. That could probably be convenient or a problem depending on circumstances.

"You okay?" Siren asked. "It took minutes to wake you."

"Yeah. I think I just needed the rest." He yawned, jaw cracking. He scanned his stats to ensure he'd fully recovered, seeing no debuffs.

"Hope you got enough. I think there's been a change of plans."

He stifled a frown, wanting to get out of this place. "Why?"

"We're not leaving Evator yet. First, we need to lead the Dark Trio into a trap."

Max blinked in surprise. "Why that instead of leaving town?"

"Evidence."

"Don't we have it?"

"Apparently not. Listen, I told my dad what happened, and he went straight to the gaming company and asked them to find the logs relating to your in-game death. They weren't sure they wanted to hand them over."

"What?" Max interrupted, annoyed. "Why wouldn't they?"

"Don't get too excited. They weren't refusing. They just wanted to think about the consequences of turning over gamer intel to the police. Many people into these games are not big on authority figures. The company worried about appearances, so they hinted they wanted a subpoena or search warrant to make it look like they didn't just hand the shit over and rat out their players, even with the situation."

"So get one."

"My dad's working on it, but it seems to be a moot point."

"Why?"

"They had someone start a search for the logs while they tried to decide how to handle the request for them, and that person came back and said the logs didn't exist."

"Wouldn't every player have logs?"

"Yeah, and you especially. You're not exactly normal."

"So then how...." Max trailed off, an awful realization dawning. "Inside job."

Siren's grimace showed agreement. "That's what my father thinks. Me, too. Someone may have deleted the logs and even updated the database to remove any XP they gained from killing you, or consequences they suffered for killing a player. My father is adding that to the search warrant. But right now, there is no evidence of who killed you in the game."

Max jumped to his feet, cursing. He started pacing as Siren watched without condemnation.

She said, "We need another fight with them. Now that the log generation code or whatever is being watched, there will be a record of it that no one can touch without being detected."

Max turned to her in surprise that grew on seeing the evil look on her face. "You have a plan?"

"You're gonna love it."

Chapter Forty-Two

Max, Siren, and her father, Akio, waited for a message from Lara, upon whom their plan hinged. Crumbling around them stood a ruined two-story building in the woods north of the cemetery, and northeast of Evator. They'd had to wait hours until Lara got off work and could do her part. The druid lived in Pennsylvania, so she was at least in the same time zone.

That morning, around 5 am, while Siren had distracted the priest at the church, Max had donned his armor, changed his name to Tyler, and cast the spell to temporarily change himself into a kryll. He'd grown six inches taller and more muscular. His attire had morphed with him. Siren had said he looked like a kryllan version of himself, but that it should be enough to fool people if he didn't dawdle. He'd tied his hair into a quick pony-tail and left the church of Kojen, the Goddess of Rejuvenation. Her priests were not the only ones able to resurrect someone, but they were better at it.

On his way out of Evator through the north gate, Max had kept to himself, walking as if unhurried or unconcerned. He'd noticed more winged riders and morkais doing aerial scouting than usual, but none had molested him. More karelia had been present but hadn't given the impression of knowing to stop look-ing for his ghost.

He'd reached this abandoned building before the *Body Morph* spell wore off. Siren had soon joined him, reporting no one following her. She had seen notes about this place online and thought it a good place to ambush the Dark Trio. But they'd had to wait for them and Lara to be in the game.

Max had spent some time working on his skills, raising *Foraging* and *Stealth* to levels 4 and 3, while adding *Climbing* and bringing it to level 2. With Siren's help, Max had practiced the Kryllan Hand fighting style, so that both raised it by one, bringing Max to level 4. He could parry blows better, faster, and more powerfully. He felt lighter on his feet. His kicks had improved, too.

He had wanted to practice with his kajina ring, but it had a cooldown of one day. That meant that if he experimented with separating his soul before the impending battle today, he wouldn't get to use it during the fight, unless he kept himself that way during the encounter. It would give him an enormous advantage, but Vixen was a sorelia who might do things to him in that state. And he didn't know what the experience was going to be like. Doing it then wasn't worth the risk, given the importance of this battle.

Finally, a message came through the *Party Screen*.

Lara: Okay, we're on the way.
Max: All three of them?
Lara: Yep. They fell for it. Should be there in 10-15 minutes.
Siren: Anything go wrong?
Lara: Not that I could see. They approached me just like we planned, so they think this was their idea.
Max: Perfect.

Siren: We're ready. Keep us updated as you get nearer.
Max: Don't forget to hang back when they attack.

"I'll be right back," said Siren, before sprinting away through the trees. Max knew where she was going.

The plan had been for Lara to go into town until finding the Dark Trio, using their gamer tags to positively identify them. Then she was to find an opportunity to loudly tell a few adventurers that she knew the whereabouts of Maestro Max, who had a bounty on his head. And most importantly, he was alive again. That would get the Dark Trio's attention.

Her story was that being a druid had led Lara out into the woods for spell materials. She'd caught sight of Max in this ruined house. She wasn't strong enough to take Max on herself, so she was asking them to join her and they'd share in the reward. But the group she told had refused because she'd purposely chosen guys who were too low level to risk it. By design, she was to have this talk within earshot of the Dark Trio, who would overhear and hopefully approach her so they'd think it was their idea to do this with her. This had been Max's concept, to lower any suspicion from Lara outright asking about the Dark Trio.

"I'll be right back," said Akio, and Max watched in envy as he vanished by logging out. He was back a minute later. "Okay, the screen recording is working."

"Great."

"It may not count as evidence, but it will still help me identify them. There will also be proof of this event, including their gamer tags. At worst, I can release it to the public to get help in identifying them."

Max felt excited and pulled out his Lyre of Murryn. He hadn't used it while alive, but a summoning would give them another advantage. They would outnumber the Dark Trio 2-to-1. They expected Max alone, not Siren, her father, and the druid, who would betray them. They might've been expecting the undead based on Max's reputation, but no one knew how he was doing it. Maybe they thought he needed to be dead. By being alive, he removed the sorelia's ability to have a special affinity for screwing with him.

He received a private message from Siren while she was on her errand.

Siren: Hey, I forgot to tell you before, but I looked up this shit about players moving a dead player's body.

Max: What did you find? The game allows this?

Siren: Yeah, but the penalty is steep. Each time you move a body to interfere with the player respawning, your chance of being sent to E'kainum the next time you die goes up 25%.

Max: The oblivion afterlife? Your character is deleted?

Siren. Yep.

Max: Wow. So if you do it twice, there's a 50% chance.

Siren: And if you do it 4 times, the next time you die, you're gone. 100% chance.

Max: That's a serious penalty, but it makes sense. I wouldn't take that risk even once, if I gave a shit about my character.

Siren: And don't forget that you *are* your character.

Max: Yeah. Though I have wondered if something like that would make me wake up.

Siren: Too risky.

Max: I know. What about if you capture the player's soul? That would stop them from respawning, too.

Siren: Also allowed, mostly to make the game consistent. Karelia and sorelia can do it in the lore, so therefore players can. They could've made only NPC spirits able to be captured,

but they've experimented with letting players do it to each other and see what people think.

Max: That has to piss people off like it did me.

Siren. Yeah. But there are differences between players and the game's NPCs doing it to players. NPCs forcing quests on players exist in lots of games, especially in starter areas, where you have to kill all the little monsters to leave the area, as one example.

Max: I remember that from other games.

Siren: For the players, there are severe limits on detaining another player's spirit. I think you can only do it a few minutes, which can stop them from respawning and rejoining a battle. You can't make them do much, either. Players can't make other players do a quest, for example. I'm done at the cemetery. No one there. Closed the gates.

Max: Great. Hurry back.

Siren: On the way.

Max ended the private chat and got a group update from Lara that the Dark Trio and she were almost here. He exchanged a nod with Akio and left the detective standing inside the building's first room, out of sight. Max went behind it, taking the route he had cleared of leaves. On the other side, he'd piled more so the undead he'd summon would pull everyone's attention that way when they shuffled through them.

He was looking forward to this. The Dark Trio thought that, for the third time, they were going to ambush him. They likely knew the logs had been deleted and thought it would happen again. If only Max could be there when they learned the truth.

Lara: I can see the building now. Coming from the southwest.

Siren: I'm not gonna make it in time. I will take up a position behind you with my bow and wait for the fight to begin.

Max: That's even better. I like as many surprises for them as we can think of.

Siren: Agreed.

Akio: After you summon your undead, let me know.

Max. Got it.

They went silent. Max waited impatiently for the talk between Akio and the Dark Trio. They had discussed what to say, but the detective hadn't seemed keen on taking advice from his daughter or Max. The conversation wouldn't really matter, but they hoped for a confession of sorts.

Lara: We're stopping about twenty feet from the entrance.

"Hey Max!" Reaper bellowed in his guttural voice. "You in there, bud? It's your old friend, Reaper." When no one answered, he added, "I hear you got your body back, so I came to take it away again. Maybe this time I'll chop off something else."

Iron Heart snickered. Max had no trouble hearing them from here thanks to the Earring of Timonen.

Max: I can't wait to kill this asshole.

Akio: Easy.

Siren: I'm almost there. Going slow to keep quiet.

Lara: We're moving in again.

Akio: Okay. Here we go.

Max pulled the Lyre of Murryn from his inventory. He'd practiced how quietly he could do this and have it still work, Akio being the listener. No one would hear it from out there.

"Something I can help you with?" Akio's stern voice asked. Max presumed he had stepped up to the doorway as they'd discussed.

Lara: We moved closer, stopped again, me hanging back a little. We're ten feet from the entrance and Detective Akio.

"Who the hell are you?" Reaper asked.

"A friend of Max's," Akio replied.

"In that case, you're our enemy. Tell us where he is and maybe we won't kill you, too. I was expecting to see that Siren slut out here. Was hoping to stick something big and pointy in her."

Max: Don't try to kill him. He'll beat you.
Akio: It's going to take more than that to get a reaction.

"Akio," said Iron Heart, having likely read the detective's name. "I know that name."

Max swore under his breath, realizing the detective hadn't changed his gamer tag and was using his real surname. An oversight. They hadn't intended to admit to his identity in case that spooked the Dark Trio into logging out before anything happened.

Vixen began, "Yeah, so do..." She gasped. "Detective Akio!"

"What?" Reaper asked. "Who the fuck... Oh wait, I know this. You're the guy trying to figure out who attacked Max in Baltimore, aren't you?"

Akio said, "No. I already know it was the three of you."

Reaper snorted. "You'd like to prove that, wouldn't you?"

"I've already talked to everyone who was at the club that night," said Akio, "including each of you. I just don't know which three of you it was."

Reaper said, "Yeah, well, you're out of your jurisdiction. You can't do shit. Laws of the real world don't apply in here."

Akio replied, "Not yet, but it's only a matter of time, and you'll be the ones who set precedent for your attack on him."

"Blah, blah, blah."

"Why don't you identify yourselves and spare us some trouble? I'll ask the DA to go easy on you."

"Derek," started Vixen, "maybe we should—"

Akio interrupted. "Derek? Is that your name? There was a Derek at the club that night. Derek Sullivan."

Max stifled a shout of excitement. They had a name!

"Fuck, Vixen!" Reaper, aka Derek, snapped. "Stupid bitch! What the fuck is wrong with you? You want me to give him *your* real name, too?"

"Yeah," began Akio, "that would be very helpful. I'll be rounding you up soon enough as known associates of Derek here."

Iron Forge said, "Shit! Shit, shit, shit!"

Max: Starting it.
Lara: Yeah. Now is good. It's about to get out of hand.

Max cast *Camouflage* on himself, and since he wasn't in combat, he didn't need to wait before playing the lyre with hands that trembled from enthusiasm. A powerfully built, sword-wielding, level 1 wight climbed from the earth to stand beside him, pulling a level 1 skeleton up with it like they were pals. A level 2 zombie joined them moments later, and from seemingly nowhere, a level 2 ghost manifested next to Max, who leered in satisfaction.

"Thank you, Everett," he whispered. "I hope you enjoy this as much as I will."

Adopting a more conciliatory tone, Akio said, "Look, we know there was no intent to kill Max, so you're looking at assault and battery if he wakes up, destruction of property, and possibly theft. But it's going to be involuntary manslaughter if he dies, maybe conspiracy charges for your purposeful attempts to keep him from waking up and identifying you. You may face first degree murder charges."

Max sent the undead around the leaf-covered side of the building. Then he used his *Stealth* skill to go around the cleared side so he could see.

Max: The undead are coming around the corner. It's on. Siren?

Siren: Almost in position. Don't wait.

"Reaper," began Vixen.

The jhaikan said, "Shut up! Just shut the fuck up." He turned to Akio. "You can't do shit in here. Nothing in here matters. Not killing you, a cop, not killing Max or stopping him from respawning. It's the fucking wild west. Anything goes!"

Akio said, "I'm going to be at your house within an hour with a warrant."

"Bullshit. Nothing we say in here gives you cause."

"Reaper," Vixen began again.

"What?" he snapped.

"I sense something behind the house."

That's right, you sorelian bitch, Max thought. This was the first time Max got a good look at any of them. The night they'd killed him had been too dark outside. Before that in the tavern, he'd been preoccupied. And at the castle, the daekais fight had happened. He'd never known their importance during other fleeting moments.

The nearly nine-foot-tall jhaikan, Reaper, stood a few strides from the entrance, his black leather tight on his huge, muscled frame, the scaly skin a dark green. Since the gods of the blue sphere had created jhaikan, the blue eyes suggested he was truly jhaikan and not the reformed rhaikan race he'd been pretending to be for access to civilization. The wicked teeth and talons on each of his hands meant Reaper was well-armed even when he didn't have a weapon.

But he held Kat, the axe-shaped guitar, by the handle, the silver blade catching the late afternoon sunlight. Max would never know if they attacked him in Baltimore just to destroy Kat, but the idea made him want her back, so he added the *Disarm* spell to his hot list.

Flanking Reaper by a few feet to either side and behind were the other two. The sorelia sorcerer Vixen stood closest to the side where the undead were. She wore the same black leather, which hugged her busty, slim figure. Her long, jet-black hair framed the heart-shaped face she'd chosen, the lorenia lines around her green eyes glowing the same color now that she'd sensed the supernatural. Aside from the dagger in her belt, she seemed unarmed.

The kryllan rogue Iron Heart stood closer to Max. He also wore black leather, a jhaikan staff in one hand, the butt on the grass. He nervously glanced between his two companions, strong brow furrowed. Between this and the way he'd attacked Max from behind before, he seemed a coward, and Max had plans for poetic justice.

Ten feet behind all of them waited Lara. Max nodded. When the Dark Trio realized she was betraying them, the distance could keep her safe for a few moments. By then, the Dark Trio would have others to deal with. From here, Max could hear his undead rustling through the leaves on the building's opposite side. The Dark Trio's eyes snapped there, their demeanor becoming alert.

Max: It's time.

Chapter Forty-Three

Max commanded all four undead to rush into the open and charge Vixen, the biggest threat to everyone, especially undead. The Dark Trio all started cursing or talking at once, Reaper issuing a command to attack. Behind them, Lara acted first, her hands moving in a swirling motion as she murmured words Max ignored. He knew what was coming and watched in satisfaction as her *Impede* spell caused the ground beneath each of her targets to become a muddy morass that clung to their boots. None of them could take a step, just like when Vixen immobilized Max the night they killed him. This had been his idea.

"You fucking bitch!" Reaper snarled, twisting to look at Lara. The undead had almost closed the distance.

Akio drawled, "Not so nice being ambushed, is it?"

It had been a long time since he'd been alive and able to cast *Weapon Ward* to reduce the damage he took, but Max cast it now.

Iron Heart awkwardly threw a knife at the druid behind him, but missed. Vixen hurriedly thrust her hands toward the ghost, zombie, wight, and skeleton, only catching the last two with twin jets of liquid flames that set the grass under them on fire as burning drops struck the ground. The skeleton fell in a burning pile, destroyed, but the wight kept going despite the flames consuming it. It, the zombie, and the ghost all slammed into Vixen, knocking her down. Too many damage notifications drifted away for Max to see who did what. All that mattered was the sorcerer's health bar being deep in the red.

While everyone was distracted, a still-camouflaged Max used his *Stealth* skill to come up behind Iron Heart and stab him between the shoulder blades with his winged rider dagger. A fountain of blood shot from the kryll's mouth onto the grass. A red -36 HP floated away, leaving the rogue's health bar almost depleted when it appeared.

Critical Hit!
Stealth Attack!

"Got you!" Max shouted in sudden passion, mimicking what the rogue had said to him. "Critical hit *and* stealth bonus! Fuck yeah!"

He heard a clang to one side and saw Reaper, who had apparently blocked a sword strike from Akio, swing the axe and cut a big gash into the fighter's side, a red -12 HP floating away. Half the detective's HP were gone.

Max saw a flash of light by Vixen and thought she'd healed herself, but it didn't matter. Either the zombie or wight finished her, with Max getting half the XP from her death.

Warning: You have killed another player as the aggressor. Continued actions of this nature may affect your reputation and gameplay.

Max silently commanded his ghost minion to sail toward Reaper. An arrow struck the jhaikan in the back to protrude from the front, the impact making him almost double over. A -14 HP drifted up.

Siren: Got him.
Max: Again.
Siren: On it.

Iron Heart tried to swing his jhaikan staff at Max, but with his feet immobilized and Max behind him, the blow missed. Max stabbed him again, finishing him.

You have killed (1) Kryllan Rogue, Level 5!
You gained 1400 XP!
Loot corpse?

Max ignored the loot prompt and another warning about killing a player.

Reaper let out a grunt of pain and Max saw the ghost had done -17 HP of necrotic damage to the torso. Then Lara cast *Burn* and set Reaper on fire, doing -4 HP. Reaper was already down to 23 HP. Akio stepped nearer the jhaikan and swung at him halfheartedly, missing before stepping back. Reaper didn't bother swinging a retaliatory blow. Instead, he quaffed a healing potion and regained 12 HP, bringing him to 35. Max knew players usually only did that when closer to 0, but Reaper had to see the situation. He was now outnumbered 6-to-1. Whether or not the potion caused it, the jhaikan's feet came unstuck from the mud and he turned toward Max. At that moment, the kryllan bracers Max wore gave a pulse, and Max knew that Reaper's axe was magical. The pulse was a safety mechanism built into kryllan hands, which didn't protect against magic weapons.

The ghost touched Reaper for another -17 HP and Lara's spell dropped him -3 to 14 HP.

The jhaikan snarled at Max, "As long as I kill you as I die."

Seeing Siren approaching with a jhaikan staff in hand, Max put away the dagger and drew his sword. "You won't. Everyone else back off. He's mine."

Hearing this, Lara went to Akio and healed him.

Max cast *Disarm* on Reaper, who resisted it and swung the axe at him with one hand. Raising the sword, Max felt certain he wouldn't block it enough, but the axe seemed to adjust at the last moment and clang into his sword enough to parry.

"What the hell?" snarled Reaper, shifting his grip.

Max lunged, but the jhaikan turned sideways and used the axe to knock the sword away. He swung the axe again and Max heard it whistling as it hurtled toward his chest faster than he expected. Once more, Max felt certain he wouldn't block enough, but the axe head seemed to move downward at the last moment and just missed him.

"Fucking axe turned in my hand again!"

Max sliced across the leather-clad arm holding the axe, a red -3 HP floating up. Lara's still effective *Burn* spell caused another -4 HP, leaving Reaper at 7 HP before the flames extinguished. With a growl, the jhaikan took the axe in both hands and hurled it at Max, who braced himself for the impact. There was no dodging at this range. This time, there was no mistaking the axe did something odd, twisting unnaturally in the air so that instead of the blade digging into him, the flat of it struck his chest and knocked him on his back, a red -4 HP floating up. Kat landed beside him in the grass, and Reaper drew a sword.

"Subdue him," Max commanded the zombie and wight, "but don't kill."

The pair leapt at Reaper, who sliced the wight across the stomach with the sword before they tackled him, leaving the jhaikan at just 1 HP. With an assist from Akio and Siren, they held the huge guy down, but it wasn't easy.

Max didn't bother healing himself. He sat up. He'd gotten almost everything he wanted, but he still wanted to finish Reaper himself. Seeing the axe-shaped guitar lying in the green and yellow grass next to him, he smiled. Max hadn't needed to chop off Reaper's arm or cast *Disarm* after all. The asshole actually threw Kat at him. Expecting that he'd be able to take it, he reached for it and felt the wooden handle's smoothness as his palm wrapped around it. He picked it up and rose to his feet, holding Kat by the handle. She felt solid and lighter than expected. An excellent weapon. It wasn't the same as the real thing, but this was the closest he'd ever get to holding her again.

He'd only held the real guitar like she was a weapon once or twice, and the neck didn't change shape, making her uncomfortable to hold that way. For old time's sake, he switched his grip to hold her like a guitar and watched in amazement as the handle changed shape to a guitar neck, gleaming silver frets appearing along with strings. A black leather strap also appeared from nowhere, tempting him to put her on.

The details of her surprised him, as she even had a few small nicks that were identical to the real thing. That it wasn't the real one could've completely fooled him if he hadn't known the truth. How they'd really gotten her into the game like this made little sense to him, given that she was in pieces, unless they'd taken most of them and maybe glued them back together? Something about this felt right to him, and he walked over to Reaper, smiling about what he intended to do.

"Are you ready to die?" Max asked.

"Why? Are you gonna sing again? I'd rather die than hear *that* shit."

"You're going to jail, motherfucker, and I am going to wake up and be there to make sure it's for a long time."

Reaper snorted. "You can't wake up. We all know. You're trapped in here. And you're never getting out."

The hint of truth angered Max. "We're gonna find your pal, too. The one erasing the logs of your attacks on me."

To Max's satisfaction, a look of surprise appeared on Reaper's face. "How di—"

"A cover-up. That's really gonna make this story sing in the news, just like this guitar." Max switched his grip to hold Kat like a weapon again, feeling the neck change to an axe handle, the strings and frets disappearing. "I have to ask, was all this really because you're jealous? I mean, that's a little pathetic, isn't it, destroying your life over an insecurity?"

"No more pathetic than you thinking you're better than everyone just because you play like that, or have that fucking guitar. Or *had*. Gone now in the real world, just like you'll be soon."

Feeling contempt and pity, Max said, "You're both a dick and a pussy." After raising the axe above his head, he added, "Go fuck yourself."

"Clever. I—"

Max slammed the blade down and through Reaper's neck, beheading him. A brief fountain of gore sprayed the grass and everyone holding the body, which went still after a last spasm. He heard himself breathing hard, adrenaline pumping.

You have killed (1) Rhaikan Hunter, Level 5!
You gained 1125 XP!
Loot corpse?

Max made a face, but it wasn't about losing probably more than half of the XP due to others helping with the kill. His expression prompted Siren to ask why. "The class said rhaikan," he began, "but he was jhaikan. Can people change what this notice says, like the way I changed my name?"

Siren said, "Sort of. If you're playing a species with multiple races, you can change it to say whichever race of that species you want. Otherwise, people wouldn't be able to masquerade as a different race. The game would reveal the truth."

The idea of doing something with Reaper's head appealed to Max, but he didn't want to bring more trouble down on his own. He saw everyone, even the undead, looking at him expectantly. He thanked his minions and told them they were free to go. The ghost vanished, and the others walked off into the woods behind the building.

"Well," Max began, "that all kind of went like I expected, except the part about him throwing the axe at me." He looked at it, noticing that the blood had dripped right off to leave it pristine, the black finish highly polished, the silver edge gleaming.

Akio came over to him. "Okay, Max. You did a good thing with all of this. We should have a recording of it, but even without that, I have a name."

"Derek Sullivan," Max said, just in case anyone had forgotten.

"Right. I don't think you need me in here anymore, so I'll logout and get started on arresting him for questioning."

"Wait," Siren began. "Walk back to Evator first. Otherwise, when you enter the game again, you'll be out here by yourself."

Her father frowned. "I don't want to wait on this. Odds are good I don't return here, anyway." Siren seemed about to protest, so he added, "Okay, I'll logout for a few minutes and set something in motion, then log back in and run to town before logging out again. Good enough?"

She nodded. "Yeah. Thanks, Dad."

"Yeah," Max started, reaching out to shake his hand, "I can't thank you enough for this. Everything, really."

Akio gripped his hand. "Just doing my job."

Max shook his head. "No, having Siren in here has been invaluable. You have no idea. And you did this. You should be really proud of her for everything she's been doing for me. I'll be a family friend of yours for life." He made a rueful face. "Hopefully that will be a lot longer than it seems right now."

Akio looked him in the eye and got all adulty on him. "That needs to be your focus now, Max. You've gotten these three caught. Justice is just a matter of time, which you don't have a lot of in here. You only have one thing left to do. I want you to focus on waking up. Stop playing this game, if that's what it takes."

"I know. I'm trying."

Akio let go of his hand, nodded farewell at everyone, and logged out.

Curious about what he'd get for looting the corpses, Max tried it with both Iron Heart, from whom he didn't have to share, and Reaper. While he'd split the XP from Vixen's death because of his undead doing all the damage, he got the first pick of loot for being the party leader. In all, he only acquired minor supplies like two Iluvien candles. He also got various coins and gems, but not as much as he expected until remembering that the game didn't let players loot each other for much.

Akio suddenly reappeared right where he'd been, announcing that he'd made a few calls but needed to hurry and get out of here.

"Um," began Lara, "is it okay if I go with you? I think I'm done for today and don't want to respawn out here either."

Akio shrugged. Max and Siren exchanged a look and thanked her for her role once more, then watched as the pair ran toward Evator. They were still in sight when Max examined Kat.

Bardic War Axe: Axe/Guitar.

Description: This one-of-a-kind bardic war axe is made from asyander wood and namaerian steel, making it nearly indestructible, lightweight, and able to enhance magic. It is both a hunter's axe and a guitar. As a weapon, it is equally suited to chopping objects or creatures. As an instrument, its beautiful sound will inspire even the most hardened listeners.

Quality: Very high.

Rarity: Unique.

Speed: Medium.

Physical Attack: +10%.

Magical Attack: +15%.

Bonuses: +5 Dexterity, +5 Charisma, +5 Constitution.

Abilities: The bardic war axe can transform from a hunter's axe to a guitar and back again, based on the way the wielder holds it. When used as an instrument, spell songs performed on it are more effective in every way.

Special: This item has acquired sentience and the ability to affect the wielder's accuracy when used as a weapon. As it can now learn, it may gain additional abilities in time.

"Huh," said Max, a few questions popping into his head. He went to Reaper's body and started removing the black leather axe holder from the jhaikan's back.

"What?" Siren asked.

"A couple things. For one, it's made of namaerian steel, which is pretty rare. I don't know how they got this into the game, but this must have cost them a lot of game money."

"I guess it was important to torture you by having it."

Max shook his head, though he agreed. "I hope it cost them a fucking fortune in the real world. It's mine now."

"Wouldn't worry. They'll be in jail soon."

Max straightened with the axe holder. "The description says the axe has gained sentience."

Siren's eyebrows shot up. "What? That's interesting."

"What does that mean?" he asked, donning the holder, which changed size to fit him snugly over his chainmail.

"I don't know. Talking axe?"

Max laughed. The infamous talking sword of epic fantasy was a big no-no in the genre. "If so, it hasn't said anything."

She smiled. "Well, she's a girl, right? Maybe you need to say hello first."

Grinning, Max held up the axe body to his face and said, "Hi Kat."

To his surprise, the guitar responded. "Hi, Max!"

CHAPTER FORTY-FOUR

Max nearly dropped Kat on hearing the axe talk. "What the hell?"

"Wow," said Siren, chuckling. "I didn't think that would actually work." She came closer, visually inspecting the black and silver weapon.

Max wasn't sure what to do. Like so many things in the last few days, this wasn't something he had experience with. But he reminded himself this was a game in a fantasy setting with magic. He'd seen weirder than a talking item. Still, he couldn't think of anything to say except...

"Um, Kat?"

"Yes, baby?" The axe purred in a rich soprano, the strings vibrating slightly when she spoke.

His eyes widened, and Siren's shoulders shook with silent laughter before a huge grin appeared on her kryllan face. "How are you, uh, alive?" He wasn't sure that was the right word.

"That's an interesting story. A painful one. Are you sure you want to hear?"

"Yes. Definitely."

Kat said, "Okay. I guess you deserve to know. When those bastards killed you that night outside the tavern, the sorelian bitch tried to raise you as undead, but it didn't work. She wasn't strong enough, or skilled. I think that's something for higher-level players."

Max nodded, noticing she seemed well spoken, didn't like the Dark Trio, and had some sense of being in a game. "Probably."

"After that, they took you out into the fields north of town to bury you, but they tried to animate you one more time before digging the grave. And Reaper put me down near your body. They didn't think the spell worked that time either, but it did. On me. I just said nothing, partly because I was confused. I didn't know who I was, what I was, or what I was doing here. I watched them bury you. It didn't bother me then because I didn't know how important you are, but I do now and it makes me so mad."

Max had a ton of questions, but the one he asked was, "Why am I important?"

Kat laughed. "You built me, silly! I heard them talking about it. I learned a lot from listening to them, which is why I continued to say nothing. Some of it I had to piece together, like the stuff about when they killed you." She made a snort of anger. "I can't believe they used me to kill you, my creator. What an insult, which is what they meant it to be, isn't it? As soon as I learned that, I wanted to kill them all, but I haven't been able to move at all until earlier today. Even now, I can only do a little. Watch."

She twisted in his hand a little, first one way, then another. That made Max realize something.

"You were interfering with Reaper's attacks on me just now."

"Of course! I wasn't going to let that asshole kill you *again*, and using me to do it! It's outrageous! By the way, thank you so much for beheading him, especially using me. That was awesome. I'm so glad to be reunited with you."

"Same."

Max looked at Siren, seeing her mouth hanging open like his was. So Kat was loyal. Maybe a little bloodthirsty? She was a weapon, after all, so maybe he couldn't blame her. He couldn't decide if this was the coolest thing he'd experienced yet or just the weirdest.

He asked, "What happened after they buried me?"

"Not much, just sitting around a lot. It took me a while to figure out a lot of things they said. They already knew how to hide your body on the map. I found out you were a ghost somewhere and needed to get back to it, and they were trying to prevent that. There was something about them attacking you in the real world. I never understood what they were talking about. Is this some sort of alternate reality where people can come and go? Sometimes they talk about logging out and suddenly they just disappear and I feel like I go to sleep. Then I wake up and I'm usually on Reaper's back or something. And time has passed. I don't understand."

Max pursed his lips. "I'll have to explain that some other time."

Siren nodded. "We should probably head to the cemetery. With the gates locked, there's no rush, but still."

"Yeah. Okay. Let's go." Max cast a last look at the bodies they were leaving. It was too bad he couldn't take a picture.

They set off at a jog, Max carrying Kat in one hand. He wasn't ready to let go of her and wasn't sure how it would feel to run with her on his back. The tree cover and underbrush were thin here so that they had no trouble loping along. Since he hadn't gone this way and Siren had, he just followed, trying to process the emotions of the past half hour.

Having gotten Derek's name certainly made him feel better about so many instances of injustice that had been eating away at him since he'd learned why he was in here. Derek was the leader, too, the architect of all that was wrong now. Cutting his goddamn head off had felt fantastic. Kat was right about that. And while he could never have the guitar back in the real world, having her in here lifted his spirits. On that thought, he checked the logout button, but it was still greyed out. He sighed. How far of a journey did he need to make to escape this place?

"What's at the cemetery?" Kat asked, interrupting his thoughts. "What's the plan? I want to help."

Max filled her in, that he was hoping to control the Dark Trio's ghosts and make them turn themselves in to whatever karelia was stationed down the road, where he'd met Ardyn. Everett had given him this as a quest and he wanted to complete it for that and because it was one way to get their characters potentially deleted. Akio might cause that, too, but the more chances, the better. Kat loved the plan and said the only reason she wanted to see the Dark Trio again was so Max could chop them into pieces... using her.

Max asked, "Do you know how they got you into this, uh, world?"

Kat replied, "Something about a 3D printer for VR games so they can bring items into here. It works from pictures, too, if those are good enough. They were trying to figure out what else they can bring in."

"I heard about those," said Siren. "Those printers have to be expensive. Where did they get... You know, it seems more and more likely that they work at the gaming company. I mean, those people could be testing something like that. I haven't heard of it really being available, not that I've been paying attention to that."

Max said, "I guess your father will find out soon enough."

Siren remarked, "I'm surprised Vixen could animate her, but I guess that's one thing about sorcerers. They aren't using spells that restrict what they can do. She must've gotten lucky."

As they jogged between the trees, Max thought of something and asked, "Kat, did you ever hear them use their real names?"

"Oh yeah," she replied. "Derek, Simone, and Marcus. Or as I like to call them, Asshole, Bitch, and Dickhead."

Both Siren and Max started laughing.

—◆ ◆ ◆—

Max was still smiling as he eyed the graveyard, but he saw something that took the expression off his face. "The gates are open!"

Siren sighed. "I guess we should've hurried after all. What were the odds of someone who isn't dead visiting in the time that passed since we killed them?"

"Apparently good. Let's see if they're still here."

"Doubt it."

Max stifled any disappointment. It didn't really matter. Siren had closed the gates earlier at his request, and she had told him the warning she'd gotten—that doing this was an act of evil that could cause her character entering an unpleasant afterlife the next time she got killed. Both knew that could include E'kainum—character deletion. But she could always come back with a new character. Max couldn't, as far as he knew, though he still wondered if the oblivion of E'kainum would cause him to wake up in the real world or die.

Most of the cemetery lay ahead and to the left or east as they faced south. They climbed over the fence, Max casting a regretful look at the open cemetery gates to the right along the front wall. He'd forgotten how dark the night could be without his superior ghost vision. He sensed nothing supernatural anywhere, including on the road that stretched away. As a non-ghost, he longer had an enhanced sixth sense. The Dark Trio could still be here. They posed a threat, but he had a plan, which prompted him to put Kat on his back and pull out the Lyre of Murryn, the *Song of Gathering* at the ready.

"What do you need *that* for?" Kat demanded, her voice too loud. "You have *me*."

"Keep your voice down!" Max whispered, worried the enhanced ghost hearing would've made the Dark Trio aware of them now. His own ears picked out sounds coming from their left, farther into the back of the graveyard. It sounded like chanting and grunting, possibly from different sources. The flap of wings made him look up to see a winged rider glide overhead atop a giant bird. He and Siren ducked.

"I forgot you have that earring to help your hearing," Siren whispered.

Quieter, Kat said, "Max, answer me."

He didn't really want to explain now, but said, "The spell I need to use will only work on the undead if I use this lyre."

Kat grumbled but said nothing. A suspicion that she was sulking popped into Max's head. He brushed it aside.

He'd only seen part of the cemetery when he was here, as he hadn't dawdled. The place was longer and deeper than he remembered, with a greater variety of vegetation and graves, though most were headstones. He and Siren were on the downward slope of a gentle hill that they now crested to reach flat land. Taller structures and random trees blocked their sight of whatever was making the sounds. Siren nodded at him and moved off to his left to go around the nearest tree, and Max went right. He soon had his back to the gates and still saw no sign of ghosts. The Dark Trio had almost certainly left. He and Siren should've just gotten out of here, but curiosity drew him forward. The voice grew louder, as did the occasional moans, and when he came around another mausoleum, he saw the source. He quietly trotted across the ground to stand behind a rectangular grave as tall as him.

A black-robed figure stood with its back to Max, gesturing with both hands at the ground before it, where a tombstone jutted from the earth. Beside the figure slumped a level 1 zombie. It stood idly and started aimlessly shuffling in his general direction, not because it had seen him, but as if unsure what to do with itself. Then Max set his sights on the figure.

Name: Necrodude of Evator.
Type: Player.
Class: Wizard.
Species: Karelia.
Level 5.
HP: 50/50.

There was no sign of the Dark Trio and Max conceded they were gone. Had this guy seen them? What was he doing, anyway? A moment later and the question was answered at the familiar sight of a zombie climbing up from the earth. Was this guy just practicing raising the dead or planning something? Max thought the player had to actually be a sorelia, since no karelia would raise the dead.

A loud moan sounded behind him, and Max turned in surprise. Another zombie stood there about twenty feet away, pointing at him. The wizard must have summoned it and then let it wander off. Now the thing had blown Max's cover. The wizard turned around.

"I can see your foot, dude," the guy called. "Might as well come out."

Max: Did you hear that?
Siren: Yeah. Got an arrow trained on him.

"I don't like this," whispered Kat, and Max realized she wasn't part of the party and therefore could not see text exchanges with Siren.

"Shhh," he whispered.

"Don't shush me!"

Max sighed. Did her personality really have to be this way? "Come on, I need to focus."

Kat grumbled but didn't reply.

Not liking his position in between potential enemies, Max put the lyre into his inventory. He also swapped a few spells on his hot list, including a great way to stop someone from casting spells. Then he climbed atop the rectangular, above-ground gravestone that was shaped like a coffin, only wider, with decorative stonework providing convenient hand and footholds. When he reached the top, he saw it had been smashed open from within, pieces of the stone flung aside and off to the ground on the far side. An unmoving corpse still stood in the coffin inside, the upper body bent over and face down on the top. It didn't seem to be alive, or whatever word applied to zombies that weren't animated anymore. Had the wizard started here?

"Up for a little night summoning?" he asked, grabbing Kat from his back.

The wizard looked at him and then squinted. "Tyler, huh? Yeah, not buying it. I recognize you. You're Maestro Max. Got a good bounty on your head. Seeing as how you're outnumbered, I think it's time to collect."

Before Max moved, Necrodude ordered the zombies to attack. The two nearest began shuffling in his direction, while the one just raised from the earth seemed a little confused.

Max: Shoot him. I can't get to him and need to deal with the zombies.

He thought of summoning his own undead and sitting back to watch some zombie-on-zombie carnage, but with the lyre put away, using Kat was faster. He switched his grip to hold her like a guitar. She transformed in his hands and he flipped the strap over his head. With meaning to, he assumed his best rock guitarist stance.

Then a bolt of lightning struck his right should and traveled down his leg, the pain making him gasp. A red -23 HP drifted away, and he glared at the grinning wizard.

"Are you okay?" Kat asked.

"No time to talk," he replied, his voice strained.

An arrow struck the wizard in the leg, wiping the smile from his face as a -6 HP floated up. They'd have to do more to take this guy out.

Max called up the *Don't Tread on Me* spell he'd received so long ago. The music floated before his eyes as he rhythmically struck the lone chord in short bursts on Kat. As he did so, the guitar strings glowed purple, and Kat let out a sigh of pleasure. After five seconds, an arc of purple light in the form of a treble music staff with notes on it shot from his guitar, lighting up the darkness.

When the beam struck the zombie in front of him, it severed it at the waist, setting it on fire and knocking back the lower body so that it flew twenty feet away. The torso fell in the grass below the grave, the zombie's arm still reaching up for him. A shockwave pulsed outward in all directions, knocking over the zombie behind him. But the wizard and remaining zombie there were out of range.

"That was awesome!" Kat yelled, trembling in his hands.

Max agreed and heard a shout behind him. A glance revealed a group of over twenty people approaching from the road leading here. They were still outside the cemetery, torches dancing as they broke into a run. Among them seemed to be the faces of karelia, based on the green glow near their heads. Max assumed it was from the lorenia lines as they sensed the supernatural in effect. The return of flapping wings above made him look to see a winged rider turning overheard.

Max: We're about to have company.
Siren: More undead?
Max: No. Seems like a mob of the living coming to stop us and this guy. And a winged rider.
Siren: You should go.
Max: Not yet.

Whether the lightning spell had a longer cooldown or the wizard just wanted to try something else, a different spell hurtled toward Max—fireball. The flames raced at him, but a little too high.

"Look out!" Kat yelled.

Standing atop the grave, Max's only move was to duck. He felt the searing heat as it whooshed by a foot over him, no direct contact happening, but he still took -5 HP of damage from the heat.

"Damn," said Kat, "that was hot, and not in a fun way."

"I could do without the commentary," Max said.

While the two hurt zombies on the ground were still clawing their way across the grass toward his position, the remaining zombie had run into range of *Don't Tread on Me*, but Max had something else in mind.

"Gather air!" he yelled, right hand raised. He threw the *Orb of Doom* straight at the running zombie—and over its head. The wizard's eyes widened on realizing too late that he was the target. As he frantically turned, the glowing ball struck him in the shoulder with a sickening crunch, knocking him to the ground. A red -20 HP appeared, the wizard's health bar more than halfway down. Kat let out a yelp of approval. Siren's next arrow dropped the wizard another -6 HP. When enraged eyes turned on him, Max suspected what was coming. The lightning bolt hurt just as bad the second time, dropping him to 25 HP as Kat again asked how he was doing. It was time to stop this.

"Sing for me, earnestly!"

The wizard scowled as if in confusion. Then he looked startled as he started singing. Max was too far away to hear the words, but the melody wasn't half bad. The guy kept singing even when another arrow from Siren struck his chest. Kat was laughing. Dangerously low on hit points, the wizard quaffed a potion and his health bar shot up by 15 HP. Cursing, Max saw two morkais approaching while the winged rider circled and had come lower, a bow in one hand. The mob on the road had reached the gates and was entering the cemetery.

Max: It's time to get out of here.
Siren: Okay.

Max: I'm not sure anyone realizes you are here. Head south. I'll draw them north.

Siren: I need to be the one they go after.

Max: Will never work. They see magic coming from me or at me. No time to argue.

Siren cursed, but didn't disagree. The last zombie that was still on its feet had nearly reached him. Max didn't want to deal with it, so he performed *Don't Tread on Me* on Kat once more and watched it get blown back and set on fire, nearly destroyed.

"Good spell," Kat approved, "and I love it when you play me."

"Time to go." Max jumped down from the tomb and chanced a look at the wizard, who was still singing and now turning away to run. Max frowned. The guy was going in the same direction as Siren and might trail her until he could cast again, so Max cast *Orb of Doom* at him one last time and nailed the guy in the back, flinging him forward and killing him.

You have killed (1) Karelian Wizard, Level 5!
You gained 500 XP!
Loot corpse?

Max hit *Yes* and didn't bother to look at the result.

Warning: You have killed another player as the aggressor. Continued actions of this nature may affect your reputation and gameplay.

"Okay," he said, "*now* it's time to go."

He strapped Kat to his back and took off to the north at a sprint, casting glances at the sky and the mob, who were perilously close. If they had a wizard with a good range spell, he might be in trouble. He heard some shouts about zombies, since he'd left three of them near death on the ground. It gave him an idea. Pulling the Lyre of Murryn from his inventory, he tried summoning them as he ran, and felt relieved when it worked. He didn't check their levels but got two ghosts and two wights, whom he promptly ordered to run at the mob and slow it down. Kat protested about his use of an instrument besides her, but he didn't respond.

Siren: I think I'm in the clear. See no one following. I'm out of the cemetery.

Max didn't answer as he sprinted around tombstones and mausoleums. He felt reasonably safe from the ground pursuit now unless he ran into a kind of bramble dead-end, but the aerial trouble posed a problem. As if to prove it, a crossbow bolt shattered on a grave marker just after he passed it. He jumped the cemetery fence and raced for the nearby trees, small rocks from above hitting the ground near. The forest wasn't that thick here, but he made it inside and kept going. The winged rider wouldn't have much luck, but the morkais could fit in between the trees and did so now, someone getting close before having to pull up. Two rocks struck him but did minor damage.

Max thought of spells he could use, like *Camouflage*, but he was still in combat and couldn't cast anything not already on his hot list. He hadn't planned for this.

He headed for the buildings where he had ambushed the Dark Trio, only because the path to there was familiar and he wouldn't trap himself in a ravine or something. A bad feeling had come over him. Only two morkais and one winged rider appeared to be after him now, but more would come, the ground pursuit unlikely to stop altogether. Even if he survived this pursuit, what then? Where could he go? He at least had some hunting and foraging skills, the very first ones he'd chosen in the game. But he was going north, deeper into the Kingdom of Andra and toward the capital, in exactly the wrong direction.

That mob had him wondering—what brought them there? Had the karelia stationed outside the cemetery sensed something happening? Had the Dark Trio been detected or even caught? Or had that wizard's necromancy caused the mob? They might have been expecting Max, but he didn't think they did. He half suspected being blamed for the wizard's actions. His reputation was destroyed here. He'd worn out his welcome. The cemetery stunt had backfired as much as the Dark Trio ambush had been a success.

As his HP inched upward, his stamina took a hit and slowed him. Another crossbow bolt crashed through the leaves to land near him, but it had come from in front. They could see where he was going and easily get ahead. He veered to one side and a hail of rocks tore through there, as if to convince him not to go that way. There were more than two morkais up there now. He ignored the apparent warning and continued on that way. Now more missiles struck, but always behind. Was he outside whatever trap they'd quickly set?

A dark-winged morkais dove through an opening in the trees to his left side and behind, firing an arrow that just missed him. Max moved right and jumped a log, desperation growing. He was off the chosen path now, but not by much. He knew a big clearing was ahead somewhere, and it wasn't wise to enter, but with some tall bushes ahead, he came upon it suddenly, stopping at the sight before him.

The winged rider had landed and dismounted the huge florin bird, which stood behind him in the grass with wings outstretched as if to say Max wasn't getting past there, not that he was thinking of trying. It could bite him in half or rake him with those talons. Or knock him over with the wings. The rider held a crossbow aimed at Max's head. The cold brown eyes suggested he wouldn't hesitate to pull the trigger and made him seem formidable despite the short stature.

Name: Flight Leader Parmon of Evator.
Type: NPC.
Class: Winged Rider.
Species: Human.
Level 18.

Another rider hovered on a bird in the night sky to the right, while a third circled, both with crossbows drawn. Two morkais flanked the rider on the ground, both with arrows pointed at him instead of slings. Several more were aloft around them but now landed. Behind, Max heard small footsteps land in some leaves that scattered, presumably from the last beat of little wings. The sound of a bowstring being drawn made him purse his lips about being shot in the back. He sighed and took a few steps into the clearing until the winged rider spoke.

"I know you are Maestro Max, even though you've changed your name."

Was there any point in denying it? "Did you want an autograph?" Max asked, and while the words were sarcastic, he just felt resigned.

Parmon continued, "You are being arrested for murder and other crimes. Will you come quietly to stand trial?"

He shrugged. "What's the alternative?"

"We fight and subdue you, possibly killing you in the process. If you're thinking your ghostly abilities will help you afterward, look behind."

Max turned and saw the morkais he expected to be there, an arrow trained at his torso. The ground pursuit had neared, a dozen members of the Karelian Guard that were usually stationed south of Evator approaching amid others. At their front walked Ardyn, a hard glare on him. Max felt bad for letting down the karelia who'd helped him, but shrugged it off. He regretted little of what he'd done. Not really. It had been necessary. But now it seemed like he was about to pay the price.

He surrendered over Kat's objection.

Chapter Forty-Five

Wearing only his tunic, Max sat up on his cot beneath Castle Evator, feeling sleepy and more than a little irritable. He had a fatigue debuff and his jaw cracked on yawning. The green wool blanket atop him hadn't been enough to counter the cold that seemed to reflect from the lichen-covered, grey stone walls on three sides of him. The smell of his piss in the wooden bucket near the floor-to-ceiling bars on the other side didn't help his mood. Sometimes Llurien Online could do with a little less realism.

Though all of his magic items were gone, he'd still been placed inside a special jail cell with a magically created magic void, one floor down from where Norus had been imprisoned. Nothing supernatural would work in here. Such voids were naturally existing, and he'd been told that prisons were sometimes built on them, but the odds of such a void existing at an ideal spot to build a castle weren't high. Using something from a Sira void cat, a rare animal that naturally emitted such voids around them, someone had figured out how to make such places wherever they wanted. And Max wasn't the only one in one.

In the cell across from him sat a similarly attired and smirk-ing Tiardyn. The sorelian bitch had spent the entire night making noises to keep him awake. Her species needed far less sleep—only four hours a night—thanks to the god of vitality being one of their creators. Once a week, they could also skip an entire night without suffering a debuff. That probably made them ideal traveling companions for night sentry duties, but a sorelia who had a grudge against you was an awful person to be jailed near.

"You can shut the fuck up now," Max muttered, glowering through the bars where a fourth wall would've been.

"I will haunt you for forever," she said, leaning against a wall as she sat on her cot, legs swinging idly.

"I doubt it. I killed your asshole boyfriend and I haven't seen a sign of him since." That felt good, especially the look of shock and growing anger it produced. Her legs stopped moving. He'd wondered if she'd been told Kiavalon was dead and that he had done it. Her mouth worked in silent fury, but she seemed unable to respond. Maybe he should've told her that sooner so he could get some sleep. Then she started to rant, but he tuned her out.

The night before, he'd been disarmed and bound, then car-ried in the claws of a florin bird to Castle Evator. The brief flight had been alarming as he dangled, though the bird's vise-like grip gave a weird sort of comfort that he wouldn't be dropped. Siren had escaped notice and made it to town, even witnessing the sight of his aerial escort, which had spared him from being pa-raded down the street. He didn't know if they did that sort of thing, or anything about the legal system here. Siren had then logged out to learn what to expect and get an update on real world concerns. Now, that reminded him to check the logout button. No change.

Life Counter: 1 Day, 0 Hours, 7 Minutes.

It was almost 9am. By this time tomorrow, Dr. Thompson pulled the plug. But he still had three days before dehydration killed him. Was it a bad way to go? How would it be inside the game? Maybe he would just fall asleep in here before expiring, if he became too weak or disoriented to think or be connected. Would he disconnect? Was that how he'd wake up? He hadn't thought of that before, but it seemed plausible. It reminded him of a computer that was hung up and nothing but a hard reset would change that. Unplugging a laptop sometimes didn't work. You had to also remove the battery to make it go off. Was it like his mind had some connection to this game and he couldn't sever it himself? Maybe that was the problem. A technical glitch. Not his will to live or something.

He sighed, tired of the guesswork.

But he received an answer about his in-game fate moments later when a guard arrived to hand him a meager breakfast of day old bread and water, plus a juna fruit, which seemed like a yellow orange. His *World Lore* skill warned him not to eat the poisonous skin, as if he would have. Minutes later, he was shackled hand and foot and hauled away. With the guards walked a level 30 wizard who worked for the duke and whom Max knew better than to mess with. He assumed the moment he tried magic, now that he'd been taken from the void, they'd club him or cast a spell on him.

As they left the prison area and into the castle's lower floors, Max saw increasing numbers of servants, nobles, and more guards, all watching him with looks of fear, disgust, or contempt. Some moved away, which he ruefully admitted to preferring to the two who spat at him. He heard a large crowd before turning the corner to step out into the morning sunlight of the courtyard. His eyes scanned for a gallows or other means of immediate execution but didn't see one, which only relaxed him a little. He knew he'd be found guilty, just not how long before he'd die in here.

A worn wooden platform, painted blue and brown in Evator's colors, had been erected in the center, two thrones upon it. To his surprise, the Duke of Evator already sat there. Max had the impression that the proceedings were underway before his arrival, which caused a chorus of boos and jeers. And vegetables to be thrown at him before the guards made the crowd stop it. People filled the entire courtyard and overflowed past the gates, as if the whole town were here.

He saw familiar faces, including Sergeant Kari, who gazed at him with a mixture of triumph and anger. The kryll Malonir stood scowling with arms folded. Kella pursed his lips, hands inside the sleeves of his robe. The princess he'd saved long ago appeared to be crying as she dabbed at her eyes. The duke sat frowning. It wasn't until Max ascended a lower but similar platform across from the duke that he saw Lara had pushed her way to the front, her eyes worried. He flashed her a smile she reluctantly returned. Then the guards turned him to face the thrones as his trial got underway. As it started, he changed his name back to Maestro Max. If he was going to die, might as well do it as himself. He'd been positively identified by a score of people, anyway.

As he listened and the crowd often jeered, charges were announced one by one, a kryllan Solon Judge in a red robe overseeing everything. The priests of the god of fairness arbitrated throughout most of Llurien. The kryll were known for impartiality, and this one was among the few present who did not wear an expression revealing he'd already decided. But Max knew this was going to end badly.

The crimes included having abandoned his post as a serving guard member of Evator. Word had returned from Rook that the town had never heard of him and that upon confiscating his armor last night, they discovered it belonged to the missing guardsmen he had presumably killed, along with others. He had been impersonating a soldier of the kingdom, which was itself a serious crime. Norus was considered an accomplice in the deaths and subsequent ruse. And of course, Max had freed the hunter and another prisoner, the niquerra, attacking and sometimes killing multiple guards in the act.

They saw his other actions as a ghost the most reprehensible. He'd wounded and killed several people at the training grounds, then more north of the town, and a sorelia just blocks from here. They also suspected that he had killed three others by an abandoned building to the northeast just yesterday. He decided not to point out that he'd been alive for that one. Max had possessed Kella and unlawfully used a Moon Pass to enter a Moon Gate without permission, visiting the City of the Gods of all places, in defiance of a kingdom-wide ban on going there without the king's approval. He had also summoned undead multiple times—at the cemetery, the training grounds, and in town. They believed he had disturbed the kryllan burial tree, a statement that caused Malonir to glare in muted fury.

At least they don't know I asked Siren to close the cemetery gates yesterday, he thought wryly.

Max had to admit that the list of charges against him was pretty convincing, in no small part because they were all true. For some reason, he found the sheer number of actions funny and struggled not to laugh. He was a monster in their eyes, but he couldn't blame them. One thing was certain—he had to get much better at covering his tracks.

They finally asked him to confess, so he decided to just admit to some of it despite increasing jeers and pelting with foodstuff. He was doomed, anyway. Making himself a sympathetic figure wouldn't work, but he hoped for some leniency. As he pointed out, he'd been murdered, and the criminals had hidden his body so he couldn't be resurrected, a serious offense. Then the sorelia, Kiavalon, had captured him and tricked him into doing many of those crimes. He had recovered Tiardyn and gotten her captured, which was a good deed they should recognize. Then he killed Kiavalon to guarantee his own freedom. Some of the other deaths had also been self-defense, and he killed the apparent necromancer last night for that reason, too. He surmised the guy was really sorelian, too, which someone admitted, so he had outed a forbidden person once again. The Dark Trio was another instance of self-defense and had the added benefit that he had exposed a jhaikan pretending to be a rhaikan, and a sorelia pretending to be a karelia, and they should be thankful he revealed the truth.

"That part is true," Ardyn admitted, his high voice soaring over the murmuring crowd. "I encountered them outside the graveyard last night and could see their true nature. Their spirits have been sent to the Orb of Souls for cleansing."

Max sighed in satisfaction. Hopefully, the pricks wouldn't be back. He added, "I also took part in the castle's defense and rescued the princess. And four soldiers of the town were attacking a hunter from Gitarna when I came across them and intervened, so while I was not defending myself, I was aiding an outnumbered individual. I am not an evil person. I am a victim of circumstance, Your Highness, and while I admit to my actions, I did not feel I had any other choice."

"A confession!" the crowd yelled. It took a minute for them to quiet, at which point the duke talked quietly with a few people, including the princess, who finally looked at Max tearfully. And he knew what was coming. The Duke of Evator turned to him and raised his voice.

"Maestro Max," the duke began, "any of the crimes for which you have been charged carries a serious penalty, often death. The sheer number and magnitude of them leaves me little choice, even with your reasons, to find you guilty of murder, unholy spiritual acts, and supernatural crimes against the kingdom. You are hereby ordered to be hanged until death at sunset this evening."

The crowd roared.

And Max flushed in sudden humiliation that made sweat break out across his body and drip down his temple. Other people had often hated him for unjustifiable reasons. He had earned this sentencing today, but hearing so many people cheer for his execution struck a nerve. Max wanted to tell them off, but he kept quiet as guards roughly yanked on the shackles to lead him away. The food began pelting him again, and this time, no one made the crowd stop so that by the time he was inside, all sorts of juices were dripping down his body from head to toe. Fortunately, the duke wanted him cleaned up before his death and given a last meal, so he was unceremoniously shoved into a bath, allowed to shave, and make himself presentable... all so he could soil himself as hanged men sometimes do, in front of a crowd, hours later.

A short while later, he once again sat in his cell, a grinning Tiarydn gloating across from him. He wondered why she hadn't been punished in some other way. He got her to reveal she was being extradited back to the capital for her trial.

A message from Siren broke his thoughts.

Siren: Hey. Where are you?

Max: In jail, awaiting execution at sunset.

Siren: Yeah, I figured the trial would be quick. It already happened?

Max: Yep. Dead man walking. In this world and in the real one. Ain't life grand?

Siren: Don't get too sad. I have an update for one and plans for the other.

Max: I need some good news.

Siren: The first update is about your friends. The gaming company has the logs of the Dark Trio fight and has the identity of all three.

Max: Sweet!

Siren: Yeah, but they wanted a warrant to turn the info over, to appease anyone who objects to them just freely turning customers into the police. It's not that they aren't cooperating. They're covering their butt, but it's a moot point, though the warrant is under way.

Max: Why a moot point?

Siren: Derek has been arrested and refused to cooperate, but thanks to Kat, my dad could figure out who the others were from their first names. He corroborated those with witness accounts of who was with Derek in Baltimore. He brought them in for questioning. They wouldn't talk, but he told them that if they confess now, the judge might be lenient on them. He said as soon as he has that warrant and gets the data from the gaming company, any deal was off the table. Both confessed.

A wave of relief made Max let out a long breath. *Got you, assholes.*

Max: This worked out even better than I hoped.

Siren. I know. And there's more. All three have had their player accounts frozen and are currently banned. We expect this to become permanent. They won't be bothering you again in here. Their names are already being splashed all over the news this morning.

Max: This just keeps getting better. Did one of them work for the gaming company?

Siren: No. Derek's older brother did.

Max: Did? He's gone?

Siren: Fired. The gaming company put it together, partly because his brother's badge number was used on the company's 3D printer VR prototype. He obviously used it to bring Kat into the game. They can't prove he deleted the logs, but he's able to do such a thing, being a game programmer there.

Max: Not anymore!

Siren: Yeah, his ass is gone and his name has been leaked, too, so with any luck, he won't be working any time soon. Many people at the company are really pissed about him, so I bet they leaked that part.

Max: God, this is awesome. He's been arrested, too?

Siren: No. Technically, he hasn't committed a crime. I mean, he did a coverup, but as Derek pointed out, nothing done in here is a crime.

Max shrugged that one off. He didn't really care about that guy, but him getting fired and the notoriety was some justice.

Max: Any update on the legal stuff?

Siren: Yeah, and it's a big one. What's your Life Counter say? When did you last check it?

Max: Just looked now. It ends tomorrow at 9am. Why?

Siren: They're resetting it, but I guess they haven't made the change yet. It doesn't technically affect your game play.

Max's heart leapt. Even if they only reset it to seven days, that was huge.

Max: Why are they resetting it? Did my lawyer get somewhere?

Siren: Your legal challenge worked. Really resonated with people, too. This is playing out in the court of public opinion, not just the legal courts. The President even got involved.

Max: Of the United States?

Siren: Yeah.

Max: Holy shit.

Siren: I told ya you were famous.

Max: Still. So what they are resetting it to?

Siren: Another seven days. The President called this unprecedented and said she believes no laws apply to your situation and you cannot and should not be unplugged. She said this is a legal, ethical, and moral issue. Most people are on your side in this.

Max: Who is *not* on my side?

Siren: Mostly fringe people or those who've had the plug pulled on someone else who didn't get the same opportunity. They're saying it isn't fair, but someone had to be first. People are demanding their loved ones in a coma or whatever get the same chance.

Max: Huh. That's interesting. This could really change things, assuming it works for anyone.

Siren: Yeah, I'm sure there are all sorts of technical and legal issues that need to be worked out. It's going to be a cluster fuck, but it's not your problem. In the meantime, you can't be unplugged. We expect that the next seven-day period would also get extended. You still need to focus on waking up.

Max: No shit, Sherlock. Sorry. Didn't mean that in a mean way.

Siren: I know.

Max: XOXO!!!

Siren: Quit.

Max: Come on. I'm in a good mood, thanks to you. But now I'm thinking.

Siren: Just what the world needs.

Max. LOL. Maybe I shouldn't wake up yet and let this play out in the courts. If I wake up, legal cases end and maybe someone creates a law to stop all of this instead of allowing it.

Siren: Maybe. But do you really want to risk your life for strangers? You don't owe anyone that.

Max: I know. But wouldn't it be great to do that for people? I mean right now, I'm probably just the subject of pity, which I really hate, by the way. I didn't sign up for that.

Siren: Get over it, Max. And sure, there are some who pity you, but it's mostly empathy and sympathy.

Max: I'm not sure there's much difference. But what I was saying is that I like the idea of helping other coma patients get hooked up in here, communicate with their families, all that shit. Maybe some will get their life extended and wake up, even if I can't.

Siren: I get it.

Max: Do you? I'd rather be a hero than someone considered pathetic. Maybe I shouldn't admit it.

Siren: No, it's fine. My dad's a cop and he won't admit it, but he loves helping people, making a positive difference. I kind of do, too. It's why I'm in here helping you.

Max: We sarcastic and bitter types don't admit that we like helping people, but we do.

Siren: I'm not bitter. Or that sarcastic. You just bring out the worst in me.

Max: I think you meant "best." :)

Siren: There's something else, to help you in the game. The gaming company has decided to let you change your species, class, gender, and name.

Max: Really? I could already change the name.

Siren: No, this is different. It won't be only how it appears, but for real. Even the name the system views you as. They want to prevent even employees, except a trusted few, to know which player you are.

Max: Yeah. My parents could sue them, I just realized, for them not protecting me better.

Siren: Good point. Are you going to change your gender?

Max: Why do I feel like I can sense you laughing?

Siren. I have no idea what you're talking about.

Max: Uh-huh. But no, I'll stay a dude if it's all the same to you.

Siren: Nothing would please me more.

Max: Why are they letting me change my species?

Siren: They didn't let you choose when you started, but too many people are looking for a human bard with your name in this area.

Max: They won't be after I'm publicly executed, but I suppose I can respawn. I don't think I want to change the class, but the species I could see doing.

Siren: Okay, but don't do either until you are gone from Evator or it becomes a moot point because everyone will know you changed things, and into what.

Max: It's already a moot point.

Siren: I have an idea for that.
Max: Okay. Let's hear it.

CHAPTER FORTY-SIX

Hours had passed, with Max waiting in his cell. As he'd sometimes done, he researched the game with his *World Lore* skills. It helped him tune out Tiardyn, though she had less to say now that he was awake. But she kept reminding him how much time remained before his demise, her only objection being that she wouldn't get to kill him personally.

In the wake of Siren's revelations, Max felt renewed determination to survive. His real world stay of execution seemed to be the catalyst, despite that removing some urgency. Siren's plan for him to escape here was sound and wouldn't be foreseen. She just had to be careful and practice her abilities. If he got out of Evator, a new life awaited him in Llurien Online, one where he could feel safer.

He noticed he was looking forward to another life in here more than waking up. Llurien Online seemed full of possibilities. But the real world? He didn't know what awaited him. Lots of TV interviews? A book deal? The wrong kind of fame? But preferring being in here to real life was stupid. He meant what he'd said to Siren, that staying in here could help people. He didn't have a hero complex, but he'd rather wake up to being a hero than viewed as a jerk. He could give other people a second chance like he had, just by not waking. Let this shit play out in the courts. Do something positive with this. He could change the world. How many people got that opportunity? How many blew it? Maybe he could even find these other coma patients in the game and protect them, if they ever got in here.

What he really wanted, he now knew, was to be recognized for what he was—a good guy. Obnoxious people treating him badly after assuming the worst about him had caused that. But it had also given him a chip on his shoulder, making him sarcastic, snide, and negative. The result was that nicer people who might've assumed the best of him didn't really like him anymore than the hateful ones who assumed he was a jerk because he played guitar well or was socially awkward. And so he'd become a loner, feeling rejected and disrespected by everyone. Any pity for him being in here felt like more contempt.

He wanted to change that. For good. He needed a respite. He just wanted to be someone else for a while. To pretend. Was that why he wouldn't wake up?

Regardless, he made a decision.

He would still try to awaken to get that option. Then he could decide whether to do it. If the logout button became available, he wouldn't tell anyone. He was in no danger of the plug being pulled. He'd stay to gain new legal options for coma patients. If they entered Llurien Online, he would try to find and help them. Maybe no one would ever know what he'd done, but he sensed it would help him lose that attitude he carried in his heart. He wanted to do something good. He needed to. For him.

Max nodded to himself, feeling clearheaded. He felt something in him had just changed. He wasn't worried about his life anymore, whether dying or just the way it was going.

Before long, he ate a late lunch of roasted terrin and baked rosun, which tasted like chicken and potato. He supposed his would be his intended last meal. While eating, he received a notice from Siren that she was in the game and setting things in motion. He knew that this meant they wouldn't be able to communicate anymore until she was right before him, so he once again gave her some sincere thanks until she told him to stop being mushy.

He looked over his spells and rearranged his hot list. In doing so, he realized he had *Soul Bind Item*, but he'd have to wait until he had Kat in his hands again to do that. The spell would mean never really losing her, even if he dropped her. No one else could equip or take her, unless he let a party member do so. He also realized he still had a music proficiency point he'd been saving. He spent it on fretted string instruments to raise that to 2 now that he had Kat. It was unlikely he'd want to use it on something else. He also braided his long hair so it wouldn't interfere with the plan.

With three hours until execution, he heard a commotion and a muted scream.

He smiled at Tiardyn. "There's a good chance you won't see me dead today after all."

From her reclined position, she said, "Good. I'd rather find and kill you myself. I will escape on my way to the capital and track you until we meet again."

Max blew her a kiss.

The air grew chilly around him. The familiar and yet unfamiliar figure of Siren's ghost floated into view, having bypassed all physical barriers between them the easy way, now that her father had killed her character on request. That might've been awkward, but Max had decided not to make jokes about it.

Siren had focused on the ability to touch objects, so she didn't appear alive or walk on the stones, her figure glowing white. She also couldn't speak, but she didn't need to. They knew the plan. A ghost couldn't enter a magic void, so she stopped short and raised the cell keys in her hand, carefully eyeing the distance to throw them before making her lone attempt. If it didn't work, Max would die in hours.

The keys landed close to the bars of his cell, but not close enough. Max reached through with one arm, to no avail. But then he tried using his leg, which reached, but he couldn't grip it until removing his boots and using his bare toes to grasp the key ring, carefully pulling it to himself. Before long, he had the door open, his boot back on, and he stepped into the dim hall.

"Goodbye, bitch," he said to Tiardyn.

"I will find and kill you."

On hearing it again, Max made a decision as he walked down the hall, up the stairs, and reached the room where his gear was stowed, Siren observing. It took only a minute to put it all on and strap an elated Kat to his back. He didn't fail to notice that the cabinet had other items in it, so he looted them all, including a hand crossbow and two dozen bolts, which he had an immediate use for. Though he didn't have time to waste, he rushed to Tiardyn.

"Say hi to your boyfriend for me," he said. Then he unloaded enough bolts into her to kill her. He'd intended to use his bow despite the confines, but this was easier. Max wasn't having an enemy stalking him. He'd had enough of that. He got over 2,000 XP for her, and looted her corpse, the big prize being a hooded *Night Cloak +2*, which boosted his ability to hide in shadows. He donned it, but since it was sorelian, it only reached his knees.

"A hero to some, a villain to others," he joked as he walked away, a notification appearing.

You achieved Level 7!

You gained 27 Hit Points!

You gained 5 Mana Points!

Class bonus: You gained Dexterity +1, Intelligence +1, Charisma +1!

You gained (2) proficiency points!

You have (5) unassigned proficiency points!

You have (1) additional spell you can have in your hot list!

Max went back to the guard station, nodding at Siren on seeing her give him two thumbs up. He paused at the stairs, needing to make final preparations. Then he put Kat on a rickety table.

"I'm going to cast a spell on you."

Kat asked, "What does it do?"

"Bind you to me so we can't be separated."

She gasped. "That's badass! I love it! Do it!"

Max cast it and saw an icon of a knot next to her on his inventory list. He also felt a strange affinity for her when he picked her up again, one that surpassed any real-life comforts he'd long felt with her familiar feel.

With that done, he looted the guard bodies but only got some coins and useless stuff like dried tosk meat. As he pulled out the Lyre of Murryn, Siren disappeared to do the next part of the plan. He summoned undead and got five—a ghost, two wights, a skeleton, and a zombie. Most were level one and followed him up the stairs. The way to the Florin Tower wasn't far but had a few servants and soldiers along the way, so he sent the ghost out first. The servants ran screaming, at which point Max and his undead charged. Soldiers saw this and ran, so Max entered the Florin Tower moments later and sent his friends ahead of him.

When he was halfway up, he heard screams and shouts above, plus a call or two for the karelia. Then running footsteps could be heard. Max paused with a smile, waiting for the scream of realization as they encountered the undead he had just sent up. It didn't take long. He listened to the fighting for a minute, and when the commotion grew quieter and he received several notifications about dead guards, he climbed again until reaching the bodies and his undead.

Siren bowed, but now her work was done. They had figured a ghost might spook any florin birds up there, so she'd been careful in her movements and hadn't gone all the way to the top before scaring guards down the stairs. They made a pretty good team. Despite their precautions, they heard the scraping of giant talons on stone and screeches of fear. The ghosts had to stay behind, and Max decided the undead would, too. He couldn't risk it. The rest was up to him.

He unslung Kat and sent his undead down to keep reinforcements from arriving that way. Up he went, only pausing at doors long enough to ensure no one would attack him from within. Near the top, he worried that Siren had made the birds too upset for him to deal with. Peeking into one room, he saw a rider trying to calm a bird, which nipped at him with its huge beak. If even a highly trained rider couldn't calm them, what chance did Max have?

He paused on a landing just before the top, a guarded door around the corner. A quick peek showed only one person there, and she was looking around nervously. Not wanting to risk anything, Max cast *Sleep* and she fell to the floor with a clatter as he gained a minor amount of XP for not killing her. He stepped over the body and opened the door. To either side, as he faced south, a stone stairwell curved up to the top, but a door across from him was closed. He frowned, wondering whether he should check if anyone was in there, but he decided not to and ascended on the western side to his right.

The late afternoon sun beamed across him from the right as he looked at the Haigan Forest that held his destination—Gitarna, where Norus had gone. No one was up here except the bird equivalent of a stable boy who hadn't seen him. Wearing a tunic and trousers, the kid knelt facing away, whacking a saddle blanket with a stick. Dust jumped into the air, caught the sunlight, and floated away with each strike. Max saw no birds to mount. He scanned around and saw no winged riders, just two morkais in the distance, north of his position. He wondered how long he could afford to stand there waiting for one to approach if a rider was near. It wouldn't matter if the boy saw him and raised the alarm. Max hoped his *Stealth* skill would let him sneak up behind the kid. He started moving, Kat held like an axe in his hands.

"You're not gonna a kill a child, are you?" Kat whispered.

"No."

The spring air buffeting him in small gusts, Max made it most of the way to the boy, the stone surface as pockmarked with talon damage as he remembered. He was so focused on being quiet that he didn't realize the sun behind him cast his shadow toward the kid, who turned in surprise on seeing it. The boy opened his mouth to shout and Max jumped at him, clapping one hand over his mouth. The boy struggled, but Max put Kat down and soon had the kid bound, gagged, and partially hidden under the blankets he'd been cleaning.

"Now what?" Kat asked as he picked her up.

"We wait."

Max looked around again and saw a winged rider to the south, so he went back to the nearest stairs and hid himself a few steps down. But the guy didn't come near, opting instead for a circuit out to the east as Max muttered to himself. Minutes passed as he nervously waited for something else to go wrong. When the rider finally swung back, Max sensed he would land and was right. But he didn't land on the top where Max was. Max belatedly remembered what his trainer had told him—only novices did that. The riders always landed on a perch below.

He was about to go down when the door below—the one across from the stairs into the tower—opened, so he quickly went up before anyone saw him. But they were coming up the stairs he was by. He raced for the opposite stairwell, intending to descend even if someone was coming up, but no one was there. Down Max plunged, reaching the bottom as the voices made it to the top on the other stairs. He made it into the stairs, where the snoring guard remained unmoving.

Max jumped over the sleeping guard and went down a flight, slowing as he neared the correct open doorway. With a glance inside, Max saw that the rider already stood in the rectangular stone room, straw strewn across the floor, cabinets of supplies in one corner and a table in the center where he stood. Beyond him, the huge opening to the outside revealed the green and brown florin bird still on its perch and saddled. Now Max just had to get past the guy in the way, and he had little time. As if to prove it, he heard a commotion from below as footsteps rapidly ascended. He received several notifications of his remaining undead being destroyed.

"Now Max!" Kat whispered.

"Wait." He eyed the rider.

Name: Bordun Hammerblow of Evator.

Type: NPC.
Class: Winged Rider.
Species: Human.
Level 8.

"Where is everyone?" Bordun asked of an empty room as he placed a quiver and bow on a wooden table. He drew a sword and put it down, too, so at least he was disarming himself.

Max was hoping the guy would turn away for a *Stealth* attack to speed this up, but it wasn't happening.

"Gather air," he whispered.

Chapter Forty-Seven

Holding the swirling orb in his hand but behind his back, Max walked into the room as if he belonged there, all grins. Bordun looked up and smiled, then scowled as if sensing something was off. And Max hurled the *Orb of Doom* into his chest from five feet away. A red -35 HP rose as the rider flew backward and slam into the wall for more damage. A message that Bordun had been stunned appeared. Max grimaced as he took advantage and killed the defenseless man with Kat, who had no problem with this, whereas him hitting a kid bothered her. At least she had *some* conscience.

Max ignored the notification about the death and dragged the guy out onto the perch after looting the body, but he only got non-magical items and money. Then he shoved him down into the netting between the stone platform he stood on and the wooden perches to either side, trying to hide the body. The footsteps from below neared. He stepped farther out of sight until they went past the doorway and up. Putting Kat on his back, he turned to the bird and calmed himself for a moment, then climbed the rope ladder hanging from the side. It didn't take long to strap himself in and pull it up, then gather the reins, but he was facing north over the castle and town, not south over the forest. He was about to go when he heard a shout behind him. A quick glanced revealed two guards having spotted him and running his way.

With a yank on the top reins, Max got the bird to take off with a powerful leap. They dropped for a few moments, the castle rushing up as the giant florin spread its wings. When they caught the air, he pulled up again, and they rose as the mostly empty courtyard fell away below, the gibbet for his hanging already erected. He smiled at his escape.

…Until an arrow whizzed past his head from behind. Banking right, Max turned for the woods as more arrows fired from the Florin Tower nearly struck him. A bell there began tolling, and he knew the pursuit would come. He issued every command he could think of to make the bird fly faster as the treetops came underneath them. A glance behind showed three morkais already in pursuit, but he knew they wouldn't be fast enough.

But a nearby winged rider behind them might be. Max eyed the sky all around, hoping for clouds, but they were high above. He only ascended to a few hundred yards as he flew southwest toward Gitarna, not entirely sure where it was, but knowing he wouldn't get there for hours at least. And it would be full dark, with him possibly going right past it.

First, he had to lose his pursuer, who blew a horn Max didn't know the meaning of. Trusting his instinct, he rose for the clouds and cast a glance behind. The rider had overtaken the morkais, who had tripled in number. Worse, the pursuer had gained on him. Max felt certain losing them in the clouds was his best chance. The winged riders were skilled archers, and he was not. Using magic meant being far closer than either the long bow or crossbow his attacker would use. He wouldn't win a fight. But he had ideas and remembered to cast *Great Seat* to improve his lower body control of the bird and make him less likely to lose balance. Or, God forbid, fall off.

Max couldn't tell how high the clouds were, but he guessed several thousand feet. The air grew colder as he neared, and the top of Bier Peaks to his left and behind caught the setting sunlight on their snowy peaks. Before him stretched a seemingly endless green canopy that he knew crawled with jhaikan and riven. And possibly daekais.

If he could outrun or hide from the rider long enough, he might lose him in the darkness, but another look showed there would be no time. His pursuer was just three hundred yards behind, but Max saw he'd enter the clouds in time.

As he vanished into them, the pursuer blew the horn again. The guy almost had to be summoning someone, but who was out here? They weren't in the Kingdom of Andra anymore, but flying over Karendi Kingdom. Feeling stupid, Max realized he might get help, but he had no way to summon anyone. How closely was the sky watched? He knew those of Castle Evator flew into Karendi's territory all the time and weren't contested because he'd seen it himself. There were probably winged riders at Gitarna, but did they patrol this far? More important was whether they were out here now. He knew he was on his own.

Within the clouds, Max altered course, trying to be less obvious than flying in a straight line. The Earring of Timonen gave him an advantage, as he could hear the flap of wings from behind, steadily climbing and gaining. Then they went silent for long moments. He guessed they were gliding like him now.

After several minutes, from below and to his right, the sound of a crossbow being fired made Max bend forward over the bird, but he heard the bolt miss by 15 feet on that side. Was the rider just guessing? Max knew they were very close and made the bird slow and descend, a spell on his lips as he pulled a piece of straw he'd collected from his jail cell from inventory. He had to time this perfectly and be within fifteen feet, which meant the other bird would almost certainly sense them. On realizing that, he changed his mind and put the straw away. It would never work.

But suddenly it was too late. A break in the clouds revealed the rider also gliding, a crossbow in the right hand. He flew just above them, to the right, and ahead by a bird's length. This was far enough for the rider to see Max from the corner of his eye, the head snapping around. They saw each other at the same moment, but Max had the advantage because the rider couldn't turn to fire behind like. Max raised his hand.

"Gather air!"

Whether or not the rider recognized the spell, he shouted, and his bird banked awkwardly to the right and down. Max gauged the flight path. Would the atmosphere alter the *Orb of Doom's* path? He flung it at them before grabbing the reins, his bird turning sharply in pursuit. The magic orb missed by several feet and plummeted through the clouds to disappear.

A new plan in mind, Max called up another *Orb of Doom*. He still missed, but it spooked the bird, who veered sharply, Max closing the distance. He pulled a feather from his inventory as the rider tried to dive. Max cast *The Flock* and from seemingly nowhere, two dozen Antarian sparrows flew right into the other florin bird's face, causing it to shriek and pull up. The sparrows continued to pester the larger perrin, which beat its wings as if trying to pull back.

Max yanked on the lower reins to bring his bird under the rider, pulling the straw from his inventory just before he came within feet of the sharp talons now above him.

"Be free!"

He tore the straw in half, pointed at the bird's belly, and banked his mount hard to one side and down, not waiting to see if it worked. Suddenly, he exited the cloud, a flash of sunlight blinding him. He turned again to keep being unpredictable, and that's when he heard a man's scream of horror from above. A moment later, the human body plummeted past him, arms and legs flailing, crossbow tumbling, too. The giant saddle followed, a riding blanket, bedroll, and other loose items right behind. The *Unbind* spell had worked on the saddle fastenings. The winged rider fell out of sight.

Relieved, Max looked around and saw morkais coming. He could now identify them by their orderly body language in flight. To another side were several daekais, but Max could outrun them and all and did just that, racing toward Gitarna. A final glance behind revealed the riderless florin bird flying back toward Evator. He knew they were trained to do that. Apparently, they weren't trained to catch their falling rider. Or at least, this one wasn't. He ignored a notification of the rider's death.

Max rose into the intermittent clouds again, the golden light of sunset on him when they parted. The coming darkness worried him, too many unknowns beneath the dark treetops below. How hard would it be to find the town? It wouldn't be lit up like a modern metropolis. The few fires likely to be lit would be visible from above, he figured, but he'd have to fly right over it. It didn't seem probable. He was not aware of any Winged Towers out here where he could safely spend the night, and he wasn't sure what his bird would need, or even do, if they landed and he tried to camp. Was it even safe to do so? He was finally free of Evator and all that was there, but still not exactly safe.

As he flew, he received a message.

Siren: Hey. Where are you?

Max: Glad to see you've respawned. On the way to Gitarna. Lost the pursuit.

Siren: Great.

Max: Not sure where the town is, though.

Siren: Yeah. Just get as close as you can. The closer you are, the safer, since you'll be farther from the mountains and anywhere infested with riven or jhaikan. And nearer to areas that Gitarna has made safer, if they did.

Max: Good point. Maybe I can see a road to follow through the trees, but nothing so far.

Siren: Might need to be farther south. I'm gonna log out and see if I can find out anything about the woods or milestones you can use.

Max: That's great. Thank you.

Siren: Sure. Nice work back there, btw.

Max: You, too.

They stopped chatting and Max decided to change his species now. He'd known for a while what it would be. The nefarious species of daekais, riven, and jhaikan were out, including any positive counterparts like morkais, dariven, or rhaikan, though the latter could've been interesting. But it would attract attention he didn't want. Of the benevolent species, querra weren't good fighters, mandeans were mostly sea-dwelling, and he'd had enough of karelia for now, while also having some of their skills, anyway. That left kryll like Siren. He pulled up the species' description one last time.

Species: Kryll.

Summary: One of the seven original species, kryll exhibit the traits of the four Red Sphere neutral gods who created them: curiosity, aspiration, fairness, and peace. Lovers of nature, they are excellent singers with powerful, agile bodies. Some are pacifists while other strive to balance good and evil with action. They excel at melee and ranged combat, especially with their traditional enemies, jhaikan, but their endurance is poor. While skilled magic-users, they can be reluctant to draw energy from the environment to cast spells.

Species Strengths: +2 Strength, +2 Agility, +2 Dexterity, +1 Intelligence, +1 Morale.

Species Weaknesses: -1 Constitution, -10% Regeneration, -1 Reputation, -10% Mana

Species Bonuses: +10% Luck, +5% Magic Resistance, +15% Speed, +10% Physical Attack, +10% Reaction Bonus, +1 Spear Bonus. They receive bonuses for using kryllan weapons. Balance Bonus, Befriending Animals, Calming Presence, Direction Sense, Hide, Leave No Trace.

Class Restrictions: None. Dual classes permitted.

Proficiency Points Bonus: None.

Max poked around in his screens before finding the option to change his species, a button that hadn't been there before. He made the selection and felt himself get a little taller and more muscular. He'd have to land to see how it affected his abilities. He was asked to choose a designation of which kryll type he was and chose solonon kryll, the ones who made things fair. It sounded right.

For his name, he decided to just change it to Max and drop the Maestro part. He didn't want to be called something else and a variation like Mayhem Max wasn't going to fool anyone. Done with his changes, he glanced at himself in the Character Screen and saw that he looked like a kryllan version of his human appearance, with thicker bones. He also removed Lara from the party, just so there was one fewer person who knew his new game identity. He'd have Siren explain why to her and once again give thanks on his behalf.

Then he reviewed his revised stats.

Name: Max

Species/Race: Kryll (Solonon).

Class: Bard, Level 6

Reputation: -11—Escaped (Serial Killer) (Andra), 1—Accepted (Karendi)

XP: 17,775

HP: 106/106

MP: 32/32

Strength: 11

Dexterity: 23

Agility: 10

Constitution: 16

Intelligence: 15

Wisdom: 13

Charisma: 23

Morale: 15

His reputation in Andra once again leapt out at him, and he laughed ruefully, especially as it contrasted with his newfound desire to show he was a good guy. He'd looked a few times since it had first gone -4 to Accused. While he hadn't checked at each change, he'd seen it move down through Wanted, Imprisoned, and Convicted. That they considered him a serial killer probably shouldn't have surprised him, but the idea was still startling. Killing was part of these games, but not in town and, for Llurien Online, killing other players was apparently frowned on unless they were trying to kill you first. He'd have to watch that.

For the first time, he wondered if anyone could see his reputation. It probably only mattered if he was in that location. He wouldn't be going anywhere in Andra Kingdom. Ever. That could be an issue. And what if someone from Andra ran into him outside of it? Would they see his reputation? Would they realize he was the Maestro Max of Evator fame? Maybe. Maybe not. It could be that they just knew he was a bad guy without knowing exactly where and why he'd gotten that reputation. It didn't really matter except for someone realizing who he was.

He'd need to get his agility up to perform better as a kryll when fighting with the Kryllan Hand style, but now that he had Kat, he might not use it much. His negatives from choosing human at the start were undone. He felt pretty good about the change.

Maybe because he was distracted, he didn't keep his guard up. A sudden bird scream made his head whip up and to the left even as his mount banked sharply on its own. But the perrin bird's huge open talons hurtled toward his bird's neck, one closing around it and the other right in front of Max, into the bird's shoulders. The blow rocked them sideways and down as they plummeted in the perrin's grip. Max gripped the pommel with both hands, afraid of being knocked out of the saddle, which he continued to hold. The ground was rapidly rushing up.

"Max!" Kat called. "Use me to hit its leg!"

But Max didn't dare let go. He thought of using *Orb of Doom* because he wouldn't miss at this range, but the perrin was controlling their descent. What would happen if it let go? Was his bird able to recover, or would they just crash land even harder? He wasn't willing to find out. It was too late anyway.

Bracing himself for the impact, Max eyed the saddle straps, knowing a new way to get out of them quickly. A small clearing lay below and the perrin guided them toward it as he pulled a straw. He'd heard the perrins were smart enough to know riders were a bigger threat than florin birds. Just before impact, the perrin let go.

With a jarring crash, they smashed into the ground with a sickening crunch of breaking bird bones. Max's back hurt as a -10 HP floated away, his head whipping up at the perrin. Its huge wings flapped once as the giant talons came for him.

"Gather air!"

Max hurled the orb up toward the perrin's belly but somehow missed at this close range. It gave the bird pause, and he cast *Unbind* to free himself from the saddle just as the talons snapped at him. Max frantically rolled off, his foot bouncing off a talon as he somersaulted to the grass, landing on his shoulder and rolling to his stomach.

"Max! Use me or run!"

Getting to his knees, he unhooked Kat and brought her around to block the perrin's beak as it snapped him. The bird landed. Max stood, the beak coming for him again while he backed away and blocked. It was so fast that he couldn't get off another spell and kept retreating. He finally stepped in between two trees, the perrin still advancing and attacking. Did it know that a steady barrage would stop Max from casting a spell? How smart were they? He almost tripped on a root but couldn't look back to watch his step. The bird snapped at him again as Max blocked. Then he stumbled, caught his foot on a root, and fell onto his back, a rock jabbing into his spine.

The perrin hesitated and Max saw branches above him blocking its access to all but his feet, which it appeared to eye. He pulled both legs up and moved away. The bird titled its head as if trying to determine how to get to him, and just as Max was about to gather air, the bird turned away. It went to the florin and left no doubt what its beak could do as it snapped the dying bird's neck.

Max pulled himself back a few more feet and then laid down again, the pounding of his heart dimming. That had been a little too close. And where would he have spawned if he'd died in the wilderness? Or in the air? The nearest graveyard could've been far. For now, he was safe from the bird. He contemplated killing it, but he wouldn't get much in XP. Maybe when it was gone, Max could get some supplies from the saddle pack. He healed himself and sat up, wondering what to do. Something had probably heard the commotion and might be approaching even now. He needed to get out of here. He didn't feel like dealing with whatever was about to happen and wished he could just leave the game.

For the hell of it, he pulled up the logout button and blinked in surprise. It glowed yellow, the black letters in the middle standing out. For a second, he wondered if he was imagining it, or if he'd hit his head in the excitement and didn't remember. Was he hallucinating? No, it was definitely real, casting its golden glow on him and the ground. It was not greyed out for the first time. What had caused that? His last stint of pondering what he wanted while in prison? That must have been it. He should have checked then but let out a sigh of relief.

"What?" Kat asked from his lap. "What is it?"

Max opened his mouth to respond, then shut it. She'd be gone again out there. But he could always see her again in here.

But he noticed his reluctance to logout. If he left, his new mission of helping other coma patients died with his rebirth. Did it really matter that much to him? He sensed that it did. Most of his life, with music the only thing going for him, he'd figured it was his lone chance to make a mark on this world and earn some respect, maybe even be liked. It now seemed shallow by comparison. And it had certainly backfired.

And yet, in a warped way, it could indeed cause what he wanted if he remained. Leaving only offered a body that was probably too weak to walk right now, and a fame that bothered him. Then it would be gone and he'd be back to dealing with the haters. It seemed stupid to stay, but since he could now log out at any time, he didn't feel particularly rushed to do so. He was not going to die because he was in this game. On the contrary, Llurien Online might have just saved his life. And he could save the lives of others. How could he leave now? Maybe this self-appointed Ascension Quest wasn't for him, but everyone else.

Beyond the logout button, the larger perrin bird gave up on the dead florin and took to the darkening sky. Maybe it had just been defending a territory, not looking for a meal. Or the Kriserian Amulet around his neck, intended to inspire friendliness from wild animals, had finally worked. Before that, the bird had probably been diving at him before coming within range, and its aggression had been too strong until its attack ended.

Max went to the florin and took the supplies he could find, looting the body and gaining a solid amount of food. Danger had to be drawing near. But it was just a game to him now, not his life, and he could give a second chance to others. He was not the Death Singer, but a Life Bringer. Seeing his kajina ring, which would let him be alive and undead at the same time, he grinned. Maybe he was a little of both.

"Don't click it, Max," Kat said, strain in her voice. "Don't leave me."

"I won't. We're soul bound, just like we're supposed to be."

"That's right. I love you, Max."

He smiled in genuine amusement. "Love you, too, Kat."

Max looked one last time at the logout button, dismissed it, and then walked away into the sunset.

GLOSSARY

For more information on the world of Llurien, including maps and pronunciation audio files, please visit the official site, http://www.llurien.com.

GENERAL

Antarian: can refer to either people from the continent Antaria or the common language.

Coiryn Riders: named for the god of courage, these expert horsemen are a major unit of defense for almost all cities and major towns.

Daedrite: this rare store is only found in the Status of Daedras, the god of inspiration.

Deal of the Gods: an agreement between the gods to allow ghosts to happen, to create morkais from a male and female daekais, to give magic to the species, to grant healing powers if species create religions, and give the karelia supernatural talents to resolve matters of undead and roaming spirits.

Jhaikan Staff: a quarterstaff developed and used by kryll against jhaikan, it can be disassembled into three pieces for easier transport. Blades can be made to protrude from either end like a scythe, spear, or both.

Kajina: the karelian ability to separate the soul and body without dying.

Kriserian: a designation for kryll, it indicates that the individual is a pacificist. It is contrasted with solonon kryll.

Kryllan Hand: a magical pair of bracers over the forearms. With a word, a metal gauntlet covers the hands, allowing for hand-to-blade combat. Also a fighting style of martial arts.

Kryllan Sword: equivalent to a bastard sword.

Lorenia lines: the karelian species has lorenia lines on their faces, radiating outward from their eyes. The lines react to supernatural phenomena.

Magician: anyone with magic talent, whether they've become a full-fledged wizard or sorcerer or not. The term can be an insult to anyone of skill and power, since they should be referred to by their proper skillset: wizard or sorcerer.

Magicry: a store specializing in items needed for magic.

Moon Gates: powered by the moon, Moon Gates are portals that allow nearly instantaneous travel to another location, which must usually have another such gate.

Namaerian: items, which are very rare, that are made from both niquerrium and valenium ores are called namaerian, which is indestructible and was first invented by niquerra on the continent Namaera.

Niquerran steel: the strongest metal on Llurien, made from niquerrium ore. The official name is niquerrantine. Such items are black with a greenish tint.

Priest: members of a religious order. Within a priesthood, clerics and healers are more specific roles than the generic term priest, which not only refers to all of them, but to those who conduct ceremonies, listen to people's problems and console them, and interpret the will of the gods for the common people, though clerics and healers can also do this. Priests are the figureheads of a religion, while clerics administrate the religion and healers heal the wounded.

Scrying: the ability to detect the supernatural.

Solonon: a designation for kryll, it indicates that the individual will intercede to maintain or create fairness in disputes. It is contrasted with kriserian kryll.

Sorcerers: the class of magician which is capable of performing magic through force of will, rather than needing a spell.

Valend cards: a set of cards, in five suits, used for games, readings/divination, and magic items. The pack can teach people the gods and species, who are depicted on them in the valend (the first seven cards of each suit).

Valenders: simple spells that any magician can usually do whether they've trained to become a wizard or not (or developed their talent for sorcery).

Valendry: the art of creating magical items.

Valend wizard: magicians who failed the tests to become wizards and are not allowed to perform magic except by creating magic items, known as valendry.

Valenium: an ore that more efficiently and powerfully holds supernatural power.

Valentium steel: items made from valenium ore are called valentium steel, a soft metal that results in strong magic items. The steel is not suitable for weapons or armor.

Winged riders: flying the great birds and affiliated with a settlement or sovereign power, these warriors act as protectors, scouts, and messengers.

Wizards: the class of magician who needs spells to work magic.

PLACES

Antaria: a continent in the northern hemisphere of Llurien, usually depicted on the left/west of world maps.

Daeijonen: an afterlife of rebirth, as conceived by the gods of the yellow sphere, it is reserved for the least good.

E'kainum: the afterlife created by the gods of the orange sphere, reserved for the evilest, whose souls are shredded into oblivion without hope of recovery.

Everland: a supernatural land ruled by the Ever Fiend and accessed directly via Ever Gates, or indirectly via Moon Gates. Everland, and everything in it, like the Ever Fiend, is not believed to be real by most people.

Ever Pathways: another name for Everland.

Ever Gates: portals from Llurien to Everland. They are naturally occurring but hard to detect without the Reveal Ever Gate spell. Karelia can sense them. From within Everland, they are always open, but from Llurien, a spell must be used to open one.

Leisiran: the afterlife conceived by the gods of the indigo sphere, reserved for the moderately good, who enjoy a paradise for eternity.

Llorus: a large continent lying mostly on the southern hemisphere of Llurien, south of the continent Antaria.

Llurien: the planet.

Lochiare: the afterlife conceived by the gods of the blue sphere, for the moderately evil, who suffer eternal torture.

Maeryndor: an afterlife conceived by the gods of the violet sphere, for the least evil, who suffer boredom everlasting.

Namaera: a large continent lying east of the continent Antaria, in the northern hemisphere.

LIFE

Adarra: neutral summer and fire goddess of aspiration, red sphere, co-inventor of kryll and myrradim afterlife.

Araiya: nefarious autumn and earth god of cunning, blue sphere, co-inventor of jhaikan and Lochiare afterlife.

Ash fiend: undead created from the ashes of corpses.

Asyander: a deciduous tree growing 30-150 feet tall, used for syrup and bows.

Banoth: a large, four-legged herbivore with huge tusks and thick fur, banoth are found in colder climates and used as pack animals.

Blaekynor: nefarious spring and air goddess of haste, violet sphere, co-inventor of riven and Maeryndor afterlife.

Coiryn: benevolent autumn and earth god of courage, green sphere, co-inventor of karelia and Sorrairyn afterlife.

Coren: often fed to livestock, this fruit is covered in tight leaves, under which lie kernels that are boiled and consumed.

Daedras: benevolent spring and air god of inspiration, yellow sphere, co-inventor of querra and Daeijonen afterlife.

Dariven: a reformed race of the riven species.

Darra: benevolent summer and fire goddess of empathy, yellow sphere, co-inventor of querra and Daeijonen afterlife

Daekais: one of the original seven species of Llurien but now a race of the kais species. Created by the gods of the orange sphere: deception, greed, jealousy, and fear. Their teeth and claws are poisonous. See "kais" and "Deal of the Gods" entries.

Devourer: undead that feed on those with supernatural powers.

Enoni: A small lizard with sharp teeth, enoni attack in packs that can devour any humanoid in minutes.

Evenorr: enormous trees that kryll often building settlements in.

Everett: nefarious winter and water god of fear, orange sphere, co-inventor of daekais and E'kainum afterlife.

Ever Fiend: the Ever Fiend is rumored to rule the Ever Pathways and use Ever Gates to appear on Llurien to terrorize people.

Fjora: benevolent summer and fire goddess of passion, indigo sphere, co-inventor of mandeans and Leisiran afterlife.

Florin: a large bird of prey often tamed, trained, and ridden by winged riders and others, and bigger than perrins.

Hart: a forest-dwelling carnivore with sharp tusks, antlers, and four long, powerful legs.

Humans: the eighth species of Llurien, humans were created by all twenty-eight gods and are the most variable species in temperament and disposition. Also called Antarians after the first man and woman, Antar and Taria respectively.

Ilioth: nefarious autumn and earth god of cynicism, violet sphere, co-inventor of riven and Maeryndor afterlife.

Jaegar: a large omnivore with stocky legs, shaggy hair, a long snout, and big paws with retractable claws.

Jhaikan: one of the original seven species of Llurien. Created by the gods of the blue sphere: wrath, cruelty, cunning, and domination. They stand seven to nine feet tall, have a sinuous tail and reptilian skin that can change colors at will. They are man-eaters and are synonymous with evil.

Juna: a yellow citrus fruit with skin that is poisonous to consume.

Kais: this humanoid species has two races: daekais and morkais. Aside from disposition, they are largely the same, about four feet tall with feathery wings.

Karelia: one of the original seven species of Llurien. Created by the gods of the green sphere: truth, exuberance, courage, and intuition. They need only four hours of sleep a night and have a well-developed sixth sense that varies from one to another in just what they can sense and do. Appointed by the gods to resolve supernatural disturbances.

Kerr: an ill-manned mountain bovine with two curved horns that are used to ram anyone or anything entering its territory. Prized for milk (used for cheeses), skins, and their wool. Their waste is known to be especially smelly, resulting in the popular expression, "kerr shit."

Kojen: benevolent autumn and earth goddess of rejuvenation, yellow sphere, co-inventor of querra and Daeijonen afterlife.

Krairon: nefarious winter and water god of domination, blue sphere, co-inventor of jhaikan and Lochiare afterlife.

Kriseri: neutral winter and water goddess of peace, red sphere, co-inventor of kryll and myrradim afterlife.

Krisira: benevolent spring and air goddess of innocence, indigo sphere, co-inventor of mandeans and Leisiran afterlife.

Kryll: one of the original seven species of Llurien. Created by the gods of the red sphere: curiosity, aspiration, fairness, and peace. They prefer to live in large Evenorr trees and are extremely acrobatic, athletic, and masters of weapons. Every kryll has a subject to which they devote themselves, becoming an expert.

Kyson: a bush with red berries and violet flowers, and which is often planted as riven bane.

Lierein: benevolent autumn and earth god of expression, indigo sphere, co-inventor of mandeans and Leisiran afterlife.

Linganore Trees: believed to only grow in Everland in a grove surrounding the Ever Fiend's Black Tower. Black trunks and blood red leaves. The trees are sentient and can move, barring passage, trapping people, or killing them.

Loiria: nefarious summer and fire goddess of malice, blue sphere, co-inventor of jhaikan and Lochiare afterlife.

Lonnieri: neutral spring and air god of curiosity, red sphere, co-inventor of kryll and myrradim afterlife.

Mandeans: one of the original seven species of Llurien. Created by the gods of the indigo sphere: innocence, passion, expression, and unity. They are water dwelling and rarely seen on land except by the shore.

Moiryn: nefarious spring and air goddess of deception, orange sphere, co-inventor of daekais and E'kainum afterlife.

Moon wraiths: an undead that results from a ghost entering a Moon Gate and being stuck in the Ever Pathways.

Moragul: a large carrion bird with corrosive spit.

Mooryndal: nefarious summer and fire goddess of hate, violet sphere, co-inventor of riven and Maeryndor afterlife.

Morkais: a race of the kais species, they resulted from the Deal of the Gods and were created by all twelve "good" gods from a male and female daekais. See "kais" entry.

Mosk: a large canine found in packs in the wild, but loyal once tamed.

Mynx: a large, maneless, carnivorous cat (some as large as a horse) that can be trained in battle tactics and bonded to its owner. Mynx can wear armor, follow commands, and communicate threats to their owner with different vocalizations.

Myrradim: one of the Seven Fates, reserved for those perfectly neutral, these immortal, supernatural beings live among humans and do unto others as is done unto them.

Nig: a small, yellow, salty nut with a hard brown shell that must be pried open.

Niquerra: a nefarious race of the querra species.

Neistrum: nefarious summer and fire god of greed, orange sphere, co-inventor of daekais and E'kainum afterlife.

Okier: nefarious spring and air god of wrath, blue sphere, co-inventor of jhaikan and Lochiare afterlife.

Olin: a fruit used to create semi-sweet white wine. Its leaves can be smoked to achieve a hallucinatory state.

Pence: a cereal grain and staple food, pence is fermented for alcohol and used in making bread, pastas, and more.

Perrin: a large bird of prey, smaller and wilder than florin birds, rarely used as a mount.

Querra: one of the original seven species of Llurien. Created by the gods of the yellow sphere: inspiration, empathy, rejuvenation, and patience. Three to four feet tall, they are playful, wise, and beloved by many.

Raekynlor: nefarious winter and water god of sloth, violet sphere, co-inventor of riven and Maeryndor afterlife.

Reanimators: a spiritual undead who drains the life force from the living to reanimate their body.

Rhaikan: a benevolent race of the jhaikan species.

Riva: sometimes called querran riva, this rice is a staple of Llurien.

Riven: one of the original seven species of Llurien. Created by the gods of the violet sphere: haste, hate, cynicism, and sloth. Three to four feet tall and often carrying diseases.

Riven bane: a variety of plants that worsen any maladies, and which are planted to keep riven away.

Ronkainen: nefarious autumn and earth goddess of envy, orange sphere, co-inventor of daekais and E'kainum afterlife.

Rosen: a starchy vegetable baked or boiled, used to brew alcohol, fed to animals, and carved into thin wafers.

Scrylyn: benevolent winter and water goddess of intuition, green sphere, co-inventor of karelia and Sorrairyn afterlife.

Serine: prized for their meat and eggs, this small, colorful bird is a nuisance at ports but can be trained to carry messages.

Siaran wingfish: a footlong, blue fish with golden stripes and retractable wings, it has eight poisonous spines on its back.

Sira void cat: a small feline that radiates a magic void for several feet.

Solanaen: a highly poisonous plant in the darkshade family.

Solon: neutral autumn and earth god of fairness, red sphere, co-inventor of kryll and myrradim afterlife.

Sorelia: a corrupted race of the karelian species, they were created when the goddess of corruption, Ronkainen, read the passage about creating karelia from the Book of Creation. Sorelia look just like karelia but have more variable eye colors. They are considered malevolent.

Sorrairyn: those who have ascended upon death to become demi-gods, which is one of the Seven Fates (an afterlife). They live in the city of the gods, which is named after them.

Sorrin: benevolent summer and fire god of vitality (and magic), green sphere, co-inventor of karelia and Sorrairyn afterlife.

Species: while this can refer to animals, it usually refers to the humanoid species: karelia, mandeans, querra, kryll, kais, riven, jhaikan, and humans, some of which have multiple races.

Tarrera: benevolent spring and air goddess of truth, green sphere, co-inventor of karelia and Sorrairyn afterlife.

Timonen: benevolent winter and water god of patience, yellow sphere, co-inventor of querra and Daeijonen afterlife.

Tosk: an aggressive, four-legged animal with curved tusks, very territorial, and prized for their meat.

Vandin: a poisonous spider whose silk is highly prized.

Vylorn: benevolent winter and water god of unity, indigo sphere, co-inventor of mandeans and Leisiran afterlife.

ABOUT THE AUTHOR

Randy Ellefson has written fantasy fiction for decades and is an avid world builder, having spent three decades creating Llurien. He has a Bachelor of Music in classical guitar but has always been more of a rocker, having released several albums and earned endorsements from music companies. He's an IT professional in the Washington D.C. suburbs. He loves spending time with his son and daughter when not writing, making music, or playing golf.

Connect with me online

http://www.RandyEllefson.com
http://twitter.com/RandyEllefson
http://facebook.com/RandyEllefsonAuthor

If you like this book, please help others enjoy it.

Lend it. Please share this book with others.
Recommend it. Please recommend it to friends, family, reader groups, and discussion boards
Review it. Please review the book at Goodreads and the vendor where you bought it.

JOIN THE RANDY ELLEFSON NEWSLETTER!

Subscribers receive a FREE book, discounts, exclusive bonus scenes, and the latest updates!

www.ficiton.randyellefson.com/newsletter

Randy Ellefson Books

Talon Stormbringer

Talon is a sword-wielding adventurer who has been a thief, pirate, knight, king, and more in his far-ranging life.

The Ever Fiend
The Screaming Moragul

www.fiction.randyellefson.com/talonstormbringer

The Dragon Gate Series

Four unqualified Earth friends are magically summoned to complete quests on other worlds, unless they break the cycle – or die trying.

Volume 1: *The Dragon Gate*
Volume 2: *The Light Bringer*
Volume 3: *The Silver-Tongued Rogue*
Volume 4: *The Dragon Slayer*
Volume 5: *The Majestic Magus*

www.fiction.randyellefson.com/dragon-gate-series/

The Ascension Quest Series

When Max awakens in the VRMMORPG game Llurien Online, he doesn't know how he got there or why he can't logout. And a Life Counter no other player has is steadily descending to zero. Can he escape before he dies?

Death Singer

www.fiction.randyellefson.com/ascension-quest-litrpg-series

THE ART OF WORLD BUILDING

This is a multi-volume guide for authors, screenwriters, gamers, and hobbyists to build more immersive, believable worlds fans will love.

Volume 1: *Creating Life*
Volume 2: *Creating Places*
Volume 3: *Cultures and Beyond*
Volume 4: *Creating Life: The Podcast Transcripts*
Volume 5: *Creating Places: The Podcast Transcripts*
Volume 6: *Cultures and Beyond: The Podcast Transcripts*
185 Tips on World Building
3000 World Building Prompts
The Complete Art of World Building
The Art of the World Building Workbook: Fantasy Edition
The Art of the World Building Workbook: Sci-Fi Edition

Visit www.artofworldbuilding.com for details.

Randy Ellefson Music

Instrumental Guitar

Randy has released three albums of hard rock/metal instrumentals, one classical guitar album, and an all-acoustic album. Visit http://www.music.randyellefson.com for more information, streaming media, videos, and free mp3s.

2004: The Firebard
2007: Some Things Are Better Left Unsaid
2010: Serenade of Strings
2010: The Lost Art
2013: Now Weaponized!
2014: The Firebard (re-release)

www.ingramcontent.com/pod-product-compliance
Lightning Source LLC
Chambersburg PA
CBHW061607210726
48287CB00001B/33